THE MYSTERIES

Lisa Tuttle

Jo Fletcher
BOOKS

First published in the USA in 2005 by Spectra Books
Also published in Great Britain in ebook in 2012 by Jo Fletcher Books
This paperback edition published in Great Britain in 2015 by

Jo Fletcher Books
an imprint of
Quercus Publishing Ltd
Carmelite House
50 Victoria Embankment
London EC4Y 0DZ

An Hachette UK company

A CIP catalogue record for this book is available
from the British Library

PB ISBN 978 1 78206 961 4
EBOOK ISBN 978 1 78087 962 8

10 9 8 7 6 5 4 3 2 1

Typeset by Ellipsis Digital, Glasgow

Printed and bound in Great Britain by Clays Ltd, St Ives plc
Clays Ltd, St Ives plc

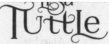

'A deft and daring blend of mystery and dark fantasy . . . Richly imagined and beautifully written'

GEORGE R.R. MARTIN

'A clever and engaging blend of folkloric fantasy and the detective novel'

THE HORROR HOTHOUSE

'Its seductive charm pull[ed] me in . . . I want to read more of [Lisa's] books'

BOOK GIRL OF MURY-CASTELL

'One of the more unique fairy-centric novels'

FANTASY BOOK REVIEW

'Lisa Tuttle has been writing remarkable, chilling short stories and powerful, haunting novels for many years now, and doing it so easily and so well that one almost takes it, and her, for granted'

NEIL GAIMAN

'The sort of slow-burning, haunting novel that digs its claws into the reader and never lets go'

LOVE READING

'I'd undoubtedly put Lisa Tuttle on my must-read authors list'

OVER THE EFFING RAINBOW

'Such a great read . . . It is a tale that feels timeless'

UPCOMING4.ME

Also by

The Silver Bough

Available in ebook only:

Familiar Spirit
A Nest of Nightmares
Gabriel
A Spaceship Built of Stone
Memories of the Body
Lost Futures
Virgo: Snake Inside
Panther in Argyll
The Pillow Friend
Love On-line
Ghosts and Other Lovers
My Pathology

To Rob and Sarah,
dear friends and generous hosts

We can see the people upon all sides,
But by no one can we be seen;
The cloud of Adam's transgression it is
That prevents them from seeing us.

– Mider to Etain

They did not know her – gods are hard for
mortals to recognise.

– Homeric Hymn to Demeter

mystery   n. a secret doctrine;
anything very obscure;
that which is beyond human knowledge to
explain;
anything artfully made difficult;
a sacrament;
a miracle play;
a shiftless, drifting girl.

Joe

The strangest memory of my childhood concerns my father's disappearance.

This is what I remember:

It was late September. I was nine years old, and my sister Heather was seven and a half. Although summer was officially over and we'd been back at school for weeks, the weather continued warm and sunny, fall only the faintest suggestion in the turning of the leaves, and nothing to hint at the long Midwestern winter yet to come. Everybody knew this fine spell couldn't last, and so on Saturday morning my mother announced we were going to go for a picnic in the country.

My dad drove, as usual. As we left Milwaukee, the globe compass fixed to the dashboard – to me, an object of lasting fascination – said we were heading north-northwest. I don't know how far we went. In those days, car journeys were always tedious and way too long. But this time, we stopped too soon. Dad pulled over to the side of a country road in the middle of nowhere. There was nothing but empty fields all around. I could see a farmhouse in the distance and some cows grazing in the next field over, but nothing else: no park, no woods, no beach, not even a picnic table.

'Are we here?' asked Heather, her voice a whine of disbelief.

'No, no, not yet,' said our mom, at the same moment as our dad said, 'I have to see a man about a horse.'

'You mean *dog*,' Heather said. She giggled. 'See a man about a dog, not a horse, silly.'

'This time, it might just be a horse,' he said, giving her a wink as he got out of the car.

'You kids stay where you are,' Mom said sharply. 'He won't be long.'

My hand was already on the door handle, pressing down. 'I have to go, too.'

She sighed. 'Oh, all right. Not you, Heather. Stay.'

'Where's the bathroom?' Heather asked.

I was already out of the car and the door closed before I could hear her reply.

My father was only a few feet ahead of me, making his way slowly towards the field. He was in no hurry. He even paused and bent down to pick a flower.

A car was coming along the road from the other direction: I saw it glinting in the sun, though it was still far away. The land was surprisingly flat and open around here; a strange place to pick for a comfort stop, without even a tree to hide behind, and if my dad was really so desperate, that wasn't obvious from his leisurely pace. I trailed along behind, making no effort to catch up, eyes

2

fixed on his familiar figure as he proceeded to walk into the field.

And then, all at once, he wasn't there.

I blinked and stared, then broke into a run towards the place where I'd last seen him. The only thing I could think of was that he'd fallen, or maybe even thrown himself, into some hidden ditch or hole. But there was no sign of him, or of any possible hiding place when I reached the spot where he'd vanished. The ground was level and unbroken, the grass came up no higher than my knees, and I could see in one terrified glance that I was the only person in the whole wide field.

Behind me, I heard shouting. Looking back, I saw that a second car had pulled off the road beside ours: an open-topped, shiny black antique. This was the car I'd noticed earlier coming along the road from the other direction. My mother had got out and was now in agitated conversation with a bearded man in a suit, a woman wearing a floppy hat, and two girls.

My mother called me. With a feeling of heavy dread in my stomach, I went back to the car. Heather was still in the back seat, oblivious to the drama. Seeing me approach, she pressed her face to the window, flattening her nose and distorting her face into a leering, piggy grin. I was too bewildered to respond.

'Where's your father, Ian?'

I shook my head and closed my eyes, hoping I would wake up. My mother caught hold of my arms and shook me slightly. 'What happened? Where did he go? Ian, you must know! What did you see? Did he say anything? You were with him!'

'I was following right behind him, then he wasn't there,' I said flatly.

'Yes!' The cry came from the woman in the old-fashioned car. She nodded eagerly. 'That's exactly what happened! He just *winked* out of existence.' She snapped her fingers in emphasis.

'I was watching the road, of course,' said the man, sounding apologetic. I had the feeling he'd said this before. He cleared his throat. 'So I didn't exactly see what happened. But I had noticed two figures in the field, a man and a boy, and when I looked again – just after Emma here cried out – there was just the boy.'

My mother's face settled into an aloof, stubborn expression I had seen before when one of us kids, or my father, was being difficult. It meant that she wasn't going to waste time on argument.

'Take me to him, Ian,' she said. 'Show me *exactly* where he was when you lost sight of him.'

I did what she said, although I already knew it was hopeless.

We searched that whole field, over and over again, at first quietly, then, in increasing desperation, calling loudly for 'Daddy!' and 'Joe!' The people in the other car, the only other witnesses to what had happened, stayed with us to help.

Finally, when it began to get dark, we gave up, driving to the nearest town to report my father missing. Here again the people in the old-fashioned car were helpful: the man was a judge called Arnold Peck, his wife was a Sunday school teacher, both of them well-respected pillars of the local community – even their two solemn, pretty little girls had a reputation for honesty – and so the impossible tale of my father's disappearance was treated seriously. Search parties were organised, with dogs; a geologist was summoned from the university in Madison to advise on the possibility of hidden underground caves or sinkholes beneath the ordinary-looking ground.

But no trace of my father, or what might have become of him, could be found.

It's strange, after all these years, how vividly I still recall the events of that day: the heat of the sun on the back of my neck as I plodded around that desolate field; the smell of earth and crushed grass; the low buzz of insects; the particular shape and hue of the little yellow flower that my father stopped and picked before he started his endless journey; the despairing sound of my mother's voice calling his name.

What's really strange about it is that none of it actually happened.

My father *did* disappear – but not like that.

My 'memory' came from a book about great unsolved mysteries, which I'd been given as a present for my ninth birthday, just a few months before my father vanished. One of the stories in the book was about David Lang, a farmer from Gallatin, Tennessee, who disappeared while crossing a field near his house in full view of his entire family and two visiting neighbours one bright sunny day in 1880.

How long I believed I'd seen the very same thing happen to my father, I don't know. At least I seem to have had the good sense not to talk about it to anyone, and eventually the fantasy fell away like a scab from an old cut.

But there's another twist in this tale of unreliable memory.

More than twenty years later, when I'd gone about as deeply into the subject of mysterious disappearances as it is possible to go, I discovered that the story of David Lang's disappearance was a complete fiction, probably inspired by a short story by Ambrose Bierce, but certainly with absolutely no basis in fact. It first saw light as a magazine article in 1953, and was picked up and retold in dozens of other places. Although later researchers conclusively proved that there never was a farmer named David Lang in Gallatin, and that everything about him and his mysterious disappearance was made up out of whole cloth, the story still survives, floating around on the internet, popping up in books dedicated to the unexplained, while other, genuine, disappearances are forgotten.

Although David Lang did not exist, real people vanish every day.

Let me tell you about some of them.

Laura

At the time, it felt more like the end, but looking back, I think this was the beginning:

The body of a woman found in a South London park at the weekend has been identified as that of Linzi Slater, a sixteen-year-old schoolgirl who went missing more than a year ago.

As I read those words on the *Guardian*'s website, a terrible numbness spread through me. I read the opening paragraph again, more slowly, but it was still the same. Linzi Slater was dead.

The old leather office chair creaked as I leaned back, turning my eyes away from the screen. I wasn't ready for the rest of the sordid details. I stared, unseeing, at the wall of books to my left and heard the sounds of life that filtered into my dusty, cluttered office from the world outside. Laughter and applause from my next-door neighbour's television, the screech of air brakes from an HGV on the street outside, the more distant rumble and

7

whine of a train approaching the nearby station. Life went on as usual. Of course, I had suspected for some time that Linzi was dead, but suspecting is not the same as knowing.

My throat ached. I found it hard to swallow. I felt sorry for the young girl I'd never known, sorry for her mother, and, more selfishly, sorry for myself. I had failed Linzi and her mother.

The police, it was true, had failed them, too, with less excuse. At least I could say I had tried. The police, with far more resources than I could hope to muster, had preferred to believe Linzi was in little danger. They had decided she was just another runaway. Young people go missing every day, and most of them vanish by choice. They run away from difficulties at home, or they go in pursuit of some barely understood dream. Linzi was sixteen, rebellious, moody, often truant from school. She had been seen last on a winter's evening within half a mile of her home, leaving a corner shop where she had bought a pack of cigarettes. After that, nothing, until a few days ago, when an unlucky dog walker had stumbled across a decomposing body under a bush in Sydenham Hill Woods nature reserve.

I'd been there often myself, since a school friend had mentioned it was a favourite hangout of Linzi's. She'd enjoyed the gloomy romanticism of the paths that wound past ruined houses and a disused railway cutting. I remembered the dim winter light, the smell of damp earth and leaves, the eeriness that always attaches to a place once settled and civilised, but now reclaimed by the wilderness. Reasoning that if she remained in London, Linzi might return to at least one of her old haunts, I had gone there several times. And as I'd tramped along those shaded woodland pathways I felt I was getting to know her, that just being there was bringing me closer to her. As it turned out, I'd been right, only not in the way I'd imagined. I must have walked past her hidden body more than once. She might have been dead within hours of vanishing. Almost certainly there was nothing I could have done to save her by the time her mother came to me three weeks later.

I read on, fearing, but needing to know how she had died. Murder? Suicide? An accident, even? Sydenham Hill Woods was a strange place to go on a winter's evening. It was a long walk – more usually, a bus ride – from Linzi's home, a destination for a Saturday or Sunday afternoon when the sun was shining. Still, people did do things on impulse – teenagers, especially.

Had it been arranged? Had someone asked her to meet him there, intending to kill her?

Another image came to my mind: a girl crawling through a low, hidden opening, into a cavelike space. I recalled reading about an early suicide attempt by Sylvia Plath: after leaving a note saying she was going for a long walk, she had crawled into the tiny, almost inaccessible, space beneath the house, with a bottle of pills, and huddled there, entombed, to wait for death.

Had Linzi been suicidal?

Her mother hadn't thought so. Janis Lettes, Linzi's

mother, was convinced Linzi had no serious problems. Sure, she wasn't terribly happy at school, but there was nothing bad enough to make her run away. She'd been insistent that theirs was a close relationship, that she would have known if Linzi was depressed. As I recalled it, Mrs Plath, too, had believed her relationship with her daughter was exceptionally close. But there would always be secrets even the most loving daughter didn't share with her mother, whether casual experiments with drugs and sex or the careful plans for her own death.

I heard the bubble and hiss of the coffeemaker in the next room and thought of getting myself a cup. Instead, I forced myself to read on, anxious to know how and why the girl had died.

But that was something no one knew yet. Forensic examination was under way. The next sentence shocked me.

Police say they have not given up hope.

Linzi was dead – how could there still be hope?

I was soon enlightened. Despite its lead, this story was not about Linzi Slater. Not really. The great newspaper-buying public had never heard of her. Linzi's disappearance had been a local story. It never made the national news, never lodged within the general consciousness as some crimes did. Maybe, if she had been a couple of years younger, or prettier, with a matched set of middle-class parents, the hacks might have turned her into a *cause célèbre* instead of ignoring her. But the press had not been interested in Linzi Slater when she vanished, and they weren't much more now. The point of this story was not that Linzi Slater's body had been found, but that someone else's hadn't.

This story was about the Nicola Crossley case.

Nicola Crossley, a fourteen-year-old from Kent, had vanished two months ago on her way home from school. Her parents had not come to me, or to any other private investigator, for help: they didn't have to. The police had made finding Nicola Crossley a top priority, and the media and public had responded. Her parents had made an emotive appeal for her return on television, her last-known movements had been reconstructed on a special episode of *Crimewatch*, and her brother had set up a website devoted to gathering information he hoped would lead to her return. But, so far, every hopeful new lead had come to nothing. When an early-morning dog walker in South London stumbled across the decomposing body of a young girl, every journalist in the country had thought of Nicola Crossley.

I thought of poor Janis Lettes and wondered how she was coping. I wanted to express my sympathy, but I didn't have the nerve to call her. She'd had faith in me once, and I'd let her down. Although I'd had nothing to do with Linzi's death, and couldn't possibly have saved her, I still felt guilty.

Instead of picking up the phone, I logged onto a few more news sites, searching for information, but everywhere I found only the same few sad, bare facts about Linzi, and a rehash of the Nicola Crossley case. Within a few days, I was willing to bet, there'd be a thoughtful piece in the *Guardian* on the subject of unsolved missing persons cases, or teenage runaways, and maybe Linzi's story would finally be told. Maybe her killer, if he existed, would be caught. But that wasn't my job, and this wasn't my case, although it had haunted me for more than a year.

Another question ate at me, one more grimly personal than the mystery of how and when she had died. Maybe I'd been given the case when it was already too late to save her. But why the hell hadn't I found her?

Janis Lettes could barely pay for a week of my time, but I'd worked a solid month for her, off the books, in my supposedly spare time: looking all over London, talking to everyone who had known Linzi, following up everything that looked remotely like a lead. There were precious few. If she'd had a secret life, or nurtured dreams of leaving, they'd remained hidden from the girls who called themselves her friends. Trying to get a feel for who she was, I'd spent hours in all her usual haunts and hangouts, nowhere more than Sydenham Hill Woods. I'd felt instinctively that it was significant, so I'd kept going back. I must have come within a few feet, if not inches, of her body, without knowing.

I'd failed before. I don't mean to imply that I was such a hotshot investigator that I'd found everybody I went looking for, because I certainly hadn't. Observational skills, intuition, dogged persistence all played a part in my success, but so did serendipity, and you couldn't count on that. Normally when I drew a blank, I just moved on to the next problem. The unsolved case remained open in my mind, a burden I would always carry with me, but it didn't stop me from taking on more. But somehow this failure felt different, and weighed more heavily. Maybe it was just the timing, because over the past year there had been a string of cases I couldn't solve, people I couldn't find, and it was making me reassess my whole career.

Maybe, after all, I wasn't any good at it. Maybe, for the better part of a decade, I'd been coasting along on luck, not skill, and now that luck had run out.

It didn't help that I was flat broke, and suddenly aware of middle age staring me in the face. I'd had a good, long run at my fantasy of being a great detective – with a base in London, no less! – but maybe fantasy was all it had ever been. I'd never made any real money out of it; it was more like a self-sustaining hobby. Maybe it was finally time to give it up, grow up, and find a new line of work.

I was distracted from my gloomy thoughts by a familiar soft, pattering sound, followed by a sharp metallic slap. I looked up in time to see the postman, transformed by the thick, frosted glass to a blurry grey ghost, bobbing away from my door.

The surge of hope that sent me bouncing up out of my chair to get my mail was irrational, but as inevitable as the tides. Even though these days I did most of my business by phone or e-mail, the regular morning arrival of the mail set off an anachronistic flutter in my chest, the feeling that my whole life could be about to change.

Unfortunately, the positive feeling rarely lasted long.

That morning, the most interesting envelope came from my publishers, Wellhead Books.

This turned out to contain a short letter, signed by someone I'd never heard of, informing me that as sales of *Taken!* had slowed to a trickle, they'd decided to remainder all unsold stock. They were offering me the first chance to buy all or some of the copies at an 80 per cent discount. Orders in multiples of twenty, please, and kindly let them know how many were required before the end of the month.

The news was not exactly a shock; I knew I was lucky my book had survived for as long as it had. Most books these days are allowed only a few months of shelf life before they disappear forever, and mine had been published nearly six years ago. Wellhead had been a small firm with an old-fashioned approach (small advances; personal relationships with authors; keeping books in print forever), but last year they'd been bought out and turned into an imprint of a much bigger media corporation. I couldn't blame them for wanting to dump me; I'd never managed to deliver a second book to my long-suffering editor. My career as an author had been even shorter and more inglorious than my life as a private eye.

I set aside the monthly bank statement unopened and tossed all offers of loans, credit cards, and private financial services onto the pile on the couch awaiting my next trip to the paper-recycling bin. That left only a Lands' End catalogue and a pale blue envelope postmarked Milwaukee, WI.

I knew before I opened it what it would be, and at the sight of the card my spirits plunged even lower.

Happy Birthday, Son.

Another unnecessary reminder that I was no longer young. Two weeks early. Inside the card my mother had sent a cheque for five hundred dollars. The sight of it made me feel both relief and guilt. Relief, because now I dared open my bank statement; guilt because what kind of forty-year-old man still needs handouts from his mother?

Just a loser like me.

I was converting dollars to pounds in my head and trying to figure out how much would be left after I'd paid this month's bills, when a small sound made me look up.

Through the frosted glass of the top half of the door I glimpsed a diminutive figure in green. The door handle rattled again.

I had a disorienting flash of *déjà vu*, the shadow of a shade, like the memory of a dream. I stared at the door unmoving, trying to remember.

There was a tapping sound, tentative at first, becoming a firmer knock against the glass. The little person outside wanted in.

Finally, still feeling as if I'd slipped back into a dream, I got up and went to open the door.

The woman on the doorstep was small, barely five feet tall, slim and lightly built. She wore a leaf-green linen dress. Her hair, just covering her ears, was a dark blonde sifted with silver. She tilted up a heart-shaped face and looked at me out of golden brown eyes that reminded me, for one heart-stopping instant, of Jenny Macedo, the love of my life.

I knew that this woman was a stranger, but for a moment, ambushed by memory, I couldn't speak or move, couldn't do anything but stare at this vision, seized by the irrational idea that Jenny had finally come back to me.

My silence made her nervous. I saw her pupils dilate, and she leaned away from me. 'Excuse me, I was looking for Ian Kennedy. Do I have the right address?' She spoke with an American accent, with a faint Texas twang – again, like Jenny's.

Her eyes shifted away from my too-intense gaze. She looked past me, into my front room. With its book-lined walls and stacks of books and box files everywhere, it looked more like the abode of a particularly messy academic, or even a small secondhand bookshop, than anyone's idea of a private investigator's office.

Finally I saw that apart from her height and the light brown eyes, she was nothing like Jenny. And although she was still attractive, she had to be nearer fifty than forty.

'Yes! You're in the right place. I'm Ian Kennedy.' Trying to make up for my slowness, I spoke too heartily.

'I'm Laura Lensky?'

I didn't understand the rising inflection, but she was obviously still wary of me.

I took a step back, gesturing to her to come in. 'Please.

I'm sorry the door was still locked; I've been at my desk for an hour already, but I'm a bit slow this morning. Please, take a seat.'

I shut the door behind her, then moved to open the blinds, letting daylight flood through the big front window. When I looked back, my visitor was still standing because there was nowhere to sit: the couch was littered with old newspapers and junk mail waiting for recycling, and even the chair that's supposed to be kept free for clients had a copy of the *Fortean Times* on it. I swept it away as quickly as I could, embarrassed by the garish cover.

'There. I'm sorry. I wasn't expecting anyone. Never mind. How can I help you?'

She took a step backward, nearer the door. 'I thought we had an appointment?'

Finally, it clicked. I groaned and screwed up my face. How could I have forgotten? It wasn't like I had that many potential clients these days . . . I couldn't afford to alienate this one.

'Laura Lensky, of course. Forgive me – you booked by e-mail. Said you'd be in between eight-thirty and nine. I'm really not with it this morning – I'm sorry. I'm not usually this bad, I promise. I just had some bad news . . . ' I waved my hand at the computer monitor. 'To do with an old case. I was thinking so hard about the past, I'm afraid I kind of lost track of the present.'

My babbling seemed to reassure her. Some of the tension eased out of her posture, and when I invited her again to sit down, she sat.

I started for my side of the desk, then stopped. 'I've made some coffee—'

'No, thank you.'

'Tea?'

She gave a brief headshake, occupied with settling a large leather shoulder bag onto her lap.

'I have herbal teas.'

'How nice for you.' She shot me a glance and softened her tone. 'I'm fine. And I need to make this meeting short because I'm on my way to work.'

'OK. Let's roll.' I settled down at my desk and opened her file. So far, it contained only her two e-mails and my replies. 'You're looking for your daughter.'

'Yes. Peri.'

'Full name?'

'Peregrine Alexandra Lensky. But we've always called her Peri.'

'What age is she?'

'Twenty-one, last week.'

'And when did you last see her?'

'Two and a half years ago. It was just before Christmas.'

I felt something heavy drop, that inward feeling that said it was hopeless, I should refuse this case. I didn't want another failure. Two years was too long.

Not taking my eyes off the screen, I said softly, 'You know, even after a few *months* the chances of—'

'But I talked to her about five months after she disappeared.'

That surprised me into meeting her eyes. 'You talked to her?'

'On the phone. She called me, collect, from a pay phone in Scotland. She said – all she said was, she wanted me to know that she was happy. And she loved me.' Laura's eyes were very bright. 'I tried to keep her talking, to tell me more, but she wouldn't. She said she couldn't stay. We talked for maybe, I don't know, two minutes.'

'You're sure it was her?'

The golden eyes flashed. 'I know my own daughter.'

'Yeah, sure, I didn't mean—' I raised my hands helplessly. 'I have to ask.'

'It was Peri,' she said quietly.

'And she's never called you since?'

She shook her head.

'Did you get the feeling that she was – I don't know . . . making the phone call under some sort of pressure? That somebody was making her say she was OK?'

Looking a little puzzled, she shook her head. 'Why?'

It seemed unlikely to me as well, but I was feeling my way. 'Was there a big search for her when she disappeared? A police hunt?'

She shook her head. An old bitterness twisted her mouth, and I knew in advance what I would hear. 'Peri was an adult, over eighteen, and there was no evidence of any crime, or force . . . The police always assumed she'd left of her own free will. That she'd had enough of me and her boyfriend and just went off to live her own life.' She sighed. 'And, well, maybe she did. Except there was no reason for it – she wasn't unhappy, in fact, everything was working out just as she wanted. There was no reason for her to run away, none at all.'

I left that one for the moment. 'Why do *you* think she called?'

She sat up a little straighter. 'Because she knew I'd be worried. I mean, she *could* have thought of that months earlier, but, well, better late than never. She didn't want me to worry – she wanted me to know she was happy. But she didn't want me trying to interfere, talking her into coming back, which is why she didn't give me any way of getting in touch with her.'

So far, so ordinary. It was an old, old story; only the details would be different. Peri had fallen in love with a stranger, or she'd joined a religious cult, or maybe she'd just gone on the road to find herself, in her own way, in her own time.

'And you believed that she was happy? That she was OK? How did she sound?'

She considered the question carefully, kneading the soft leather of her bag between her hands. 'Alive. Herself. Um. Emotional – very ...'

'Scared?' In my mind's eye, there was a man in a phone booth with the girl, a little snub-nosed pistol pressed into her back.

As if she could see this melodramatic image, Laura frowned and shook her head. 'Not scared. Happy, but ... I thought once she was on the brink of tears. Maybe a little homesick? Torn two ways? She did say she missed me, but ...' She sighed and gave her head a shake. 'I'd like to think I'm more important to her than I obviously am. Maybe I'll never know what made her leave the way she did. But I think she meant it when she said she was happy. I don't think she said that under threat.'

I nodded slowly, as if I understood. 'So you accepted that she was OK and let it go at that?'

'Of course not!'

Her astonished, angry glare made me feel like a complete idiot. I was wise enough to keep my mouth shut rather than make things worse.

'She's my daughter,' Laura said slowly, explaining the facts of life to a half-wit. 'My only child. Of course I couldn't let it go. I wouldn't try to force her to come home – even if I could. But I wanted to know for myself that she really was OK. I got in touch with the police again, and they traced the call for me. Once I found out where she'd been, I went there myself, the next day.

'There was no sign of her, but I managed to find this woman who had talked to her – she'd given Peri the coin she'd used for the pay phone. She'd felt sorry for her, she said. She said . . .' Laura paused, her eyelids fluttering, and drew a steadying breath before going on. 'She said Peri didn't look all that well. She offered her a meal, but Peri wasn't interested. She said she didn't need anything but a coin for the call.' She fixed her eyes on mine, willing me to understand. 'But she didn't have *anything*. Not a penny. Her clothes were in rags. She wasn't even carrying a bag, she didn't have ten pence to stick in the phone, and – at least, the woman thought – she was pregnant.'

I felt a jolt of vindication, almost triumph. It was like fitting the vital piece of a puzzle satisfyingly into place.

I was careful not to reveal my feelings, and spoke gently, aware that this could be a sore point: 'Could that be why she ran away?'

'Peri didn't have to run away!' It was a cry from the heart. Laura bit her lip, composed herself, and said, sounding resigned, 'I guess you need to know a little more about what the situation was when she left.'

I gave her my most sympathetic look. 'Please.'

She gave a small sigh and settled as best she could into the chair. It was a cheap, secondhand piece of mass-produced office furniture, impossible to really feel comfortable in. Usually I didn't care – after all, this was an office, not my living room, and I was only a cheap detective. But already I felt that Laura Lensky deserved better, much better, than anything I could provide.

'Peri and I were always close,' she began. 'Then I got offered this job in London, when she was in her senior year of high school. We agreed that the most sensible thing was for her to finish out the year, living with her best friend in Texas, while I came over here. She'd already been accepted by Brown University – her first choice. The plan was that she'd spend the summer with me in London, then fly back to the States when school started.'

Her eyes roamed restlessly about the room, along my bookshelves and up to the old, dusty cobwebs in the corners of the ceiling.

'Peri loved London, as I knew she would. But then something happened that I hadn't expected. She fell in love with a London boy. A young man, I should say. Hugh.'

'You didn't like him?'

'I *did*.' She caught my eye, to stress her sincerity. 'He's great; a really nice guy. He was completely smitten by her, and he made her happy – it was so sweet to see them together. I was fine with it, really.'

I thought she was protesting too much. 'But?'

She sighed. '*But* this was not the nineteenth century. I wanted something more than a good marriage for her – and I'd always thought she did, too. But now, the first time she falls in love, she just loses interest in everything else. She didn't want to go to college. She didn't want to leave Hugh. I guess if he'd had his own place, she would have left me and moved in with him. But he was still living with his mom and his stepdad and a couple of sisters – so she was stuck staying with me.'

'You argued.'

Her shoulders slumped. 'Well, of course we did. I couldn't bear to see her throwing everything away for an infatuation. Not even for true love, if that's what it turned out to be.'

She straightened up. 'And Hugh took my side. He didn't like the thought of being separated from her, but he was sensible, a responsible young man – and more in touch with reality than Peri was. He knew she ought to continue her education. Finally, under pressure from us both, she agreed to go away to Brown as planned. Meanwhile, Hugh was going to look into the possibility of a job in America, and she could apply to transfer to some English universities. I figured that would give her an incentive to keep her grades up. She'd be back in London for Christmas, and at that point we'd all discuss what would happen next. I admit, I was hoping that after a few months apart they'd find it easier to go on like that – eighteen is awfully young to tie yourself down for life – but I wanted the best for her, whatever it turned out to be.'

'So what happened?'

'As soon as I saw her get off the plane I knew I couldn't send her away again. She was so miserable she looked ill. She didn't come back to life again until Hugh hugged her.'

'True love.'

She couldn't quite manage a smile in response. 'She needed him, that was obvious.'

'And that was OK with you?'

She made a sound somewhere between a laugh and a sigh and shook her head. 'I guess you don't have any children.'

'Not that I know of.'

'Maybe it's different for a man. For a woman, the baby is part of you. At first, she can't survive without you. And then, more and more, she can. Until, finally, it seems that she can't survive *with* you – everything you try to do for her is wrong – so you just have to let go, and stand back, and let them make their own mistakes, and realise, maybe, they aren't mistakes, they're just somebody else's life.'

I waited, but she was finished.

'So. You were going to let her drop out of college, stay in London, do what she wanted. What about the boyfriend? Had his feelings changed?'

'Of course not. Hugh loved her as much ... more than ever.'

'So why did she run away?'

She was silent, looking down at the bag in her lap.

I pressed. 'If all she wanted was to be with Hugh and nobody was standing in her way, why leave? Did they have a fight?'

'No ... at least, I don't think so ... '

'If she was pregnant by someone else ... '

'What?' She stared as if I'd said something unthinkable.

To me, it seemed obvious. 'She'd been away for months. Even if she loved Hugh, something might have happened while they were apart. I'm not saying it was her fault. Who knows how it happened. Maybe she couldn't bring herself to confess. Maybe she was afraid Hugh would reject her, so she ran away first.'

'She didn't run away. I'm sure. She was taken.'

Taken!

My nerves vibrated like a struck bell.

I took a breath. 'Tell me everything that happened on the day she left. Everything you remember about the last time you saw your daughter.'

She chewed her lip, then shook her head. Her hair bounced and shimmered, strands sparkling, in a shaft of dusty sunlight. 'I don't have time today. Anyway, you need to talk to Hugh. He was with her the whole evening, and according to him, the things that happened – well, the police could never make any sense of it, but somehow it's got to be connected. You've got to hear his story before I tell you mine.'

'His *story*,' I repeated. 'Do you think he made it up?'

'No! Well . . . ' There was pleading in her gaze. 'Hugh's honest. I'm sure he is, he means to be, but he's an artist. Imaginative. He, well, he fantasises, and he's not always aware that he's doing it. It means he has a different take on the world. He doesn't always see things the way you or I would. But he's not a liar. And he tried his best to find her. He's helped me so much. He was devastated when she disappeared.'

I was getting a bad feeling about this guy. 'He was with her when she disappeared?'

'No.' She shook her head in emphasis. 'He brought her home. And then he left. She was last seen in my flat.'

That seemed a strange way of putting it. Last seen by whom? Before I could quiz her, though, Laura had extracted an envelope file from her bag. 'This should have everything you need. Hugh's phone numbers, some pictures of Peri, her notebook, the detective's report—'

'Detective? You've got a copy of the police report?'

'No, a private detective in Scotland. I hired him after she called, when I realised I couldn't get any farther on my own.'

I sat up straighter in my chair, competitive. 'Did he find anything?'

'He found a few people who had seen her at the campsite, or on the road nearby, and took statements from them. But there were no sightings of her after that day. The trail went cold. He was honest with me. He said that without any leads he didn't know where to begin. He wouldn't give me false hope. He could have gone on taking my money for years without ever finding her.'

'I'll be honest with you, too. After two years, your daughter could be anywhere. She probably has a new identity, a whole new life. Even if I do manage to track her down, she may not want to come back. She's made certain choices. She's an adult, not your little girl anymore.' It had to be said, even if she would ignore it, and probably blame me in the end.

'I know that,' she said quickly. 'I don't expect to get her back. I just want to know what happened. And I want her to know that I still love her, that I'll always love her, and that I'm always waiting for her call.'

She ran her fingers through her shining hair, pushing it away from her face. 'The Scottish detective said something. He said there are only two kinds of disappearances. Either someone is a victim, or they *want* to disappear. He said if it was the latter, I had to respect Peri's choice. She hadn't called to ask for help, but to tell me she didn't need it.'

'Maybe.'

Her eyes flashed up to mine, and I saw the need in them clearly: the anxious, needy hope.

'What do you mean?'

I don't believe those 'only two kinds of' formulations. People are more complicated than that, life more ambiguous. There was such a thing as a willing victim – but did that mean she should be left to her fate? What if her call *had* been a cry for help? I had no idea why Peri had made that phone call, and I didn't think the Scottish detective knew any better than I did.

'I just mean we don't know yet. Why Peri disappeared will be a mystery until we find her.'

'Thank you,' she said quietly, hoisting her bag onto her shoulder and starting to rise.

It would have been nice to end our first meeting on such an upbeat, positive note, but I got greedy.

'Wait – just a few more questions.'

She glanced at the watch on her slender wrist, then back at me, not very patiently, but still sitting.

'Peri's father.'

She stiffened. 'She doesn't have a father.' Her tone was glacial.

I raised my eyebrows, all innocence, ignoring her clear signal. 'Quite often, when a child goes missing – even an adult child – there's an estranged parent at the back of it.'

'Not this time.'

'You can't know that. If she decided to try to find him, or he made contact with her ...'

'Impossible.' She made it sound like her final word.

I waited.

She couldn't wait as long as I could. 'Peri doesn't have a father.'

'Ms Lensky, if I'm going to help you, I need to know everything, and that includes personal details. Just because you've decided certain things aren't relevant doesn't mean you're right. Even if Peri never knew her father, she would know she must have had one, and—'

'It's not just Peri who never knew him.' She looked me straight in the eye, but I was damned if I knew what she was telling me. Had she used a sperm bank for conception, or was Peri the child of rape? Either possibility said something very different about her, and about her relationship to her daughter, and I'm not sure which I found more unsettling. There was a time when I would have bulled ahead and insisted on having her spell it out for me. But I'd been in England for too long and had adopted the local manners and mores. Now they were no longer camouflage, but an integral part of me, and so I backed down before her distress and respected her privacy as she expected me to, like a proper English gentleman.

I told myself it didn't matter, because however it had happened, the man who'd provided half of Peri's genetic makeup wouldn't be aware of her existence and couldn't be involved in her disappearance.

And yet there was still a niggling little doubt at the back of my mind telling me I was missing something important here.

'Is there anything else you need to know?' Her tone was cool and impatient, and I felt bad that I'd forfeited her earlier warmth.

I told myself it was part of the job. 'I'm curious about why you've come to me now, two years after another detective let you down.'

She took a deep breath and held herself very still. 'I want you to help me because this could be my last chance. I'm leaving, you see. The London job was for three years.

Now my company is sending me back to America. I don't even know where I'll be a year from now – probably New York. If Peri wanted to get in touch with me again, she wouldn't know where to find me.'

Her words were carefully chosen, but I could hear the anguish vibrating low in her voice, and I felt a sympathetic pain in my own chest.

'I'll do my best to find her for you, Ms Lensky.'

'Thank you.' She rose in one fluid motion. 'Call me after you've talked with Hugh.'

Ancient lessons in now-outdated etiquette pushed me onto my feet, and I hurried around the desk. My mother had done a good job on me: I opened doors for women *and* called them 'Ms.'

She gave me a brief, social sort of smile and slipped out of my office, leaving behind only a faint trace of her summery, green-smelling perfume.

It was only then, my hand still on the door handle, that I realised I hadn't taken a credit card impress, or a cheque, hadn't even remembered to get her signature on a standard boiler-plate for my services. But none of that mattered. I was back in business, with a new mystery to solve.

Benjamin

Austria, 1809

The country was full of French spies after Napoleon's recent victory over Austria. Britain was at war with France, and life was not safe for Benjamin Bathurst, the British envoy to Vienna. Before leaving the city, he took the precaution of obtaining false passports for himself and his Swiss manservant. Travel from the Continent to England, especially for someone known to the authorities, a man bearing important papers, was necessarily a slow, dangerous, circuitous progress. Bathurst was determined to reach Hamburg, a still-independent city, where he thought he would be safe.

On the twenty-sixth of November, Bathurst's coach stopped in the small town of Perleberg for a change of horses. In the coach with Bathurst and his servant were two other travellers. All four dined at the inn while they rested. At nine o'clock, the travellers returned to the courtyard, where the coach was being readied. They waited as their luggage was loaded. Then, for no reason anyone could later explain, Bathurst moved away from the others, walking briskly around the horses as if to check something, or speak to someone on the other side of the coach.

He was never seen again.

The two other travellers boarded the coach. Bathurst's servant called for his master, then went to look for him. But he was gone.

The other travellers were annoyed at the delay, thinking that Bathurst had gone off to relieve himself and perhaps missed his way in the dark. Maybe he'd had too much to drink, or had made an assignation with that pretty barmaid ...

Only his servant knew that Bathurst had feared for his life and how desperate he had been to move on. He roused the others to search for his master, while he raced off to see Captain Klitzing, the Prussian governor of Perleberg. Unknown to the other travellers, Bathurst had earlier requested protection from Klitzing during his stay, which had been granted in the form of two soldiers, who had spent the evening hanging about the inn, eyeing everyone suspiciously.

When questioned, the soldiers had noticed nothing amiss. No one waiting in the dark and chilly courtyard had seen or heard anything unusual. Although some ruffian might have crept unseen into the yard under cover of darkness, surely the sounds of a scuffle would have alerted the others.

Klitzing arranged for the three remaining travellers to lodge at the nearby Gold Crown Hotel and started an investigation immediately. Every inn and tavern in the town was checked, fishermen were instructed to explore the local river, while gamekeepers and huntsmen with dogs were sent out to search the surrounding countryside. Bathurst's servant unpacked the luggage and discovered his master's sable cloak was missing. It was eventually found hidden beneath a pile of logs in the inn's woodshed. An employee was questioned about this and held briefly, but his questioners were convinced he knew nothing of Bathurst's fate.

A pair of Benjamin Bathurst's trousers was found by huntsmen on a forest path. The trousers had been turned inside-out and shot at with a pistol – but not while Bathurst was wearing them. In one pocket was a scrap of paper, a scribbled letter from Benjamin to his beloved wife in which he mentioned the name of one Comte d'Entraigues as implicated in his trouble.

When the British government learned of Bathurst's disappearance, they offered a thousand-pound reward for his return or certain news of his fate. Despite this substantial reward – which Bathurst's family agreed to match – there were no takers.

Benjamin's wife appealed directly to Napoleon and, despite being at war with Britain, the French ruler granted her special permission to travel throughout France and Germany in search of her husband.

On her travels in the spring of 1810, Mrs Bathurst

managed to pick up a number of conflicting reports and rumours about her husband's fate: he had escaped to the north coast of Germany, but drowned there; he had drowned while trying to cross the Elbe after escaping his abductors; he had been killed by a servant. The governor of Magdeburg Prison had been heard to boast, 'They are looking for the English ambassador, but I have him.'

When Mrs Bathurst confronted the prison governor, he did not deny his words, but said that he had been mistaken about the identity of one of his prisoners. He would not explain further, nor would he allow her to meet this man. In the end, she was forced to return to England sadly, none the wiser as to her husband's fate.

At home, she was visited by the Comte d'Entraigues, the double agent who had been named in her husband's last letter to her. The comte told her that Benjamin Bathurst had indeed been imprisoned in Magdeburg, and, when she asked for some proof, he promised to try to obtain it. However, a few days later, both the comte and his wife were assassinated at their house in Twickenham.

The general assumption at the time and also later was that French agents were responsible for abducting and disposing of Benjamin Bathurst; yet how they managed to accomplish this with such utter secrecy, in front of so many potential witnesses, has never been satisfactorily explained. As an early commentator on this famous case wrote, 'The disappearance of the English ambassador seems like magic.'

Joe

Being a private investigator is not a normal sort of job, nor is it a career that many people choose. In fact, I'm not sure it's a choice at all. I've often felt I was chosen for this role, rather than the other way around; and my dedication to it makes it seem more of a vocation, or an obsession, than ordinary work.

My calling is to look for missing persons, and you don't have to look very deep to figure out the reason why. My first case was my father.

He disappeared when I was nine years old. In my childhood imagination, the disappearance of Joe Pauluk was on a par with the great unsolved mysteries of all time, like whatever happened to Benjamin Bathurst, Owen Parfitt, or the crew of the *Mary Celeste*; but in reality he was just another guy who didn't come home from work one day.

When my mother called the service station where he worked as a mechanic, to find out why he was so late, they said he'd called in sick the day before. She discovered shortly that he'd cleared out their joint account, and emptied the joint savings account that was supposed to be our college fund. Luckily, she had her own private savings account, earmarked for emergencies, as that was exactly what our daily life had suddenly become.

A few weeks later, Dad's car was traced to a dealer in Chicago, who had bought it from a man matching my father's description. At that point, the police said there was nothing they could do. If my father had decided to sell his car and move to another state without telling anyone, that was his right. My mother couldn't even sue him for desertion or child support because they weren't married.

He could have left her any time, as my mother's mother liked to point out.

'Yes, Ma, I know. Of course he could have left me – we both knew that. He didn't need the state's permission to move out. That's just it: why sneak away like that when he didn't have to? Why steal money from his own kids?' Dropping her voice still lower (my ear was already pressed hard against the door; now, I held my breath in order to hear) Mom confided into the phone, 'Ma, I think he must be in some kind of trouble. I think maybe he *had* to go on the run. I just wish he would have told me . . . '

My father didn't gamble, take drugs, or drink to excess. He had few debts, which were budgeted for. He had no obvious enemies, and his friends (such as they were) had no idea where he'd gone, or why. My mother always claimed that they had been getting along just fine, and, as far as I knew, that was true. They argued sometimes, but who didn't? There was none of that constant, strained tension in our house, that invisible poison in the atmosphere that reveals an unbearable unhappiness. So why did he leave? And why leave like that?

He must have had to leave. It was the only thing that made sense. Some great outside force compelled him.

Sometimes I thought he'd been carried off to oblivion by a mysterious, incomprehensible power, like the Tennessee farmer, vanished into nothingness, that I'd read about in *Great Unsolved Mysteries of the World*. But although the weirdness attracted me in a story about someone else, closer to home it was just too scary. Mysteries should always have a solution. Despite the fantasy that haunted my childhood, in which I saw my dad wink out of existence before my own eyes, I needed to believe there was a rational explanation for what had happened to him. I'd been raised by my parents to be a sceptical humanist, and I already knew from television how easily people could be misled.

My father had never spent a lot of time with me – dads didn't, as a rule, back then – and as far as the outside world was concerned he was just an ordinary guy, but to me he was a hero. As a regular viewer of TV shows like *Get Smart!* and *The Man From U.N.C.L.E.* (and too young to realise they weren't meant to be taken seriously), I found it entirely reasonable that my dad could be a secret agent, his job at the service station a cover like the dry cleaners that hid the entrance to U.N.C.L.E. HQ. He wasn't allowed to tell us, of course, but he had a mission to save the world. The thought of it made me glow with pride.

A secret government agency had the money, the equipment, the skills, and the reasons to make one of their operatives disappear in the most spectacular way. I'd never seen any of the James Bond movies at that age; but the stories were well-known on the school playground, and I'd been particularly impressed by Bond's resurrection after his totally convincing murder followed by a burial at sea in *You Only Live Twice*. I felt grateful that nothing so apparently final had been done to my dad. He'd just 'gone away,' as my mother put it, and I expected, no matter what else she said, that one day, his mission accomplished, he would come back to us with no more warning.

My mother told us we'd just have to get on with our lives without him. She expressed no anger at my father's desertion. Even now I don't know what her innermost feelings were, but if not dictated, they must have been complicated by her feminist beliefs. She was, and still is, a strong-willed, quixotic individual, one born outside her natural time. Ever since I was old enough to read about them, I've realised that she was more like Emma Goldman, or the 'New Women' of the 1890s, than she was sister to Betty Friedan or Gloria Steinem or any of the new-wave feminists who came along later. She believed in free love and equated marriage with prostitution at a time when the average American girl went to college to get her 'MRS' degree and thought pregnancy out of wedlock the most horrifying fate imaginable. My mother wouldn't even pretend to be married, not even – as her own mother would plead – for the sake of the children. Before the term 'Ms' was coined, she was always, emphatically, *Miss* Kennedy, and gave her surname to her two children so everyone always knew that our father was not married to our mother.

She was a staunch individualist, and she believed strongly in love. Love was too important to be denied and could not be compelled. If love died within a relationship, people had the right – even the obligation – to leave their partners and seek it elsewhere.

My father knew the rules. If he no longer loved my mother, he had only to tell her so, and she would have let him go. He could have abandoned us honestly.

His disappearance was the great mystery of my childhood, one which I was eager to grow up and solve.

The chance came sooner than I'd expected.

When I was sixteen I wrote an essay for my civics class ('Dissent Makes Good Citizens') that won me a trip to a student conference in Minneapolis. I got to stay in a motel, and even though my civics teacher was right across the hall, and I had to share a room with a strange kid from Oshkosh, this was a thrilling novelty that seemed the height of grown-up sophistication. I examined the miniature toiletries and paper-wrapped tumblers in the bathroom, and bounced on my bed while my roomie hunched over the end of his, flicking through the TV channels. There was a telephone on the stand between the beds, and the local phone books were in a drawer underneath. I picked up the white pages and automatically turned to the *Ps* to look for my father's name. I wasn't expecting to find it, but there it was: *Pauluk, J*, just above *Pauluk, M*.

My heart turned over. I felt dizzy. I took a deep breath and mentally talked myself down. OK, it wasn't a common name, but that still didn't mean it was *him*. *J* could stand for Jane instead of Joe.

I reached for the phone and got the front desk.

'I'd like an outside line, please.'

'You'll have to come down to the front desk and give us a credit card imprint.'

'Credit card! It's just a local call.'

'I'm sorry, sir, but company policy requires that we take credit card details in advance from any guest wishing to make calls from their room.'

'But I don't have a credit card.'

She paused. I heard someone else speaking to her. Then she said, 'There's a pay phone in the lobby.'

I hung up without thanking her. My heart pounding, I tore out the page with *Pauluk, J*'s address and phone number and grabbed my jacket.

'Hey, man, where you going?'

I turned and saw the kid from Oshkosh staring at me, his mouth hanging open slightly.

I gave him the same, mysterious reply my father used to give me: 'Have to see a man about a dog.'

Scarcely a minute later I was dialling the number on the lobby pay phone.

A woman picked up on the third ring.

I took a deep breath. 'May I please speak to Joe Pauluk?'

'He's not back from work yet. Who's calling?'

My mind went blank. I had not planned for this; I hadn't planned or expected anything. 'Uh, that's OK, I can call back.'

'Well, don't call during dinner, all right? We eat at six. And if you're trying to sell something, don't bother. We don't have any money, and we never buy anything over the phone.'

'No, ma'am, I'm not selling anything. I just . . . I'll call back later.'

She hung up.

Looking at my watch, I saw it was just past five o'clock. She'd said they ate at six. He might be back any minute. I tapped my foot, nervous and impatient, wondering how long I ought to wait before trying again.

And what would I say if *he* answered this time? Would I recognise his voice after so many years? How could I be sure this was *my* Joe Pauluk?

I realised I would have to go and see for myself.

I went to the front desk. 'Could I get a taxi, please?'

'Ian? You're not going out?'

Caught. My shoulders stiffened, and I turned at the familiar voice to see my teacher, Mrs Charles, looking at me with furrowed brow. 'Is anything wrong?'

'No, no, nothing's wrong.' I tried to smile. My mind was racing. 'I've got relatives in town. I promised my mom I'd see them while I was here.'

'But not now.'

'Yeah, they've invited me for dinner.'

'Oh, Ian!' She shook her head in dismay. 'You can't! The opening ceremony starts at six. It's the first chance for all you students to meet and talk together. You can't miss that!'

'The banquet is tomorrow night. I thought that was the important thing.'

'They're both important! Look, you'll have some free time tomorrow afternoon, couldn't you visit them then? Surely you don't have to have dinner with them. If you explain, they'll understand. Would you like me to talk with them?'

She smiled with such kindly concern that I felt my soul shrivel. I shook my head. 'No, no thank you. I'll explain. You're right, they're bound to understand. I'll try to get back here by six, six-thirty latest.' I had no idea how big Minneapolis was, or how long it would take to get from there to the address I clutched in my hand and back again, but one minute would be more than enough to show me if this Joe Pauluk was my father.

'Why do you have to go? Why not just call?'

'It's too late for that – they've already left, to meet me – I have to go and meet them, I said I would.' I gabbled and grimaced, desperate to convince her. 'It's OK, really, I'll rush straight back. But I have to go. My mom gave me money for taxis and all that,' I went on, as easily as if I'd been lying all my life. My mother had given me fifty dollars for emergencies, but I knew she expected me to bring most of it back home. We lived to a very strict budget, every spare dollar going into the college fund for me and Heather.

From Mrs Charles's expression I saw she'd accepted my story, even though she didn't look happy about it. Unfortunately, she stayed with me until the taxi arrived, chatting about the weekend's schedule. I had meant to ask the desk clerk for a map of the city and some idea of what the taxi fare might be, but I didn't dare do that in front of Mrs Charles, fearful of rousing her suspicions. I wasn't used to lying. Beneath my down jacket, my armpits ran with sweat while I concentrated on looking relaxed.

Luckily, the taxi driver had no problem with the address. Mrs Charles waved, beginning to look a little anxious again, as he pulled away. 'I'll be back as quick as I can,' I said, and sat back and tried to think of nothing.

It was completely dark, and very cold, when the taxi stopped in a quiet residential street. It looked like a fairly recent development at the lower end of the price scale. Except that the houses were newer, it reminded me of my own neighbourhood back in Milwaukee. I paid the driver what he asked, barely registering the cost, then got out.

'You want me to wait?'

'No, no.' As the cab drove away I realised that I didn't know how I was going to get back to the motel, but I couldn't worry about that just then.

I took a deep breath, feeling the cold air bite my lungs, and stared at the ordinary ranch-style house in front of me. It looked snug and sealed against outsiders, the curtains drawn against the dark and prying eyes. A yellow light shone above the front door, but it looked less like a welcoming beacon, more like a warning: yellow for caution.

Parked on the driveway, in front of the garage to the left of the house, was a light-coloured, late-model American car. I could hear the ticking of the engine as it cooled and knew it hadn't been parked there very long. On an impulse, I walked over to it and opened the door on the driver's side. The warmth of the interior was like a caress. I felt a powerful urge to slip inside, behind the wheel, to start 'er up and back away from this house and whatever life went on behind its walls, to drive away from this neighbourhood and this city, to hit the highway and go. I could drive, even though I wasn't yet licensed. I could drive and drive . . . I think, if the keys had been left in the ignition, I would have done just that.

I let the door slam shut and held my breath because it had been so loud, I couldn't believe it wouldn't alert someone to my presence. Far away, I heard a dog bark. I stood there beside the car and waited to be caught.

But nothing happened.

My breath huffed out in a pale cloud, and I followed the yellow beacon to the front door, and knocked.

The man who opened it wasn't as tall as in my memory; his hair wasn't so thick and black, and there was a heavy softness around his middle, the start of a beer gut. He'd changed a little in seven years, but not as much as I had.

Daddy! cried the little boy inside me, but the detective I'd made myself kept quiet.

He looked at me blankly. 'Yeah?'

I moved a little, to give him a better view of my face in the weird yellow light. 'Remember me?'

He frowned a little, impatient. 'You the paperboy?'

'I'm Ian.'

Something flared in his shadowed eyes. He shook his head, pulling back. 'Sorry, wrong house.'

'You're my dad!'

I was talking to the door. All at once, I was possessed by self-righteous anger. How *dare* he shut me out, deny me. All at once, I knew that my fantasies about spies and secret missions were so much bullshit. Joe Pauluk had abandoned us deliberately, because he wanted to, because he could, because he didn't care. I pounded on the door with my fist and shouted. 'Hey, you, let me in! You listen to me! You're my dad, and I know it!' I saw the doorbell, and stabbed it repeatedly, alternating the melodic electric chimes with the brute thudding of my fist.

The door opened so suddenly I nearly fell.

My father's face, contorted with fury, was almost demonic as he thrust it into mine. 'Stop that!'

'I need to talk to you.'

'Who zat?' A tiny child clutched my father's leg and peeped up at me with bright, merry eyes.

'Mikey, get back inside. Go on, back to Mommy.' He gentled his voice to speak to the infant, and the familiar tones made my throat ache.

'What's going on?' A woman appeared behind him, shooting me a hostile look. She was very thin, with bleached blonde hair in a bad perm. She looked twenty-five going on sixty, and I hated her.

'I'm dealing with it, don't worry.'

45

'I have to talk to you.' I was not going to leave, and he saw it. His eyes darted around, searching for a way out, well aware that in another second or two I might say something he didn't want her to hear.

'Joe, I am *cooking* your *dinner*. I can't do that unless you look after Mikey and Sammy and keep them out of the kitchen.'

'I'm sorry, hon, but something's come up. I'm afraid I'm going to have to go out.' He spoke in leaden, unnatural tones, as if I was holding a gun to his head, but she didn't seem to notice.

'Go *out*? But what about your dinner?'

'I can eat later.'

'Can't this wait?' She looked at me, and frowned. 'He's just a kid.'

'It can't wait,' I said flatly.

'Just hang on a minute; I'll get my keys; we can talk in the car,' said Joe. He turned away from me, herding the woman and child ahead of him, and dropped his voice to a pleading tone: 'I'm sorry about this, hon, but it won't take long.'

I heard them talking as they went away – her high, irritable whine, his lower, broken rumble – but paid no attention. They'd left the front door open. I felt constrained from actually going in without an invitation. Without stepping across the threshold, I leaned my upper body into the house and gazed around, drinking it all in. I caught a faint whiff of frying onions, and the sound of the Coca-Cola song, but both of those came from other rooms beyond my ken.

This front room, clearly, was a formal space reserved for special occasions, not the ongoing daily life of the house. There was a big, new-looking pink couch and two matching armchairs. Between them, a shiny coffee table displayed a stiff arrangement of artificial flowers. Shelving units lined the far wall. No television, but I saw a stereo system and a line of LPs on a low shelf, along with two oversized books. On second glance they weren't books, but photo albums. There wasn't a single book in sight. All those shelves, which in my mother's house would have been stuffed to overflowing with books, here held only a frozen display of china knickknacks, silver-framed photographs, more artificial flowers, and a set of gold-rimmed wine glasses.

'OK, let's go.' My dad came through, shrugging on a grey windbreaker, still avoiding my eyes.

Neither of us said a word as we got into his car. He backed swiftly out of the driveway, drove down the street and around the corner, then pulled to the kerb and stopped. He put the car in park but left the engine running. Staring straight ahead he said, 'How'd you find me? Did your mother send you?'

'She doesn't know anything about it. I found you myself. I've been looking for you ever since you disappeared. I didn't know what had happened. I thought—' I broke off, unable to tell him what I had thought, unwilling to confess how much of my life had been given over to childish fantasies. I folded my arms and stared ahead, frowning hard.

'How did you find me?'

'You're in the book.'

He exhaled noisily and shook his head at his own stupidity. 'Oh, yeah. I never thought. For two years, three, I was so careful, but after so long ...' He turned to me, frowning suspiciously. 'But what're you doing here? Aren't you still living in Milwaukee?'

'Mom's still there. And Heather.'

'Don't tell me you ran away from home!'

'Like you did?'

'I didn't run away.'

'Oh no?'

'You don't know anything about it.'

'Of course I don't – how could I? You never told us anything – you didn't even say good-bye. What were we supposed to think? We were *worried*. Scared. We thought you might be in trouble.'

He stared at me. In the dim light I couldn't be sure of his expression, but I thought he looked stunned; that our long-ago anguish was an unsought revelation.

After a while he said, quietly, 'I'm sorry. I never wanted to hurt you.'

'Why did you go?'

'I had to. To save my own life. I was in so deep, I couldn't see any other way out. I had to leave, to start over again. It seemed like the only thing to do.'

I felt a surge of excitement. 'What do you mean – were there people after you? Like gangsters? Did you owe them money? Or did you know something secret, or ... ?'

He sighed and shook his head. 'No, no, nothing like that. No debts or drugs; nobody was after me. It was just . . . I couldn't stand my own life. I had to get out. You know, a wolf will gnaw off its own paw if it has to, to get out of a trap. That was kind of what it felt like I was doing.'

What was I in that scenario, I wondered: his paw, or part of the trap? How had he been trapped? I didn't understand, and I said so. Finally, after all these years, I'd found my father, and I wasn't going to let him go until he'd explained himself.

'What was it you didn't like? If you didn't want to live with us any more, you could have just moved out, like a normal person. You were free; you weren't even married. You could have quit your job, too – it's not like you were some indentured servant. You didn't have to sneak away like a criminal and disappear and make everybody worry.'

'I'm sorry.' He didn't sound it. If anything, he sounded bored with the whole business. He drummed his thumbs against the steering wheel. 'I just did what I had to do. Sometimes, you have to look out for number one, even if other people get hurt. Surely you can understand that?' He gave me a hopeful look. I stared back, stone-faced, and he sighed. 'Well, maybe when you're older. Maybe you'll be able to forgive me then. Now look. I'm going to drive you down to the bus station and get you a ticket to Milwaukee, and you can call your mother and tell her where you are—'

'She knows where I am.'

His eyes widened with shock. 'Did she send you here?'

'She doesn't know about you. I mean she knows I'm in Minneapolis – I'm here for a student conference.'

'You didn't run away?'

I shook my head.

He looked disappointed. I felt I had let him down, then hated myself for caring. He wanted me to be a runaway, someone like him, who could disappear without a word of explanation and let people down. But I wasn't like that and didn't want to be.

'Why didn't you ever call us? Once you got out of your trap and knew you were safe, I mean,' I added sarcastically. 'Didn't you care what happened to me and Heather? Didn't you miss us at all?'

'Of course I did – I missed you terribly.' He spoke with a sudden, intense sincerity which, I decided angrily, had to be fake. 'You don't know how many times I started dialling your number—'

'You're right, I don't know. Don't care, either.'

'Of course you're mad at me for leaving. I don't expect you to understand why I had to do it. But, Ian, believe it or not, I've always wanted the best for you. Mary's a great mother. I knew she would look after you fine. And after a couple of years I thought, what right do I have to get in touch? You'd been managing all right without me. You'd probably nearly forgotten me. For all I knew, you might have a stepfather or something by then. It wouldn't be right, it wouldn't be fair to *you* for me to come barging back into your lives just because I wanted to see you again. It was better if I stayed away.'

I felt like my head would explode if I listened to another second of his self-justifying crap. I yanked the door open.

'Ian, where are you going?'

'Away.' I got out and slammed the door.

He lowered the window on my side. 'Come on, get in. Tell me where you're staying, and I'll take you there.'

'I can get back on my own.'

'Don't be silly. Get in.'

'Don't you tell me what to do.' I marched off, and the car rolled slowly after me, my father telling me to get in.

I really did want to walk away and have nothing more to do with him, but I was miles from where I should be, with no idea of how to get back there, and it was dark and very cold. After a brief struggle with my pride, I got back into the car and told him the name of the motel.

He tried asking me about the conference, and how I was doing at school, and what my interests were, but I wouldn't play, and after a few attempts he gave up and just drove. When we reached the motel, at least he didn't try to pretend that this was the ending of a sentimental made-for-TV movie, or apologise, or explain. Not a word about how someday we might see each other again. I didn't even say good-bye, just shut the door and walked away without looking back.

When I got home on Sunday night, I told my mother that I'd found my runaway father. I waited until Heather was in her room, and I had my mother all to myself, eating grilled cheese sandwiches at the kitchen table.

'Ah,' she said quietly, searching my face. 'And was it all right?'

I shrugged, then shook my head. 'It wasn't like I always thought it would be. I thought I'd be solving this great mystery, and all I did was to find a guy who didn't want to be found.'

'People are mysteries,' said my mother. 'There are no solutions.'

'File under the Wisdom of Mom,' I said, but not in a nasty way. I scowled at my sandwich and felt my pulse rate speed up. 'You don't seem very surprised.' I looked directly at her. 'Did you already know where he was?'

She looked uncomfortable. 'I'm sorry, Ian. Your grandmother told me about two years ago.'

'Why didn't you tell me?'

'Because . . . you didn't ask. No, really, I mean it. I didn't want to force it on you, stir up painful feelings. You were doing so well at school and all, I thought you'd got over it. Especially since I had no intention of getting in touch with him. I decided that if you asked, or were obviously, you know, thinking a lot about it, then I'd tell you.'

I was shocked, but tried not to show it. How had she not realised that I had never stopped thinking about and wondering what had happened to my dad? It was an obsession with me, and yet she had not known anything about it. As the first shock faded away, I was more relieved. There were plenty of things in my mind that I wouldn't want my mother knowing about. People were mysteries. Thank goodness for that.

I stuffed the rest of my sandwich into my mouth and, as I chewed, thought about my paternal grandparents. We'd never seen that much of them. They lived, frugally, in Madison, in the same two-bedroom house they'd owned since my father was in grade school. They had never approved of my mother and didn't visit us, their excuse their reluctance to take their deteriorating old Ford out on the highway; but we went to them at least twice a year, and they'd always been very generous to me and Heather at Christmas and on our birthdays. They had seemed as worried and as clueless as us when their only son disappeared.

'How long did Grandma know?'

'I didn't ask her that,' said my mother, pulling her crusts apart and nibbling at the cheese.

I thought of something else from two years ago. 'He wasn't at Grandpa's funeral.'

My mother nodded, looking sad. 'He didn't want to meet us. He knew we'd be there. He'd been in Madison with Grandma just the day before. She tried to talk him into staying, but he wouldn't. He wanted her to promise she wouldn't mention that she'd seen him.' She shook her head.

'So that's when she told you. Has she even met her new grandchildren?'

'Ian, that's between them. It's none of my business, and I don't care – but I *do* care about Grandma's feelings, and I don't like seeing her hurt. Joe didn't have to create this big mystery and hurt everybody else just because he'd stopped loving me.'

'I don't think it was about you,' I said. 'I don't think he wanted to be a dad any more. Or a son. He wanted to disappear out of the world and start all over again, fresh. That's more or less what he said, I think.'

She nodded as if this was old information, and reached across the table to hold my hand. 'Then I hope you know it wasn't about you, either. You're a wonderful person, Ian. Your dad doesn't know what he's lost.'

After finding my father, I lost all interest in being a detective. For years, just remembering my fantasies of solving mysteries was even more embarrassing than listening to my mother talk about love. Looking for people who didn't want to be found – and, let's face it, that had to be most people who disappeared – was a thankless task, at best.

Owen

Owen Parfitt had been something of a rogue in his youth. Although safely apprenticed to a tailor, he ran off to be a soldier. But after many years spent roaming the earth, he returned to his origins in the little English village of Shepton Mallet, where he settled down and shared his house with his older sister, Mary, who had never married. And so life went on well enough until, in his late sixties, he had a series of strokes that left him semiparalysed.

Tailoring and travel were alike impossible for old Owen now. He was incapable of moving without assistance, a bedridden cripple utterly dependent upon the care of his older sister. Mary herself was past eighty, so she hired Susannah Snook, a young girl from the village, to help her with the nursing, housework, cooking, and other chores.

The Parfitts' cottage was on the high road out of Shepton Mallet, with the main street of the village running past the end of the garden, so they saw a fair amount of traffic every day as people on foot, on horseback, or in wagons passed by.

One sunny morning in June 1768, Mary and Susannah carried Owen from his bed and settled him into a chair outside in front of the house. Over his nightdress they draped his old greatcoat – for even on a warm summer's day, old men could feel cold – and they left him there, resting upright in the warm sunshine and gazing at the road.

He was out of the two women's sight for, at most, a quarter of an hour, while they made his bed, tidied, and aired his room. When Mary returned, she saw that the chair in the front garden was empty, the greatcoat lying on the ground beside it. At once she began to call his name, but there came no reply.

The alarm was raised and a search begun throughout the village. Haymakers working in a field across the road had seen no sign of the old man, nor had they noticed any visitors calling at the cottage or heard anything untoward. Search parties combed the woods and fields for miles around, witnesses were called for and questioned, but no one had any useful information to offer, and no trace of Owen Parfitt, or clue to his fate, was ever found. Many villagers were of the opinion that old Owen had been carried off by demons, and there was certainly no evidence to say that he hadn't.

In 1814, a new investigation into the mysterious disappearance of Owen Parfitt was launched. By this time, of course, Mary Parfitt was long dead, as were most people who had known them well. But Susannah Snook still remembered the events of that long-ago June day very clearly, as did some others who had been part of the search parties. During this new investigation, human remains were discovered buried under a wall not far from the Parfitts' cottage; however, upon examination, these were declared to be the bones of a local girl, more recently missing and presumed murdered.

The investigators also found reports from June 1768 of an elderly man, matching descriptions of Owen Parfitt, seen wandering in the lanes near Frome, more than ten miles from Shepton Mallet. This raised the question of whether or not the old man was *totally* paralysed, as was generally believed, or if he would have been capable of walking a bit. Yet, even if he still possessed some power of movement, it seems unlikely he could have walked so far unaided, and unseen, and the mystery of why he should do so, and what happened to him after that evening, remains.

Peri

When I was alone again, I went to get my long-delayed cup of coffee but found it nearly undrinkable, simmering away on the hot plate. I didn't bother to brew up a fresh pot because I was suddenly ravenous. Even though I'd neglected to get a formal retainer out of Ms Lensky, I was back in business again, and with that five hundred dollars from my mother, I figured I could afford to treat myself to breakfast at the Turkish-Cypriot café around the corner. I decided to make it a working breakfast and gathered up my phone, notebook, and the folder with details about the missing girl and stashed them inside the capacious leather satchel I'd bought for the purpose years ago when formally launching my career as a finder of missing persons.

I worked out of my home in a funky, run-down, ethni-cally mixed area of North London. My house was built originally as a single-family dwelling, but sometime in the 1970s, when most of the bigger houses along the same road were being cut up into flats and bed-sits to suit the needs of a changing population, mine had been reclassi-fied as commercial premises, and the downstairs became a corner shop with the owners living upstairs. But the conversion had been done on the cheap, and in a very halfhearted way: there was no separate entrance to the upstairs rooms, and the small, dark, ancient kitchen remained inconveniently downstairs, separated from the rest of the living quarters by the shop; also, the only toilet was upstairs, separated by a partition wall from the narrow, chilly bathroom.

When it came up for sale again in the early nineties – at a time when property prices were dropping precipi-tously – it was an obvious white elephant, neither a family home nor a useful commercial premises, and had to be 'competitively priced'. I knew as soon as I saw it that it would suit me very well. It was much cheaper than any of the one-bedroom flats I'd been looking at, and although the council tax was higher on a commercial property, I would save money by not having to rent office space else-where. If it was a little out of the way (I admit, I'd had fantasies of hanging my shingle from a picturesquely seedy walk-up in Soho) that didn't matter: I wasn't expecting to be dependent on passing trade, and I was in easy walking distance of both a tube station and a railway line.

Over the past few years London property prices had been rising steadily until now they were through the roof. Although I'd done absolutely nothing to make my odd little office/home more saleable I knew I could sell it for considerably more than twice what I'd paid for it. Local estate agents and property developers had taken to shoving flyers into my letter box on an almost daily basis, tempting me with free estimates and the promise of a quick sale. Whenever I felt gloomy about my financial situation I knew there was an easy way out: I could sell up and move back to America with enough money to make a fresh start.

But this was not one of those days. I crumpled the latest flyer into a ball without looking at it and tossed it onto the recycling pile before I set the alarm and double-locked the door. It wasn't so much that I had things worth stealing as that I couldn't afford the hassle of having to replace my computer again.

There were lots of good places to eat in the neighbourhood, some of them even cheap. One of my favourites was the Turkish-Cypriot café less than a five-minute walk away. From the outside it didn't look inspiring, being small and starkly decorated, but its charms had grown on me. I liked the laid-back, family attitude, loved the freshly baked Turkish bread and the strong, delicious coffee. Men gathered there at all times of the day to talk to each other or read their newspapers while they smoked cigarettes and sipped numerous cups of the thick black coffee or mint tea. What seemed to be a Turkish radio station was always playing softly in the background, and I rarely heard anyone speak more than a few words of English. I suppose I should have felt out of place there, but I liked being the foreigner, alone in the corner with my English papers or book, surrounded by the incomprehensible buzz of a language and culture I knew nothing about.

One or two regulars nodded at me when I came in, and the owner seemed pleased, as always, to see me. I ordered coffee and a bacon sandwich on Turkish bread, and settled down at an empty table with the new file.

The photographs it contained were the first revelation. Peri Lensky was extraordinarily beautiful. In the pictures, at least, there was something almost unearthly about her looks; I wondered that she hadn't been talent-spotted on the street and flown off to become the face of some international cosmetics company. How had someone so stunningly gorgeous managed to stay hidden?

These weren't studio shots with light used to highlight and conceal, or with flaws airbrushed out; they were just snapshots taken on a summer's day in London.

One showed Peri with her mother, posing in Trafalgar Square with pigeons clustered around their feet. The daughter loomed over her tiny mother, the amazon with the elf.

In another, Peri hung on the arm of a young man and laughed into the camera as he gazed sideways at her, clearly besotted.

Hugh? I peered at the unexceptional profile. He looked thoroughly ordinary, but the boyfriends of gorgeous women generally did, if they weren't hideous gargoyles.

I went looking through the papers to find out more. He was called Hugh Bell-Rivers, and this hyphenated young personage had two mobile phone numbers. The first connected me with his voice mail, but he answered the second.

'Bell-Rivers.'

I introduced myself and explained what I was doing. 'Ms Lensky said you could fill me in on what happened the night Peri disappeared. I'd like to meet and talk with you about that.'

'Sure. Happy to. Maybe sometime next week?'

'Today would be better.'

'That's impossible. I'm sorry but I'm very busy just now.'

'I'll come to you. Any time. If not today, how about tomorrow? It shouldn't take more than an hour.'

'Look, I'll be happy to help you, but I can't just now. Next week . . .'

'I can't leave it that long.' His accent and brisk yet languid manner irritated me even more than his double-barrelled name. 'Ms Lensky insisted that I had to hear your story first. Which means I'm stuck; I can't even start to work until I've talked to you.'

He sighed into the phone. 'Frankly, I don't see the urgency. What difference does a week make after all this time?'

'I'm sorry that you're finding this such a chore. Ms Lensky's going back to America soon, and she'd like some sort of results before she leaves. She thought you'd want to help me. If you won't, of course I'll have to go back to her.'

Silence. Then another sigh. 'Oh, all right. Lunch today. I'll be needing a break then, anyway. I'm in Soho. There's a noodle bar nearby, Kingly Street. Say one o'clock.'

'One o'clock,' I said agreeably, and was startled to realise he'd ended the call. Well, the hell with that. I reckoned I could track down a noodle bar in Kingly Street without any help from him.

I put my phone away and turned my attention to the Scottish detective's report. This seemed thorough, if ultimately pointless, as he listed and detailed his failure to find any further trace of Peri Lensky after a last sighting on the day of the phone call, on the road leading away from a campsite in the Scottish Highlands. I worked my way through his compilation of witness statements.

MRS MORAG BROWN: (IDENTIFIED PERI FROM PHOTOGRAPH)
It was early evening, around about teatime. I'm not sure of the exact time – you do tend to lose track during your holidays, don't you? And this time of year, it doesn't get dark until really late. This was the last day of May, that's right. It had been a nice day, mostly, very warm, and with a nice bit of sunshine in between the showers. I'd just walked up to the shop to get some soft drinks for the kiddies, and I noticed this girl hanging about by the telephone box.

She was hard not to notice. Well, she was pretty, and young, and pregnant. And her clothes! It was as if she hadn't noticed she was pregnant, or maybe she didn't have anything better. They certainly weren't maternity clothes, they were stretched all out of shape and didn't fit her properly, much the worse for wear. She wasn't staying on the site – I'd have noticed her before. I thought she looked a bit lost, frankly, so I asked if I could help. I have daughters myself, you know.

She said she wanted to make a call but she couldn't get the phone to work. I asked her what coin she'd put in, and she said she didn't have any money, but that she wanted to make a reverse-charged call, her mother would pay for it. Well, you have to put a coin in to make the phone work at all – I gave her a twenty-pence piece to use. When I saw she'd got through to the operator all right, I went away into the shop – I didn't want to be eavesdropping or anything, you know.

When I came out, she was still there, and tried to give me back the twenty pence, but I wouldn't have it. I invited her to come back to my caravan for tea; I told her I had a daughter about her age and that she'd be most welcome. Frankly, she looked like she could use a good meal. But she sort of backed away from me, shaking her head. She said she couldn't stay, that she had to get back to her husband. I noticed then that she sounded American. She seemed a bit nervous, and she looked so, well, so ragged that I just came right out with it and asked if she was in some kind of trouble, and could I help.

She looked surprised then, and she laughed and said no, no trouble – but she wanted to get back, and she couldn't risk being late. She thanked me again for the coin – she tried to give it back but I made her keep it, poor soul – and she waved me good-bye and walked off down the drive, towards the gates. I didn't see her again.

WILLIAM MACDOUGALL (IDENTIFIED PERI FROM PHOTOGRAPH)

Yes, that's her, that's the girl, all right. She wasn't dressed so nice when I saw her – she looked a bit of a scarecrow, really, and she was trudging along the road like she was dead beat. That's why I stopped the car. I only stopped because I thought she was a poor cow – sorry – who needed a lift. It's a long walk from there to anywhere.

Where? About a mile from the campsite, maybe a bit less. I was staying in Tayvallich. I'd just been down on the beach, parked my car at the campsite because it was convenient. So I was heading back to Tayvallich when I saw her.

She said, 'No thanks,' when I offered her a lift. She said she'd rather walk. Well, I was only trying to be friendly. I left her to it.

No, I'd never seen her before, or since.

ANNE MACDONALD (IDENTIFIED PERI FROM PHOTOGRAPHS)

Yes, that's her, I think. She looks more glam in the photos, though. She was really much more ordinary-looking in real life. And pregnant, of course. I could see she was pregnant from the way she was walking, even from the back, and I told Ewan – that's my husband – to slow down and offer her a lift.

He asked her where she was going, and she just shook her head without saying anything. So I leaned over and said we could give her a lift to the village – it was about five or six miles away – or farther, as we were going all the way to Lochgilphead. She said no, thank you, she only had a short way to go.

About a mile farther along the road I noticed a farmhouse that did bed-and-breakfast, so I thought maybe that was where she was going; that seemed to make sense.

That was all. Only four people had seen Peri on that evening in May, two years ago, all in the space of perhaps an hour, within a few square miles in the middle of nowhere. The Scottish detective had thoughtfully included a photocopied map of the area, with red Xs to mark the spots where Peri had been seen. The campsite was off a single-track road, nine miles from the nearest village. On one side of the road was hilly heathland and forest; on the other, the sea. One obvious explanation for her abrupt disappearance was that she had been travelling by boat with the man she'd referred to as her husband. I imagined a suave, James-Bond-type figure in a dinner jacket, powerful and rich, waiting for Peri to rejoin him on an elegant yacht anchored in a hidden bay somewhere along that rocky coastline. Yet that hardly fit with the ragged girl who didn't have a mobile phone or a credit card, who'd had to beg a coin in order to call her mother collect.

Far more likely that Peri had hooked up with some wretched, anachronistic vagabond who liked to keep his woman barefoot and pregnant. She'd made her way off the cramped, dingy fishing boat and found the nearest telephone in an attempt to put her mother's mind at rest about her; but she was so thoroughly under this goon's spell that she was terrified in case she was gone too long, and he sailed off without her.

Why did wonderful women fall in love with horrible men, make unnecessary sacrifices, give up everything for them?

It was one of the great mysteries of life.

But I was getting carried away. I didn't know that Peri had done any such thing. At the beginning of an investigation, everything is wide-open. Anything is possible and it's too temptingly easy to build up elaborate stories that one solid fact would demolish. The truth of what had happened to Peri might be much, much stranger, or utterly banal.

I picked up an A5 hard-bound book covered in a sort of paisley pattern in dark pink, blue, and white – Peri's diary? Inside the front cover she had written her name and two different addresses. The Texas address had been lightly scored through; beneath it was an address in West Hampstead.

I flipped through the pages, noticing the careful, rounded handwriting of a good girl student, the same throughout. Only about the first third of the book had been used, and most of that as a sketchbook. This, like her handwriting, was schoolgirl stuff, and repetitious. She had only three subjects: horses, dogs, and elaborately coiffured Barbie-doll women. There was no evidence here of any great artistic talent; most twelve-year-olds could do as well. Although there was something oddly obsessive about the style and subject, I guessed there was nothing more sinister behind the pictures than a bored teenager passing the time.

After the drawings came about twenty closely written pages. There was no heading, no time or date to introduce it. Flipping through to the end of the text I saw a small drawing of a butterfly beside the initials P.L.

Ordering another cup of coffee, I made myself as comfortable as the hard chair allowed and settled down to read.

I know Ca was there from the beginning, because there's a picture of him in my crib, all fluffy and white and new-looking, with a bright pink ribbon tied around his neck. He must have been a present when I was born, but Mom can't remember who from.

'Probably Polly,' she said. 'She was the only real friend I had when you were born. We didn't get many presents.'

Wherever he came from, Ca was the first of the Guardians.

Mocky came next. There's a picture of me, age two, clutching the little purple pony with the flying pink mane and tail. Mom thinks we got her at a garage sale.

Queeny was naked, one-legged, and half-bald, not a doll anyone would give as a present or pay money for. I brought her home with me from day care: Mom remembers trying to take her back while I screamed my head off. In the end, she was allowed to stay. Mom gave her a good washing, braided her sad hair, and made her a dress out of an old purple silk scarf. I thought she was beautiful.

How did I know they were Guardians?

I guess they must have told me.

They weren't like other toys; they could talk. Not out loud so other people could hear them, but just to me, secretly when we were alone.

Once I asked them where they came from.

Ca said he couldn't remember. Mocky told me it didn't matter.

Queeny said they'd been sent by Him to watch over me.

But when I asked who 'He' was she wouldn't say His name.

I tried to reason it out. Who else got a capital-H Him? 'You mean God?'

She got mad: it was a jangling sort of noise inside my head that made my teeth ache. If I'd thought first, I would have known it was a stupid question. The Guardians didn't have anything to do with God; they wouldn't let me take them into a church – not that I went into one myself very often. That didn't mean they were bad, though; they just weren't Christian. I didn't dare ask Queeny what they were. She scared me a little, to be honest. Ca and Mocky would love me no matter what, but I had to be careful with her.

One day, as I was getting ready to go to school, Ca asked me to take him along.

Yeah, sure.

'No way!' I laughed. Then: 'Sorry, Ca, but you haven't come to school with me since first grade! Too babyish! What's up?'

'I like to be near you,' Ca said, low and mournful. 'I know you don't really need me any more, but . . .'

I grabbed him and cuddled him close to my chest: my baby-toy, my sleepy-time doggie, my coo-coo Ca, and said, 'Of course I need you, I'll always need you   don't ever leave me, any of you!'

'Oh, my dearie, you'll have much finer horses than me when you're married – a whole stableful. Proper horses you can really ride, not like little me,' said Mocky. 'And you won't miss raggedy old Ca when you've got the finest hunting hounds in the world.'

They'd never talked like this before.

'I'll always love you—all the best, no matter what. Don't you know that?' I looked Ca right in his soft, furry face. 'Promise me you'll never leave me – promise!'

'I'll never leave you of my own will,' said Ca, the faithful hound. 'I'm yours forever.'

'Mocky?'

The little purple pony gave a deep chuckle. 'I'd die for you, my deario, if you asked it. And if you ask me to live, why, I'll do that, too.'

'Queeny? What about you?' I had to ask, but I felt nervous.

'You won't be needing me much longer,' said Queeny, and her voice sounded different, farther away already.

'But what if I want you to stay?'

'You won't want me when you're married.'

'What if I do?'

'I can't go with you to your husband's house.' There was no arguing with that tone.

'OK, then, but as long as I'm not married, you'll stay with me?'

'I will.'

So that was OK, since I didn't plan to get married, ever.

I would be like my mother and just have a daughter someday, to keep me company.

I went off to school as usual, and did the usual sorts of things until it was time to go home on the bus. It was one of the days when I didn't have any after-school activity, which meant I would get home before Mom. Whenever this happened, I went next door to the Stahlmanns.

Ray and Regina Stahlmann didn't have kids, but Regina didn't have a regular job. She went all over the state, buying and selling at flea markets and collectors' fairs at weekends; but during the week she was home every day, and she always seemed really happy to see me.

I liked going there. Regina collected dolls and old-fashioned toys, and even though you weren't supposed to play with them, she let me look at them. She made delicious snacks, plus there were the dogs, Pancho and Cisco.

This particular day, though, was different. As soon as I got off the bus and walked over to their house I saw that Regina's red station wagon was missing from the garage, and Ray's shiny black pickup truck was parked on the driveway. It winked at me beneath the dazzling sun, and dangerous black animals raced through my head: sharks, panthers, spiders, snakes.

But that was just stupid. Ray was OK. I didn't feel as comfortable with him as I did with Regina, but I liked him fine. For an old guy, he was good-looking, with thick, dark brown hair, well-muscled arms, and a flashing grin. His chocolate-brown eyes were just like the eyes of his sweet-natured mongrel dogs.

Thinking about the dogs made up my mind, and I marched on up to their front porch like nothing was wrong.

The front door was open. I looked through the dark wire mesh of the screen door into the familiar living room, and this is what I saw:

Ray was lying on the couch, stretched out on his back. His eyes were closed, and his chest was rising and falling evenly. I could hear the slow, steady whisper of his breathing. Regina always kept the television on, a constant background to whatever she was doing, but not today. The room was utterly silent except for Ray's breathing. He looked naked, with only a cotton throw draped across his middle.

I stared, fascinated and repulsed. I'd never seen him without a shirt on, and I guess he didn't often go out bare-chested, because his dark suntan stopped at his neckline. The skin on his chest was as pale as a peeled potato, but heavily sprinkled with coarse, springy hairs. Some were as dark as the hair on his head, others were white. His nipples were reddish brown. There was a curving, puckered scar high on his belly. His legs were very hairy.

Was he really asleep? What if he opened his eyes and saw me looking at him? I felt a crawling, wormy sensation deep inside, and my heart began to pound.

I backed away from the door, turned slowly, biting my lip with agony as my school bag creaked and my shoes slapped too loudly against the steps. I launched myself off the bottom step and ran flat out across the springy grass and didn't stop until I was on my own front porch, sweating and fumbling to find the key.

Even inside my own room, door shut and locked, and the outside door locked and bolted, I couldn't relax. Only as I cuddled Ca did I finally calm down.

Then I felt like a total idiot.

What had happened?

Nothing.

Ray was probably off work sick. Regina probably went down to the drugstore to get some medicine for him, and she'd left the front door open so Ray could talk to me from the couch, and explain - only he'd fallen asleep. The wrongness was only in my head. I didn't say anything about it to Mom, or to Regina when I finally saw her.

One week later the same thing happened. I got off the bus from school and once again there was Ray's pickup and no sign of Regina's car.

My stomach gave a queasy lurch, and I walked slowly around to the side of the Stahlmanns' house, avoiding the front porch with the open front door.

The two little dogs, Pancho and Cisco, were in the backyard, shut in behind the chain-link fence. They whined with pleasure when they saw me approach and wagged their stumpy little tails. I poked my hand through the fence and let them kiss me. I talked to them for a while, loudly, hoping my voice would carry inside. If Ray was lying on the couch, and he heard me, he might come out. He'd have to put his clothes on to come out.

The dogs left off licking my hands. Their ears pricked as they stared alertly behind me.

I turned around and saw a man. For a second I thought it

was Ray. Then, with a feeling like a roller-coaster drop, I saw he was a stranger and looked nothing at all like Ray Stahlmann.

I thought he had to be the best-looking man I'd ever seen in my life. At the same time, although he was a stranger, I was absolutely sure I'd seen him before. Maybe on television? He looked like he ought to be famous: tall and fair and young and strong and handsome, with something about him . . . There's a word older people sometimes use, 'vibes'. That's what he had. Powerful vibes. Special vibes.

Even the dogs knew he was special. They always barked at strangers, and sometimes at people they knew, but they hadn't barked at him. They were just standing quietly, their tails shyly wagging, hoping he would notice them.

I didn't feel scared or nervous at all. Afterwards, I thought this was odd, because I generally do feel at least a little bit wary about strange men, no matter what they look like, because . . . well, because. But that old warning of 'don't talk to strangers' didn't even cross my mind.

'Who are you?' I asked.

'Don't you remember me?'

I shook my head. 'When did I meet you?'

'In another country, long ago.'

I laughed. 'I've never been to another country – not even to Mexico!'

'I'm talking about the life you had before you were born into this world. You were my wife then.'

It looks crazy, written down, but not when he said it. Then, it seemed absolutely right. It was like something I'd

74

always known. And yet it was a shock.

How could it be both familiar and strange? Well, I guess because it fitted in with something I'd thought about, although no one had ever said anything like it to me before. I had always thought that birth could not be the beginning. I didn't talk about it much, but I had the feeling that I'd had another life before I was born. I'd read some books and things about reincarnation, but they never told me what I really wanted to know.

Now, looking at this familiar male stranger, I felt I had finally met someone who could explain my feelings to me.

I stared hard into his blue, blue eyes. 'How did I die?'

'You didn't die. You are immortal, like me.' He said it like it was totally ordinary. In the same way he explained: 'My first wife was a sorceress. In her jealousy, she separated us. She turned you into a fly and caused you to be blown out of our world and into this one. Here, a mortal woman swallowed you in her drink, and nine months later you were born again. Once you were called Etain; now you are known as Peregrine Alexandra Lensky.'

That sent a shiver through me. Not many people knew my full name. It was almost like a secret. Even on official forms, my mom usually put down my name as 'Peri Lensky', or 'Peri Alexandra Lensky', and so I did the same. Only someone who'd seen my birth certificate would know my mother had once upon a time given me the hippie-ish name of Peregrine. I liked Peri for all sorts of reasons – not just because it was easier to spell – but I liked having a secret other name, too.

A peregrine is a type of falcon, so named because it was

taken not from its nest, but while in flight. To peregrinate is to travel about; to live in a foreign country; to wander or go on a pilgrimage. A peregrine is a wanderer, a stranger in a strange land.

A peri is a Persian fairy.

When I learned that (from the same dictionary that had given me the meaning of peregrine), I got a thrill. I looked up 'Persian'   'of, from or relating to Persia (now Iran).' That was less thrilling; Iranians were not a group much loved in Texas. But the fairy part was fine; I'd always loved fairy tales.

The handsome stranger standing in front of me in the Stahlmanns' side yard seemed to have stepped out of a fairy tale, especially when he said, "I've been searching for you throughout many mortal lifetimes. Now, finally, I've found you. Will you come with me, back to our own land, and rule beside me as my queen?"

I shut my eyes, but when I opened them again, he was still there, right in the middle of the familiar, ordinary neighbourhood where I'd lived for the past five years. I looked around at the Stahlmanns' house and, beyond it, to my own. A squirrel suddenly dashed across the lawn and up a tree; I could hear the faint scrabble of its claws on the bark, and the leaves shivered as it plunged into them, out of sight.

The hot Texas sun beat down on me, out of a blue sky cloudless but faintly hazed by the city's pollution. Perspiration soaked my cotton shirt. I was hot and tired and hungry. Mom wouldn't be home for at least another hour, and inside the

Stahlmanns' house, instead of Regina with her dolls and ice cream and freshly homemade lemonade, a naked middle-aged man was dozing on the couch.

I felt like bursting into tears, so I got mad and yelled, 'You're crazy! I live here! Why should I go anywhere with you?'

'I can give you everything you want. In my country, you'll live and be young forever. And you'll always be safe with me. I'm very powerful, Peri. Who do you think made Ray fall asleep?'

'I guess you mean you did.'

He nodded.

I shrugged. 'Why?'

'To protect you.'

'To protect me from Ray?'

'The man is sick with love for you. He's been waiting all day for you to come. And, if not for me, there'd be no one to stop him having his way.'

'That's sick. That's totally sick. He's an old man. I'm just a kid!'

'You're a beautiful woman. But love can be a sickness, that's true. Don't worry, I've given him a healing sleep, and when he wakes, his sickness will have passed. He won't ever try to bother you again.'

'He'd better not! It's totally illegal, you know. I could call the police.' My face was burning, but I started to shiver, feeling cold and hot, disgusted and excited.

'I've taken away Ray's sickness, but other men will fall in love with you, whether you will it or no. That is your fate. But, I promise you, I won't let you be harmed or dishonoured. I'll always watch over you, even if you don't return my love. When you are ready to take a lover, it will be by your own choice entirely.'

My feelings changed again. I noticed how handsome he was, how noble and sad. Maybe, once upon a time, in another country, I really had been his wife. I said, 'Can I see you again? I mean, I'd like to. When I'm older.'

He smiled 'When you are ready for a husband, I'll come again. I've waited more than a thousand years; a few more years don't matter to me.' He smiled, and his bright eyes were looking into mine, seeing me as I'd never been seen before. He was so handsome I could hardly stand it, it was like a sweet ache in my bones.

And suddenly I was scared, not of him, but of the way I was feeling about him. I turned around and ran back to the safety of my own house.

I took a big breath, and stood quietly for a few moments in the living room (in shape, exactly the same as the one next door), breathing in the familiar smell of home, listening to the slow ticking of the old-fashioned clock on the plain white wall, feeling the cool breath of the air-conditioning.

I yawned. Then I wriggled and stretched, blinking and feeling sleepy. Did I fall asleep on the bus, or what? Maybe the whole thing had been a dream.

I went to check out the refrigerator. It looked to me like we were going to have to eat out that night, unless Mom remembered to stop off at the supermarket on her way home from work There was some half-flat Diet Dr Pepper left, so I drank that, and made myself a jelly sandwich and wolfed it down.

Feeling better, I went back to my bedroom.

Ca lay on my pillow, as usual. I flopped down and hugged him. 'Ca! Darling Ca, you'll never guess! I met a man. He said he used to be my husband in another country, before I was born — what do you think of that?'

Ca said nothing.

I stared at his sleeping face, frowned, and shook him. 'Wake up, sleepyhead!'

He had nothing to say. Loyal he was, but sometimes a bit slow. I picked up Queeny from her throne on the tissue box on the bedside table.

'Who was he, Queeny? What's his name? Was it true, what he said?'

The silence rang in my brain as Queeny stared back with her blind, painted eyes, and did not respond. Sometimes, to tease or punish me, she would delay answering, but this time, I knew, was different. She didn't answer because she couldn't. She was just a doll.

'Mocky?' The little purple pony smiled at me, looking shy and sweet and as loving as ever, but I knew as soon as my fingers closed around her soft, rubbery body, that she had changed, too.

It had happened. They'd left me in spite of their promises.

Or had I left them?

Into my loneliness rushed the memory of him.

He said he would watch over me.

I believed him.

I didn't even know his name, but he was my future as well as my past. He had promised to come back for me, when I was ready.

I'm ready now.

P.L.

James, Donald, and Thomas

Joseph Moore, James Ducat, Donald McArthur, and Thomas Marshall, four retired seamen, took up their posts as lighthouse keepers in the newly constructed lighthouse on Eilean Mor in December 1899.

It was a lonely place; one of the loneliest in the world. Eilean Mor (the name means 'big island' in Gaelic, but it is barely five hundred feet wide) is the largest of the Flannan Islands, twenty miles west of the island of Lewis in the Outer Hebrides. Before the building of the lighthouse, no one had lived on the Flannan Islands for centuries, although they were regularly visited by Hebridean shepherds, who ferried their sheep across the sea to graze on the rich grass, and hunters intent on catching a few of the many birds who nested there. Yet visitors were reluctant to pass a single night ashore on the Flannans, for they'd heard legends of spirits and fairies haunting these lonely outposts in the sea. The islands took their name from St Flannan, who built a chapel and his hermitage on Eilean Mor in the seventh century.

The only way on or off the island was via the supply boat *Hesperus*, which (weather permitting) called every two weeks to bring the mail, food, fuel, and other necessary supplies. The lighthouse keepers were to work in a team of three for six weeks on the island, taking turns for two weeks' leave on Lewis. Each time the *Hesperus* called she would bring one man back from his time off and take away another.

On 6 December, 1900, Joseph Moore left on the *Hesperus* for his two weeks off. After his first year as a lighthouse keeper he was not looking forward to another, and the others felt the same. The lighthouse provided shelter from the wind and rain and cold, and their duties as lighthouse keepers were not arduous, but there was little to do on the tiny, rocky island. The long hours passed slowly as they read and reread the same books and papers, played draughts and dominoes, talked to each other, or thought their own thoughts and gazed out to sea. After six months they all knew each other's stories inside out and backwards, and were starting to long for different company. Only the two weeks off every six weeks kept the job from being any different to a prison sentence, thought Joseph. Still, it was safer than his previous life as a sailor, and the pay was better: a man would be a fool to complain about such safe and regular employment.

Joseph Moore again boarded the *Hesperus* on 21 December, ready to return to his duties. But although the weather had been calm throughout his leave, shortly after *Hesperus* left port, a storm blew up. For the next three days the supply boat rode the storm off the coast, as the winds and waves made it too dangerous either to go on or to turn back.

Finally, on Christmas Eve, the weather calmed, and the boat approached the Flannans. Moore was alarmed when he realised that the lighthouse was not showing a light, but the sea was still dangerously rough; it was another two days before the weather eased enough to allow the *Hesperus* to moor at the island's east dock.

There were no mooring ropes on the dock, as there should have been, and repeated blasts on the boat's foghorn brought no response. When Joseph Moore finally went ashore he found the lighthouse cold and empty. Everything was neat and tidy. The lamps had been filled with oil and their wicks trimmed, yet they had never been lit. On the shelf, the clock had stopped. Two of the three sets of oilskins and rubber boots were missing, but one remained. With a creeping feeling of dread, Joseph read the most recent entries in the log, written by Thomas Marshall:

12 December: Gale, N by NW. Sea lashed to fury. Stormbound.
9 p.m.: Never seen such a storm. Waves very high. Tearing at lighthouse. Everything shipshape. Ducat irritable.

Moore frowned. There had been no storm reported on Lewis at that date. And it was most unusual for the log keeper to comment on anyone's temper. Perhaps in a private letter, but this was an official report that anyone might see. He read on.

> *Midnight: Storm still raging. Wind steady. Stormbound. Cannot go out. Ship passing sounding foghorn. Could see lights of cabins. Ducat quiet. McArthur crying.*

Moore blinked and read the words again, but there was no mistake. He tried to picture stolid, steady Donald McArthur in tears, and could not.

> *13 December: Storm continued through night. Wind shifted, W by N. Ducat quiet. McArthur praying.*
>
> *Noon: Grey daylight. Me, Ducat, and McArthur prayed.*

What a man did in the solitude of his own soul was between himself and his God. Moore had never known Marshall, Ducat, or McArthur to pray, publicly, alone or together. They were well used to extremities of weather – any man who had been to sea, or grown up on the coast of Scotland, had seen plenty of wind and weather. He could not imagine the storm that would have driven any of the men to tears or prayer. To swearing, blasphemy, maybe, but . . . He swallowed hard and shook his head, wondering what on earth had happened there in his absence. With a nameless dread coiling in his stomach, Moore read the final entry:

> *15 December: 1 p.m. Storm ended. Sea calm. God is over all.*

What, Moore wondered, had happened on the fourteenth? Why was there no entry for that day? Even more urgent was the question of what had happened on 15 December. When the sea was calm and 'God . . . over all,' what strange disaster had befallen the three men?

Could a sudden, freakish sea swell have swept all three men from the jetty?

Yet regulations were clear: three men staffed the lighthouse at all times, because it was a stern requirement of the post that *one* man, at least, must always remain inside. This rule was always obeyed.

Might Ducat and Marshall have gone out in their oilskins onto the jetty to perform some task and been caught by a sudden high wave that swept them out to sea? If McArthur had rushed out in a futile attempt to save them, and been swept away himself, they could all have perished, and it would explain why his oilskin was left behind.

But it didn't sound right to Moore. He knew that if he'd just seen his two companions swept off the jetty in a storm, he'd hardly rush out unprepared and meet the same fate. Only a fool would jump into a raging sea in a doomed attempt to save someone else, and his colleagues were not fools.

And what to make of all those reported tears and prayers before the fatal day?

Was it possible that one of the three men had gone insane, killed the others, then leaped into the sea himself? Although every knife, axe, and hammer that might have been a weapon was clean and in its proper place, and there was no sign of blood or human violence anywhere, it was not impossible that the killer could have used his own hands, or a rock, and afterwards thrown the bodies into the sea.

Theories have been put forward, possibilities suggested, and fictions contrived to explain the disappearance of the three keepers of the Flannan Lighthouse, but it seems unlikely that the whole truth will ever be known. Today, the lighthouse on Eilean Mor is, like most lighthouses, automatic. No one lives there. The mystery remains.

Hugh

Peri's story was familiar to me. Not in every detail, but I was certain I had read something very like it before in a book of fairy tales or old legends.

I closed the notebook and stowed it away in my brief-case. I was unsettled by it, uneasy for a reason I couldn't quite pin down. What did it tell me about Peri? That she was a fantasist? A plagiarist? A budding author? Or just a bored kid who longed to believe there could be magic in her very ordinary American suburban life?

Yet when I took another look at her photograph I couldn't believe she'd ever been ordinary, or even imagined herself so. I wished I knew when and why she'd written it. An assignment for school? Or something she'd felt compelled to write for her own reasons, something she maybe even believed . . .

'More coffee, sir?'

Lost in my thoughts, I hadn't heard the waiter approach. I looked up. No, not a waiter – the café's owner. I felt embarrassed, and a little guilty, that I didn't know his name. I glanced at my watch and was startled to see that most of the morning had gone.

'No, thanks, I'd better get going. What's the damage?'

When I got home there was just time to deal with my e-mail and a couple of other small chores before I had to shower and change my shirt (which reeked of fried bacon and other people's cigarettes) and head into town for my meeting with Hugh Bell-Rivers.

The air felt close when I went out again, warm and moist, the sky like dirty white cotton massed overhead, bearing down on the grey-and-green city, threatening rain. At the tube station, I bought a paper from the newsagent and read the story about Linzi Slater as I might have probed a wound. Once upon a time, I reminded myself, I had imagined Linzi alive and that I could find her, save her. Was I heading down that same self-deluding road in my search for Peri?

I left the train at Piccadilly Circus and walked through Soho, past Golden Square with its statue of George II and benches adorned with bare-armed office workers munching sandwiches from Boots or Marks and Spencer, enjoying their lunch *al fresco*. It wasn't raining yet.

There was just one noodle bar on Kingly Street, and as I approached it I thought I recognised the young man crossing the street. We reached the door at the same time, and our eyes met. He spoke first.

'Ian Kennedy?'

'That's me.'

I put out my hand and, after a hesitation, he shook it,

rather limply. He seemed unpractised at handshakes. *Young people these days*, I said to myself in an old-codger voice. A gloomy sense of my own mortality really had a grip on me: his youth and fitness seemed to emphasise that I was past it. Even without Peri's beauty to cast a shadow he wasn't what I'd call handsome, but young he certainly was. His hair, a pale, no-colour brown, had been shaved off close to his head, and his blandly symmetrical features were dominated by enormous blue eyes. I find that neonate look freakish and slightly disturbing in a grown man, but have noticed that women like it. His chin was faintly stubbly, which made me suspect he shaved only a couple of times a week, and he wore three small silver rings in one ear.

We went into the steamy little café and took a table beside the window.

'Drink?' I asked.

He shook his head. 'I have to work. You go ahead. The Japanese beer is nice.'

I was intending to work later, too – in fact, I was at work then – and didn't think one bottle of beer would incapacitate me. There seemed a challenge implicit in his comment. I'm not a particularly macho guy, and he gave the impression, with his earrings, trendy casual gear, and mild blue gaze, of being a modern, sensitive young chap; yet from that first moment of meeting there was something charged in the atmosphere between us, something that seemed to demand dominance displays. Or maybe I'd just made up my mind not to like him, suspecting that whatever had happened to Peri would turn out to be his fault. If it's not the father, it's the boyfriend, in cases like these, more often than not.

'What kind of work do you do?'

'I'm a filmmaker. Writer-director. We're in postproduction now, but the filming took longer than we'd thought, and time is getting tight. I'm under a lot of pressure.'

I must have looked surprised – I certainly hadn't expected this kid would be doing anything so grand – because his eyebrows went up. 'Laura didn't tell you?'

'She didn't tell me a whole lot. She said something about you being artistic; I didn't ask for details. I was more concerned with learning about Peri than about you. No offence,' I said blandly.

'Fair enough.' He shrugged. 'Only, I thought she might have shown you my first film. Not because I made it, but – Peri's the star. Anyway, it won a few awards, and led to my getting backing to write and direct my first feature. Which is what I'm working on now.'

The waitress arrived to take our orders. Hugh didn't need to consult the menu. Not having much experience with Japanese food, I said I'd have the same, plus a Kirin.

He got right down to business. 'You want to know about the last time I saw Peri. It'll be three years in December, but I remember it like it was yesterday. She'd just come back from college in America, so we hadn't seen each other for more than three months. I saw her the day she got back, but her mum was there, too, and she was tired from travelling, so the Friday night was our first date, the first chance we'd had to be together.'

'How was it? You were happy?'

'Of course.'

'You didn't find it awkward at all? Your feelings were the same?'

'I was totally in love with her,' he said flatly. 'Nothing had changed, not for me. I wanted to spend my life with her.'

'And she felt the same? As far as you could tell.'

He nodded, eyelids briefly dipping to half-mast, a slight curl to the lip. 'As far as I could tell, yes.'

'But you didn't talk about it?'

He sighed. 'We'd never stopped talking. E-mails, instant messaging, and phone calls every day. My phone bill was positively gigantic. Caused a huge row with my mum, even though I said I'd pay it off.'

'So you think, if she'd met someone else in America, or changed her feelings towards you, you would have known.'

'I thought so.'

He fell silent as the waitress arrived with our drinks.

I prompted him. 'Where did you go that night?'

'I had a couple of comp tickets to a club in Soho. I didn't know anything about it, except it had to be some kind of music gig. I was working as basically the tea-boy for a TV production company for almost no pay. That sort of job's about making contacts, and there were perks, invitations and free tickets floating around. Those just happened to be the tickets I had for that Friday night. It didn't matter to us where we went. If I'd had my own place, I'd have taken her there. But we couldn't spend the whole evening in at my mum's, with all my sisters, and . . .' he trailed off, looking vulnerable. 'But, God, I wish I'd thrown those tickets away! I wish we'd gone anywhere else.'

Our food arrived at this interesting juncture: enormous steaming bowls of soup full of noodles, meat, and vegetables. Each would have served a family of four.

'So where did you take her?'

He stripped the paper wrapping off his chopsticks and snapped them apart. 'The address was in Golden Square.'

'A club? In Golden Square?' This seemed unlikely.

He shrugged. 'Yeah. Twenty-three Golden Square, that's what it said on the card. From 9 p.m. That was another odd thing. Nine o'clock is incredibly early. So I thought, well, maybe it was a party to celebrate the opening, or maybe it was an early gig; I thought—' He stopped, shook his head. 'No, I didn't think. I really couldn't think about anything except being with Peri again. Maybe if I'd—'

'Don't beat yourself up. Just tell me what happened.'

He had picked her up from the flat in West Hampstead at about half past eight.

It was a clear, cold night. Their breath puffed out in clouds before their faces, their heels rang on the cold pavement as they walked along, their arms about each other, snuggling close for warmth, high with the happiness of being together. They took the underground to Green Park and, rather than change to another stuffy, crowded train, emerged from the underground to walk along Piccadilly.

Everything was bustling and brightly lit, humming with activity in the run-up to Christmas. Stores had extended their opening hours, and every pub and restaurant was packed to the gills and boisterous with parties. Soho, when they reached it, was like one enormous street party from the pub overspill.

But the address on the card took them away from all that, into a quiet pocket without shops or pubs, where there were only empty office buildings shut for the night. There were a few people on the benches in Golden Square, doing low-voiced deals with each other or drinking from bottles in paper bags.

Hugh brought the card close to his face, checking the address in the yellowish light of the streetlamp on the corner, sure it had to be wrong.

Then Peri squeezed his arm and pointed out a set of metal stairs leading below street level. On street level, the building housed some sort of media company, but the basement had a separate entrance. Yet it looked just as locked up and empty. Hugh felt uneasy, but before he could stop her, Peri went clattering down the metal stairs.

The door opened as soon as she put her hand to it. Hugh, pressed close against her, breathing in the flowers and citrus scent of her hair, was astonished by the room revealed. It was a surprisingly large, long space, with a gleaming parquet dance floor in the centre. Small round tables, covered with white cloths, clustered in a rough semicircle on the dark red carpet surrounding the dance floor, and faced a small stage. It was like an elegant nightclub from some old-fashioned movie, and not the sort of place Hugh had ever been in himself.

Nearly all the tables were occupied by couples, every single one of them dressed to the nines: the men in dinner jackets, the women in elegant long dresses. Hugh had worn his usual casual-smart club gear, hoping and expecting to blend in. Beneath her puffy down jacket Peri was wearing a short black dress with patterned tights and a glittery, beaded cardigan in silver and purple. She looked great, she always did, but their clothing marked them both as outsiders.

He wanted to back out, but already a black-suited waiter had bustled up to greet them, beaming with welcome.

'How good to see you, sir, madam! I've saved you a table near the stage.'

'May I take your coats?' A young woman, also wearing a black suit and bow tie, was at their side, smiling and helping Peri off with her jacket. Peri did not resist. Her face glowed with excitement and curiosity.

When he saw that, he didn't feel so bad and handed over his own coat. He'd let everyone laugh at his inappropriate gear, anything to make her happy.

The waiter led them to an empty table. In the centre, a candle glowed through ruby-coloured glass.

'May I get you something to drink?'

'What sort of beer do you have?' Hugh looked at Peri's happy face and felt a rush of reckless generosity. 'No, make that champagne.'

'I'm sorry, sir, but we're not licensed. I can offer you

Perrier or Evian water, Coca-Cola, or orange Fanta. On the house.'

'Terrific.' Hugh laughed in disbelief. 'OK, Perrier water for me. Peri?'

'Fine.' When the waiter had gone, she leaned across the table and grasped his hand, murmuring, 'We can go to a pub after. But I'm so glad you brought me here. This is so cool!'

He didn't understand why, but all that really mattered was that she was happy – and that he had been able to make her happy by doing this simple thing. It had happened before, that she'd been blown away by something he'd taken for granted, or had never noticed. London, the big, grimy city where he'd lived his whole life, was a fabulous theme park to her.

He looked around the nightclub, trying to be cool about it and not look overly interested. Although he guessed Peri was the youngest person in the room, no one appeared to be over thirty. A whole room of twenty-somethings dressed up like bright young things from the 1930s. There'd been no mention of a dress code on the invitation. And they were all good-looking, and nearly all of them were white. As his gaze flitted from face to face, he saw something else: they actually looked alike, with similar features and colouring. Were they related? Was this a family event? Maybe the invitations had been meant for someone else. His stomach plunged as he considered the trouble he might be in at work for snaffling an invite meant for somebody else.

The waiter returned with a big bottle of Perrier and two heavy red glass goblets. He asked their permission before breaking the seal on the bottle and pouring it. Then, with a bow, he backed away.

Peri smiled at Hugh, and the candle flame danced reflected in her eyes.

'Welcome back.' He lifted his glass.

'To us.' She clinked her glass against his.

'Forever.'

He was happy gazing into her eyes, breathing her perfume, luxuriating in her physical nearness after the long, frustrating weeks apart. They held hands, and he caught her knees between his beneath the table.

The lights went down and the murmur of voices died away as a spotlight revealed a man standing on the stage.

Hugh's narrative, fluent and full of detail until this point, now faltered.

'Obviously a folksinger, dressed up like a gypsy, or one of those pop singers from the early eighties, what were they called? New romantics, something like that. But the music he did was older than that, moany old folk songs, not my sort of thing at all. But Peri loved it.' He scowled and fiddled with his chopsticks.

'Anyway, this singer turns out to be the owner of the club, and he's the one, the one who took Peri, or at least she went off with him – he disappeared, too. Find him, you'll find her.' He sounded as if he'd finished.

'Describe him.'

He sighed. 'Big. Handsome. Almost ridiculously good-looking. And blonde – hair down to his shoulders. Silk shirt, knee-high boots. Very theatrical.'

Very mechanical. I said impatiently, 'Forget the costume. I want to know what *he* was like.'

Hugh shut his eyes and I saw the colour drain from his face. He swallowed hard, and whispered, 'Monster.'

'What?'

Blue eyes blazed at me out of a white face. He gave himself a little shake.

'I can't explain.'

'Try.'

'It was his presence – charisma, power, whatever it is; I've met people with it before; some are gorgeous with it, like he was, others, it's more to do with being powerful, and knowing it – it's like you'd expect a king would be.'

I thought I knew what he meant. 'OK. Powerful vibes. But – a monster? You mean, like Hannibal Lecter?'

He shook his head. The colour was coming back to his face. 'Not evil. But not human. I don't know what I mean, really.' His shoulders slumped. 'I'd know him straight away if I saw him again, no question. Even in disguise, I'd sense him. There's no point me trying to describe what he looked like – the way he appeared that night was just something he'd put on. He'd look different every time.'

'Heavily made up?'

'No. Not at all.'

'So . . . what do you mean? Why can't you describe him?'

He shook his head in frustration. 'The truth is, I can't

remember much about how he looked. The hair, the stupid clothes ... but nothing for a composite sketch. When I think about that evening – and I have some *very* vivid memories of it – when I try to remember *him* all I can think of is *me*: how I felt, how he made me feel.'

'That's perfectly normal.' I was getting impatient with all this agonising, although I had to admire his honesty. In my experience, witnesses who gave the most precise and vivid descriptions, absolutely certain of what they had seen, were most often the fantasists. 'What was his name?'

'Mider.' His pronunciation, more or less, was 'mither,' but he spelled it out for me. 'That was the name of the club on the invitation, and that's what the singer said his name was. It was his place.'

The name was familiar, although I couldn't think why. I stored it away to consider later, and concentrated on Hugh's story.

While Mider sang, accompanying himself on guitar, Hugh tuned out and speculated about the rest of the audience. It was unlikely to be a family gathering with everyone belonging to the same generation, but something more than chance had brought them all there. The more he looked around the room, the more certain he felt that everyone was related somehow.

By the time the singer had finished his set, Hugh had finished the bottle of water and had to go off in search of the toilets. There was just one, unisex, with four enclosed stalls and a purple carpet on the floor, every bit as posh as the rest of the club. He had it all to himself, and took his time washing his hands with lavender-scented soap, checking out the progress of his stubble in the ornately framed looking glass above the sink.

When he came out he saw that his place had been taken by the singer, who leaned across the table, much too close to Peri, his eyes fixed upon hers, his lips rapidly moving: clearly no casual conversation.

His gut clenched in a spasm of jealousy, and Hugh felt ready for a fight as he strode across the room.

Then Peri got up so suddenly she knocked her chair over. She whirled around, and Hugh saw she wore a panic-stricken expression. He caught her quickly in his arms and glared over her head at Mider. But the singer had turned away, presenting the back of his golden head to Hugh's angry gaze.

'What happened?' he murmured, pressing his lips to her hair.

She relaxed in his embrace and peeped up at him. 'Where's the ladies' room?'

'Peri, what's wrong? What did that bastard say to you?'

When she didn't respond, he let go. 'Right, I guess I'll have to ask *him*.'

'No!' She grabbed at him. 'Don't make a big deal out of it! Please, Hugh, just show me the restroom.'

'Tell me what he said.'

She was tense, her eyes wide and fearful. 'Nothing!'

' "Nothing" made you run away from him, looking scared to death?'

She pressed her face into his chest. Hugh felt embarrassingly exposed, standing in the middle of the room, but, to his relief, no one paid them the slightest attention. They might have been wrapped in a protective shell. Whoever these people were, they were experts at ignoring others, that particularly British form of politeness.

'Come on, we're leaving.'

'No! Hugh!' She looked up, shattered.

He sighed. 'We're not staying here if he's made you uncomfortable.'

'He wasn't. He just said something . . . that reminded me of a dream, and it scared me.'

'A dream?'

She nodded. 'There was this dream I used to have all the time when I was little. I never forgot it. You could say it haunted me. I even wrote a story about it, just before I met you. That man over there reminded me of my dream. He said something and it was kind of like *déjà vu*, you know? My dream all over again, coming true. It freaked me out.'

Hugh didn't know what to say. He shook his head. 'You're sure he didn't say anything . . . unfriendly? Or nasty? Or . . .' He flailed around. 'Was he hitting on you?' But that was such a stupid question. Of course he had been. It was almost inevitable. Somebody as gorgeous as Peri . . . Only a psycho would try to pick a fight with every hopeful who tried to get off with his girlfriend. As long as he hadn't crossed the line in some way, turned what might be flattery into offence.

'He was really nice, honestly.'

He glanced across at that golden head, still turned away. It was as if everything had frozen. He had the odd feeling that time had stopped for them, and nothing would progress until he'd sorted this out with Peri.

'What were you talking about?'

She looked vague. 'Oh, I don't know ... I asked him about one of his songs. I thought I knew it from somewhere, but he said he wrote it himself.'

'So what was your dream like?'

He saw from the set of her chin, the drift of her eyes, that she wouldn't tell him about it, and was hurt that she still wanted to have secrets from him. He would have told her everything, stripped his soul bare for her inspection, if she'd asked.

'Can we go to the restroom?' She squeezed his hand.

It would give him a chance to talk to the singer on his own. He stood a little straighter. 'Go on, then. It's just back there.'

She clung to him. 'Come with me.'

So he did. It was a relief, after all, to delay the confrontation. When they reached the restroom, Peri pulled him inside and pushed him against the wall and almost before he knew what was happening, they were fucking.

Telling me, Hugh hunched down in his seat, avoiding eye contact. It excited him to think about it even now, and I'd bet he'd thought about it a lot. But no matter how many times he'd replayed it on his own internal screen, he'd probably never shared it with anyone. And who was I, to deserve this intimacy?

'It was like something out of a movie, man. She was all over me. She really wanted it.'

'She didn't usually like sex?'

He looked at me as if I'd crawled out from under his plate, waving my feelers. 'Of course she did. But this was a public toilet – even if it was awfully nice – no lock on the door, anybody could have come in. We'd never done it like that before, up against the wall, somewhere we might have been caught. I wouldn't have thought she—' He flushed and dropped his gaze. 'But it was her idea, it was what she wanted, and . . . It was exciting. She was totally hot. I guess she'd missed me so much . . . ' Entranced again, he drifted for a few seconds before coming back to the present, to me, to finish, flatly, 'It was all over in about three minutes. Then she made me leave.'

In a happy, relaxed stupor, he went back to the table, where Mider was waiting. He'd added a third chair, and on the table there was a fresh bottle of Perrier, and, unexpectedly, a gaming board with piles of white and black stones.

Hugh found that his annoyance with the man had totally vanished. Well, after all, Peri had just proved how little reason he had to be jealous.

Mider nodded. 'Will you have a game with me? I had the impression that my singing was not to your taste.'

'Oh, it was fine. You sing really well,' he said awkwardly.

Mider raised an eyebrow. 'Shall we play?'

The board and stones were for the Japanese game Go. It had been a passion of his once; he'd been very good at it. He'd started playing with some friends in his final year of school, as a protest against the popularity of computer games and the snootiness of the chess club, and he'd grown to become something of an expert player.

Hugh looked at his host more closely, wondering if they had met before. How had he known he played Go?

'What do you say? Will you give me a game?'

'It wouldn't be fair to my girlfriend. She'd be bored just watching us play.'

'She won't be bored. Someone else will be singing soon.'

Peri returned, bright-eyed and golden. His heart ached with longing. He wanted to rush off with her then and there, but Mider was waiting. He felt curiously obliged, unable to refuse, and turned to Peri: 'I honestly don't care; we can leave any time you like.' He scanned her face, her posture, for any sign that she was uncomfortable. She smiled into his eyes as intimately as if they were alone.

'Let's stay for a while. If there's going to be more music, I'm happy.'

The new singer was one of the beautiful, elegantly dressed women from another table. She looked enough like Mider to have been his sister as she took his guitar and his place in the spotlight. She sang 'fa la la' and 'my love has gone,' and as Peri sighed happily, sinking into the ballad as into a hot bath, Hugh tuned it out and concentrated on the game.

Time flew by, enjoyably, and quite suddenly it seemed, Hugh had won. It hadn't been an easy game; his opponent was good. He could feel proud of himself.

'Name your forfeit,' said Mider.

'How do you mean?'

'You've won. Since we didn't name stakes beforehand, that's your privilege now.'

'Oh, that's OK,' said Hugh. 'We were only playing for fun.'

'There's no fun in a game without a stake.'

'I don't agree. And since nobody said anything about it beforehand—'

'Careless, you.'

The arrogance stung, as it was meant to. 'Careless *you*. I'm the winner, after all. I can ask for whatever I want?'

'Yes.'

'Anything?'

'Do you doubt me?'

'I'm just checking out the rules. You'd give me whatever I asked?'

He expected a laying out of boundaries, some more reasonable definition of 'anything', but Mider said only, 'I would. On my honour. And you're then honour bound to grant me another game.'

'Ah, I see. So you can win it back.'

The faintest frown touched the handsome face. 'What you win, you may keep. Likewise, whatever I win from you. I don't always lose.'

'No, I'll bet you don't.' It had to be a scam, although

he couldn't see how it was supposed to work. Hugh was not by nature a gambler. He didn't even waste his money buying lottery tickets. He couldn't guess the object of this con, if it was one. So Mider let him win a couple of times and lulled him into a false sense of security before sweeping the board – so what? Hugh had forty pounds on him, money that had to see him through the week ahead. There was no way he was going to blow it all on a bet with a stranger. He shrugged. 'How many games?'

'Three.'

'OK. Shall we say ten pounds a game?'

The other man's eyes narrowed, his face darkening. 'Are you mocking me?'

There was no music. When had the singer stopped? There was no background buzz of conversation, either. Hugh had the feeling that everyone in the room was watching them, listening with bated breath. And these were Mider's people, not his.

He held up his hands. 'No! Look, I don't know how you're fixed, but I'm on a tight budget. I have a lousy job and can't even afford to run a car. Ten pounds might be nothing to you, but it's a lot to me. Really.'

'But Hugh,' said Mider gently, as the tension eased out of the room, 'you don't have to pay me – you've won this game! You can ask for whatever you want.'

'Sure, great. And if I don't win the next game, it would be your turn to ask me for something. Would it be *honourable* of me to ask you for something I couldn't match?'

'Ask for what you want.'

There was some trick to this that Hugh couldn't see. Lessons absorbed long ago from stories, fairy tales, and jokes jostled in his mind with enlightened self-interest, logic, and greed. There must be some moral strategy involved, a right and a wrong. Ask for too much and get nothing at all; ask for too little and lose even more . . .

Mouth dry, he gazed around the dimly lit room. He noticed that although all had the ornate red goblets, theirs was the only table with a bottle on it. Peri had asked for a Coke, and the waiter had brought her a can. None of the other tables had anything but goblets. Now that he thought about it, Hugh recalled seeing waiters moving among the tables carrying large, opaque decanters. The liquid in the other goblets might have been anything, but from the way the other people drank, he was willing to bet it wasn't water.

'All right,' he said. 'I'll tell you what I want: a drink.'

'You already have one.'

He shook his head. 'No. I want what *they're* drinking.' He waved his arm. 'It's wine, isn't it?'

'Yes, but—'

'But you don't have a licence. At least, that's what the waiter told me. Is this a private club?'

'It's my place.' The man did not look happy.

Gleefully, Hugh pressed on. 'So you can make me a member, or you can give me a drink, as a friend. You're the boss here, right? Go on, pour me a drink. Even if anybody was to find out, you wouldn't get done for it – you're not charging me.'

Mider didn't seem to be following Hugh's argument. 'Ask me for something else. There are things you want. I can give you money enough to buy a car, to buy your own house, to leave your little job. Just ask.'

'I want that drink.'

They stared at each other. Hugh felt triumphant; without understanding it, he'd found his host's weakness. He would make him do what he didn't want to do. He really had won. Finally, Mider stood and walked away.

'Oh, Hugh,' Peri whispered. 'Was that smart?'

Hugh shrugged. 'I don't know. I don't know what's going on here, at all. Do you?'

Slowly she shook her head. They held hands.

Mider came back carrying a goblet. As he stood beside the table he said, 'Think: a glass of wine is soon gone. Will you not ask me instead for something of real, lasting value in your own world?'

'Are you going to let me taste that wine?'

Without another word, Mider set the goblet down. Hugh let go Peri's hand to raise the glass.

The scent hit him first, and his nostrils flared with pleasure. When he drank, the wine was rich and heavy on his tongue, smooth and delicious in his mouth. It tasted the way he had once imagined grown-up drinks might taste, but he had certainly never tasted anything like it. It must have been a very rare and expensive vintage. It was so much nicer than any wine he'd ever had before that he immediately took another mouthful to make sure.

'Wow.' He felt a wide and foolish grin stretch his lips.

'That is really good stuff. No wonder you wanted to keep it to yourself. Tell me the name so I can buy lots of it.'

Mider's face was set like stone. Hugh's spirits soared; he felt invincible. He didn't understand why, if the man really could hand over a car or a wad of cash, he should begrudge this single glass of wine, however valuable it might be. It must be that Hugh had confounded him, spoiled whatever scam he was attempting to run.

'Confusion to our enemies,' Hugh pronounced, raising the glass before taking another drink. He set it down and slid it across to Peri. 'Here, try it.'

She glanced at Mider. This annoyed Hugh – why did she think she needed a stranger's permission? Anyway, he didn't respond, and after a brief hesitation, Peri picked up the glass in both hands and took the tiniest of sips. Then, looking surprised, she gulped more. 'I thought I didn't like wine. I could get addicted to this!'

He laughed and took the glass away from her. 'Easy! This is *my* prize, remember?' He drained the rest of it and smiled at Mider. 'I guess you'll want a rematch now, huh? Even though you'll never get *this* back.'

The wine had gone straight to his head. It was powerful stuff. Yet he didn't feel fuzzy; there was no alcoholic haze wrapping his senses. Instead, all his senses felt sharper than before. It seemed he could hear whispering from the people at the other tables, and there were colours and movement at the corners of his eyes ... he couldn't quite make it out, but it was all tremendously suggestive and fascinating. Everything reminded him in brief, charged flashes, of something else. He remembered what Peri had said about *déjà vu* and Mider reminding her of a childhood dream. He turned to her, meaning to ask her again, but she shook her head, frowning, and he realised that Mider had already set up the board for a new game.

He looked down at the board, then at his pile of white stones. He thought of the patterns he could make with them, and what they might symbolise ... Everything he looked at seemed more than itself, suggested so many other things, all of them intensely interesting. It was very distracting. He felt the urge to let go and follow his impulse, let the images well up in his head unrestricted, fall into a dream. And then it occurred to him that the wine had been drugged.

What was it, a psychedelic? LSD? Mescaline? Hugh wasn't averse to a little chemical experimentation now and then. Only not *right then*, surrounded by strangers, with Peri depending on him to steer her safely home ... Maybe he hadn't been so terribly clever after all. And maybe all of Mider's emotion had been an act, pushing him into a more vulnerable position.

Anxiety worked on him like a cold shower. He resisted the pull of the drug with all his might, shutting it out. It was absolutely vital that he concentrate.

Hugh played his best, and in the blink of an eye it was all over, and he'd won again. Mider asked him to name his forfeit and this time, although his heart pounded, he didn't hesitate.

'Five hundred thousand pounds.'

Peri's hand gripped his thigh, her fingernails digging in. He didn't look at her. All his attention was fixed on Mider's face. The singer, club owner, whatever he was, didn't look surprised or discomfited. He snapped his fingers, and a waiter came over with a chequebook and a gold pen.

Hugh watched the other man write out the cheque. As he read the figure – £500,000 – he had to struggle not to laugh. How could it be so easy? He should have asked for a million. This had to be a fake, anyway.

Coolly he nodded, folded the cheque, and stuffed it into his shirt pocket.

'One last game,' said Mider.

'Act Three: in which mine host wins it all back.' Hugh wasn't sure that he'd spoken aloud. His mouth was dry with a thirst the Perrier could not quench. He longed for another glass of Mider's wine.

The game seemed to go on for a very long time – for hours, although in retrospect he realised that was impossible. Mider was quick and decisive as he placed his pieces on the board; Hugh agonised over his strategy. But in the end it didn't matter what he did or how long he thought about it: there was no beating his host. It was almost a relief when he had to concede at last.

He reached into his pocket and pulled out the cheque. 'Here you go.'

'I don't want that. You won it fairly; it's yours to keep. I'll name the forfeit.'

Hugh crossed his arms. Now they were getting to the

point of this whole charade. 'Go on,' he said grimly.

Mider canted his head toward Peri. 'I want her.'

Hugh looked at Peri. Her reaction shocked him even more than Mider's outrageous demand. She should have been laughing that wild, infectious laugh of hers. She should have made fun of the anachronistic old hippie who had the nerve to talk about her as if she were property. Or she might have been furious: Mider's implication being that she was for sale, and Hugh was her pimp. But Peri looked neither angry nor amused. She sat with her eyes cast down and a blush on her cheek like some innocent maid from the reprehensible, sexist past.

He was appalled. If she wouldn't defuse the situation and refused to stand up for herself, it was up to him. He had no choice; he had to protect her. But he hated fighting. It had been years since he'd been in a physical brawl, and Mider had about him the air of a man who was well used to taking care of himself and might even enjoy hurting others.

'She's not mine to give away,' Hugh said shortly.

'Isn't she your wife?'

'She's not my wife, and even if she were, that wouldn't make her property. Ask me for something else.'

Mider was silent. Then he said, 'Grant me a kiss from her lips and the right to put my arms around her in an embrace.'

Hugh trembled. He clenched his fists beneath the table. Peri wasn't holding his hand or touching his leg, by then. She wasn't looking at either of them. She'd withdrawn into herself, as unreachable on the other side of the table as if she'd still been on the other side of the Atlantic Ocean. He was aware of how little he knew her and how much longer they'd been apart than they had ever been together.

He took a deep breath. 'I told you, I'm not her owner. If Peri wants to kiss somebody, that's her decision. You can't ask me to make her do anything.'

'Then do I have your word that you won't try to stop me?'

'Like hell I won't.' Hugh's self-possession deserted him, and he jumped up, rocking the little table. 'You stay away from her! I love her, and she loves me – tell him, Peri!'

Finally, Peri looked up, a drowning expression on her face. That sleepy, helpless look irritated him even as it tugged at his heart. 'Tell him,' he repeated sharply.

'I love Hugh,' she said to Mider. Her voice was very faint.

'There,' said Hugh, throwing the cheque down like a challenge. 'Here's your money back.'

'It's yours. You won it.'

'And now you've won it back. So we're quits.' He grasped hold of Peri, pulling her up out of her chair. 'Come on, love, I'm taking you home.'

She didn't resist, but she was not exactly travelling under her own steam. She was like a big doll he had to walk across the floor. He was very aware of their audience, all the people in the big, dim, underground room, silent, watching, and he knew it would only take a word from Mider to set them all against him.

A waiter stood at the door with their coats. He was blank-faced, unsmiling; but he opened the door, and no one tried to stop them from leaving, and no one followed.

He marched her up the metal stairs and steered her along the dark, empty street, back towards the lights and the throngs of people. He'd expected the streets would be nearly deserted by now, but there was the usual crush at all the entrances to the Leicester Square underground station, so the trains must still be running. As they paused on the corner, Hugh checked his watch. He stared in disbelief as the digital display changed from 23:03 to 23:04. Still an hour till midnight, when he felt they had been in that basement club for hours, for a whole, long night.

He thought of the wine, and his suspicion that it had been drugged, and suddenly Peri's silence and her stumbling walk took on a more sinister aspect.

'Are you all right, love?'

She gazed up at him, yet seemed unable to focus. Her blue eyes were cloudy and far away. 'Hmm? I was dreaming . . .' She smiled a private smile.

He held her tight, kissing the top of her head, breathing in the scent of her clean hair. 'I'm going to take you home now.'

'Mmmm, that's nice.' She leaned against him, in a world of her own, utterly relaxed.

She hadn't had as much to drink as he had, but she was smaller, lighter. Anything in the wine would affect her more strongly. He'd been tense and suspicious, which might have helped him fight off the effects, whereas Peri, relaxed, would have been more vulnerable to any drug.

He felt furious at himself, and thought they'd been lucky to get away. But they *had* got away, and he got her home, delivering her safely to her mother's door at twenty minutes to twelve.

'She went inside, and that was the last time I saw her.' He looked drained and sad after this partial reliving of the longest night of his life, but I had no sympathy for him. My subconscious had finally responded with the information I'd wanted. I'd recognised the story, and remembered that Mider was a character from ancient Celtic myth. The story in Peri's notebook was from the same source.

Imaginative, Laura Lensky had called Hugh. *Artistic. He fantasises.*

Oh, yes, all of that. But how she could square this fairy tale with the idea that he was honest and trustworthy was beyond me.

'So that's the end? You let him take her?'

That surprised him. A frown wrinkled his brow. 'What do you think I should have done?'

'Oh, I don't know.' I made a pretence of thinking. 'Maybe ... if you'd gone and dug up his *sidh*, the king of the underworld might have been forced to come out and deal with you.'

'Shee?' he repeated blankly.

'Spelled s-i-d-h, or s-i-t-h. The Gaelic word for fairies, and for the ancient burial mounds and artificial hills which were presumed to be their homes. Don't try and tell me you've never read about the *Sidhe*.'

'I didn't know that was how it was pronounced.'

'Right. But you *do* know the story of Mider and Etain.'

'Ai-deen?' He copied my pronunciation carefully. 'Huh. I thought Eee-tain, to rhyme with Elaine. Sure, I read "The Wooing of Etain" when I was researching *The Flower-Faced Girl*. My film,' he explained, taking my dropped jaw for curiosity. 'The short subject I made after Peri – disappeared.'

'After,' I said sourly. 'You're sure about that?'

He ate some more noodles, handling the chopsticks as deftly as if he'd been born to them. 'You're very well-read for a detective. Or well-informed in some unusual areas.'

'I suppose you've met loads of detectives.'

'The police certainly hadn't heard of Mider.'

'You told *them* that story?' I was staggered. 'I thought you only entertained me and Peri's mother with that fairy tale.'

He gave me a hard look. 'It's what happened. If I was going to make something up, it would be a lot more believable, believe me. Maybe this Mider guy expected me to recognise what was going on and play along a little better. Or maybe it was all for Peri's sake.'

'You mean, the story she wrote.'

He looked blank. 'What story?'

'In a notebook. Her mother gave it to me. You never read it?'

He shook his head. I found myself inclined to believe

him. It was one thing for him to mess me around and waste my time, but if he'd told the *police* that fairy tale, maybe something like it really had happened to him. Or he'd been made to believe it had.

'So, what did the police say?'

'You can probably guess.'

'Tell me anyway.'

He sighed and pushed his bowl to one side. 'There was no club downstairs at Number 23 Golden Square, and there never had been. On Monday morning, it was all offices, upstairs and down, just as it had been at close of business on Friday. There *was* a separate entrance to the basement, but nobody ever used it. The gate at the top was bolted and chained shut, and the door at the bottom was alarmed. Even if somebody did have access, they'd have had to clear out all the desks and computers and stuff and redecorate the whole place like an elegant nightclub in about two hours, without anyone noticing. Sounds like a job for the *Mission: Impossible* force, yeah? And even saying there was somebody with the money and the manpower to do it, you'd have to ask how it could possibly be worth it, all that just to confuse me and kidnap Peri.'

'So you think she was kidnapped.'

'I don't know. Abducted, seduced . . . ' He let his shoulders fall, defeated. 'Maybe she was willing. I still think there was something in her drink. Maybe the wine I had, or maybe something separate in her soft drink. She acted so weird, afterwards; I'd never seen her act like that. Maybe it was that date-rape drug, so she wouldn't struggle when he came for her later.'

'From her mother's place.'

He nodded.

'You left her *with* her mother?'

'Yeah. I didn't go in with her – she didn't want me to – but I waited, and saw her go in and the street door shut behind her. Their flat was upstairs, and what she always did if I didn't go in, was go to the front window and wave down at me. That night, Laura came and stood next to her. They had their arms wrapped around each other's waist, like sisters, and they looked so cosy and happy there in the warm, lighted room, waving down at me. Then they drew the curtains. I stood there for a little while longer. I don't know why, but I didn't want to go, even though I was expecting to see her in the morning. Plus, it was bloody cold. Anyway, that was the last I saw of her, standing there with her mother, the two of them smiling down at me. And I told myself I was a lucky bastard, then I went home.' He dropped his face into his hands.

'Finished?'

I looked at the waitress, who was looking quizzically at the great mass of noodles still in my bowl.

'Take it,' I said. 'But I would like another beer.'

Hugh raised his head. 'Just the bill, please.'

'So you think he came back and took her while she was too drugged to struggle.'

He sighed. 'I just don't know. Maybe there was no drug. Maybe there didn't have to be. Maybe he kind of hypnotised her into submission— I think of how I saw them together at the table, and that weird thing she said about her dream. And there's another thing. What she said to him in the club. I kept thinking about it afterwards, and I just couldn't be sure. You know, I thought she said "I love Hugh." But her voice was so faint, maybe what she *really* said was "I love you." And maybe I just heard what I wanted to hear.' He rubbed his head, looking miserable.

I waited, trying to compel the truth from him with my eyes.

He stared back challengingly. 'And even if he took her by force, she could have fallen in love with him after. What do they call it? Where victims identify with their kidnappers? The Stockholm Syndrome. And, after all, if he got her pregnant—'

'If *he* did? Are you sterile or something?'

He scowled. 'OK, we didn't use protection that night, it's true. But once I started thinking how weird that scene was, how out of character for her, I had to wonder why it happened. Maybe she was already pregnant and wanted me to think it could be mine. Maybe she'd already got together with Mider in America, and everything that evening was a show put on for my sake. No, I know that's paranoid, and I know it's unlikely, but what the hell am I supposed to think?'

The waitress returned with a fresh cold bottle of beer and the bill on a saucer.

Hugh snatched the slip of paper as if he expected me to fight him for it. Then he stood up, took his wallet from his back pocket, and laid a couple of notes on the saucer. 'Enjoy your beer.'

'Hey, you're not leaving!'

'I am. If you've got any more questions—'

'Of course I do.'

'Good luck.'

It pained me to abandon a drink that had been paid for, but I followed him out into the street. I talked to his back. 'For a man in love, you give up awfully easy.'

He stopped and turned, frowning. 'I'm not in love with her. I was, but she left me. That was years ago. It's over.'

'Even if she didn't want to leave you? Even if she was taken against her will?'

'Stop trying to make this my fault, OK? I didn't *let* her go. Anything I could have done to get her back, I would have. Six months later, she called Laura, remember, not me. She didn't even mention my name. We're history.'

'So, you're going to leave her to her fate just because she hurt your feelings?'

His scowl deepened. 'I made time to come and see you. I didn't have to. I've told you everything, for all the thanks I get.'

'Have you really?'

'If you've got something you want to say, just say it.'

We both shifted uneasily on the pavement, bristling at each other like a couple of dogs, each wanting to be at the other's throat, both wary of the consequences.

'Hugh!'

The voice, clear as a bell, made him forget about me. I

saw a tall young woman charging across the street at us, a wide grin splitting her narrow face. She was a young amazon, nearly as tall as I was, and strong and athletic-looking. She threw her arms around Hugh and gave him a smacking kiss.

'You told me you'd be locked in the editing room all day. Liar!'

He wrapped his arms around her, smiling sheepishly. 'I shouldn't be here now. I had to meet someone.'

She looked at me with clear grey eyes shining out beneath arched brows. Although not a great beauty like Peri, she was a very attractive young woman. 'Hello, someone.'

'Ian Kennedy.' I held out my hand. She took it in a firm, tennis player's grip. 'Fiona McNeill.'

'Mr Kennedy's a private detective,' said Hugh. 'Working for Laura Lensky.'

Something in her eyes shut down. 'Looking for Peri?'

Hugh pulled her firmly away from me. 'Come on, walk me back to work.'

'I've got your number,' I called after him. Childishly, I hoped it sounded like a threat. 'I'll have more questions later.' Neither of them turned to look back at me. I watched them go, leaning on each other, clinging together, Peri's discarded lover and her replacement trying to make a life together.

I wondered if Hugh still dreamed about Peri as I dreamed about Jenny, wondered if he ever passed a single day unhaunted by loss and regret. The passage of time was meant to heal all sorrows, but for some, I thought, centuries would not be enough. It was said that people still felt pain in amputated limbs, that the mind never really adjusted to the loss. It was the same on the rare occasion when another person became part of your life. After she left, you learned to limp along, you made new friends and pretended life was just dandy, but at night you'd wake up in agony, feeling pain in your phantom limb, a pain no one could explain or heal.

The afternoon had grown steadily more overcast and humid, and the air felt about as wet as it could possibly get without actual rain. I took a deep breath of the city's damp, odorous exhalation, and continued walking down the street until it doglegged into Golden Square.

Number 23 was part of an eighteenth-century brick terrace, four storeys high, that lined one side of the square. It had a large display window to the left of the front door, and it was immediately obvious that the ground-floor property was empty. A sign fastened to the black iron railings in front advertised a business property to let. I went up to the railings and peered over the spikes. The basement windows had security bars across them, and although there were net curtains still hanging inside, they hid nothing, for there was nothing to hide. There was a black metal door without an outside handle, and a very visible alarm box attached to the top lintel. The metal stairs leading down to the basement area were practically as steep as a ladder, clearly not meant for regular use. The gate in the iron railings was locked shut as Hugh had told me. He hadn't mentioned the windows.

I straightened up and wandered over to the door, which was set in an archway of white stone, with a fanlight above. The one modern touch was a grubby plate with buzzers to operate the entry intercom system. There were seven buttons, but only three occupants listed: a film production company (two floors), a publisher, and something that went by the initials IMP.

High in the wall to the right of the doorway was an old Greater London Council blue plaque:

GREATER LONDON COUNCIL

THESE
TWO HOUSES
WERE THE
PORTUGUESE EMBASSY
1724-1747
THE
MARQUESS OF POMBAL
Portuguese Statesman
Ambassador
1739-1744
lived here

I wandered back to the front window and gazed inside at the empty space. Then I peered over the railings again at the veiled windows below. I assumed that basement and ground floor were treated as one property. I wondered when the last tenants had moved out and how long they had stayed. Had they felt it haunted? My own reflection in the dusty glass looked as dim and wavering as a ghost, but I couldn't believe there were any ghosts inside. I didn't feel anything weird about the place, no strangeness hanging over it or emanating from it. Not that I'd know – I don't have that sort of sensitivity, much as I'd tried to develop it over the years.

I got out my notebook and jotted down the name and number of the letting agency. I knew it would be easy to talk my way inside and have a good sniff around the basement; I just didn't know if there was really any point.

I felt jittery, anxious, and my mouth was dry. With regret, I thought of the beer I'd left behind in the noodle bar. I turned away from Number 23 and crossed over to the tree-lined square. I sat down on a bench and recalled Hugh's description of his mental state after drinking Mider's wine, his comment that everything had seemed intensely significant and meaningful.

That was how I felt now, and it worried me.

There's always the temptation, when you've heard only part of a story, to finish it in a way that makes sense to you – even if it's not true. I had to remind myself that I didn't know enough about Hugh and Peri yet to make assumptions. I had to resist that slide into the past.

I sat down on that bench meaning to think about Hugh and Peri, but very soon I was thinking again about Jenny.

Jenny

Sometimes people want to disappear.

Sometimes they just leave, for reasons which you would never understand.

And sometimes, of course, you have to let them go. It's the stalker, rapist mentality that refuses to accept a lover's decision to end it. That was why I was wary of accepting missing person cases from husbands or wives of the vanished. I preferred reuniting parents with lost children, or vice versa.

I'd had an English girlfriend once who thought I was just like Holden Caulfield.

I'd told her that was crazy, that being a private investigator specialising in missing persons had nothing in common with being 'a catcher in the rye,' and she was just confused by my goddam American accent and all.

And yet I'd never forgotten her teasing comment; maybe there was something to it.

It was true that what I liked about my job was when I managed to restore families and bring people who cared about each other together again. I also liked solving mysteries. What I didn't like was finding out that people were dead and there was absolutely nothing I could do about it.

Before I became a private investigator I had a job in information systems technology. I went to work in Chicago, straight out of college, which was terrific, but all too soon the company transferred me to Dallas. I hated everything about that place until I met Jenny Macedo.

I'll never forget the first time I saw her. I was feeling hot, bored, and alienated at a party full of strangers, to which I'd been dragged by somebody I worked with. I went into the kitchen for a beer, and there she was, this tiny little woman in a tight red scoop-necked top, with a mass of shiny black hair curling around her lively face. She seemed child-sized, barely five feet tall, but she had the most fantastic, womanly figure, and a wonderfully dirty laugh. I couldn't stop looking at her; it was like she was in colour, and everyone else was just black-and-white. I was smitten from that first moment and, amazingly, she seemed to feel something similar for me.

I wasn't sure at first: she had a mouth on her, sharp and sarcastic, and she was so scornful of my every opinion that I thought she must despise me. Only the fact that I didn't want to go back into the living room, where some satanic heavy metal band on the stereo made the walls vibrate, kept me standing there trying to impress her, and trying not to stare too obviously down her shirt. Anyway, I soon found I preferred being insulted by her to exchanging banalities with anyone else. Eventually I plucked up the courage to ask her out.

Within a month of our first date we were living together. I bought her a diamond ring. We became officially engaged. This was it, I thought, the rest of my life, side by side with this woman – and I was happy.

Jenny wanted a big wedding. She had very definite ideas about what she wanted, and how to ensure that it was affordable (her parents would help out, of course, but she didn't expect them to foot the entire bill), and all of this was going to take some time to plan, so we set a date well into the future. Long before we got there, Jenny's mother became seriously ill. The wedding plans were put on hold, and somehow, after Mrs Macedo died, Jenny didn't have the heart to go back to them. Perhaps it would be better to have a quiet ceremony, with just family and a few close friends. After all, we'd been living together for more than two years now; what was the big deal about marriage?

I agreed to whatever she wanted. All she had to do was set the date. But she never did. And, as time went by, we fell into a rut. We got along fine. But romance and passion were things of the past. I began to wonder about missed opportunities, and I fantasised about other women. Not that I actually *did* anything – I still loved Jenny and didn't want to lose her. But I was restless. My job was both demanding and boring – a deadly combination – and life with Jenny, once an escape, had become just another set of routines.

Our snug little life was *too* snug. The two-bedroom apartment that had seemed so spacious when we first moved in was packed to the gills with *stuff*. Jenny's job, like mine, was with computers, but her private passion was weaving. Her rugs, tapestries, and cushions were everywhere. And from the craft fairs where she displayed her work, she'd brought home things by other artisans: bowls and vases and pots for plants, stained-glass hangings, wind chimes, and hand-turned furniture and ornaments and little boxes until there was hardly room to move.

One day I said we needed more space.

Jenny, in her practical way, said we should buy a house.

Not for the first time, she pointed out what a waste of money it was to rent when we could be buying. I'd resisted the idea before, but now it began to seem inevitable. She had all the arguments on her side, and I'd even admitted I wanted to move.

'Well, maybe we should get married first,' I said.

Jenny looked at me. Her brown eyes looked almost black, and she wasn't smiling. 'If that's your idea of a proposal, you can stick it up your butt.'

'Say what? I proposed years ago! You're the one who kept changing her mind.'

'I didn't change my mind.'

'I'm glad to hear it.' I took her hand. She let me hold it. I said, 'Run away with me. To Vera Cruz. We could get married down there.'

She didn't smile, exactly, but her mouth and eyes

relaxed. 'And come back to this, after?' With her free hand, she made a small, circumscribed gesture, careful not to brush a potted plant or knock over a bowl or a vase. 'Weren't you saying you wanted more space?'

'Yeah.'

'We have to find a house, Ian. After that, we can go to Mexico.'

'After we buy a house, we won't be able to afford to go anywhere.'

She took her hand away and tucked her hair behind her ears. 'We will so. We can use my rug money for the honeymoon. I've been saving it up.'

I knew, of course, that Jenny sold her rugs and tapestries at craft fairs. Back at the beginning, which was when I'd last paid attention, she'd barely made enough from them to pay for her materials, but gradually she had gained a reputation as an artist. She'd attracted a following. The rugs and tapestries she wove by then were nearly all commissioned pieces, and I was surprised at how much she was able to charge for them.

I was surprised, too, when we started discussing finances, by how much she'd managed to save over the years. We both pulled in roughly the same salaries, we each had a car, and we split the rent and utilities right down the middle. I didn't think I had any particularly expensive habits, and yet I had less than six thousand dollars in the bank. She had much more.

But as soon as we started to look at house prices, Jenny's

savings shrank in significance. Even burdened with loan repayments of more than twice what we were currently paying in rent, we couldn't afford to live in any of the areas I'd be willing to consider; instead, we were consigned to the hell of the 'starter home' in some soulless little subdivision in the outer circles of suburbia.

Jenny went through real estate ads in the paper while we lay in bed, and read me the details of whatever she thought sounded like a possibility. I vetoed nearly all of them, sometimes on practical grounds (too far to commute), sometimes political (I refused to live in a place called White Settlement), but most often out of personal prejudice: against Baptists, rednecks, gated communities, or bad design.

Eventually my invention flagged, and I couldn't think of anything convincing to say against a visit – 'Just to look, Ian' – to a model home in a brand-new subdivision called Apache Springs.

The highway turnoff was identified by a billboard featuring a fantastic vista of misty green hills and tumbling waterfalls proclaiming WELCOME TO APACHE SPRINGS! Needless to say, there were no actual hills or waterfalls anywhere in sight, just empty prairie land in the process of being parcelled up and tamed to meet the needs of the overflow from the city.

Newly laid streets gleamed beneath the searing sun. Half-finished houses reared up out of the raw, churned earth. There were no trees or grass anywhere, although a brilliant green carpet of Astroturf had been carefully laid in front of the two model homes.

Nothing else was finished, but these buildings demonstrated the two styles of house on offer: the 'ranch' and the 'villa'. The ranch was one storey, the villa had two. Either could have three or four bedrooms, two or three baths. Both were timber-framed and clad in a pale composite stone, and had probably been thrown up in about eight weeks.

We were met by a woman who introduced herself as Dawney. She was straight out of the TV version of *Dallas* with her big-shouldered power suit and even bigger hair. She showed a lot of gum when she smiled and she spoke with a slow, Western twang.

'Notice the cathedral ceiling in the entrance, y'all. Such a lovely feelin' of space! And how about that chandelier? Mind, it don't come with the house – like all the fittin's and furnishin's here it's just to give y'all an *ideal* of a real home. Everybody always likes to customise their own home, o'course. Y'all can get a chandelier just like this one down at the Home Depot, if y'all like it, though.'

Ideal. I wanted to grimace sarcastically at Jenny, but she was gazing raptly at the boring light fixture.

The living room, too, was an ideal. In fact, it was perfection, of a sort. The walls were a pale neutral shade ('Linen' perhaps, or 'Biscuit'), and the furniture was restrainedly modern and minimal apart from the one comfy couch overburdened with cushions. Bowls of potpourri released a spicy, almost Christmassy scent into the air, and there was something by Bach tinkling quietly in the background. On the walls hung arty black-and-white photographs of London and Venice. There was no hint here of the dull Texas landscape baking outside. This room, with blinds carefully slanted down to keep out the scorching sun, could have been anywhere in the world. It was all in the best possible taste, and it all spoke to the higher aspirations, not to the lowest common denominator as in too many other sales pitches. You were invited to imagine yourself living in this room, this house, being the sort of person who was artistic and musical and very, very tidy.

I saw the yearning in Jenny's eyes, and my heart was like a lead weight in my chest.

'Mmm, very nice, but Apache Springs is really out in the middle of nowhere, isn't it?' I said.

Dawney never missed a beat. 'Not at all, not really, not for long now,' she said, crinkling her eyes and flashing her gums. 'This is one of the fastest growin' areas in the whole entire state. It's attracting lots of families, too, lots of young couples just like y'all. Prices are still low, but you want to get in now, while you can, because they are set to ex-*plode*! And Apache Springs is right at the very epicentre of the boom.

'Did y'all notice all the buildings going up alongside the highway? A lotta business is coming out here now, taking advantage of the low, low property taxes. There's talk about a new shopping centre. We've got good family values, too: there's a Baptist church five miles away, and also a Pentecostal, and one or two others not far away. And a brand-new elementary school is set to open next year, just three miles from here!'

'Oh, that's wonderful,' I said. 'I won't have to go far to get myself educated. Thanks for the advice.'

Dawney blinked. 'I meant if y'all had children ...'

'Well, we don't. As a matter of fact, we're not even married. I'm more interested in bars and liquor stores than I am in schools and churches. This isn't a dry county, is it? How far do you have to go to get a drink around here? And you were talking about churches, but you never mentioned the Church of Satan. Isn't there anything around here for devil worshippers?'

Jenny sucked in a breath. I was sure she was going to tell me off, but she didn't. Instead, she turned and walked away, her footsteps snapping against the bare wooden floor like gunshots.

My heart raced. I gave the blankly staring Dawney a big smile. 'Oops, my girlfriend hates it when I talk about religion. Gotta run!'

I hurried out to the car and saw Jenny standing on the driver's side, rooting in her bag, uselessly searching for her key.

'I'll drive,' I said, steering her round towards the other side.

She was trembling, I thought with anger – I knew I

deserved it, and was braced for her fury – but as we drove off she suddenly burst into tears. That took the wind out of my sails. 'What's wrong? Oh, hell, I'm sorry. But we really couldn't live there.' Her sobbing – so rare – pierced me. All my hot, angry exhilaration rushed out and left me limp.

'Oh, God. Oh, hell. I'm sorry. You liked it. I didn't. I'm sorry, but I just didn't. I mean, the house was OK, but not where it is. I couldn't live out here. This is suburban *hell*. I'm sorry. We'll find a place we both like. We'll keep looking, I promise. Jenny, come on, don't cry. Please don't. Talk to me, Jenny, please.'

She stopped crying after a few minutes and snuffled into a tissue she found in her bag. But she wouldn't talk to me. I got the silent treatment all the way home.

Later, of course, we talked. I gave her a whole spiel about how I felt about such smug, white-bread, commuter-belt suburbs. It was the worst kind of ghetto. And as long as we were on the subject of where I wanted to live, I went on to confess that I'd never imagined myself settling down for good in the Dallas–Fort Worth area. I'd much rather go somewhere else. How did she feel about that?

Jenny was a Texan born and bred, but she came from San Antonio. She had no deep sentimental roots in North Texas. It was a job that had brought her there, just like me.

'I wouldn't mind going somewhere else,' she said. 'I hear Dell is hiring.'

Her knowledge of this took me by surprise. I wondered if she'd been making her own private investigations, thinking thoughts and having dreams I knew nothing about. 'Austin?' I thought about it. Austin reminded me a little bit of Madison, and could be a pretty appealing place to live, if you had to stay in Texas.

'That would be better than here,' I agreed. 'But I was thinking of another state. I miss city life. I mean, a *real* city.'

Our eyes met, and for the first time in ages we were back on the same wavelength. Memories of past romantic vacations came bubbling up. The most romantic thing I'd ever done – maybe the only really big-scale romantic thing I'd ever done – was the time I'd surprised her with an anniversary trip to New York City. For a few seconds, we entertained the notion of it, then she said, 'We couldn't afford to buy a broom closet in Manhattan.'

'A room in Queens?'

'Ha-ha.'

'How about Chicago? Chicago is a great city. You liked it, didn't you, when we were there?'

She shrugged. 'I don't know. It was so *cold* that weekend.'

'I'm sure you'd like it. Well, we can think about it. It doesn't have to be Chicago. There are lots of other places. Why don't we start looking for jobs, see what's out there, what do you say?'

She compressed her lips and cast her eyes down thought-fully, then nodded as if she agreed. So I thought it was settled. I thought we'd agreed to go forward, to start over again in a new place, together.

Together: that was the important thing.

But a week later, Jenny disappeared.

Armando

Armando Valdes Garrido, corporal second class in the Chilean army, was out on manoeuvres with seven recruits stationed at Pampa Lluscuma, near Putre, in the spring of 1977. At 4:15 in the morning of 25 April, Valdes abruptly and inexplicably vanished before the startled eyes of his men.

Fifteen minutes later, while they were still trying to figure out what had happened to their leader, he reappeared. He had no memory of what had happened to him; no awareness of having been absent for even one minute, never mind fifteen. And no one could explain how, in those missing minutes, the calendar on his watch had advanced by five days, indicating 30 April, or why the formerly clean-shaven corporal now sported what was obviously a five-day growth of beard.

Etain

Rain finally drove me out of Golden Square. I was soaked before I reached the shelter of the underground station at Piccadilly Circus, then I had to stand in a crowded carriage, moist and gently steaming, all the way to Turnpike Lane.

Leaving the station, I noticed a young woman huddled in a blanket at the top of the stairs to the street. It was a prime site for beggars, but I hadn't seen her before. Life on the street had aged her, making it impossible to say if she was sixteen or twenty-six. Although it was June, she was dressed in heavy winter layers and wore a dark, knitted cap atop her long blonde hair. She had a metal stud in her nose, and her blank face was dirty. She might have been drugged or half-asleep from the way she stared into space and mumbled almost inaudibly. I couldn't make out if she was talking to herself or asking passersby for spare change, but a yellow styrofoam food container, open by her side, held a few coins, so I dropped in a couple of pounds as I went past. I couldn't help wondering how she

had come to this, and if, in her mind, it was an improve-
ment on the life she'd left behind. Was anyone in the wide
world searching for this girl? And if they were, would she
want to be found?

The memory of her empty gaze haunted me during the
short walk home. What did she think about all day? What
did she make of her world? If you asked her, she might
have said she was happy – I'd met people like that before.
However bare and uncomfortable her life appeared to an
outsider, it was probable she had no wish to be rescued.
Peri Lensky could be living a similar half-life on the streets
of any big city in the world. She might be a prostitute, a
drug addict, a homeless beggar – or, on the other hand,
she might have a completely new identity, be the pampered
wife of some rich gangster, a well-paid porn star, or the
mainstay of a small religious community, doing all her
chores by hand and looking forward to the coming end.
Even wanted criminals sometimes managed to create new
identities for themselves and vanish into an alternative
life. For someone like Peri, with an American passport and
a clean record, once she'd managed to give her mother
and boyfriend the slip, there were no limits to her freedom.

When I got in, after I'd changed my clothes yet again
and brewed a fresh pot of coffee, strong and hot to clear
my head, I settled down to work.

First, a list of questions to ask Laura Lensky. What did
Peri take with her? When she flew to London for the
Christmas holidays, did she have a single ticket or a return?
And I needed some names to work with: Peri's friends

from Texas, people (besides Hugh) she might have hung out with during her summer in London, and anyone who'd known her during her brief residence at Brown University.

It was possible, even probable, that Laura had done the basic legwork back when her daughter first went missing, but she might have overlooked something, or been side-tracked by her conviction that she knew Peri. As an outsider, it might be easier for me to see the truth.

Next, I ran some simple name and address searches, using the internet and some databases I had on CD-ROM. There is nothing romantic or specialised about that kind of detective work, and anyone can do it; but it takes time and the willingness to sift through lots of dull, unrelated material. It could all be a waste of time if Peri had changed her name. That would seem to be the logical course for someone trying to hide out, but I had only to think of my father to know that lots of runaways never bothered with disguise. If Peri had gone back to America and needed a job, nothing could be simpler than to use the social secu-rity number she'd already been assigned. Of course she might be using her husband's name, but she would have needed to provide some ID to get married, in which case the name of Peregrine Alexandra Lensky would be awaiting discovery, along with her husband's name, in public records.

After more than four hours of searching I hadn't found anything that seemed like a lead, and I thought I'd better take a break before I folded. I was hungry, but I didn't feel like going out again, and I never feel like cooking.

Fortunately there was one ready meal remaining in the freezer – Sausage and Mash, Tesco's Finest.

There was no room in the narrow little kitchen for a table and chairs, and I found I was not in the mood for my usual fine dining experience upstairs, slouched on the couch with the remote in one hand and a fork in the other, so after I'd nuked the frozen dinner I took it back to my desk with a glass of *eau de* North London. My stomach was starting to protest at the amount of coffee I'd poured into it, and there was nothing else to drink.

Ever since parting from Hugh Bell-Rivers I'd very deliberately *not* thought about his strange story and what it suggested to me. I'd told myself that Peri, like Jenny, had simply wanted a life in which her boyfriend played no part. She wasn't the predictable child her mother imagined, but a complex young woman who had gone off in pursuit of her own dream. We might never understand why she'd done it – possibly she couldn't even explain it herself – but, given enough time and a little bit of luck, I would find her living a more or less ordinary life somewhere, just as I'd found my father. I'd concentrated on the practical, tried-and-tested methods of tracking down a missing person.

As I munched away at my dinner my gaze swept along the stuffed bookshelves lining the walls of my office. It was something I often did, admiring certain choice finds, luxuriating in the accumulated knowledge, or despairing a little at the useless, dusty weight of all those pages I'd never read again, thinking of all the money I'd spent and wondering how much I'd get if I put them up for sale. Yet my eyes were drawn magnetically to a few particular books: *Myths and Legends of the Celtic Race*, an impressive volume, more than eighty years old, but with the gold lettering of the title still shining out of the dark green binding like new; and also the tattered black spine of an ancient Penguin Classic, *Early Irish Myths and Sagas*. Not far away were several other compilations of Celtic mythology, including Lady Gregory's *Gods and Fighting Men* and a thick, scholarly tome by W. Y. Evans-Wentz, and, the weirdest scientific treatise of all, Robert Kirk's brief yet mind-blowing *magnum opus* of 1691.

Those books, and several others grouped nearby, were the legacy of my first case. They had been left to me by a woman who had disappeared in Scotland nearly ten years ago.

That recollection made my heart pound harder and my mouth go dry. It had been years since I had looked inside any one of them, or had any need of them. More recently, they'd become a slight embarrassment to me, as I'd grown to doubt my own memories. And yet I'd have to be crazy to ignore the connections between Hugh's description of his last night with Peri and what had happened to me all those years ago in Scotland.

I had to clear more books off the library ladder before I could use it to reach the top shelf. Then I blew dust off the books I wanted and carried the stack back to my desk.

'The Wooing of Etain' was a longer and more complex story than I'd remembered. It fell into three separate sections, and there were some important variations to the basic tale. How it ended depended on who was doing the telling, and for what purpose it was being told. Yet certain basic things remained the same.

In all the stories, Mider was one of the Tuatha de Danann, immortal magic-users who were traditionally supposed to have ruled Ireland until their overthrow by the human Milesians forced them underground. The Otherworld in which they lived was perceived by the ancient Celts as a realm that could occasionally be visited by humans, although it also had connections to the afterlife.

The first part of the story began with Mider's decision to take to wife the most beautiful woman in Ireland, Etain Echrade, the daughter of Ailill. He sent his foster son (or half-brother) Angus to negotiate the bride-price and bring her back.

However, Mider already had a wife, a powerful sorceress called Fuamnach, and when she saw Etain invading her space, she turned her into a pool of water. From the pool of water a worm was formed, which then turned into a red fly.

But what a fly! 'This fly was the size of the head of the handsomest man in the land, and the sound of its voice and the beating of its wings were sweeter than pipes and harps and horns. Its eyes shone like precious stones in the dark, and its colour and fragrance could sate hunger and quench thirst in any man; moreover, a sprinkling of the drops it shed from its wings could cure every sickness and affliction and disease.'

Mider felt so happy in the fly's presence that he didn't even want another woman. When Fuamnach found out how happy the fly made Mider, she conjured up a storm to blow it out of his palace. The wind blew the fly into Angus's palace. One immortal could always recognise another; he knew the fly was actually Mider's wife, and kept her safe in a crystal bower, until the jealous sorceress came to hear of it and again summoned a mighty wind. The poor fly was blown about for years and years, never able to find rest, until at last it landed on a house in Ulster where people were feasting. It fell into a drinking cup and was swallowed by the wife of a warrior named Etar. Nine months later – one thousand and twelve years from her first begetting by Ailill – Etain was born again.

Echu Airem was the king of Ireland, and determined to have the most beautiful woman in the land for his wife. In addition, she must be a woman no other man had known before him. Etain the daughter of Etar seemed his perfect match, so he took her as his bride to the high court at Tara.

There his brother, confusingly named Ailill, no sooner set eyes on Etain than he fell in love with her. He could not dishonour his brother, so he said nothing of his feelings to anyone and dwindled into an illness caused by his unrequited love until it seemed that he would die. Echu had business to attend to, so he left Etain with instructions to tend Ailill, to do everything possible to make him well, and to perform the proper funeral rituals for him when he died.

With Etain visiting him every day, Ailill quickly grew better, so that she began to suspect the cause of his illness and questioned him. 'You should have told me sooner,' she said, when he confessed. 'If it is in my power to heal you, I shall. Come to me tomorrow morning.'

Ailill lay awake with excitement all night, but then, at the hour agreed for their meeting, he fell sound asleep.

Etain went onto the hillside at the agreed time and saw a man who looked like Ailill. But he said nothing to her, and when she looked more closely, she saw he was a stranger, and went home. There she found Ailill just waking, lamenting his weakness. She told him the next day would do just as well for their tryst.

Three times Etain went to the hill, and three times she saw the man who looked like Ailill. Finally she demanded to know who he really was. He replied that his name was Mider and he had been her husband in another lifetime. He explained that he had made Ailill fall in love with her, and had now removed that desire. He asked her to come away with him, but she replied that she would not leave the king of Ireland for a man she did not know. She went home and found Ailill was cured.

One fine summer morning Echu was startled to discover a strange young warrior within the ramparts of his fortress.

The handsome young man introduced himself as Mider of Bri Leith, and proposed a game of chess. 'If you win,' said Mider, 'I will give you fifty dark brown horses, strong, swift, and steady, all finely bridled and saddled.' They played, and Mider lost, and he went away.

The next morning Mider returned leading the fifty horses, just as he had promised, and asked for another game. Again, Echu won, and this time he set Mider four hard tasks: to clear a field of stones, to drain a bog, to build a great road, and to plant a forest.

'You ask too much, but I shall do it,' said Mider. He went away and, after a year and a day, all four hard tasks were accomplished. Mider returned to Tara, in a much sterner mood this time, and challenged Echu to another game.

'The winner shall name the stake,' he said.

Mider won. For his prize, he wanted Etain.

Echu scowled. 'I will not sell you my wife.'

'Then grant me the right to put my arms around her and receive a kiss from her lips.'

Echu felt he had no choice, in honour, but to agree. But he knew from past performance that Mider was very powerful, so he was careful. 'Very well, but not today,' he replied. 'Return in a month's time and you shall have what you ask.'

On the day appointed for Mider's return, Echu made sure his palace was surrounded by heavily armed men. All the doors were locked, and his best warriors stood guard along the walls. Surrounded on all sides, Echu and Etain sat at the table in the centre of the great hall when suddenly Mider appeared before them, looking more splendid than ever.

'I have come for what you promised me,' said Mider to Echu. 'I have come to take Etain.'

Etain turned red with shame and anger.

'There is no dishonour to you in this, Etain,' said Mider. 'You would not abandon your husband, but he has agreed to give you away.'

'I have not agreed to give you my wife!' Echu hotly objected. 'I said only that you might put your arms around her and have a kiss from her lips. And *that* you may have only if she is willing.'

Mider looked at Etain. 'Will you?'

'I will not go with you unless Echu sells me,' she said. 'But you may take me, if Echu sells me.'

'I will not sell you,' Echu said. 'But, as I promised, he may put his arms around you here in the centre of my house.'

'I will do that,' said Mider. As Etain stepped forward to meet him, he put one arm lightly around her, and they immediately rose up into the air together, and out of the skylight. Echu and his men rushed outside but all they could see was a pair of swans flying away to the north.

Recognising now where Mider had come from, Echu gathered his men and headed north to the *sidh* of Bri Leith, where they began to dig. But after a year and three months they were no closer to finding the people who lived there, for whatever they dug up one day was filled back overnight. They took advice from their druids and certain spells were cast and men set to dig day and night until eventually, after nine years of digging, Mider appeared before them and demanded to know why they attacked his home.

'I want my wife back,' said Echu.

'I won her from you fairly.'

'That you did not.'

'Very well. I will send her out.'

Fifty women, each one the very image of Etain, came out of the hill. And no matter how hard he looked at them, Echu could see no difference between them, nothing to tell him that one was his own long-lost wife.

'Choose one to stay with you and let that satisfy your grievance,' said Mider.

Echu set the women a task of serving wine, for he considered his wife to be the best server in all Ireland. After that, he was able to whittle the contestants down to two, but between them he could not decide: 'This is Etain, but she is not herself.' Pressed again to choose, he consulted with his men and finally took one of the two identical women home with him.

Some months later, Mider appeared again, to make Echu promise that he was content with the woman he had taken and would never seek revenge on Mider or his people. Echu promised, and Mider then revealed how he'd tricked the mortal king: 'Your wife was pregnant when I took her from you, and she bore a daughter, and it is your daughter who is with you now.'

Echu was horrified to learn he had slept with his own daughter, especially as she was now pregnant. When she in turn bore a daughter, he instructed his men to cast the baby into a pit with wild animals. However, the baby didn't die, but was rescued by a herdsman and his wife, who reared the girl as their own. When grown, her beauty aroused the passion of the warrior-king Eterscelae, who took her by force, and also that of an unknown immortal, who came to her in the guise of a bird and impregnated her. Her son Conare would become a legendary king of Ireland, but was fated to meet a violent end: his story was told in 'The Destruction of Da Derga's Fort,' to which 'The Wooing of Etain' was an introduction.

I found it a strange and disturbing story, even more so now than the first time I had read it. I wondered what about it had spoken so strongly to Peri that she had adopted it as her own myth.

Of course, it was more than a mere fairy tale: At its heart was a myth about regeneration, about the eternal mystery of life itself. Ordinary human motivations scarcely entered into it.

The most 'complete' version had not been discovered and translated until the twentieth century. Most popular retellings, not feeling required to link Etain to the later King Conare, left off the sour little payback entirely. Some preferred to end it with the two swans flying away: the immortal Etain reclaimed by her immortal lover. For those who detailed Echu's determined assault on Mider's stronghold (described by one writer as 'the earliest recorded war with Fairyland') the story was complete when the mortal side of Etain won out and she gave her mortal husband a sign by which he might know her.

I supposed Peri had read the story as a romance and

identified herself with Etain because she was a magical, immortal beauty. Nobody wanted to be merely human these days. Kids imagined being Harry Potter or Buffy or Sabrina the teenage witch, with magical powers their birthright. But Etain wasn't a person at all, certainly not a role model. Unlike a modern girl, she was merely a possession. She could be bought or sold, won back or stolen. She seemed to have no emotions about her fate and no desires of her own. She would do as her husband-owner bid, and even her daughter lacked the simple ability to tell her father that he'd made a terrible mistake.

I remembered what Hugh had said about how unlike her usual self Peri had been in Mider's presence, how meek and quiet and lacking in will. But was that true? Could I believe anything he said? He might have got the story of Mider from Peri, and while I couldn't think of a good reason for anyone, guilty or innocent, to tell such an unlikely tale to the police, to come to me with that fairy tale was very different. I'd been assuming that to Hugh – and even to Laura Lensky – I was just another private investigator. But what if I was wrong? What if they knew something about my first case? What if they knew quite a lot about the missing person case that had first sent me to Scotland and led to my whole subsequent career in this country?

Anyone who knew that much would also know that I'd find the hints of Celtic mythology in this disappearance impossible to resist.

Amy

My whole life changed when I was thirty. The same month that Jenny left me, my grandmother Pauluk died. She'd been old and ill and I'd never known her very well, so this news would not have caused a ripple except for the fact that she'd left all that she owned to my sister and me. Even more surprising was the fact that she had anything to leave.

I'd always thought of her as poor; at least as poor as we were after my dad left. She would sometimes try to help us out, but my mother always refused those wads of ten- and twenty-dollar bills with a firm, 'You need this more than we do, Anna!'

But it turned out that she'd been frugal and thrifty all her life, long after there was any need to be. When Grandpa died, his insurance policy left her a tidy fund, which she ploughed back into careful investments. She didn't need much to live on, and she never touched her capital.

By most standards, I suppose, what she left wasn't a fortune. But it was more than enough to set me free.

Without Jenny, there seemed no point to staying in Dallas. I quit my job and moved back to Milwaukee. I figured I'd just stay with my mom while waiting for the will to go through probate, before deciding what I wanted to do next.

It was my mother's idea that I should travel. I'd never been that crazy to go to Europe, especially not by myself, but she had these wonderful memories of bumming around France and Italy and Spain when she was young, and she thought I was missing out. She urged me not to settle down right away but to travel and enjoy myself while I had the chance. I didn't say I would, but I didn't say I wouldn't, either. I was finding it hard to get focused. I slept late every day, watched a lot of TV, sometimes went out for a beer or three with some guys I'd known in high school. There was nothing I had to do, no urgency about anything. With so many choices before me, it was somehow impossible to fix on just one.

Maybe Mom was afraid that I never would decide on my own, and never move out of her house again. At any rate, she started bringing home brochures from a travel agency, and canvassed her friends for suggestions, telling them that I was planning a trip, but couldn't decide where to go first. So word got around, and one day at the beginning of September Nell Schneider turned up at the house to offer me a new role in life.

I recognised the tall, rather imposing woman with close-cropped, greying hair as Mrs Schneider who lived down the block. She and her husband had three or four kids, all much younger than I, and I recalled that my sister used to do some babysitting for them.

I was a little surprised that she should drop in while my mother was out at work, but she said she wanted to talk to me, so of course I invited her in. She got down to business right away.

'Mary tells me you're thinking of going to Europe. I wonder if you would do a favour for me, if you'd go to Scotland. I'd be happy to pay, at least to cover all your expenses while you're there, and your airfare, too.'

'What sort of a favour?' I asked, surprised.

'It's my daughter, Amy. I don't know if you remember her?'

'Not really,' I confessed.

She was digging around inside her handbag. 'Here's a recent picture; you can keep it.'

She gave me a studio photograph of a young woman wearing a black gown and a tasselled mortarboard perched atop her thick blonde hair. The girl had a long, plain, Scandinavian-looking face whose essential seriousness was unmoved by the rather pained half smile she'd put on for the occasion.

'She's twenty-one,' Mrs Schneider told me. 'She graduated from college in May and went to Scotland as a volunteer on an archaeological dig. It was for six weeks. Then she was going to spend a week in Glasgow. She should have been home ten days ago.'

'You haven't heard from her?'

'Just a postcard, saying she had decided to stay for a

while. No explanation and no address. It wasn't like her at all. So I called the university that had sponsored the dig, and talked to Dr Deere, Dr Martin Deere, the head archaeologist. As far as he was aware, Amy had left with the other volunteers. He gave me the number of the girl who had been her roommate. An English girl, Jasmine Beccles. So I called her. I didn't get much out of her. Amy hadn't left on the bus with the others, but she didn't know why she'd stayed behind.' She wrinkled her nose. 'I had the feeling that maybe she would have said more to somebody who wasn't Amy's mother. I'll give you her number.'

She reached into her handbag for a piece of paper, and for all her dry, composed delivery, I saw that her fingers were trembling.

'I'd go there myself, if I could. But the boys need me, and my mother's just had a stroke, and Don can't take any more time off work. And maybe it wouldn't do any good, if I went.' She stopped, pressing her lips tightly together. 'Maybe that Jasmine girl knows something. If Amy went off with some boy ... well, she's twenty-one, she's a free agent, she can do as she likes. But something's not right. That postcard ... If she'd fallen in love, why not just tell me? I'm not a monster.' She clasped her hands tightly in her lap and looked at me hard.

'You're closer to her age. She might talk to you. If not, well, you can still scout the territory. Let me know the situation. I'm afraid there's something wrong. I'd like to be reassured. But if – if she *is* in trouble, I want to know that, too. You could let her know that we love her, we'll always love her, and we're here for her, if she needs anything.' She stopped, biting her lip.

I thought I'd learned my lesson; I thought I'd given up all my fantasies of playing detective, but past disappointments were wiped out in a second by Nell Schneider's unexpected request. She needed me. Until that moment I hadn't realised how important that was, and how much I missed having a job to do.

'I'm going to Scotland,' I said. 'I'll find your daughter for you, Mrs Schneider.'

Before leaving I made a couple of phone calls. The first was to Jasmine Beccles, the girl who had been Amy's roommate. Talking to her was my first experience of hearing *real* British English. It was like nothing I'd heard in the movies. The strange accent was bad enough, but her intonation was the real killer. I understood about one word in five.

She must have thought I was a moron, as well as being incredibly deaf. She had no trouble understanding *me* and after I'd asked her the same question four or five times, her patience became understandably worn.

Fortunately, she was eager to help. Unfortunately, she knew nothing of any consequence. What I managed to interpret of her replies was all opinion and suspicion.

Amy Schneider was not a very friendly girl, not outgoing like most Americans. She'd kept her thoughts to herself and preferred going for walks on her own to having a drink and a laugh with the others in the pub after the day's work was done. Towards the end, she was even getting up early in the morning for her walks and not turning up at the dig until late, which made Jasmine suspect there was something fishy going on. She must have met someone. And, since she was so secretive about it, her lover was probably a married man.

My other long-distance phone call was to Dr Martin Deere at the University of Strathclyde in Glasgow. His voice was low and musically Scottish and completely comprehensible. He regretted there was nothing he could tell me: he hadn't known Amy well; in fact, she'd remained more of a stranger to him than some of the others. 'Not a very social animal' was his verdict. Towards the end he had noticed that she didn't always turn up for work until quite late in the morning, but she would not be the first volunteer to lose interest: fieldwork could be tedious and unrewarding. When I asked if I could come to see him in Glasgow, he warned me again that he had no idea where Amy might be, but agreed to try to help in any way he could.

I flew out of Chicago and into Glasgow on a beautiful September day. In Chicago it had been hot and humid, the tail end of a brutal summer, but in Glasgow the air was cool and crisp, hinting at autumn. I picked up my rental car and plunged into the nightmare that is the British motorway, forced to drive on the wrong side of the road at ridiculous speed.

Once in the city, movement became slower. This was a

relief: I didn't care if it took half an hour to travel three miles. Martin Deere had given me directions for finding the university; he'd even faxed me a map with the likeliest parking lot marked with an X. I hadn't liked to push my luck by specifying an exact time, and he'd assured me he'd be in his office all day.

Martin Deere was a tall, lanky man with a short grey beard and curly reddish grey hair. He showed a friendly smile as he shook my hand.

'Ian? I'm Martin.' He had sharp blue eyes behind scholarly-looking bifocals. 'Welcome to Scotland. Your first time? Good trip?'

'Yes, thank you.'

'Can I get you something to drink? Tea?'

'That would be great,' I said, realising how dry my mouth was.

'Sugar?'

'Yeah.'

'I'll just be a minute,' he said, moving towards the door. 'Please, sit down, make yourself comfortable.'

I sat in a chair made of leather and tubular steel and looked around the office. It was a small cubicle in a big modern building, but it was comfortably cluttered and had the friendly aroma of old books and paper. On one wall was a large map of Scotland; on another, a blown-up photograph of a misty landscape: in the foreground, a low, lichen-covered stone wall, and what might have been part of a gravestone; in the background, dominating the grey skyline, a rounded, tree-covered hill.

'Here you go.' Martin thrust a steaming styrofoam cup into my hand.

I took it, bewildered. In the first place, I'd been expecting a cold drink, and in the second, this opaque, tan-coloured liquid didn't look or smell like the Lipton's Jenny sometimes brewed on a winter afternoon. Then I noticed that a woman had come into the room behind him, so I stood up.

'Ian Kennedy, Margaret Campbell,' Martin said.

She was a slim, fair-haired woman about my own age. 'Sit, sit,' she said, fluttering a hand at me, before perching on the desk.

'Margaret is a colleague, a lecturer in history,' Martin explained, slouching back against the wall. 'She wasn't involved in the Kirkton dig, but she has a house only a few miles away. She was there last weekend, and she thinks she might have seen Amy.'

'Actually, it's my parents' house,' she corrected, leaning towards me. 'I have a flat in Glasgow, but I go up to Aberfoyle most weekends. I was there last weekend, and I went up Doon Hill.' She gestured at the misty photograph on the wall. 'Now, I can't say that the girl I saw was your friend, because I never met her, and I didn't even talk to this one – she ran off as soon as she saw me.'

'Ran off? What was she doing?'

I took a cautious sip of my drink. It seemed to be some sort of sweetened, flavoured milk.

'Well – I think she was camping out on the hillside. I found a bender.'

'What's a bender?'

'You know, a makeshift tent. Like the women of Greenham Common?'

I had no idea what she was talking about.

'Anyway, from the way she acted, I thought maybe she wasn't supposed to be there. I wouldn't have thought twice about it if I hadn't overheard Martin here talking about an American girl who went missing.' She looked at Martin in a flirtatious way, then back to me. 'She was blonde, the girl I saw – long blonde hair, and quite young.'

While she was talking, I drank some more of my drink. The taste didn't improve with familiarity, but I was thirsty and it was wet.

'It could be Amy,' Martin Deere said. 'Doon Hill seems to have been her favourite place for walking. From what I gather, she went up there most evenings.'

'That's Doon Hill?' I pointed at the photograph on the wall, and they both nodded. 'How near is it to the dig?'

'Lowering over it. I took that picture from Kirkton,' Martin explained. 'From the churchyard itself. It's an easy walk, maybe half a mile, with a well-marked path right to the top.'

'I don't know why she'd be camping out,' I said.

'How's she fixed for money?' Martin asked.

I shrugged. 'She has a credit card. But her mother said she hasn't used it.'

'Maybe she doesn't want to be found,' Margaret offered.

'Then why stick around Aberfoyle? Jasmine Beccles thinks she was having an affair with someone.'

'Yes,' said Martin dryly. 'I was treated to Jasmine's romantic theorising at some length.'

'So you don't think it's true.'

He shrugged. 'It's possible, of course. But there's absolutely no evidence. Jasmine had to admit Amy never even hinted at a romance, and that she'd never seen Amy with anyone. She just liked the thought of a love affair.'

'She couldn't imagine any other reason for a sane person to want to stay in Aberfoyle,' said Margaret. 'But why, if she's got a lover, isn't she with him? Why's she sleeping out on the hillside by herself?'

'He's married?'

'And he doesn't have a car? Or the means to put her up in a warm, dry room somewhere? No, I don't believe it. I don't think it's her heart she's lost – more like her mind.'

Her words came out with peculiar force and seemed to hang in the air. Martin said nothing, and I drank the rest of my tea-milk like someone taking medicine.

Margaret Campbell slipped off the edge of the desk. 'I must go. I have a class,' she said. She looked at me. 'I'm sorry, I haven't helped. It probably wasn't your girl at all.'

'You've been very helpful,' I told her. 'At least this gives me somewhere to start.'

When she'd gone, Martin wandered over and peered at my empty cup. 'More tea?'

I repressed a shudder. 'No, thank you.'

'Well.' He gnawed a thumbnail thoughtfully, then went around the desk and took the seat there, directly opposite me, underneath the map of Scotland. 'I don't know what else I can tell you. I spoke to all the others, volunteers and staff alike, and no one – except Jasmine – had any ideas. The others hadn't even realised she was missing. For whatever reason, she hadn't made any friends. No enemies either.'

A silence fell.

'If there's anything else I can do to help?' He peered at me over the top of his glasses.

I got up. 'I'll let you know.'

A few minutes later I was back in the car, a map spread open on the seat beside me as I made my way slowly through the congested city streets towards the Great Western Road. Every once in a while a shock of astonishment, a tingling thrill, would run through me: *I'm in a foreign country!* But the prosaic need to concentrate (to add to my problems, the car was a stick shift, which I was out of the habit of driving) kept me from getting too carried away.

Once I was out of the city, traffic became lighter and I could relax a little. The rolling countryside, the high hills, lushly green, splashed with purple and streaks of rusty brown against a soft blue sky, made my spirits soar. The light kept changing, and the hills grew higher, the landscape more and more something out of a romantic poet's dream: it was like driving into a beautiful painting. If it weren't for the other cars, hurtling at insane speeds along the narrow, winding road, I could have believed I was travelling back in time. It was all so unlike anything I'd ever seen.

I'm in another country!

Aberfoyle was only thirty miles from Glasgow, but it was another world. It was a little village – not much more than one main street and a few clusters of houses – nestled in the foothills of the Trossachs. The gorgeous scenery was obviously its major asset: there were two hotels on the main drag, as well as a large, modern tourist information centre. I followed signs directing me to the free parking lot and got out of the car at last with relief. I took a deep breath of the cool air, smelling woodsmoke and damp earth. My legs trembled and I felt weak and hungry.

Behind me was the Scottish Wool Centre, with a sign advertising the Spinning Wheel Coffee Shop, but I turned my back and made my way to the main street, where I found a pleasant-looking café. It wasn't noon yet, so most of the tables were free. I sat down next to a rack of brochures for the various local tourist attractions and read through them while I waited for my toasted cheese and ham sandwich.

'So wondrous wild, the whole might seem
The scenery of a fairy dream.'
Visitors to the Trossachs are still discovering the truth of Sir Walter Scott's description of the region. Aberfoyle, with the Trossachs Discovery Centre and Scottish Wool Centre, as well as many pleasant shops, cafés and restaurants, is an ideal place to begin your exploration of this uniquely beautiful area.

I set the brochure aside when my food arrived and stared out through the big plate-glass window at the passing traffic while I ate. There were quite a few people around. I guessed that the ones who walked briskly were locals, and the ones who dawdled were visitors trying to find something to do in this quiet little place. A Japanese family paused beside the window to inspect the menu, then moved on. They were followed by a cluster of blue-haired ladies who decided, after much discussion and gesturing towards the hotel across the street, to come in. A tour bus rumbled past. I saw the Japanese family go into the hotel across the street, then emerge a few minutes later. Two blonde, healthy-looking young women wearing tank tops and shorts and hiking boots went striding by.

Before arriving, I'd imagined a young American woman in a small Scottish village would be immediately noticeable, but now, even though Aberfoyle was smaller than I'd expected, I wasn't so sure.

I'd booked myself a room in the bed-and-breakfast that had been Amy's last officially recorded residence, and although it was still early, I thought I might as well go there now. The owner, Mrs MacDonald, had given me careful instructions on how to find it.

'Go out of the main car park and turn left onto the road to Kirkton. You'll cross a bridge over the river. *Don't* turn off at the Covenantor's Inn – a lot of people make that mistake! Stay on the road until you've gone past the ruined church and graveyard, and when you come to the *second* Y-junction, take the left-hand turning. Our house is the third on the left. It's called "The Rowans". There's a sign with the name on the gate, but you'll probably notice the trees before that. If you have any trouble, ask anyone. Or give me a bell from the village and I'll send my son to fetch you.'

Kirkton – I needed no special fluency in the Scots language to guess it meant 'church town' – was no more than half a mile from the centre of Aberfoyle, but maybe the fact of its being on the other side of the river had made people consider it a separate entity from what in Sir Walter Scott's day had been 'the clachan at Aberfoyle'. The name also reminded me that Martin Deere had referred to 'the Kirkton dig', and I realised that, in my fixation on finding Amy, I hadn't asked him anything about it. I still had no idea where it was, or what it was about. I felt annoyed with myself. Although I didn't think it could have anything to do with Amy's disappearance – according to Mrs Schneider, Amy had only a mild interest in archaeology, it was the idea of a working vacation that had appealed to her, and Scotland had been a second-best choice after Ireland – it had been a stupid oversight.

As I drove past the ruined church I recognised the hill on the horizon behind it and stopped the car.

Today, beneath clear skies and in sunshine, the heavily forested hill was more sharply defined against the sky than on the misty day when Martin Deere had taken his photograph. And, I realised, looking at the low stone wall surrounding the graveyard, this was probably the very spot where it had been taken.

I parked in front of the iron gates and went in to have a look.

The church might be a ruin, but it was obvious that the graveyard was still in use. The grass was carefully trimmed, the gravel paths edged and neat, and a couple of the graves, with newer marble headstones, were decorated with fresh flowers.

Making my way towards the remains of the church, I noticed a couple of what looked like heavy iron coffins, resting above ground on stone blocks. Later, I learned these were mort safes, used to protect against grave-robbing body snatchers.

It was nice to be out in the sunshine and fresh air, in the peace of the countryside. I could hear the faint, distant sound of hammering – maybe, somewhere in Aberfoyle, a house was being built – and from somewhere a bird called; otherwise, it was silent. I gazed across at Doon Hill, so green and soft-looking in the afternoon light, and wondered if Amy could be camping out up there. Maybe she'd fallen in love with this place and decided to stay.

In no hurry to move on, I wandered around the graveyard, the gravel of the path crunching beneath my shoes, pausing to read the occasional inscription. TO THE MEMORY OF . . . IN LOVING MEMORY . . . The oldest had phrases in Latin, or were illegible after years of wind, rain, and lichen.

I was feeling fine until a wave of weariness flooded me, and it was all I could do not to stretch out and go to sleep on one of the soft, green graves. I hurried back to the car and continued on my way.

The Rowans was just around the bend, out of sight of the graveyard and closer to the foot of the hill. I saw two slender trees, heavy with bright orange berries, and, just beyond, the modest, stone, two-storey house named after them.

I parked on the drive and followed the path to the front door, admiring the neat and blooming garden.

Mrs MacDonald was a brisk woman in early middle age who seemed rather taken aback to find me on her doorstep.

'Mr Kennedy? Oh, my, you are early! I wasn't expecting you quite so soon – no, never mind about that, it doesn't matter,' she went on, cutting me off. 'Just you come in and sit down. You can have a nice cup of tea and put your feet up in the lounge. Your room would have been ready, only the washing machine broke down yesterday, so that put me a bit behind. But don't worry, the sheets are clean, and they'll soon be dry. I wanted to make sure they were properly dry before putting them on the bed, of course. Come in, come in! Is that your bag? Leave it here in the hall, yes, just there.'

She ushered me into a very warm, pink, and fuzzy living room. The walls were cream-coloured, but practically everything else, from the thickly napped carpet to the velvet curtains to the soft, plump sofa and matching armchairs was one shade or another of rose or plum or peach. The pictures on the walls were framed reproductions of rosy naked children and half-dressed women washing themselves. A coal fire burned in the gleaming grate, and, sitting as close to the fire as she could get without catching herself alight was a little old lady, who looked up as we came in.

'This is my mother-in-law, Mairi MacDonald,' said Mrs MacDonald. 'Everyone calls her Granny Mac. Granny,' she went on, raising her voice, 'this is Mr Kennedy, come all the way from America!'

She patted my arm. 'Sit yourself down, Mr Kennedy. I'll just make the tea.'

I sat down and smiled uncertainly at old Mrs MacDonald. She was possibly the oldest woman I had ever met. She was very small and thin, as if she had dwindled with age. Her skin was very pale white except where it was mottled with brown spots, and there was no fat on her; the skin fit tight against the bone. Her eyes were a faded blue-grey behind thick, round glasses, and her fine white hair had been spun into a wispy bun like a ball of cotton on top of her narrow skull.

She stared at me in silence until I began to wonder, nervously, if she *could* speak, but finally she opened her mouth.

'What brings you to The Rowans, Mr Kennedy?'

I was relieved. She looked and sounded perfectly *compos mentis*. 'It's Ian, please. Actually, I'm looking for someone. A girl, Amy Schneider. She stayed here for a few weeks during the summer. I don't know if you remember—'

'Yes, I remember Amy,' she said sharply. 'So, she's gone missing, has she?'

I looked at her more closely. 'Do you know anything about it?'

She moved her head. Firelight reflected off her glasses, making them flash, hiding her eyes. 'Ha. Disappeared, did she? I'm not surprised. I'm really not surprised. Nancy said she'd gone away with the other girls, but I didn't think so. She had that look.'

'What look?'

She turned her head away to stare into the fire. 'When you've seen that look, you don't forget it.'

'What look is that, Mrs Mac?'

'I hadn't seen that look in years. Not since I was a girl. But she was my best friend. Elspeth Paterson. I saw that look on her face, and watched her as she pined away and died.'

I shut my eyes briefly. 'I'm talking about Amy Schneider, the American girl who stayed here last month.'

She turned back to me indignantly. 'I know fine well who you're talking about, young man, I'm not daft! I mention my friend Elspeth because your Amy put me in mind of her. Not at first. I didn't think anything much of her at first. Not until she came back one evening from one of her walks and she had *that look*. Then I knew it would be the same as with Elspeth. She'd met him out walking, and she'd never be able to rest easy without him.'

'She'd fallen in love? Did she say anything? Mention his name?'

'Oh, no. No, she didn't. But she didn't have to say anything – I could see it.'

'I don't suppose you have any idea who—'

'Of course I do.'

The door opened then, and the younger Mrs MacDonald came in with a tray, which she set down on an embroidered footstool.

'Here you are, Granny, here's your tea, just the way you like it.' She handed a china cup and saucer to the old woman, who leaned forward eagerly.

'And Mr Kennedy. Do you take sugar?'

I saw with dismay that my cup held the same unpalatable mixture I'd been given in Glasgow, half milk, half tea. 'Um, I'm sorry, but, if it's not too much trouble – could I have coffee instead?'

Mrs MacDonald stared at me, horrified. 'You don't take tea? Oh, dear, why didn't you say?'

'I'm sorry.' I gave her a sheepish grin. 'I'm kind of slow today. Jet lag, I guess.'

She snatched the cup back, almost spilling it. 'Of course! I should have offered – I'm sorry. My son likes coffee, too. Well. I won't be a minute.'

I stopped her. 'And – I'd like it black, please.'

'Without milk?'

I nodded.

'Plain black coffee. Yes, of course.'

I felt bad for flustering her so. 'I'm sorry – I don't want to be any trouble—'

'No, of course you're not! I'll be right back.'

I turned back to the old lady. 'Did you say you know who Amy Schneider's in love with?'

Old Mrs MacDonald did not rush to reply. She was deeply involved with her tea, drinking it steadily and with obvious pleasure, like someone forced to go too long without a drink. Finally, with a sigh of satisfaction, she put the cup down.

'I have an idea who she met in the woods, of an evening. Just like poor Elspeth. They used to call him the ganconer.'

'Ganconer,' I repeated blankly.

'Yes.' She gave a birdlike nod. 'That's a very old word; I haven't heard it used in years. I believe the English for it would be "love-talker".'

This was not getting me any further. 'Any idea *who* that love-talker might be, Mrs Mac? Or where I might find Amy?'

'Yes, you must find Amy,' she said, suddenly fixing me with her faded blue gaze. 'You must find her and take her away. Help her forget the ganconer. Maybe, if you can get her back to America, she won't have to die, not like Elspeth. America is a modern country.'

'Scotland's a modern country, too, Mrs MacDonald,' I said, feeling embarrassed. 'Girls in Scotland today don't pine away and die for love.'

'Girls today don't usually meet the ganconer,' she retorted. She lifted her cup to her lips, then, finding it empty, put it impatiently away. The cup clattered in its saucer as she set it down on the tea tray.

I shook my head, confused. 'Are you saying this ganconer is a particular person? That Amy and your friend both met the same man?'

'Not a man. Not a *mortal* man, anyway. They used to say that if a maiden met the ganconer, she might as well begin to weave her shroud. He would appear to innocent country maids living in lonesome glens – the sort of place Elspeth and I lived as girls. There are still places like that in Scotland, and I suppose there must still be innocent country maids, too, in spite of the television. The glen where I grew up still doesn't get the television. No reception. The hills are too high.' She nodded, a small, satisfied expression on her face.

'That's the sort of place you'd expect to meet the ganconer, the sort of place you'll still find water horses, and a lad might find his way to Elfhame. Not here.' She cast a quick, contemptuous glance at the silent television in the far corner of the room before fixing me with her gaze again. 'Not in a busy wee village like Aberfoyle, with the buses and the cars and all the visitors, and the hill walkers, coming and going at all hours. Doon Hill was an uncanny place once, but not any more. Now the tourists come, the hikers, the dog walkers, whole families, young people in their strange clothes. Do you know, groups come to dance around the minister's pine? And they decorate the trees with hanging cloth.'

The younger Mrs MacDonald came back in with my cup of coffee. It was some cheap instant stuff – I was willing to bet it was powdered, not even freeze-dried crystals – but I was grateful for the familiar taste and the caffeine. I felt about ready to nod off to sleep in the overheated room, only the irritant of Granny Mac's stories keeping me awake.

'Just give me a few minutes to make your bed,' said Mrs

MacDonald. 'You'll be all right in here, talking to Granny, won't you?'

'Sure.'

'He's asking about Amy,' the old woman said. 'That American girl who didn't go away with the others.'

'I know that, dear,' she replied, scarcely pausing as she went out. 'And I've already told him that we haven't seen or heard from her since she checked out.'

The old woman looked at me as the door closed. 'But I saw where she went.'

I looked at her sceptically. 'Amy? When?'

'Late in the day. In the morning, she went with the others into the village. But in the evening, she came back. I was watching from my window. I saw her.'

'You're sure it was her?'

'I couldn't be mistaken. Not with that long, golden hair. Just like Elspeth's. They love golden hair, you know. And she was wearing her striped jumper. I'd seen her wearing it before when the evenings were chilly. It wasn't like her other clothes, it was handmade. She told me her own granny knitted it for her.' She paused, blinking and working her lips at the memory before she went on. 'I suppose she imagined it would keep her safe, like her granny's love. But it was an unlucky colour. Green. Her granny should have known. But perhaps in America it doesn't matter if you wear green.'

'I thought you said it was striped.'

'Green and purple striped.' She nodded, her eyes vague. 'Not a usual combination. No one else would wear a jumper like that. So, you see, I couldn't have been mistaken. It was certainly Amy I saw going up Doon Hill.'

At last Mrs MacDonald came back to tell me my room was ready and let me out of the stifling sitting room to take me upstairs. She pointed out the bathroom at the top of the stairs and turned left. 'Here you are.'

'Will you be wanting dinner tonight?' she asked outside my door.

I looked at her blankly.

'It's an extra five pounds for dinner, and I serve up at six o'clock. Plain home cooking, a family meal – but I need to know in advance how many to cater for.'

'Well, thank you, but I think I'll eat out,' I said. 'I thought there were plenty of places to eat in Aberfoyle.'

'Oh, yes. You'll have no problem finding somewhere to eat.'

I was overcome by an uncontrollable yawn. 'Excuse me. I didn't manage to sleep on the plane. I'm just going to lie down for a little while . . . ' I stumbled into the room and scarcely had time to notice anything about it before I crashed out, fully dressed, on the bed.

I woke abruptly, with no idea where I was.

I'd been dreaming I was back in Texas, with Jenny. I came home from work one day, and there she was. She couldn't understand why I was so amazed to see her; she insisted she had always been there, in the next room, working on one of her rugs. When I followed her, trying to get an explanation for her disappearance, I found that this other room was connected to a completely different apartment, which I'd never seen before, but where Jenny had, apparently, been living alongside me, unsuspected, for many weeks.

'All you had to do was come through,' she said. 'I thought you didn't want to. All you had to do, if you wanted me, was to open the door.'

I gazed into her warm, liquid, utterly honest eyes and was just about to tell her how much I really loved her when I woke up.

I sat up and looked around the room, in a state close to panic. What had happened? Where was I? This wasn't the apartment in Dallas, and it wasn't my old bedroom in my mother's house. I stared at the window with its flowered curtains, at the looming bulk of a dark wooden wardrobe, at the pale green sink in one corner and felt sure I'd never seen this place before in my life. As I looked at the picture on the wall, a misty landscape of a lake and mountains, with shaggy cows wading into the water to drink, I remembered I was in Scotland.

I'd been asleep for several hours; it was almost six-thirty, and I was desperate to go to the bathroom. I found my way there without any problem, and when I got back, I shaved and put on a fresh white shirt and the smart navy blue linen jacket Jenny had insisted I buy on sale at Neiman-Marcus.

I put a photo of Amy Schneider and a small notebook with my wallet in the inside pocket, and checked that I had the keys to the rental car before I left my room. I didn't have a key to the house. Guests were requested to 'make arrangements' with the MacDonalds if intending to be out past 11:30 p.m.

My stomach was rumbling, and I was intending to make the short drive into Aberfoyle, but as soon as I got outside the house I changed my mind.

It was such a beautiful evening, the warm, still air filled with rich, golden light, that it seemed a crime to shut myself into a car and miss the best of the day. At home, it was dark by seven, but here the summer days lingered, dying slowly in the long twilight. In Texas, summer or winter, day turned to night like the drop of a curtain.

I walked slowly down the drive, breathing in the sweet, heady fragrances from late-flowering bushes that filled the garden, and listened to a bird singing – I imagined a blackbird, but I couldn't see it and really didn't know.

It seemed the most natural thing, to walk towards the hill. There was no traffic at all on the narrow road, which took me past a meadow dotted with the shapes of grazing sheep, then, gradually, into woodland. After a few minutes I saw a wooden signpost pointing to my left advertising DOON HILL FAIRY TRAIL, ½ MILE CIRCULAR WALK.

The trail wound uphill through mixed, mostly deciduous woodland. On some trees the leaves were turning gold or brown. Occasionally a leaf would detach itself and drift slowly to the moss-covered ground.

It was damp beneath the trees even on this dry evening,

and ferns and mushrooms grew in the dips and hollows of the leaf-strewn floor. The path wound upwards, growing steeper, becoming more of a climb. My breath came harder, and between the pounding of my heart and the sound of my own breathing, I couldn't hear anything else.

For some reason, that bothered me. I was afraid of missing something.

I stopped suddenly and looked around while I struggled to control my breathing. I thought I saw something – someone – moving off to the side, but when I turned there was no one there. Movement glimpsed from the corner of my eye made me look the other way, but, again, nothing. The strange shapes of trees, the gathering shadows, the movement of leaves all conspired to tease and mislead. Was there someone there, or no one? Had I seen anything at all?

Darkness gathered as the sun went down behind the hill. Twilight was a tricky time. How much light was left? I didn't want to be caught there after nightfall. The sensible thing was to turn back immediately.

But I wanted to get to the top. Surely I could manage that before sunset. In any case, it wouldn't be pitch-black. All I had to do was stick to the path and it would bring me back. I started walking again, concentrating now on covering ground instead of fantasies glimpsed in the undergrowth. This was Scotland, not Transylvania.

When I reached the summit I had the brief, disorienting impression that a crowd of silent people waited for me there. Then I realised the grove of trees was decked with scarves, socks, and strips of material, and remembered what Granny Mac had said.

But I wasn't alone. There was a woman standing beside a tall pine tree.

She was half in shadow and too far away for me to see her face, but the last rays of the sun made her hair gleam gold. She wasn't as tall as I'd expected, and she wore a neutral-coloured jacket buttoned over jeans and a pair of muddy boots, but she was young and blonde.

I swallowed hard and walked towards her.

She stepped away from the tree and came to meet me, raising her eyes to my face, wearing a tentative smile.

She didn't look anything like the photograph in my pocket.

I asked anyway: 'Amy?'

The smile died on her face. She thrust her hands into her coat pockets and turned away with a jerky, angry motion.

'I'm looking for Amy Schneider. Do you know her?'

'No.' It was a furious grunt.

'She's been seen up here. Do you come here often? Maybe you've seen her.'

'So what if I have? What do you care, anyway? You ought to leave people alone. I came up here to meet someone and now it isn't going to happen.' She was furious; she also had a strong Scottish accent.

'Do you live around here?'

'What does that matter to you?'

'Look, it's almost dark. I don't think anybody else is

going to come now—' I realised she'd left me talking to myself and hurried after her. 'Hey, wait a minute, I want to talk to you!'

'Maybe I don't want to talk to you.'

'I'm trying to find Amy Schneider.'

'I told you, I don't know her.'

'But you might have seen her. She's American, and she was supposed to go back home almost three weeks ago. Her mother sent me to try to find out what happened. Let me show you her picture.' I reached into my breast pocket just at the very moment when a stone slipped under my foot. Unbalanced, I fell heavily.

'Ow.'

The strange Scottish woman burst out laughing. 'Och, I'm sorry! Are you OK?'

'I've got a bruise the size and shape of Scotland on my butt, but, apart from that, yeah, perfect.'

She laughed again, a soft, snorting sound, then gave me a hand and pulled me roughly to my feet. 'Better mind how you go. You're lucky you didn't break something.'

'Thank you for that priceless advice. I suppose you work in one of the caring professions. Nursing? Mountain rescue?'

'You're the one who wants to rescue people, not me.'

The next bit of path was particularly steep, so I concentrated on negotiating it. When we reached a gentler stretch, where the path was wide enough for us to walk side by side, I said, 'I'm only up for rescuing Amy if she *wants* to be rescued. She's old enough to make her own choices.

Her mother just wants to know if Amy's all right. I told her I'd find out and let her know.'

'So you're not Amy's boyfriend?'

'Never met her. I wouldn't have mistaken you for her if I had. But you know her.'

'No.'

'You've met her, though. Seen her.'

She said nothing.

'Come on, why are you being so protective of somebody you don't know?'

'Maybe I just feel sorry for her. Maybe I'm just naturally sympathetic. Some people are, you know.'

'But you have no sympathy for me.'

I listened to the sound of our feet slapping and crunching down the trail. It was getting dark, but we were nearly out of the forest.

'Can we start over? My name is Ian Kennedy. I'm a great big stupid bumbling American, but I have a good heart. I mean well, honestly. I'm not going to hurt Amy. I just came out here to find out what happened to her, to try to set her mother's mind at rest. If she doesn't want me around, all she has to do is tell me, and I'll go away. May I take you out to dinner?'

'You want to take me out to dinner?' She sounded both startled and deeply suspicious. 'Why?'

I sighed. I wasn't at all sure I did, if she was going to be such hard work. 'I was just going out to eat. It would be nice to have company. I don't know anyone around here. Maybe you could recommend a good place to eat?'

She stopped at the edge of the road. It was too dark to read her expression, but she seemed to be thinking about it. 'All right. You can take me out to dinner. But I have to warn you, I really *don't* know your Amy.'

'That's OK. You can tell me about Doon Hill.'

Rhys

Rhys and Llewellyn, two farm labourers in South Wales,
were driving some horses back to the farm one night when
Rhys stopped still and listened.

'Hear that music?' he asked.

Llewellyn strained his ears, but heard nothing out of
the ordinary: wind in the trees, some late birds singing,
a faint rush of water from a nearby stream. He shook his
head.

'Someone's having a party,' Rhys declared, nodding
enthusiastically. 'There might be pretty girls.' He began
to tap his foot. 'I fancy a dance, don't you?'

Llewellyn was bone weary after a long day of ploughing,
and all he fancied was his bed. He shook his head.

'Well, I mean to find out where that music is coming
from,' said Rhys. He gave Llewellyn a slap on the shoulder.
'You go along home to bed, you. I'm for dancing, me. I'll
tell you all about it tomorrow.'

Llewellyn watched as Rhys set off across the fields,
following a music only he could hear. Then he shrugged

his shoulders and plodded off after the horses. He slept soundly that night, as he usually did, and in the morning when he woke up and saw that Rhys's bed was still empty, he wasn't bothered. He supposed that his more impetuous workmate had stayed out all night. Either he had found an accommodating girl at the dance, or had drunk too much to make his way back to his own bed. Surely he would turn up at work later in the day, boasting of his conquest or complaining of his sore head.

But Rhys did not turn up; not that day, or any other day that week, and no one else in the surrounding countryside had seen or heard anything of him. Llewellyn told his story to universal scepticism. There had been no parties, no music playing, anywhere in the region on the night in question. Why would a man lie, unless to cover up a crime? To his horror, Llewellyn was accused of murder.

Luckily for him, there was one dissenting voice. Another farmer (who didn't think Llewellyn smart enough to make up stories) recalled that there had been tales in the past of people who heard strange music. He suggested that Llewellyn should take them all to the spot where he had last seen Rhys. They arrived at twilight. And this time, when Llewellyn stood on the spot where Rhys had stopped and listened, *he* heard the music.

When the others stood close enough to touch Llewellyn, they, too, heard music – and saw a crowd of little people dancing in a ring. Among the crowd was the familiar figure of farm labourer Rhys, towering over his tiny companions.

Llewellyn called to his mate, but the man kept on dancing around the circle, a vacant smile on his face. The next time Rhys came near, Llewellyn grabbed him by the arm.

'Help me hold him!' he cried, and everyone else seized hold of Rhys and dragged him out of the ring. It took half a dozen strong men to keep hold of the mesmerised dancer and pull him away; not until they were several yards down the road did Rhys stop struggling, and ask, querulously, 'Why won't you let me be? I only want a little dance!'

He could hardly believe it when they told him he had been dancing for nearly a week; it seemed to him that only a few minutes had passed since he had parted from Llewellyn.

Alas for Rhys, although his friends managed to rescue him, he did not remain in this world for long. He could never forget the sound of that mysterious music, and wandered the lanes and roads and fields at all hours, hoping to hear it again. He could not do his work, or think of anything else, and in a short time he pined away and died.

Peri

I'd written an entire book devoted to mysterious disappearances, but I had not included Amy's. In fact, I'd never told anyone the whole story of how I'd found her, and I knew there was no reasonable way Hugh could have guessed, which suggested that what he'd told me about his last night with Peri was true – or at least was what he believed had happened.

Still, there was no sense in being *too* trusting, so when I settled down to work the next morning I ran a computer search on Hugh Bell-Rivers. I'd never heard of him before Ms Lensky had given me his name and number, but I quickly discovered three websites devoted to him and his as-yet-unfinished, unreleased first feature film. One was the 'official' site, another I suspected of being a canny marketing tool, the third was a semicoherent labour of love from an excitable fan, which included a 'soul-baring' 'very personal' interview. I was rather surprised to learn that even first-time writer-directors of unreleased films had their fans. But that was the internet for you, making personal obsessions public.

Peri was evoked in the interview as the 'girlfriend and muse' whose 'heartrendingly sudden' disappearance had galvanised him into making his first film, a short subject titled *The Flower-Faced Girl* which was dedicated to her.

Q: Would you say you made that film to try to understand why she left, or to try to get her back?

HBR: No.

Q: Really? Not on any level? Being honest?

HBR: How could making a film get her back?

Q: Isn't that part of the reason why art gets made? Personal art, I mean, like the peacock spreading his tail to attract a mate, saying, look what a beautiful thing I've made, I'm so talented, how could you leave me?

HBR: I don't think so. People aren't peacocks, and anyway, if somebody is aroused by a film they usually want to sleep with the star – not the director or the writer or the cameraman.

Q: Well, OK. How about the other part of the question?

HBR: What? Oh, did I make the film to understand . . . well, you know, the fact is that I'd had the idea to make a short film based on the myth of Persephone and Demeter soon after I met Peri. It was something about the relationship between her and her mother, and then I came along; I was her first serious boyfriend. I was aware of this conflict, not in me, but in her, being drawn to me on the one hand, and being a woman, yet still wanting the comfort of being her mother's little girl. So even if there'd been nothing for me to come to terms with, if Peri hadn't left, I would have made the same film. Except that then it wouldn't have been the same film, if you see what I mean, because she would have played the main character, she would have been the star.

The only mention of Mider I could find was when Hugh referenced 'The Wooing of Etain' as one of several 'mythic sources' for the story told in *The Flower-Faced Girl*. He hadn't told his interviewer the story he'd told me, and nowhere was it suggested that Peri's 'leaving' was a still-unsolved mystery.

I entered the name 'Mider' into a couple of my favourite search engines. Among the more than twelve thousand references were a product, an organisation, various people who had Mider for a family name – some of them news-worthy – as well as the figure from Celtic mythology, but nothing that seemed relevant.

Peri's name, and her picture, turned up on two sites dedicated to missing persons. Although her disappearance had not made the news, she'd been featured in *The Big Issue*, the magazine homeless people hawked on street corners.

While I was at it, I ran a background check on Laura Lensky. Even without her credit card number I was able to check out her credit rating, which was high. I also found out the name of the large corporation she worked for, and her job title. The pieces slotted together, all the little details confirming the image I'd already formed. She was who and what she'd said she was; the idea that she and Hugh might be co-conspirators making up a story to draw me into some murky game was ridiculous.

One of the things common to all of the Hugh Bell-Rivers websites was an oddly murky, grainy-looking black-and-white video clip of Peri. It had probably been Photoshopped and digitally enhanced and remixed to achieve the archaic home-movie effect, but however it had been done, it was effective. She was turned away from the viewer, looking at something out of shot, a faint half smile on her beautiful face. It was like a snapshot; for a few seconds, I'd thought I was looking at a still photograph, until she slowly turned her head to stare directly, wide-eyed, right at me.

Even though I knew she had merely been staring into a camera, years ago, and if she'd been looking at anyone it would have been Hugh, still, the illusion was powerful enough to raise the hairs on the back of my neck. I felt like some credulous, ancient worshipper who'd just seen the statue of a goddess come to life.

I don't know how much of that magic was in Peri, and how much due to Hugh's video skills, but I was impressed enough to download, save, and replay it several times that afternoon. I was reminded of a short film I'd seen years ago, in college: *La Jetée*. That film, about a man from the future who is sent back into his own past, had been composed almost entirely of black-and-white stills, and the haunting, moody atmosphere had made a lasting impression on me. Although I'd never seen it since, it was still on my personal top ten list of great movies.

I wondered if the rest of *The Flower-Faced Girl* measured up to this one clip.

I picked up the phone and called Laura Lensky's office number. I was anticipating voice mail, and the usual irritating delays, but she had a secretary who put me through as soon as I told her my name.

'A quick question,' I said. 'Where could I get a copy of *The Flower-Faced Girl*?'

'You've talked to Hugh? I've got a copy, on video.'

'Could you send it to me?' I glanced at my watch, confirmed that it was still early enough. 'By messenger?'

'It's at home.'

I grimaced, disappointed. 'Well, tomorrow?'

'How about tonight? You could come over and watch it and I could answer any other questions you've got. Now that you've heard Hugh's story, you'll probably want to know what I remember and, I don't know, take a look around the place.'

'What time?'

'I'll be home by seven; if you wanted to come a little after that . . . ?'

'That's good for me.'

'Do you need directions?'

'I've got your address and my trusty *A–Z*. If I get *very* lost, I'll give you a call.'

When I lived in Texas I went everywhere by car. Dallas and its surrounding sprawl were not designed for pedestrians, and the countryside, flat and featureless, had none of the inviting pathways you find in other parts of the world. People who walked anywhere but inside an air-conditioned shopping mall, or on a treadmill in a gym, were regarded with fear and loathing.

During my first few months in Britain I had a rented car, but I gave that up once I'd moved to London. I enjoyed exploring the city on foot, and living without a car was cheaper and easier than the alternative. Being a regular walker was useful, too. You noticed things at street level that drivers seldom saw. If I needed to go out of the city, I could always add a rental car to my expense sheet.

West Hampstead was not one of my usual stamping grounds, so I set off early that evening to give myself plenty of time to scout the territory. I took my briefcase with me, chiefly as a means of unobtrusively transporting a bottle of wine, but there was room alongside the *London A–Z* and my notebook for T. W. Rolleston's *Myths and Legends of the Celtic Race*.

The previous day's rain had washed away some of the city's grime and left everything feeling fresher. In the balmy evening light lots of people were out, tidying their well-kept gardens or just taking the evening air. I passed Hampstead Cemetery. On Fortune Green joggers jogged, dog walkers scooped the poop, and kids of all ages zoomed past me on scooters and skates. I gazed without envy at the fine, big houses, feeling only a mild curiosity about the people who lived there. My English friends were much preoccupied with questions of class, and placing people according to background, accent, income, address, and other accoutrements, but although I'd learned to recognise the distinctions, I couldn't take them personally. Even after almost ten years I remained an outsider. I was like an anthropologist, there to observe the quaint customs of the British people, but not to judge or disparage them.

I walked past solid, redbrick mansion blocks and streets of Victorian terraces. I didn't go east of Finchley Road to Frognal or into Hampstead itself, where there was far more of architectural interest. I'd been there before. Today, I was sticking firmly to the limits of West Hampstead, of which the great architectural historian Nikolaus Pevsner had declared, 'The houses and streets require no notice.' They might not require notice, but I was happy to look at them anyway, and feel the tingle of happy anticipation. On even the most unpromising street I might find something previously unknown.

That evening I discovered, behind some of the most ordinary three-storey Victorian terraces, a beautiful, hidden, communal garden. This was the English passion preserved even in an area where there was no room for separate houses with expansive grounds. And it was not for me: All I could do was peer through the iron railings of a locked gate, where I found my curiosity foiled by heavy shrubberies. This wasn't a park, but a garden to which only the local residents had keys.

Laura Lensky didn't live on a street with a private garden. Her address was part of an unimpressive Victorian semi that had been converted some time ago into two flats – or maisonettes, as they were probably called. A blue-flowering bush grew beside the front wall. I paused as I went through the gate and checked my watch. It was seven minutes past seven. I looked up at the upper front window, thinking of Hugh's description of his last sight of Peri, but there was no one standing there now.

Beside the front door were two buttons, one labelled *Biggs*, the other *Lensky*. I pressed *Lensky* and shortly received an answering buzz that unlocked the door. An overhead light came on as I entered the hall: I saw another door to my left, and a staircase straight ahead. Upstairs, a door opened, and I heard her call, 'Mr Kennedy?'

'It's Ian,' I called back. 'I left Mr Kennedy in the office.'

I bounded upstairs, pleased to see her smile; pleased, to tell the truth, by the sight of her in general. She looked more relaxed than she had on our first meeting. She was casually dressed in a light cotton sweater and jeans, and her figure was as attractively trim as I remembered.

I followed her into her living room, which was modestly furnished: a couple of two-seater couches, a table and chairs, and one wall covered with shelving units which housed the TV and video, sound system, CDs, tapes, and books. Even the pictures on the walls had the impersonal air that suggested they'd come, like the other furnishings, with the flat: reproductions of old British Rail advertisements from the 1950s promoting holidays in Scotland and Wales, and one bright, Mediterranean-looking landscape. The big room was open plan, divided by a breakfast bar from the small kitchen area.

'Can I get you a drink? Tea? Coffee?'

'Well, actually . . .' I fumbled with the briefcase fastenings and pulled out the bottle of wine. 'I brought this.'

'Merlot,' she said, looking at the label but making no move to take it from me. 'Well, that's nice.' Her expression didn't match her words; she looked not just surprised, but something worse, and in that moment, my confidence completely deserted me. What had possessed me? She was a client, not my date. Although I'd had no romantic expectations of this evening, it was obvious she thought I did.

'We could wash down our popcorn with it while we're watching the movie,' I said. 'I know Coke usually goes with popcorn, but, what can I say, I like wine. But that doesn't mean I *have* to have a drink, because I don't; I honestly don't have a problem with keeping a clear head, and if you'd rather, we can stick to water. I *would* like a drink of water, in fact, right now, because I'm thirsty. Really thirsty. Probably a sign that I've been talking too much.' I stopped abruptly, tilting my head in a manner I hoped was not only nonthreatening but appealing, and waited.

Her expression was unreadable. Then, to my surprised relief, she broke into a peal of laughter.

'I'm funny?' I asked hopefully.

'You're American!'

That was the last thing I'd expected to amuse her. 'You're not telling me you've only just realised?'

She bit her lip, but that didn't stop her smile from spreading wider, and her eyes sparkled. 'It was the way you said "water" that clinched it. Because otherwise you sound so totally, totally English!'

'Not to the English, I don't, I assure you.'

'I assure you,' she said, mocking me. 'Totally! Even your name is English!'

'Please! It's Scottish.'

'But you're not Scottish?' She looked uncertain.

'No, I'm American, born and bred. Uh, could I do something with this?' I waved the bottle.

She bit her lip and her brows drew together in an anxious little line. 'There isn't any popcorn.'

'Hell, I *hate* popcorn. I don't care; I was just kidding.'

'You thought we were going to have dinner,' she declared.

Nervous again, I didn't dare speak. I walked over to the breakfast bar and put down the bottle. 'All we need's a couple of glasses and a corkscrew,' I said.

'It's my fault; I'm so stupid,' she said. 'Of course, if you invite somebody over for sometime after seven, you've got to give them a meal. I'm just so out of the habit; I've never entertained here, and I don't cook just for myself. A lot of times I don't get home until eight or nine. And if I've had a big lunch, I don't want anything else. Maybe a bowl of cereal before I go to bed. But I should have thought—'

I stopped her. 'Look, it's OK. I wasn't expecting anything, honestly. I work unsociable hours and I eat on the hoof. I can pick up a take-away after I leave. Now, do you want me to open this wine or just leave it?'

'I'll get the corkscrew.' She moved past me into the

kitchen and dug in a drawer. 'And then I can order us a pizza.'

'Only if you want it, Ms Lensky.'

Her head jerked up at that, and as she handed me the corkscrew she was smiling again. '*Ms* I should have realised you were American when you called me that. British guys don't say "Ms".'

'They don't know how to pronounce it,' I said. 'Me, I was taught by my mother.'

She put two wineglasses down on the counter. 'Anyway, since you're not a proper English gentleman, I think we are definitely on first-name terms by now.' She picked up the phone. 'What do you like on your pizza?'

'Anything but anchovies.' I don't think much of pineapple or sweet corn, either, but didn't think I needed to mention that to a fellow American.

'Pepperoni and mushroom?'

'Sounds perfect.'

I walked away from the counter, letting the wine breathe while she ordered the food, and amused myself by inspecting her collection of books and videos. Among the books were hardback novels by Larry McMurtry, Toni Morrison, and Carol Shields, some classics in Penguin paperback editions, as well as a bunch of recent travel writings. The videos were mostly undemanding fluff like *Four Weddings and a Funeral*, *Notting Hill*, and *Bridget Jones's Diary*.

'Put on some music if you want,' she called to me across the room.

I hadn't even looked at the CDs. Music doesn't play much of a role in my life, and I don't know enough about it to interpret other people's tastes.

'I thought we were going to watch a movie?' Turning to look, I saw that she was pouring the wine.

'Oh. Yes, of course.'

Her voice was steady enough, but I remembered Peri's image from the website. If those few frames had moved me, who didn't even know her, how much more powerful the effect it must have on someone who did. 'Look, it's all right if you don't want to ... I can take it away and watch it later, on my own.'

'No, I'll watch it with you. We might as well wait until after the pizza. It's not very long, anyway.' She brought the glasses across to me.

I held mine up. 'To families happily reunited.'

She managed a small smile and clinked her glass against mine. 'Come and sit,' she said, going to perch on one of the sofas.

I sat down beside her.

'Where are you from?'

'Milwaukee.'

She frowned a little. 'I don't think I know anyone from there. Where did you go to college?'

I knew what was coming, because it's a national habit. Whenever two Americans meet abroad, a certain amount of time is always spent winkling out possible points of past contact, acquaintances, or even mere landmarks held in common. It's as good a way as any of getting to know someone, but right then I decided to pass. This was not a cocktail party. I'd already blurred the boundaries with my bottle of wine, but if that had been a mistake, it wasn't irretrievable. I had a job to do, and even though she was the one who had hired me to do it, that didn't mean I could trust her unreservedly. She might have her own reasons for keeping me away from the truth, and I couldn't risk letting myself be swayed by the irrelevant fact that I found her attractive.

As gently as I could I said, 'Why don't you tell me what happened that night after Hugh brought your daughter back here.'

The sparkle in her eyes went out. 'I don't know.'

I waited, but she didn't expand upon her flat reply.

'Hugh said that the last time he saw Peri she stood in that window there, with you, waving him good-bye. You can confirm that?'

She shook her head, eyes downcast, mouth a tight line.

I frowned. 'No? What do you mean? Are you saying Hugh was lying?'

Her eyes came up to meet mine. 'No! I don't think so. I believe him.'

'But?'

She took a hasty sip of wine. 'But I don't remember.'

'You don't remember standing at the window?'

She shook her head. 'Not that. Not anything.'

'So what do you remember?'

She took another drink of wine. Watching her closely, mirroring her movements, I did the same.

'I remember that Hugh came over to pick Peri up that evening, after dinner. After they'd gone, I had some ironing to do. Peri had brought back a whole load of dirty clothes – well, never mind. Anyway, after I'd finished my chores I sat down, here, on this couch, to watch TV.'

I followed her gaze across the room to the blank eye of the television screen.

'After the programme – it was *Jonathan Creek*, you know, that mystery show? – after that was over, I just channel-surfed. I wasn't really watching anything, I wasn't inter-ested in anything else that was on, but I felt too tired to read or do anything else, and there didn't seem any point to going to bed, because I knew I wouldn't be able to get to sleep while listening for her. I was still too excited about having her home again, and I guess I wanted to hear how her date went, just to be able to spend a little more time with her, you know? So, I was waiting for her, and then, all of a sudden, I woke up.

'I knew immediately that it was very late, and I was surprised to see the TV was off. I got up and looked around.' She half turned, gesturing towards the door. 'The first thing I saw was Peri's purse, on that table by the door, with her set of keys lying on top. And then I noticed that she'd put the chain on the door.'

She made an odd little sound, half laugh, half sigh. 'Well, that did it for me. Seeing that, I just *knew* Peri was home. She had to be, right? I thought she must have come in, dumped her purse, come over and seen me asleep on the couch, and turned off the TV without disturbing me. And then she must have gone up to her room. She couldn't have gone out again, not without taking the chain off.'

Laura paused to take a drink of wine. This time, she held the glass with both hands, seeming to need them both to guide it steadily to her lips.

'Anyway, that's what I thought. And yet, I *felt* like I was alone in the flat. You know the feeling? So, I went up to her bedroom. She had been there, her coat was lying across the bed, and the light was on, but she'd gone.

'She wasn't in the bathroom, and she wasn't in my bedroom, and there wasn't anywhere else for her to be. She just wasn't here.' Laura stared at me, baffled and haunted. 'I called her name, I even yelled at her like she was a five-year-old playing a silly game. I raced back down here thinking she had to have been hiding from me, but – her purse was still there on the table, and in the kitchen I found her watch lying on the floor; she must have dropped it. She had been here, but she was gone. Yet the chain was on the door. It was locked from the inside. There was no way out.'

'Fire escape? Anything like that?'

She shook her head. 'The windows all have bolts on them so they won't open more than a few inches. I mean, you could take the bolts out from the inside if you wanted, but they were all still in.'

'Is there an attic?'

'There isn't one. The bedrooms are upstairs – I guess that was the attic, before the house was done over.'

'Could I see?'

She got up. After putting her glass down on the counter, she went to a door to the right of the one by which I'd entered. It opened onto a narrow hallway and a steep flight of stairs.

'Bathroom's here,' she said, opening a door beside the stairs. 'There was just enough room for the two bedrooms upstairs. You want to go first?'

I did, then waited for her on the small landing. It was warm and stuffy up there, with a faint smell that made me think of hot plastic. Then her scent came to me, fresh and somehow green, already surprisingly familiar, and my pulse speeded up as she squeezed past me to open one of the two doors.

'This was Peri's room.'

It was obvious at a glance that although Peri had not been there long enough to impress her personality upon it, the room had no other purpose now than to be a sad little shrine to her loss. It had been cheaply furnished with twin beds, a pine dresser, and matching wardrobe. On one of the beds was a battered, almost shapeless stuffed animal that might have been a dog. On the bedside table two other toys were perched in front of a short stack of paperbacks: a purple plastic pony and a slightly walleyed teenage fashion doll wearing a shiny purple dress long enough to hide her legs, or the lack of them.

'The Guardians,' I said.

I heard Laura gasp. Then she said, rather flatly, 'Oh, yes. They were in the story.'

'Anything else in that story taken from life? That you know of?'

'Well, the neighbourhood we used to live in, and the neighbours . . . she changed their names, but anyone who knew us would have recognised them from the description. But none of that actually *happened*.'

'You're sure about that?'

'I know the – the people concerned. Anyway, it's an obvious fairy tale.'

'Yes. You don't happen to know when she wrote it? Or why?'

'No. She never showed it to me – and she always showed me her school essays and things. I only found it after she disappeared.' She turned away. 'My bedroom is just here, across the way – you can see, there's no way out, and really nowhere to hide.'

Her bedroom was the same size as Peri's, but had far more in it: neatly organised ranks of toiletries and cosmetics on the dressing table, a couple of large square woven baskets full of sheets and towels, and, beside the book-piled bedside table, a two-drawer filing cabinet.

'I even looked behind the door and under the bed and in the wardrobe,' Laura said in a sad, small voice. 'But she wasn't anywhere.'

I followed her back down the stairs to the living room.

'What did you do when you realised she was gone?'

'I called Hugh. He was asleep.'

'What time was it?'

'Almost three o'clock. He told me he'd brought Peri

home before midnight. He told me he'd watched her go inside and that he'd seen her there in the window with me. According to him, I wasn't asleep. And, I have to admit, I didn't see how I could have been. I don't sleep that deeply anyway, and if I'd fallen asleep sitting up on the couch, I'd wake up as soon as she came in.' Moving almost like a sleepwalker, she crossed the room to reclaim her wine-glass, then stood and slowly drank.

I stood watching her. I didn't like this story, but I believed her.

'Sounds like a classic blackout,' I said. 'Missing time.'

She gave the faintest shrug, then threw her head back to drain the glass.

I thought of Hugh's goblet of wine in the disappearing nightclub, and of his speculation that Peri had been drugged. It sounded as if something similar might have been done to Laura. The same class of drug used to make someone acquiescent also affected the memory: the victim would wake up with no idea of what had happened. Maybe Hugh really had seen Peri and her mother, arm in arm before the window – but maybe not from the outside.

A sudden harsh buzzing noise cut into my thoughts. I cast a startled glance at Laura.

'Pizza man.' Moving towards the door, she stumbled slightly. It was only a moment, and she recovered almost instantly, but my protective instincts were aroused.

I caught her gently by the arm and steered her to the couch. 'I'll get it.'

As I went downstairs, the idea that Laura could have

been drugged, her daughter abducted before her vague and uncomprehending eyes, put me on high alert. But when I opened the heavy street door, it was, indeed, only the pizza man. I paid and tipped him, and made sure the lock had snicked into place before carrying the warm cardboard box upstairs.

Laura was at the bar, setting out plates and flatware and refilling our glasses with wine.

'Do you want a salad? I could make one. There might be some lettuce in the fridge – I don't know how fresh it is – and some tomatoes . . .'

'Don't bother, just pizza's fine for me.'

'Are you sure?'

'Real men don't eat salad.'

That won a smile. She shook her head. 'I must be a bad influence.'

'What do you mean?'

'You sound more American by the minute.'

'Really? That crack about salad? I thought American men were all into healthy eating nowadays.'

'Not that I've noticed. Not in Texas. Ever been to Texas?'

'Sure. I lived in Dallas for years.'

'Really! So did I, in the seventies.'

'Before my time,' I said. But that didn't stop her from rolling out a list of names, none of which I recognised. We were back to where we'd been at the beginning, but she was so much more comfortable with it that I didn't have the heart to drag her back to the night her daughter disappeared. We'd have to go there again soon enough.

For now, let her have a break. I ate my pizza and drank my wine and shook my head at every name she trundled out.

'Polly Fruell!' That one name came out with particular force, like a cry of triumph, but it meant nothing to me, and I shook my head again.

'But of course you know Polly!'

'Nope.'

She frowned. 'You must. Maybe not from Texas. You did some work for her?'

I redirected my thoughts to access old cases, but I have a good memory for names and was already as certain as I could be that I'd never encountered anyone in any context named Polly Fruell.

'Would she have used another name?'

'No, she's always been Polly Fruell.' She frowned thoughtfully. 'That's really strange. She certainly made it sound like she knew you – but I don't think she ever actually said how or why.'

'How did the subject come up?' I was more interested in the pizza I was cramming into my mouth than in this curiously abstract conversation. I couldn't see what difference it made to anything whether or not I'd ever encountered some old friend of hers from Texas.

'In an e-mail. That's how we keep in touch. I haven't seen her in years – not since Peri ... Anyway, she knows better than anyone – except maybe Hugh – what I went through at the time, and how hard it still is ... It's not like I ever got over it, but life *did* go on, after the phone call, and even though I still don't understand what happened, at least I know she's alive, and out there somewhere, and I could hope that someday she'd decide to get back in touch ... but now that I'm about to leave London, well, I could lose her forever.' She gazed sadly down at her plate. She'd taken no more than a bite or two of a single slice.

She took a deep breath. 'Polly's like a sister to me – much closer than either of my *real* sisters – and she was like Peri's second mother for a while. I didn't know where to go – I mean, where do you start, when you want to hire a detective? Look in the Yellow Pages? Polly gave me your name.'

'And said she knew me?'

'I don't remember exactly. I could look up the old e-mails to find out. She definitely knew about your work. She said you were uniquely qualified – I remember that. She said you specialised in this kind of thing, and that you'd managed to find another young woman who'd disappeared in almost the same way as Peri.'

There was a strange prickling sensation at the roots of my hair. 'I don't gossip about my cases,' I said. 'I protect client confidentiality.'

Laura looked startled. 'Oh, I'm sure! Actually, it should have occurred to me before – she wouldn't have to know you, just somebody else you'd worked for.'

'Nell Schneider?' I suggested, although I was as sure as I could be that Amy's mother still had no idea of what really happened to her, and wouldn't talk about it if she did.

Laura shrugged. 'I don't think she mentioned any names. But she was right? I mean, that you have had a case like this before?' Her eyes were full of a desperate hope. It was not just that she wanted me to be able to help her, but that she longed for her daughter's disappearance to be explicable, more ordinary than it seemed.

'Maybe. I've been getting a feeling about it.'

'Can you tell me anything? I mean, I don't want you to break confidentiality, but – anything?'

I wished I could. It was an experience I'd often longed to share. But I knew she wouldn't believe me.

Fred

The woman I'd met on Doon Hill told me to call her Fred.

'What's that short for?'

'It's not short for anything. It's what I like to be called. If you don't like it, too bad. I don't have to show you an ID card.'

'No, I guess not,' I said calmly, trying to keep the peace. 'You look like you're old enough to drink.'

We were in one of the hotel bars, Fred having said she preferred a bar meal to the formality of a restaurant, and I was having my first good look at her in the light. I immediately revised my estimate of her age. At first I'd thought she was just a kid, but now I saw she was nearer my own age, in her late twenties, at least. Her eyes were greenish grey, her eyebrows and lashes sandy-coloured. She had the pale, freckled complexion of a redhead, at odds with her brilliant gold hair, which had to be a wig.

'Definitely old enough!' She took a healthy swig of cider.

The bar was doing a brisk business in both food and drink, and we'd been lucky to snag a table at all. It was small and round, made for drinkers rather than diners, and instead of chairs there were low stools.

I sipped my beer, resisting the temptation to drink it too quickly. I was very hungry, and the smell of freshly cooked food wafting through the air made my mouth water. 'This seems like a good place. Do you eat here often?'

'Are you kidding? Never. I'm on a very tight budget. I can't afford to eat out. I wasn't expecting to stay so long, and now it looks like I'll be here for another six weeks. I have to make my money last.' She drank some more cider with obvious pleasure.

'So, what brought you to Aberfoyle?'

'A bus.' She grinned. 'Ah, go on, you don't want to hear about me. Show me a picture of your girl; I'll tell you if I know her.'

I got out the picture of Amy. She inspected it briefly, then looked at me. 'Would she have been wearing a green-and-purple woolly jumper?'

'I think so.'

She nodded. 'I saw her on the hill.'

'When?'

'Oh, lots of times. In the evenings.'

'You never talked to her?'

She scowled. 'Of course not. I never talk to any of them.'

'What do you mean, "them"?'

She shrugged. 'Trippers. Tourists. Local dog walkers. Whoever takes the circular walk, the fairy trail . . .' She said the last words with a sneer. 'Anyway, she never said anything to me, either. We both wished the other wasn't there. It was obvious.'

'When was the last time you saw her?'

'I don't know. A week ago? Maybe a little more.'

'Did you ever see her meet or talk to anyone?'

'No.'

Our first course arrived – we'd both ordered the venison pâté. Once the plates and cutlery had been set down there was barely enough room for the waitress to balance a small basket of bread on top of the empty ashtray.

The pâté was delicious, rich and gamey, and there was a sour-sweet red jelly that was the perfect foil for its richness. For a little while I forgot everything else in the enjoyment of eating.

I felt like leaning back when I'd finished, but the backless stools didn't allow it. I gazed across at Fred, who was buttering the last little piece of bread. 'Do you go up Doon Hill every day?'

'Yes.' She rubbed the bread against her plate, scouring up the last vestiges of meat and jelly, and popped it in her mouth.

'Why?'

'Same reason Amy did, I guess.'

The waitress came to take away our plates. Fred beamed up at her. 'Thanks. That was lovely.' She held up her almost-empty glass. 'Another Strongbow?'

The waitress looked at me. 'I'm fine,' I said.

When she'd gone, I stared at Fred. 'I have absolutely no idea what that reason might be.'

'Really?'

'Really.'

She rolled her eyes in disbelief and smiled at me, much friendlier now she'd had something to eat and drink, and I had a glimpse of just how deprived and basic was the life she led. 'Don't you know what Doon Hill is famous for?'

I shook my head.

'Who hasn't done his research?'

'For God's sake, I arrived in this country this morning. I'd never heard of Doon Hill before today. Give me a chance,' I said mildly.

'Fairies.'

'Oh, right, the Doon Hill Fairy Trail.' I remembered the sign, which I'd thought a piece of modern marketing whimsy. I stared. 'You're saying Amy went to Doon Hill to look for fairies? You're saying that's why *you* were there?' I knew there were people who believed in fairies, just like there were people who believed they had their own personal guardian angel hovering invisibly over one shoulder; I'd even known a woman who believed in both, but Fred didn't strike me as that type.

The waitress came back with our main courses just then, which required a great deal of shifting and juggling to fit onto the tiny tabletop. I'd ordered the homemade steak pie, Fred the lasagne. Both came with separate plates of french fries, and they required the accompaniment of bottles of vinegar and ketchup, not to mention salt and pepper. Eventually everything was settled and the waitress took the condiments away, and Fred gave me her considered reply.

'Fairies are real. I'm not talking about gauzy little Tinker Bells who sit on toadstools. They're people, full-sized, and they live in their own world, which only sometimes crosses over into ours. They're another race, different from humans, but just as intelligent. We must seem as strange and exotic to them as they do to us; maybe some of them don't believe in *us*!' She beamed, obviously taken with this idea. 'And others, well, others are scared of us and keep well away, while still others must be like me and Amy and feel drawn to us and want to know more.'

'Does this have anything to do with the ganconer?'

Her eyes went round. 'Oh! You—! You *do* know something!'

'No I don't,' I said flatly. 'I don't know anything. An old lady at the B&B where I'm staying thinks Amy met the ganconer and is going to dwindle away and die of unrequited love unless I can get her away. I think she was getting Amy confused with some girl who died when she was young, and mixing that up with stories from her childhood. She's very old.'

'That doesn't make her stupid.'

'I never said it did. But fairies, immortal, inhuman beings ... ' I shrugged uneasily. I didn't want to offend her. We still had dinner to get through, and it wasn't impossible that Fred might know something that would help me find Amy. 'I don't want to argue about the supernatural. But Amy was a science student. To assume she believed in fairies is—'

'I know why people go to Doon Hill,' she interrupted, digging into her steaming lasagne. 'There are other fairy hills in Scotland, but it's probably the most famous, thanks to Robert Kirk.'

'Who's he?' I took a cautious bite of my hot steak pie. It tasted as good as it smelled.

'Dear, dear, you haven't heard of the Reverend Robert Kirk? Aberfoyle's most famous son. You really must go into the tourist office. There's a brochure about him.'

'I'll look for it tomorrow,' I promised. But she proceeded to enlighten me while we ate.

Robert Kirk was born in Aberfoyle in 1644, the seventh son of the local minister. Traditionally, the seventh-born was gifted with the Second Sight, which offered glimpses into the future and also the ability to see fairies and other supernatural beings. Scots of the seventeenth century did not consider knowledge of the pagan supernatural to conflict with devout Christianity, and so, despite his 'gift', Kirk also went into the Church and served for twenty-one years as the minister at nearby Balquidder. He was a very learned man, a Gaelic scholar who made his reputation with a metrical translation of the Psalms into Gaelic, and a student of folklore.

Upon his father's death, Kirk took up the post of minister in Kirkton, Aberfoyle, and finished writing the treatise he titled *The Secret Commonwealth or an Essay on the Nature and Actions of the Subterranean (and for the most part) Invisible People heretofore going under the names of Fauns and Fairies,*

or the like, among the Low Country Scots as described by those
who have second sight, 1691.

This treatise, generally known as *The Secret Commonwealth*,
was in manuscript form at his death and not published
until 1815. It was the most authoritative study of the
subject ever written and is still considered important by
scholars of folklore. Yet for all its scholarly approach, *The*
Secret Commonwealth was different from standard works of
folklore, which tended to be written by outsiders curious
about the beliefs of the 'common people'. Kirk was seeking
evidence and description of something he believed in
himself, and made use of his own Second Sight to find
out more. Almost every evening he could be seen climbing
Doon Hill, which was shunned by most locals as a well-
known abode of 'the Good Neighbours'.

And it was finally his undoing, for, within a year after
completing the manuscript, Kirk was found lying dead on
the hill.

'He was only forty-eight and in perfect health. It was
said that the fairies took him because he knew too much,'
she said, pausing to eat.

'You mean they killed him?'

'No. They took him inside the hill and left behind a
stock, something that looked like his body. So that's what
they buried – either that, or an empty coffin. Word got
around that Kirk wasn't really dead and, sure enough,
after his funeral, Kirk appeared to one of his relatives and
told him he was a prisoner in Fairyland.'

'Kirk's wife – she was his second wife, actually – was pregnant when he died. Kirk said that when the child was christened, he would appear at the feast. As soon as his friend, Graham somebody, I forget the name, anyway, as soon as this Graham saw him, he was to throw his knife over Kirk's head, and that would break the spell that kept him in Fairyland.

'The christening happened, and Kirk did appear, just as he'd said he would, but his friend was so startled by the sight of him that he forgot to throw the knife, and Kirk disappeared and was never seen again.'

'So what does all this have to do with Amy?'

'Doon Hill has a reputation. It's a liminal place. People go there for a reason, and people have gone missing there before.'

'Like who?'

'Robert Kirk.'

'He didn't disappear, he *died*.'

She shrugged. 'So they said.'

After that, the conversation dwindled. I didn't want to talk about fairies, and she stonewalled my halfhearted attempts to find out a little more about her background.

I had hoped we could skip dessert and cut the evening short, but Fred insisted on a full three-course meal. She ordered treacle tart with ice cream, and coffee to follow. I gave in and had another beer.

'So how did you get to be a private eye?' she asked. I didn't correct her assumption. After all, I was conducting a private investigation, and I didn't do anything else for a living. Maybe it was at that moment, letting her believe that's what I was, that I embarked on my career.

I told her about my father and my fascination with vanishings.

'You know,' I said, becoming expansive as the level of beer in my glass diminished, 'people *don't* just disappear into thin air. There's always a rational explanation. They've gone somewhere, in a perfectly ordinary way – sometimes, of course, they're grabbed off the street and murdered – and only because nobody happened to be looking at just the right moment, only the guilty parties know what really happened, so we imagine something impossible, we say they *disappeared*. But there's always a rational explanation.'

She looked sceptical. 'What would you say if you saw someone disappear, right in front of your eyes?'

'I'd figure I'd been tricked. I'd try to work out how.'

'What if it wasn't a trick? What if they'd gone out of this world?'

'Not possible.'

'How do you know? How can you be so certain that this is all there is? That there aren't other dimensions? Other worlds? Scientists say there might be; some say there *must* be more worlds than this.'

I, too, had read popular articles about theoretical physics. 'Sure. There may be other worlds. But they're completely separate. You can't get there from here.'

'You can't know that.'

'Sure I can. It's common sense. If there was a way to

travel between worlds, there would be evidence. It would happen. People would disappear, and someone would see it. By now, somebody would have it on videotape. Instead, people only *seem* to disappear: because there are no witnesses.'

'It does happen,' she insisted. 'Just not very often. Maybe it's very, very rare because there are only a few places where the barrier between the worlds is thin enough, and even then it only opens for a little while, maybe only for a few minutes, once or twice a year.'

I shook my head. 'No. I don't believe it. Those are fairy-tale laws. I don't think the universe operates like that. People like to make up stories. Just because we *like* miracles and mysteries doesn't make them real.'

She was looking edgy again. Even the treacle tart wasn't compensation enough for my determined rationalism. She pushed the plate aside and fixed her strange green-grey eyes on mine. 'If you saw someone disappear, right before your eyes, you'd have to believe it then.'

'I don't think so. I've seen magic shows. I can be fooled, like anyone else. If somebody disappears, and I can't figure out how, that sure doesn't prove they've gone to Fairyland.'

'Oh, you're too much! An answer for everything. You're so sure you know it all. You'd never admit I could be right.'

She seemed close to tears. I hate to make generalisations about differences between men and women, but I'd run aground on this one too many times before, finding that what, for me, was an enjoyable theoretical argument, was, for her, woundingly personal.

'No, that's not true,' I said quickly, 'I know I don't know it all. I'd never claim that. I'm not saying I couldn't be convinced, just that I'd need real, hard evidence that people can go to other worlds.'

She nodded, accepting this for the apology it was, and said quietly, 'I just think, sometimes, you need to have faith.'

'I'm afraid I can't. I'm a rationalist to the core, I can't help it.' I sighed, feeling a wave of dizziness. 'It's late ... I'm jetlagged ... do you mind ...?'

She didn't look pleased. 'I really wanted a coffee.'

'OK.' I looked around, caught the barmaid's eye. 'Uh, do you want a lift somewhere, after?'

'No thanks.'

'Well, if you don't mind, I'll just pay the bill and leave you to drink your coffee. I'm fading fast.'

'You're just afraid I'll change your materialist outlook,' she said, but it was a tease; I could see a smile twitching at the corners of her mouth.

I laughed. 'Yeah, right. Good-bye, Fred.'

'Good night, Ian. Thank you for my dinner.'

I awoke thickheaded and disoriented, late the next morning. The light in my room was dim, and I could hear the steady, lulling drum of rain on the roof.

The clear skies, sunshine, and balmy air of the previous day had vanished. I peered through the curtains at a sodden world.

Mrs MacDonald's full Scottish breakfast – orange juice,

porridge, fried eggs, bacon, sausage, toast, and some limp, floury, subtly tasty triangles called 'tatty scones' – restored me to life. She warned me that normally, breakfast would not be served after nine o'clock, and I promised her that I was normally up and about by eight.

Soon after breakfast I headed off to the tourist information centre in Aberfoyle. Neither of the women working there recognised my picture of Amy, but they were as helpful as they could be, giving me free brochures about the area and a list of everyone offering B&B or self-catering accommodation. They also directed me to the local solicitor's office. In Scotland, property sales, and often rentals, too, were handled by members of the legal profession.

The solicitor was a fair-haired, suited young man called Archibald McTavish. He was certain he had had no dealings with Amy Schneider, either in person or on the phone, but had me pass the photograph around the office just to make sure.

'If she was looking to rent long-term accommodation, it's possible that she entered into an informal arrangement,' he told me. 'Several people in the town have caravans or spare rooms they occasionally let out *ad hoc*. They might put a notice in the newsagent's window, or on the bulletin board at the tourist information place. You'll have been there?'

I told him I had. 'What if Amy decided to camp out in the woods, maybe on Doon Hill – would that be a problem? Would she have to get permission?'

Archibald McTavish rubbed his smooth chin thought-fully. 'I don't think so ... it's not privately owned. Unless she was creating a nuisance of some sort and someone complained, she'd be all right. But, with winter coming on, I can't imagine anyone wanting to stay out on the hill-side.' He nodded at the window. We both watched the rain lashing down until I broke the silence. 'Is there some-where around here she could have bought a bender?'

'A bender?' he repeated blankly.

'A tent, you know, something to camp out in, keep the rain off.'

'Oh! Of course. Isn't a bender something you make for yourself? A makeshift shelter?'

I shrugged. 'Well, then, a sleeping bag, groundsheet, supplies ...'

'Around here?' He thought about it. 'I suppose you might try the ironmonger's.'

'The Wool Centre,' piped up one of the young women working at a computer across the room.

'Wool Centre?' I recalled a sign advertising the Spinning Wheel Coffee Shop. 'You mean that place by the parking lot?'

'That's it,' she said, nodding and smiling at me. 'It's not just woolly jumpers in there. It's quite a big shop inside, and they sell outdoors things for hill walkers and fishermen.'

'Thanks. Is there a place in town I can get some copying done?' I asked, turning back to Archibald.

'We have a photocopier here,' he said.

'I wanted to make a poster, with a picture of Amy and a few details, asking for information,' I explained, assuming he had misunderstood.

He nodded. 'Eight pence a sheet, A4 size, or twelve pence for A3. Morag will help you. She can even type it up for you.' He indicated the young woman who had suggested I try the Wool Centre. Then, noticing my hesitation, he explained, 'There isn't anywhere else for photocopying unless you go all the way to Stirling.'

I gave Morag the photograph and composed some text:

AMY SCHNEIDER

– MISSING! –

AMERICAN STUDENT, LAST SEEN IN ABERFOYLE.

WOULD ANYONE WHO KNOWS AMY'S CURRENT

WHEREABOUTS,

OR HAS ANY INFORMATION WHICH MIGHT HELP IN

FINDING HER,

PLEASE GET IN TOUCH WITH:

IAN KENNEDY

C/O THE ROWANS

MANSE ROAD,

KIRKTON, ABERFOYLE

I took twenty copies, probably more than I'd be able to post in this small village, but they might be useful to hand out.

I went along the main street, calling in at all the shops with my flyer. A boy in the newsagent's remembered the

American girl who had bought a hardback notebook and some bars of chocolate. That was about two weeks ago, he thought. He hadn't seen her since; he assumed she had gone home. He took the phone number of my B&B and promised to be in touch if he saw her again.

A woman working the till in the Co-op also remembered Amy. She had been in several times, quite regularly, buying provisions – fruit, bread, biscuits, soft drinks, the usual sort of thing, she said – but not recently.

No one else said they had seen her. Whatever the attractions of Aberfoyle for Amy, they did not involve her in the ongoing life of the town.

I took a break for lunch in the coffee shop, attracted by the smell of good coffee. By the time I finished my second cup, the rain had stopped, and although the day was still moist and heavily overcast, I knew I couldn't put off another trip up Doon Hill.

The shop in the Wool Centre didn't extend to tents, but I bought myself a pair of waterproof boots and a hooded rain jacket. The woman who served me didn't recognise Amy's picture but suggested I come in again on Saturday, when there would be different staff on duty.

The woods were as wet as I'd expected. It might not have been raining, but the drips from the trees were nearly as bad as real rain, and once I'd left the path walking was a constant, slow process of avoiding holes full of water and battling off the wet, clinging embrace of bushes, vines and brambles. My new anorak kept my upper body warm and dry, but my jeans got soaked and clung to my legs unpleasantly. I went slowly and kept my eyes down.

I must have been in the woods for two hours, circling back to the path and away again as I made my way slowly but steadily up and around the hill, before I finally stumbled across Amy's bender.

It was a desolate, crumpled-looking huddle of heavy clear plastic given structure by wooden sticks and wire. I hesitated, staring down at it, then looked around at the empty woods. The surrounding area was empty and quiet. Water dripped from branches. A leaf fell slowly to the leaf-strewn ground. Then I crouched and crawled inside.

Although it provided some shelter from the weather, the bender was not entirely waterproof. I found the sleeping bag half-soaked. I wondered: had the night's rain driven Amy out? She might have hitched a lift to another town.

But if she'd gone, not intending to return, wouldn't she have taken her things?

There was a dark blue zip-up sports bag in the driest corner. Opened, it proved to be full of clothes. Feeling both justified and guilty, I went through them: T-shirts, jeans, a Northwestern sweatshirt, a short black dress, socks, women's underwear. There was also a zip-up toiletries bag (a nearly empty tube of toothpaste, deodorant, body lotion, shampoo, lip balm), a pair of leather sandals, a deck of cards, a beanbag monkey, and an American paperback edition of *The Hobbit*.

On the other side of the sleeping bag I spotted a white plastic bag. Inside was a square metal box that had originally held an assortment of Danish cookies but which now contained one bar of Cadbury's fruit and nut chocolate, several boxes of matches, Band-Aids, a Swiss army knife, a small flashlight, an Ordnance Survey map of the area, an unused pad of watercolour paper, and a box of watercolours with two brushes.

There was nothing positively to identify any of this as Amy's – no passport, credit cards, diary, or personalised labels – yet I knew it was. But where had she gone? Was she coming back soon? Had she taken the few things she absolutely needed – cash and credit cards and passport – and gone off to start a new life? Or was she lying dead somewhere, her cash and ID in her killer's pocket?

A familiar noise made me look up, and I saw that the rain had come on again, pelting down against the makeshift plastic roof.

The rain was noisy against the plastic, yet there was something oddly comforting about the sound. For a moment I luxuriated in the atavistic pleasure of being warm and dry and protected from the elements. At least, I was mostly dry; the damp legs of my jeans were an annoyance I could live with. I was a little too warm, so I peeled off my new waterproof jacket and looked around. There was an unopened bottle of mineral water and a plastic cup. Once I'd quenched my thirst, I thought about the chocolate bar in the tin box, but decided that would be stealing. Water was hospitality, a necessity of life, whereas that chocolate was her private stash. Maybe, if she came back, she would offer to share. I decided to wait and see.

The next thing I knew was a disorienting lurching feeling, and a rush of fear. Opening my eyes, I realised I had fallen asleep sitting up. I also knew I wasn't alone.

I could still hear the patter of rain against plastic, but fainter now. The light, too, had faded, but, as I crawled out of the damp yet oddly cosy little shelter, I had no difficulty seeing her.

A young blonde woman in a striped sweater and jeans stood only a few feet away, between two trees.

'Amy?' I called softly as I straightened up. My heart was pounding.

She turned slowly to face me. She looked thinner and sadder than in the photograph her mother had given me, but recognisably the same girl.

'Amy, I'm Ian Kennedy, from Milwaukee. Your mother—'

'Don't touch me.'

I stopped where I was. 'I'm not going to hurt you.'

'Don't try to touch me or I'll disappear. You have to come back on Halloween. There's a chance, then, at midnight. They have to let me out, and if you can catch me and hold on tight, I'll be safe. But you mustn't let go before morning. If you let go, I'm lost for ever.'

She was very matter-of-fact as she spoke, but I wasn't sure that she was seeing me.

'Amy, I've come to bring you home,' I said, trying to make my voice gentle but firm. 'Your mother sent me to find you. I'm not going to hurt you, I don't even have to touch you, but I want you to come away with me now.'

'I can't.' Now, for the first time, she looked frightened.

Her eyes darted about. 'They're watching me. I'm not supposed to talk to anyone. They'll punish me!'

'Who? Nobody's going to punish you, Amy. I won't let them. Come on, now.'

'I can't.' She stood still as a statue.

'Yes, yes, you can.' As I spoke, I took a step towards her and stretched out my hand.

'Don't touch me!'

I let my hand fall. 'All right. I want you to start walking towards me now. Take a step, come on, just one step.'

She still didn't move, just stared hard at me. 'Come back on Halloween. *Please.*'

Then she disappeared.

Just like that, before my eyes.

Shocked, I sucked in my breath and rushed forward to where she'd been – or where I thought she'd been.

'Amy! Amy!'

As I raced around, flailing my arms in search of the girl who *must* be there, the rain abruptly poured down in the heaviest shower of the day. Of course, this made it even harder for me to see anything, but I wasn't about to give up. I fell to my knees and patted and prodded at the soaked, leafy ground, searching for a hidden pit, a trap-door, wires, mirrors, *anything.*

I looked behind bushes and trees and rocks hardly big enough to hide a cat. Amy was nowhere to be found.

Maybe because she had never been there?

I thought of her fear that I would touch her, her refusal to let me get too close. There could be trickery behind that. If she'd been standing somewhere else, before a camera, and her image had simply been projected onto that spot ...

Was that really possible? She had looked solid and three-dimensional to me. Was hologram technology that good now? And wouldn't there have to be something to project her image onto? I peered up into the trees as the water ran into my eyes and down my face, but I couldn't see anything: no wires, no screen, no hidden cameras.

I went on searching the area until it was too dark to see. I didn't want to give up, but couldn't face the alternative of spending the whole night exposed on the hillside, getting colder and wetter. I crawled back into the bender to get my jacket and borrowed Amy's miniature flashlight to help me find my way back to the path, then down the hill back to the road. As I stumbled along through the dark, making my way slowly back towards the comfort of The Rowans, I remembered what Fred had said last night: 'If you saw someone disappear right before your eyes, you'd have to believe.'

Peri

I shook my head in answer to Laura's question.

'I'm not sure,' I hedged. 'There are some things about Peri's disappearance that remind me of – this other case, but it could be coincidence, or someone deliberately trying to mislead.'

'Who?'

'Whoever's behind it. Mider, whoever he is. Or this friend of yours, Polly – I can't work out why she sent you to me.'

'I could ask her, if you want. But it's obvious: she knows somebody you worked for, and that person raved about you to Polly, so when I wanted a detective, naturally she thought of you.'

That sounded reasonable, but it wasn't. Until now, I'd never had another case remotely like my first, and I couldn't think of anyone, besides myself, who would think there were similarities between Peri's disappearance and Amy's. Who was it who'd thought I had 'unique qualifications' – and what were they?

I stared thoughtfully at what was left of the pizza.

'Go ahead,' she said.

'Oh, no, that's yours. I've already eaten my half.'

She reached over to the box and prised away another slice, which she added to her plate. 'That's all I'll want. You have the rest.'

I didn't need to be told twice. 'Why don't you tell me a little more about Polly Fruell.'

She looked doubtful, so I said, 'I've never had a fan before. This is very exciting for me.'

She laughed. 'Boy, you've really got that self-deprecating British thing, don't you. I thought you had to be raised over here to get like that. Are you telling me you don't have satisfied customers? *That's* not good.'

'Of course I have satisfied customers.' But I thought of poor Janis Lettes, Linzi Slater's mother, as I spoke, and my protest lacked conviction.

Laura rolled her eyes. 'So what can I tell you about Polly?'

'You could start with how you came to know her.'

'Well, if you really want to hear about it . . . '

Laura Lensky and Polly Fruell met when they were both students at the University of Texas in Austin in the early 1970s. They had a couple of classes together, but ran with different crowds, and might never have been more than passing acquaintances if they hadn't met again in Dallas.

Laura had moved to Dallas to be with her boyfriend, shortly after graduation. Polly came a few years later, fleeing an abusive husband. Laura had discovered her working at Kinko's, a couple of blocks from her office, and they met for lunch. Over taco salads, friendship swiftly blossomed. At first Laura, happy in her relationship and her work, within a comfortable social circle, had been the strong one, the giver: she invited Polly to parties, introduced her to people, helped her move to a better neighbourhood. But when Laura's relationship began to break down, their positions shifted. Most of Laura's other friends were in couples, and nearly all of them had known her boyfriend first. The one person she could really talk to and expect wholehearted sympathy from was Polly. They'd wound up sharing an apartment, and when Laura was pregnant, Polly had been her sole, staunch support.

'What about your boyfriend?' I asked.

'That had been over for months. He was living with someone else.'

'Did he know you were pregnant?'

'He would have known it wasn't his.'

Her dry tone forbade me to pry.

'Everybody thought I was crazy to be having a baby on my own. Like I'd planned it! Even my parents, who are rabidly anti-abortion, practically disowned me. You'd have thought from them that I'd done it just to make them look bad and hurt my good married sister, who'd been trying for years to get pregnant.'

Polly didn't question Laura's morality or her sanity, did nothing to erode her shaky confidence, and was at all times supportive and kind. Besides emotional support, she gave practical help. After Peri's birth she'd been better than family, positively heroic. When Laura had to go back to work, far too soon (maternity leave, even unpaid, was practically unknown in Texas at that time), Polly had switched to the night shift at Kinko's so she could babysit while Laura was at work. For the first few months of her life, Peri had the loving attention of two mothers.

But this seemingly idyllic state had not lasted long. Laura's voice faltered slightly when she described how one night while Polly was out at work, she'd hastily packed everything she could fit into her Volkswagen Rabbit, strapped the baby into her car seat, and fled off down the highway.

'I was crazy,' she said. 'Actually crazy. Suffering from postnatal paranoia, although I didn't know it at the time. I was so strung out from lack of sleep that I'd started hallucinating. I thought everyone was conspiring against me; I had nightmares about Peri being stolen from me, and because I *wasn't* coping so well, it seemed a real possibility that I would lose my baby, either through carelessness or because someone from social services would step in and decide I wasn't qualified to keep her.' She paused to take a drink of wine.

'And it *wasn't* just inside my head. My mother started calling. At first I was grateful, thinking she wanted to make up, but then I realised she wanted me to give my baby to my sister. She said it was the only sensible thing to do: I was single, I had to work, I could barely support myself, let alone a baby, whereas my sister was married, her husband made enough money for her to stay home and be a full-time mom, and they were good, churchgoing Christians who'd raise her right.'

Finishing the last of the pizza, I shook my head in wonder. 'Whew. I can see why you'd want to run away from *them*.'

'But not Polly. She was the best friend I'd ever had, then I turned against her. See, she was alone with my baby all day while I was out at work. Polly took her out for walks, and in the car to run errands, all that stuff. For all I knew, she might be telling people Peri was hers and they'd believe her. Why would Polly do what she was doing, for no pay, if not for love? And what if she decided she didn't want to share any more? If she ran away with my baby, I'd never get her back. As soon as I'd thought of it, I was sure it would happen. And that the only thing I could do was run away with Peri myself, before Polly could.'

Laura had driven down to Houston, where she'd had a vital bit of luck, getting a job with a company that offered subsidised day care on the premises. Peri's sleeping patterns changed, and as she began to sleep through the night, Laura's psychological symptoms eased.

By the time Peri was two years old, Laura had her new life on firm foundations and, after another year, felt secure enough to revisit her past. She repaired the broken relationship with her family – it was made easier by the fact that her older sister was by then pregnant – and tried to get in touch with Polly.

But Polly was no longer at the old address in Dallas, or working at Kinko's, and Laura couldn't track down anyone who knew what had become of her. She didn't spend very long trying.

'I knew she had a sister called Rebecca who lived somewhere around Jacksboro, and maybe I could have found her, but ... ' She shrugged uncomfortably. 'I guess I still felt guilty, and it was easier just to let it go.'

'Until she found you?'

'Yes. That was a *long* time later – nearly eighteen years.'

'After Peri had vanished, or before?'

'The same week.'

A chill ran through me. 'You didn't think that was strange?'

'It was a coincidence,' she said, her jaw set stubbornly. 'A good one. I was so grateful – without her, I don't think I would have survived.'

'Wait, wait, wait.' I waved my hands. 'Go back. *How* did Polly get in touch with you – phone? E-mail? And when exactly?'

'A couple of days after Peri disappeared. Christmas Eve, she turned up on my doorstep.'

'And you just accepted that? It didn't occur to you that the two things might be connected?' I reached for my glass, but it was empty. I poured the rest of the bottle into it, baffled by Laura's puzzled frown. Was it really possible she had never suspected her old 'friend' could be involved?

'How could they be connected?'

'Well, let's see. Once upon a time you imagined that Polly wanted to steal your daughter, so you ran away from her. Eighteen years later your daughter disappears, and, surprise, Polly turns out to be close by. She turns up on your doorstep. How'd she manage to find you, did she say?'

'She ran into somebody I knew in Houston, and when she mentioned she was going to London for Christmas, this person gave her my address.' Laura glared at me. 'Polly is not a suspect! She's been a wonderful friend. Really, she saved my life, twice.'

'You didn't always think so.'

'I told you I was crazy then. Paranoid.'

'Even paranoids have enemies.'

'Oh, honestly!' Laura pushed her plate away although most of her second slice was still untouched, and sighed. 'Look, there's a huge difference between stealing a baby and deciding to kidnap a grown woman! How could she do it? And why would she even want to try? Revenge? It's like the plot of a bad movie.'

'I don't know. And I'm not saying Polly kidnapped Peri. Just that I'd be surprised if she wasn't involved in some way.'

'How?'

'That I don't know. But she knows something. We need to find her.'

Laura shook her head unhappily. I could see that my suspicions had affected her, despite her determination that her old friend was a candidate for sainthood. 'I guess you ought to talk to her yourself.'

'Where's she living now?'

'Northwest Texas. She and her sister have a ranch out near Jacksboro. I can give you her e-mail address.'

'I might have to go out there,' I warned. Lying is too easy by e-mail, and you can't learn enough through a phone call. When you're suspicious, a face-to-face interview is the only way to go. 'I know it might seem like a big expense, but . . .'

'If you think it's necessary. But I just can't believe Polly had anything to do with it. She stayed with me for nearly a month after Peri disappeared. If she had something to hide, wouldn't she have talked me out of hiring a private eye? Why would she send me to you?'

I grimaced at my empty plate. 'The *unflattering* reason could be she thinks I'm useless.'

Laura got up. 'You're wrong about Polly, that's all. Come on, let's clear this stuff away and watch the movie.'

Washing up didn't take long, and we were soon settled on the couch in front of the TV.

The opening image was the one I'd already seen: the young woman gazing at something off-screen, a faint half smile on her face. She was luminously, timelessly beautiful – this time, I thought of one of Botticelli's goddesses.

On the soundtrack, the plaintive sound of a single flute. As if she'd heard, the girl slowly turned her head to look directly, wide-eyed, into the camera – and again, even though I'd been expecting it, I felt the same sense that she was looking at *me*, personally, and I couldn't help a fearful, delighted shudder.

The image froze there, and the title came up over her softly smiling face.

THE FLOWER-FACED GIRL
A FILM
BY
HUGH BELL-RIVERS

The scene changed to a party: loud music, young people talking, laughing, and thrashing about in a crowded room. The camera work was jerky and frantic in that contemporary way I dislike, drawing attention to itself, all odd angles and weird perspectives, the zoom function seemingly completely out of control. No particular shot mattered more than any other, the focus was all over the place, and yet – drifting through the chaos, appearing in practically every scene although visible only briefly, was a beautiful blonde girl, all the more compelling for being so unknowable.

'That's not Peri?'

'No. A young actress called Alyx Meterie. Hugh picked her because she looked so much like Peri.'

Gradually a sense of story emerged. Alyx was playing a London schoolgirl dabbling in drugs. She became addicted and left her mother's house to move in with her pusher (an improbably sleek, handsome, sinister-looking young man). Intercut with this bleak, modern tale was the myth of Demeter and Persephone. These sections were in black and white, with the same grainy, old-fashioned quality as the opening sequence, and I thought that Peri was playing the part of Persephone until Laura pointed out the way the camera moved from a close-up of Peri's face – the same close-up, mostly – to a longer shot of the actress who was her near double. Hugh had filmed Peri at the start of their courtship in the summer; later, I learned that almost all of that filming had been done in the very same communal garden I'd found so attractive on my walk through West Hampstead. It backed onto the house where Hugh's mother, and also at that time Hugh, lived. It didn't add up to a lot of film, and there was no narrative, just scenes of Peri looking pensive, or smiling, or picking flowers, or, in the longest sequence, stretching out to lie on her back on the grass, half-shaded by a bush.

Hugh had used this material for the Persephone sequences, weaving glimpses of Peri into the dramatic scenes performed by Alyx so painstakingly that it would be impossible for anyone who didn't know to pick out the splices. The careful construction gave the Persephone segments a strange, slow, ritualistic pace that seemed to belong to another age, and invested the story with an even greater sense of mystery. The modern story was backed with a track of alternative rock music – all unfamiliar to me – but in the mythic sequence the only music was brief snatches of flute-playing; otherwise, the soundtrack consisted of a woman's voice whispering in classical Greek, lines from the Homeric Hymn to Demeter.

We saw Hades tricking the unwary Persephone into eating a pomegranate seed before he sent her back to her mother, knowing this would force her to return to his realm. Then, the same scene from a different angle, and this time instead of force or trickery we saw compliance, as the girl exchanged a sexually charged look with her rapist/lover, slyly thrusting out her tongue to accept the seed he offered.

In the modern drama, the girl is just saved from death by overdose and returns, repentant, to her mother's house. Then, in the dead of night, she creeps outside, into the same iron-fenced garden where Persephone had been sitting in daylight amid flowers; there she meets her dealer-boyfriend, offering him her arm, upturned and fisted, for the needle. The camera moves to catch the dreamy ecstasy on the modern girl's face. Gradually, that face blurs to mere shadows. When it comes back into focus, it's Peri's face, and her smile gradually fades, replaced by a look of utter blankness. Even the light in her eyes seems to be extinguished, a split second before the image freezes.

The hairs rose on the back of my neck. I felt as if I'd seen Peri at the moment of her death; and the horror and sadness of it was overwhelming.

The screen went black. Credits scrolled slowly, white words against a black background, against silence.

I turned to Laura and saw tears rolling down her cheeks. Her breathing was a little ragged, but otherwise she made no sound, gave no sign that she was weeping.

I felt like crying, too. I wished I had the right to put my arms around her and kiss her tears away. Instead, I got up and went across the room to the counter, where there was a box of tissues, and brought it back to her.

Laura took a tissue and gently blotted her face. 'She must be alive. She was alive six months after she left. And she said she was happy then. She sounded all right.'

I could think of nothing useful to say, so I said nothing.

Laura sighed, crumpling the tissue in her hand. She didn't look at me. 'It's getting late. Maybe you should go.'

'When will I see you again?' That came out more ambiguously than I'd intended. I added quickly, 'I've still got some questions . . . and we need to talk about, um, a contract, expenses, stuff like that – now's not a good time.'

She nodded. 'Tomorrow. I could meet you for lunch. Somewhere near my office?'

'Sure.'

'There's a bistro place – look, I'll e-mail you the details. I'll send you Polly's address, too.' She was brisk, almost recovered, the businesswoman dealing efficiently with practicalities.

'Good.' I picked up my briefcase, much lighter without the bottle, and started for the door.

'Ian.'

I turned. She was staring at me, intent on the truth. 'That other case of yours, the one you didn't want to tell me about? Just tell me one thing.'

I waited for it.

'Did you find her? And was she all right?'

I met her eyes and fixed on them, a wide, unblinking gaze meant to convince. It was, I knew, the body language employed by liars, but I couldn't seem to stop myself.

'Yes,' I said. 'I found her, and everything was OK.' I could feel a flush rising above my collar and was eager to get away. 'See you tomorrow.'

What I'd said was the truth, so why did I feel like a liar?

Mary

Mary Campbell married John Nelson, a young goldsmith of Aberdeen, in the early 1800s, and they were a happy couple until the time came for her to be delivered of her first child. At midnight, the household heard a loud and terrible noise, and all the candles blew out. The midwife and friends attending Mary fell into a panic, and it was some time before they managed to recover their wits, restore light to the room, and return their attention to her – to find a corpse in the bed.

Many people attended the wake, among them one Reverend Mr Dodd, who took one look at the body and proclaimed it fake: 'Mrs Nelson must have been carried away by the fairies, who left this stock in her place so all would think her dead.'

But he was unable to convince them, even though he adamantly refused to attend the funeral, and so the thing from the bed was buried, and John Nelson and all of Mary's friends and relations deeply mourned her loss.

Sometime later, John Nelson was riding in his fields

one evening when he heard music, which seemed to be coming from the little grassy knoll that they called in that part of Scotland a 'knowe' or 'moat'. As he went towards it, he saw a veiled figure in white. He greeted the woman kindly. She threw back her veil and burst into tears and, with a shock, he recognised his wife.

'In the name of God, what has disturbed you?' he cried. 'And what has caused you to appear at this hour?'

'I am not dead,' she replied. 'Although you think me buried, there is but a stick of wood in my grave. I was carried away with our newborn child. I hope you may save me, but I fear I cannot bring our child away, for it has three nurses who attend it always. The greatest hope I have is in my brother Robert.'

Robert Campbell was a sailor, whose ship was due to arrive in Aberdeen within a fortnight. Mary told her husband he would find a letter addressed to her brother on his desk the following Sunday, and that he should give it to Robert Campbell when he came home.

'Do not attempt to win me away, or I shall be lost forever,' she cautioned. 'Only Robert can do it.'

With that, she vanished.

John Nelson quickly rode back to town, where he found Mr Dodd and told him what had happened. The Reverend Dodd accompanied him home and stayed with him until the following Sunday, when a letter appeared as Mary had promised. A few days later, Robert Campbell arrived, and John gave him the letter at once.

In the letter, Mary asked her brother to go, on the first

night after he received it, to the moat where she'd been seen. 'Let nothing daunt you, but stand in the centre of the moat at the hour of twelve at night, and call me, when I, with several others, will surround you; I shall have on the whitest dress of any in the company; then take hold of me and do not forsake me; all the frightful methods they shall use, let it not surprise you, but keep your hold, suppose they continue till cockcrow, when they shall vanish all of a sudden, and I shall be safe . . .'

Robert Campbell vowed he should rescue his sister and her child that very night. He set out by himself at ten o'clock, and almost immediately was confronted by a great roaring lion. He lashed out with his sword and the lion vanished. This cheered him enormously, for now he felt certain that all the threats he'd meet would only be illusions.

Arriving at the moat, he saw a white handkerchief spread on the top of it. He went and stood on it and called for his sister. At once he was surrounded by a company of ladies, all in white clothes, and the one who shone the whitest was unmistakably his sister.

Taking hold of her right hand, he announced, 'By the help of God, I will preserve you from all these infernal imps!'

A wailing broke out, and a circle of fire surrounded them, and the shapes of terrible birds swooped and dived at them. This torment went on for almost two hours, until the first, distant cock crowed. At that, the fire faded, the ugly shapes vanished, and beside him Robert Campbell saw his sister Mary, shivering in the cold dawn breeze. Giving thanks to God for her delivery, he wrapped her tenderly in his coat.

She threw her arms around him and cried out that she was saved.

However, they didn't have the baby. Later in the day, Robert Campbell stood with his brother-in-law beside the moat, discussing a plan of burning off all the brambles and thorns, then making it level with the field, when a voice spoke out of the air: 'You shall have your child back on condition that you do not till the ground within three perches of the moat and leave the thorns and brambles untouched.'

They agreed to this, and a few moments later, Mary Nelson felt the baby gently laid in her arms. They all knelt and gave thanks to God for this safe delivery.

Fred

I resisted what I'd seen on the hillside. I refused to believe my own eyes. People did not disappear into thin air. Maybe I'd dreamed the whole thing.

All night in my narrow bed in Mrs MacDonald's overheated house I tossed and turned in a delusional, dreamlike fever, and woke in the morning feeling tired but clearheaded. I went to the local police station, which turned out to be a one-man operation, and reported Amy as a missing person. I told Sergeant McAdam about the abandoned, makeshift shelter that I believed to be hers. I didn't say anything about the apparition of Amy, for Sergeant McAdam, a dark, wiry, keen-eyed man, didn't strike me as a believer in fairy tales.

He listened politely to what I had to say, then assured me, in a few, obviously formulaic phrases, that he would look into it. However, he trusted I understood that his resources were limited, and unless I had reason to believe a crime had been committed, or that she had gone missing while climbing or hill walking, requiring the assistance of the mountain rescue service, there was little he could do.

Amy had the right, with her passport, to remain in Great Britain until the end of December. As she had already told her parents she was intending to stay on for a while, perhaps I'd better accept that was precisely what she'd done. So, she'd abandoned a bag of old clothes in the woods. She hadn't left her credit cards behind. She was probably happily established in an Edinburgh hotel, busily running up a huge bill as she sampled all the fine shops there. The young ladies did enjoy the shopping, didn't they, sir? Edinburgh was a grand place for it, with only Glasgow maybe better.

I stared at him in disbelief. *Young ladies?* McAdam didn't look as old as me, yet he talked like somebody's grandfather.

'Practising a little retail therapy,' I said. 'Is that what you mean?'

'Retail therapy?' he said, as if he'd never heard the phrase before. He smiled and nodded. 'Ah, yes, that's a very good way of putting it, sir. I'm sure your young lady will turn up safe and sound in a month or so with a whole new wardrobe. I'm sure there's no cause for worry.'

Dissatisfied, but not surprised, I left the police station and went back to explore Doon Hill in the daylight. I found my way back to the bender easily. It was all as I had left it, although I noticed that in places the ground was churned up, as if someone had been digging. I felt a moment's excitement before realising that I'd done it all myself, in my frenzy to discover the trick of her disappearance.

Now in sober, if still-shadowed, daylight, my idea of holograms and such seemed straight out of an episode of *Scooby-Doo*. Surely I had been dreaming.

I spent the rest of the day driving around outlying villages with Amy's photograph and a fresh stack of flyers that I posted in Port of Menteith, Brig o'Turk, Callander and Doune. The skies cleared and the sun shone benevolently down so I almost forgot why I was there, and simply enjoyed the fabulous scenery like any awestruck tourist.

In the evening I called Nell Schneider. I didn't tell her about the bleak little bender, or any fairy tales about Doon Hill. I told her the police weren't worried.

'She's probably off enjoying herself in Edinburgh or London,' I said.

The long-distance silence went on for a little too long. Then she told me that there had been no transactions on Amy's credit card since the beginning of August. 'Of course, she may have some travellers' cheques left, but ...'

'Maybe her boyfriend is paying the bills.'

'Yes ... maybe ...'

After that conversation I knew I had to do something more focused than a random flyer-posting of Scottish villages. Sergeant McAdam had given me the phone number of a charity that specialised in helping the families of missing persons, so I contacted them the next day. They made various suggestions and I took notes.

I was wandering aimlessly around Aberfoyle, wondering

whether I had enough appetite for lunch yet (Mrs MacDonald's breakfasts took some getting through), when a flash of brassy gold caught my attention. I looked up and saw Fred trudging past the Co-op. On impulse, I rushed after her.

Up close, in full daylight, she wasn't quite as I remembered. The artificial hair was the same, but her skin had a coarseness I hadn't noticed before, and there were wrinkles around her eyes. She was obviously older than I: mid-to-late thirties, I reckoned, maybe even forty. I was struck by the odd notion that she'd aged several years for every day that had passed since our first meeting.

She looked surprised to see me. 'You're still here.'

'Still looking for Amy,' I explained, trying not to stare. 'Have you had lunch?'

She shook her head and hoisted the plastic carrier bag she wore on one arm. It didn't have much in it. 'Just about to go home and cook beans on toast.'

This sounded as mysterious and unappetising as the drink of orange squash Mrs MacDonald had offered me earlier. 'They do better than that in the café. My treat.'

She smiled. 'Great, pal. You're on.'

We both ordered the special of the day: fresh haddock fried in crispy batter with chips and a salad. Fred chose to accompany hers with the inevitable hot, milky tea, and I asked for a Coke. When the waitress had left I looked at Fred, suddenly speechless.

She put her elbows on the table and propped her face in her hands. 'So?'

'So?' I repeated.

'Have you changed your mind?'

'About what?'

She smiled faintly, mockingly. 'Are there more things in heaven and earth than were dreamed of in your philosophy?'

I took a deep breath. And then, although I hadn't planned this at all, hadn't meant to tell anyone, *ever*, it all came pouring out, all the details of my mysterious, impossible encounter with a woman I assumed to be Amy, on Doon Hill.

I finished just as our food arrived, so Fred was busy for a few moments, vigorously salting her chips and splashing the fish with drops of vinegar. When she'd dosed everything to her satisfaction she looked across at me.

'You'll go back on Halloween?'

I shrugged. 'I guess. But I wish I understood what was going on.'

'I can tell you,' she said. 'Halloween is the old festival of Samhain. In the old calendar, the last night of October was the end of the old year and the beginning of a new. It's a magical time, a time of transition. It's when the door between the worlds opens, and anything can happen. You'll be able to bring Amy back, if you're brave enough to do exactly what she said.'

'All she said was that I should hang on to her and not let go until morning.'

'It won't be as simple as that.'

'Now, why didn't I guess that? And what do *you* know about it?'

'I've researched the subject,' she said, matter-of-factly. 'In another life, I was a graduate student; old habits die hard. I've read everything I could find. What she said is pretty traditional as a means of rescuing people who've been abducted by the gentry. There was a woman in Aberdeenshire, Mary Campbell Nelson, a hundred and fifty or two hundred years ago, who was rescued by her brother just that way. The earliest story might be that of Young Tam Lin – you probably know the ballad?'

'Never heard of it.'

She raised her eyebrows, then, between mouthfuls of fish and potato, she explained:

'It's a traditional ballad, but a lot of those were based on true stories. Young Tam Lin was taken by the – fairies.' Her hesitation before saying the word was as palpable as a hiccup, which struck me as odd, but I said nothing and she went on.

'He had a habit of appearing to young maidens in a particular spot in the woods, near a well – or maybe they summoned him.'

'The love-talker,' I said.

She smiled. 'Anyway, when Janet fell pregnant, she refused to have anyone but Tam Lin for her husband, and he admitted that he was, in fact, human: he'd been taken by the Queen of the Fairies, and he had only one chance of returning to the mortal world. That was if Janet could win him back on Halloween. He'd be riding with the fairy host, and she had to pull him down from his horse and hang on tight. By magic he'd be changed into a snake, a bear, a lion, and even a red-hot iron burning brand, but if she could ignore all that, and keep hold of him, remembering that whatever he appeared, he was still her baby's father, he'd finally be turned back into her own true love, naked in her arms, and all she'd have to do then was cover him with her green cloak to keep him safe from the fairies forever.'

'Sounds very symbolic.'

'You think that makes it untrue?' she snapped back. 'I'm trying to help.'

'Yes. I know.' I poked through the crisp fried crust on my fish and watched the steam escape. 'I can't help wondering why.'

'What do you mean? Why shouldn't I help you?'

I shrugged. 'You don't even know Amy Schneider.'

'So?'

'What are you doing in Aberfoyle? What brought you to Doon Hill in the first place?'

She went on eating, not looking at me. Finally she said, 'Take a guess.'

'You're looking for someone.'

'Sort of.' She pushed her plate aside. It was empty now except for the fish skin and one pallid, undercooked french fry. 'Not so much some*one* as somewhere. I want to go where Amy went.'

I frowned. 'You want to disappear?'

She grinned mockingly. 'Oh, I've already done *that*.'

'Why would you want to go to a place that other people want to escape *from*? Robert Kirk, Tam Lin, Amy?'

'The same thing doesn't suit everyone. Some people love Scotland. Others can't wait to get away. Are you going to eat those chips?'

I pushed my plate across to her.

She picked up the vinegar bottle and gave me a questioning look.

'Go on.'

She shook out the vinegar. 'It's because of something that happened when I was wee. We came here on holiday. Two weeks in a caravan, my parents, my two brothers, and me. Luckily, the weather was good. We kids ran wild. Well, it was the country, and folks didn't worry so much then. My brothers played with some other boys, but I was on my own a lot. I didn't mind, in fact, I loved it. I never seemed to have any space to myself at home. Here, I'd go off all day by myself, just wandering, and exploring, and climbing trees, or crawling into some little hidey-hole with a book to read. And then one evening I met a lady.'

'On Doon Hill?'

She nodded. 'She told me there was a poorly baby that needed my help, and would I come with her? So I did. Of course, we'd been told not to go with strangers, but this seemed different, somehow. Well, she was a lady, and very beautiful, then there was that baby – I don't know why, but I followed.

'She went very fast; I had to run to keep up, so she gave me her hand – and then, all of a sudden we were in a completely different place. I thought I knew all the countryside around there, but this was strange.' She broke off, frowning. 'I can't describe it now – I can't even explain it. Sometimes I dream about it, but—'

'Did you want something else?'

It was the waitress, coming to clear away our plates.

'I'll have another cup of tea, please,' said Fred.

'Coffee,' I said impatiently, and leaned forward, urging Fred to go on.

'It was just getting dark when we came to a building, I think it was a big house of some kind. There was a tunnel, it seemed to be the way into this house, but the opening was down so low you'd have to crawl to get in. The lady wanted me to go in first, and then I started to get scared. I realised how late it must be – I didn't have a watch – and I didn't know how long it was going to take me to get back, but I was bound to be in big trouble.

'When I hesitated, the lady started to coax, telling me there'd be lovely things to eat and drink inside. She gave me a gold coin and promised there'd be another for me once I'd seen to the baby; and then I really did get worried. All those things they used to tell you: don't take sweets or money from strangers, don't go away with strangers – suddenly, it hit me, that's just what I'd done. I didn't want her to see I was scared, so I put the coin in my pocket, and said that I'd follow her in. She got down on her hands and knees, and as soon as she was in the tunnel, I legged it.

'I had no idea where I was, or how to get back. I ran

for a long time, in a blind panic, and when I couldn't run any more I hid myself as best I could, behind a rock or a tree or under some heather ... It got darker and darker. I never saw any houses or a paved road. Sometimes I heard voices, and once I thought I heard music. At some point, while I was hiding, I fell asleep, and the next thing I knew, my father was bending over me, furious and relieved.

'I'd been out all night, and there was hell to pay. They wouldn't believe I'd got lost less than a mile from the caravan site, and they didn't believe me about the lady. When I tried to show them the coin, all I found in my pocket was an oak leaf.'

She fell silent. The waitress brought our drinks.

'That's it?' I asked.

She poured the contents of two packets of sugar into her tea and stirred it slowly.

'And now? You've come back here after all those years to look for the lady who gave you an oak leaf?'

'To find my way back.'

'Why?' Her story made no sense to me. The bare bones of something inexplicable that had happened to her as a child and haunted her all her life. Well, I could understand about that, but why did she think she could go back? Why did she want to?

Later, when I read about historical people's visits to the Otherworld, I found them full of the details that her story had lacked: palaces of silver and gold, trees hung with fruit and flowers, the commonplace countryside transformed into an elaborate pleasure garden full of people feasting and dancing. All those lame, clichéd, hopeless attempts to express the inexpressible, to describe the land of the heart's desire – and yet, really, they made no more, or less, sense than Fred's obsessive yearning for a place she'd never seen.

'Why?' I asked again.

She shut her eyes and shook her head impatiently. 'If you don't understand, I can't explain. If I said I'd fallen in love, would you ask *why*?'

'I wouldn't ask why you'd fallen in love, but I would point out that you'd be crazy to marry a serial wife-beater.'

She scowled. 'What are you talking about?'

'Why do people have to be rescued from Fairyland? Does anyone who goes there want to stay?'

'Yes. Lots. You only hear about the ones who *want* to come back; the ones who are kidnapped, not the ones who go willingly.'

'You mean, the people who disappear and are never heard from again are happy? That's wishful thinking.'

'It's not. Anyway, sometimes they do come back, then wish they hadn't. What about Elidurus? Even as an old man, and a priest, he used to weep when he thought about the magical country he'd used to visit but could never find again. What about Gitto Bach, Johnny Williamson, Anne Jeffries, the boy of Leith – there's plenty of evidence that people have been able to come and go as they pleased. Sometimes people were "rescued" when they didn't want to be – dragged back into our world by well-meaning friends – and after that, they were never happy; they pined away and died. They wanted to go and they were happy to stay.'

'Amy may have gone willingly, but now she's desperate to come back.'

Fred shrugged. 'Well, it doesn't suit everyone. Like I said—'

'What makes you so sure it would suit you?'

'I just am.'

'And if you're wrong?'

She shook her head, took a breath. 'I'm not coming back. There's nothing left for me here.'

I felt a chill. However she dressed it up, she was talking about suicide.

'You can't know—'

She stopped me. 'I'm an adult, all right? It might not be your choice, but it's mine. I know what I'm doing. I know what I want.'

'Amy probably thought the same thing.'

'Amy didn't think,' she said sharply. 'She got seduced. And then she started to miss shopping, and watching TV and eating chips and driving a car and doing the same dull things every day, and every tedious thing about the modern world that I wouldn't miss at all.'

'Why did you run away the first time, then? You had a chance and you didn't take it. You were scared to go into the tunnel. Don't you think maybe there was a reason for that?'

'I was too young. I didn't know then what I know now.'

'How long have you been trying?'

'I came to Aberfoyle in June. I didn't think it would be so hard. I never dreamed it would take so long.' She fell silent, looking down at her empty teacup. 'Halloween's my last chance. If it doesn't happen then, it never will. I'll know they don't want me.'

I was uncomfortably aware of the depths of misery beneath her stillness. I knew I had to help her because there was no one else.

'Will you help me?' I asked.

She gave me a wary look.

'From what you say, I'm only going to have one chance of rescuing Amy. So I have to get it right. You're the expert on the subject – you can help me.'

'Do just what she told you. Grab hold of her, and hold on tight, and don't let go until it's morning – when the first cock crows, or when you see the first rays of the sun, whatever. And as soon as morning comes, cover her with your coat. You'd probably do that instinctively anyway – she'll probably be naked.'

I raised my eyebrows. 'I know you probably think I'm a useless wimp, but I think I can manage to hang on to a naked woman – all night, if necessary.'

So that was how Fred became my project. I was determined to save her.

My excuse for spending so much time with her was that I needed help that only she could give. We had long discussions about the folklore of fairies, and she gave me books to read: Kirk's, of course, and Evans-Wentz; *British*

Fairy Origins by Lewis Spence, and Katharine Briggs's wonderful *An Encyclopedia of Fairies*. I still couldn't take it seriously as she did – to me, it was myth and delusion – but, like someone wanting to get involved in a role-playing game, or becoming an expert in the trivia of *The Lord of the Rings*, I absorbed all she could teach me. Maybe it softened me up and made me more open to belief, opening cracks in my surface rationalism – I don't know.

Although she didn't complain about it, Fred wasn't just living on a budget, she was surviving on next to nothing. What had seemed like plenty to live on at the end of June had all but vanished by the end of August, and although the couple who were renting her the caravan (what I would have called a trailer) had been willing to give her a discounted rate for October, they still insisted on having the money up front. I'm not saying that without me she would have starved to death, but I made sure she had two good meals a day.

To make my charity easier to stomach, I pretended this was an all-expenses-paid job and carefully collected every receipt.

Fred was not someone I would have chosen to spend a lot of time with under other circumstances. I wasn't attracted to her, and she was too odd and prickly for an enjoyable friendship. Yet I felt responsible for her. I was possibly the only person in the world who knew she was in trouble; like it or not, that meant I had to save her.

I only wished I knew how.

I was curious about what had made her give up on this

world and pin all her hopes on Fairyland, but she wouldn't explain. Occasionally something personal would slip out – like the fact that she had two brothers – but if I pursued it, asking their names, for example, she clammed up.

'I don't want to talk about myself. I've left the past behind. It's over. Don't ask me again.'

One evening, over dinner in what she referred to as 'the posh restaurant', I asked Fred to go to Edinburgh with me the next day.

Alarm flared in her eyes. 'What for?'

'To look for Amy. Thought I might put some flyers up, maybe visit the American consulate to see if they've got any suggestions.'

'But why do you need me along?'

'I don't need you; I just thought you might like the chance to get away, do something different. You wouldn't have to go around with me all day – you could go to a movie, or a gallery, or see the sights ...' I shrugged. 'Actually, I want to see the sights myself. Maybe we should stay overnight.'

She shook her head, gazing at me tenderly. 'Oh, Ian. You're very sweet. And kind. And I do like you. But—'

'I didn't mean it like that,' I said quickly. 'You can have your own room. I'm on expenses, remember?'

'You're very sweet,' she said again. 'But I'm not going to change my mind. It doesn't matter how slowly you take it ... it's not you; it's me. I just don't want a relationship with anyone.'

'Neither do I.'

She smiled, obviously disbelieving. 'Yeah? Why do you spend so much time with me, then?'

'Because I need your help to find Amy. And you *have* been very helpful; without you—'

'Oh, give it a rest, Ian! You think it's all nonsense. You saw her with your own eyes, and still you're going to check the homeless shelters in Edinburgh?'

I shrugged. 'I'm going to be on Doon Hill on Halloween, don't worry. But until then, well, I'm not putting all my eggs in one basket.'

'Eggs being faith and baskets belief systems?'

'Something like that.'

In the end, Fred did go with me to Edinburgh. We spent two nights, in separate rooms, in a modestly priced guest house, ate Indian and Chinese meals, and visited the castle together. On my own, I visited a homeless shelter, the American consulate, and the university campus, talked to lots of people, and took out an ad in *The Big Issue*. All this meant I had something to report back to Mrs Schneider, something to disguise the fact that I was still no closer to finding her daughter.

A week later, again accompanied by Fred, I did similar things in Glasgow.

As the weeks passed, we fell into certain routines, to all appearances a regular couple, although we weren't intimate, and I still knew very little about her.

And then it was Halloween.

The day was cold, but blessedly dry. I piled on my warmest clothes – I'd need layers if I was going to give

Amy my coat – then went out for a daylight reconnoitre of Doon Hill.

At the summit, a familiar figure waited for me, standing in the centre of the grove of trees decked with strips of cloth.

'I don't suppose we'll have it to ourselves tonight,' she said gloomily.

'Kids?' I guessed. 'All dressed up like ghosts and fairies?'

She shrugged. 'Wiccans. Witches. Pagans of all sorts. Come to pay their respects to the Reverend.' She finished with a bow towards the big pine tree in which, according to one legend, the spirit of the Rev. Robert Kirk was lodged. 'Better if it was a rainy night.'

'Speak for yourself! I'd rather not spend the night out in the rain.' I looked around. 'I'm going to have a wander. Meet at the café for lunch?'

We went our separate ways. I made my way to what I thought was the spot where I'd encountered Amy, or her apparition, more than a month earlier, but I couldn't be certain. At some point, probably while I was away in Edinburgh, the bender and its contents had been removed – whether by the police, the local council, or scavenging kids, I had no idea. Maybe it had even been Amy herself.

I couldn't find anything suspicious, and after making notes of a few landmarks and familiarising myself with the area, I admitted there was nothing more I could do and walked back down to the village. I was early for my meeting with Fred, but so was she.

'Just tea,' she said. 'I'm not hungry.'

'You should eat,' I said, knowing she wouldn't have had breakfast.

But she shook her head. 'Maybe later.'

At least she drank her tea with enough sugar to power an entire classroom of five-year-olds. I ordered a bacon roll and a cup of coffee.

'What time shall we go up the hill?' I asked. The clocks had gone back a few days earlier, and I hadn't adjusted yet to just how early night was falling.

Fred didn't answer, concentrating on stirring her tea.

'What's the matter?'

'I have to go by myself,' she said. 'It won't work if you're there. I have to be on my own.'

'That's real likely, if the tree decorators are out in force tonight.'

'I can't help it if they come.'

'You can't help if I come, either,' I said, annoyed. 'You know I have to be there, for Amy.'

'Fine. I'll go on the other side of the hill, well away from the path.'

I couldn't think of anything to say to that. She sipped her tea, eyes down. As the silence went on, I felt unaccountably sad, as if we were a couple breaking up. 'Any last-minute advice?' I asked, trying to sound normal. 'Maybe we should have a pop quiz.'

'You know what to do,' she said quietly. 'Even if you don't believe, just do it.'

'And if she doesn't come?'

Fred shrugged and finished her tea. Then she got up.

'Hey, don't go!'

She heard the alarm in my voice.

'It's too early,' I added, trying to cover.

She shook her head and put her jacket on. 'We might as well say good-bye now.'

'Not yet – can't we talk?' I knew at that moment, with absolute certainty, that I had not saved her and that I could not. I had missed my opportunity if, indeed, I'd ever had it.

'No,' she said. 'It's too late, Ian. I won't see you on the hill. Let's say good-bye now.' As she spoke, she came around the table, leaned over, and kissed me, for the first and last time. It was only a fleeting touch, but firmly on the lips. Before I could respond, she'd pulled back and was winding the dark green scarf, which I'd bought for her in Glasgow, around her neck. 'Good luck,' she added, with a brief, wavering smile; and then she was gone.

I didn't go after her.

I lingered over another cup of coffee and a sweet roll, then wandered around Aberfoyle, killing time until, a little after four, it seemed near enough to twilight to venture up Doon Hill once more.

I'd told Mrs MacDonald that I'd be away for the night, possibly for a few days – she was used to my comings and goings by now. I'd packed a small bag and locked it in the boot of the rental car, which I left in the public car park in Aberfoyle.

Before it was fully dark, I was settled in the woods on my newly purchased 'car rug', with a flask of hot coffee close at hand. Despite Fred's predictions, I saw no sign of any other visitors to the hill; no wiccans or pagans, not even any guisers. Mrs MacDonald had told me that 'trick-or-treating' was not a local custom; rather, Scottish children went 'guising' – dressed up in costume and carrying lanterns made from hollowed-out turnips.

Occasionally, as the night grew deeper, I caught sight of flashes of light here and there in the woods. From farther down the hill there were shouts, cries, laughter, and the barking of dogs. I heard rustling in the undergrowth around me, but no one came near. The moon rose slowly, majestically, three-quarters full and shining brightly in the clear sky. Gradually the sounds of people and dogs grew more distant and infrequent.

By eleven-thirty I had finished the entire flask of coffee and relieved myself more than once. To stave off worried thoughts and pass the time, I recited every poem I had ever learned at school, as well as a number of scatological limericks and various advertising jingles before getting into old television theme songs. Occasionally I got up and stamped my feet to make sure I could still feel them, or ran on the spot, or marched about flapping my arms. It began to get very cold. I couldn't decide whether hypothermia or boredom would do me in first.

I'd just checked my watch for about the tenth time in as many minutes when I heard the faint sound of bells jingling rhythmically.

The back of my neck prickled. I jumped up and, despite the brightness of the moon, switched on my brand-new flashlight, sweeping it about like a light-sabre.

And there she was. Amy Schneider, only a few yards away, stumbling through the woods, looking miserable. She had on a big, saggy, knitted pullover and jeans. Her hair hung in lank rat-tails around her face. Even when I shone the light directly at her she didn't seem to notice me, far too absorbed in picking her way over the uneven ground.

I heard the bells again, and a sound like whispering, and quickly flashed the light around, looking for the source. But all I could see were trees and shadows. The shadows clustered in odd places, melted away, then regrouped, giving the impression of people moving, dashing from bush to bush, just outside my main line of vision, always faster than the eye could see.

I couldn't afford to worry about that. I knew what I had to do. I stuffed the flashlight into my pocket and stepped right in front of Amy, my arms open. She walked into my embrace like a sleepwalker. As soon as her body met mine, she stiffened, and would have pulled away if I hadn't held her tightly.

She went limp in my grasp. I staggered, and had to struggle to keep upright. She was a big girl, nearly as tall as I was, and her deadweight was a real burden. Had she fainted? I whispered her name.

No response. Seconds ticked past, lengthening to minutes, and the weight in my arms was unrelenting.

Although she pressed heavily against my chest, I couldn't feel her heart beating or hear her breathing.

My own heart began to race in terror. Was she dead? I gave her a shake.

Still no response, and her head lolled worryingly.

I'd learned about the kiss of life in a first-aid course, but I couldn't stretch her out into the approved position without letting her go. What should I do?

Go with your instincts. Do what seems right. I could almost hear Fred's gentle Scottish burr in my ear, and for a moment I seemed to feel her lips on mine again.

I took a deep breath, steadied Amy's head with one hand while gripping her firmly with the other, and pressed my mouth to hers, and exhaled.

Immediately, my breath filled her lungs, and I felt vitality surge through her. She came to life in my arms, and quite suddenly began to kiss me back. Her tongue thrust into my mouth, her arms snaked beneath mine, and she clung to me.

She felt absolutely wonderful. It had been so long since anyone had kissed me like that, and I was starved for sex, for female warmth and affection. I opened my mouth wide and kissed her back, at the same time pulling her even harder against me. We were both wearing so many layers of clothes that her body remained a shrouded mystery, yet instinct joined with imagination to make me vividly aware of her large, soft breasts. Her hands dug into my back; as she held on so tightly I thought it was safe to slip one of my hands around to fondle her breasts. Through the thickness of her sweater I couldn't even tell if she was wearing a bra, yet I was sure I felt her nipple grow erect beneath my teasing fingers.

She rose up on tiptoe and ground her pubic bone against mine: thick denim rasped against corduroy, and our belt buckles met with a grating clink. Then she began to fumble at my belt. She seemed desperate to get into my pants, and I was more than happy to let her, yet one small, rational bit of my brain raised a warning that penetrated the fog of lust:

This can't be for real.

This sort of thing happened in movies, not in real life – not to guys like me. She didn't even know me.

So what was going on? Was I being set up for something?

Visions of satanic covens and human sacrifice and blood-drinking vampires tumbled through my brain. After all, it was Halloween.

I caught Amy's hand just before she could undo my zip, and, reluctantly, pulled away from her sweet, ravenous mouth. 'Slow down,' I mumbled, gripping her hand tightly. My eyes darted everywhere, seeing threats in every shifting shadow, looking everywhere for the danger except in her face.

It happened in an instant. I realised abruptly it was a *man's* hand I held; it was not a woman but a man pressed close against me. Even as I turned disbelieving eyes to his face I recognised through some other sense – smell, perhaps, or a tactile memory going back to infancy – that the man I embraced was my father.

'Dad?'

He looked at me without understanding. Then, all at once, recognition lit his eyes, followed immediately by a look of loathing. I might have been the most disgusting creature on the face of the earth. With a grunt, he tried to pull away from my grasp.

I almost let him go, pained more than I can say by the expression on his face. But then I remembered Fred's solemn instructions, and a line from 'The Ballad of Young Tam Lin':

But hold me fast, and fear me not . . .

And I gripped him just as tightly as I had held Amy.

I stared into my father's face – knowing this was not my father but only his appearance – and held on grimly as he wriggled and writhed, panting hard with the effort to free himself. Yet he didn't try to lash out at me, to hit or kick or bite.

This time I watched closely, yet the change when it came was just as sudden and shocking as before.

I was still holding a man, but he was no longer anything like my father. He'd become a young stranger, a malevolently handsome, devilish-looking youth with golden eyes, long black lashes, and lips like Mick Jagger. And, while I blinked in surprise, he moved his arms and sent long, cool fingers to stroke my back, my neck, finally to twine in my hair.

As he moved to kiss me, I jerked my head back out of reach. He pulled me, painfully, by the hair, dragging my face towards his and, like a striking snake, he struck with his tongue. He kissed me, probingly, insinuatingly, and pressed his hard, undeniably masculine body against mine.

I've never in my life been sexually attracted to a man, but I'm not homophobic, and it never seemed to me either shameful or impossible (although, I admit, disturbing) that someday I might feel just the tiniest bit aroused by some mysteriously attractive bisexual . . .

But this was not that time.

My erection – legacy of Amy's embrace – died abruptly.

His tongue in my mouth, his hands on my body, sickened me. I felt under attack in the most revolting way and I couldn't do anything about it.

This isn't a man, this is Amy – I told myself that again and again, denying the urge I felt to fling him violently away and throw up. I kept my mouth firmly clamped shut and tried to resist his relentless assault on my body. Yet whatever I did somehow made it worse: I was aware each time I flinched or wriggled in a vain attempt to escape that my movements excited him more. I could feel his penis pressing against my leg, getting bigger and stiffer, seemingly ready to burst out of his pants.

I was so revolted, even with my endless mantra of *this is really Amy, think of Amy and hold on*, that I didn't know how much longer I could stand it. If he went much further, I'd have to sock him. How far was too far?

Hating him, hating myself, I hung on. I held him even

tighter, wishing I had enough strength in my arms to squeeze him unconscious, or break a couple of ribs ...

That was when I realised I was holding a woman again, squeezing her tightly.

But this was a different woman, bare-armed, scantily clad ...

Looking down, I saw my mother: dressed only in her underwear, and wriggling lasciviously in my arms, her eyes half-closed, a wide and willing smile on her face.

I'd thought nothing could be worse than that devilish young man wanting to rape me, but this – my own mother, begging for it – was infinitely more horrible.

Where were the snake, the lion, the bear, the burning brand that Janet had to endure before she won back her young Tam Lin? Those, I could have dealt with.

Telling myself, yet again, *this is really Amy*, I shut my eyes and held on tight, trying not to feel her nibbling at my earlobes and brushing kisses down my neck.

How long that went on, I don't know, but eventually she changed again. Suddenly she was Carl Voorhees – nasty little freckled bully, my nemesis from grade school – and then someone, or something, I don't know, reeking of sewers, hideous, slimy – then, finally, it was again Amy.

Only, this time, she was dead.

I stared down in horror at the slumped body. She wore nothing but a dirty T-shirt and underpants. Her skin was faintly blue. There was no doubting this time: she wasn't just unconscious, and she hadn't recently passed on. This thing that I held had been dead for days, if not weeks.

The corpse was stiff and cold and the smell – although I had never encountered it before, the smell of death was unmistakable.

Only the fact that I'm a stubborn bastard made me keep hanging on.

It had to be another illusion. Had to be.

I gritted my teeth, shut my eyes, and held on tightly and, although I'm not a believer, I prayed to anyone listening, anyone with the power to save her.

I opened my eyes and saw that the night had passed. Darkness had dimmed to grey, and over on the horizon the sky was getting light. And in my arms was a dead body.

I began to cry. I couldn't help myself. It was rage more than sorrow. After all that, after winning through every trial, this was what I got? It was so unfair!

I went on clutching the heavy, dead body as I wept, still unwilling to admit defeat. Maybe it wasn't quite morning yet. I hadn't heard a cock crow. The sun wasn't actually up, was it? What was the official moment when All Hallows Eve ended and all the spirits had to flee back to the Otherworld, leaving this one to the living?

Staring down at Amy's body, I wondered what had happened to her clothes. Why was she only in her underwear? Had someone killed her? Had she died of exposure?

Then I remembered the last thing I had to do.

It was a nightmare, trying not to let her go while I took my coat off, then grappling with the corpse, forcing her stiff, dead arms into the sleeves of my well-padded storm jacket, but, sobbing and cursing like a lunatic, I did it.

And then she was in the jacket, in my arms, and it was now light enough for me to see the change that rippled across her face, like a breeze over the surface of a pond. Her death had been another illusion, the final trick. Now, once more, she was alive, warm and flexible within my arms. She opened her eyes and gazed at me.

'Thank God,' she murmured. Then, pulling gently away from me, she began to shiver convulsively. 'Christ, I'm freezing! Will you take me home?'

Elidurus

In the twelfth century, there lived an elderly Welsh priest, Elidurus, who often spoke of events that had befallen him in his youth. At the age of twelve, although he loved his books, he often found the discipline of his instructors too harsh, and one day, to avoid a beating, ran away and hid in a hollow riverbank.

After he had been hidden there for two days without eating, he was visited by two small men who offered to lead him to 'a country full of delights and sports'. He agreed, and followed them along a path leading down below the earth. There he saw a beautiful country, although it was only dimly lit, and the nights were especially dark, without moon or stars. He met the king of that country, and became the friend and playmate of his son. All the men and women there were small of stature, but well proportioned, not dwarfish, and all had beautiful golden hair, which the men wore hanging to their shoulders.

After a little while, Elidurus returned home, but he went back to visit the wonderful country under the earth several times. He told no one but his mother about where he went, for his new friends were very mistrustful of the people who lived above the ground, considering them dishonest and unreliable. The boy's mother was inclined to think her son was lying when he talked about the many wonderful things he had seen. She wanted proof, so he promised to bring her a present made of gold, and the next time he played with the king's son, Elidurus stole a golden ball and quickly ran off with it.

However, Elidurus was seen by the same two men who had first led him to the underground kingdom, and they followed him, catching up to him just in front of his parents' house.

He was seized by the shoulders from behind, forced to stop. Turning, he saw his former guides, their faces no longer friendly, but now stony with disapproval.

'I didn't mean to take it,' he stammered. 'I'll bring it back. I only wanted it to show my mother.' He held the ball out apologetically.

There was to be no forgiveness. One of the men snatched the ball away from him, and both spat words at him he didn't understand but could guess were curses.

Overcome with shame, the boy ran after the two small men, but they seemed to have vanished. When he reached the usual spot on the riverbank he searched in vain for any sign of an entrance to the underground road he had used before. He continued to search for almost a year, but was never able to find it again.

Even as an old man Elidurus still had vivid memories

of the time he had spent in that underground kingdom. He remembered some words and phrases of the language they had spoken there, which he had picked up so readily as a child; he remembered the games he had played there, the taste of the saffron-flavoured, milky puddings, the beauty of the land, and the kindness of the people he had so thoughtlessly betrayed. He could never speak about his time there without weeping, and never, until his dying day, ceased to mourn his loss.

Laura

After leaving Laura's place, I walked all the way home. It wasn't that late, and I could have caught a bus easily enough, or gone by a slightly more complicated route on the underground, but I like walking, especially when I've got something to think about, and, boy, did I have something to think about.

Never, since my rescue of Amy, had I encountered a similar case. Never, since then, had I come in contact with the Otherworld, and not for lack of trying.

I'd spent years studying folklore and digging into old mysteries, travelling to ancient sites that were said to be haunted or holy, pursuing tales of vanishings and apparitions down through history all over the British Isles. In my own way, and for my own very different reason, I'd become as obsessed as Fred with finding a way through to a place or condition I couldn't describe or explain. That was why I'd set myself up in business as a specialist in missing persons, and it was why I'd never gone back home. *This* was the country where I'd caught a glimpse of another reality, so this was where I stayed, in the hope that it would happen again.

But despite all the people I'd managed to reunite with their families, despite my successes (which did outweigh the failures, by quite a bit) and even the crimes I'd been able to solve, I'd never found what I was looking for. I'd never even come close, until now.

Or was that just what somebody *wanted* me to think?

I'd never told anyone the true story of how I'd rescued Amy; and she was the only one who knew what had happened to her during the weeks she was missing.

I remembered how we'd made our way together down Doon Hill in the frosty morning. Apart from the occasional exclamation when she stepped on something uncomfortable to her bare feet she'd said nothing until she was settled in the front seat of my car, with the heater turned up as high as it would go, when she'd given me a slightly nervous smile and said, 'Thanks for rescuing me. Can you take me to the airport or something?'

I had stared in disbelief. 'Amy, what happened to you? Where've you been?'

She frowned. 'How do you know my name?'

'Are you kidding? I've been looking for you for weeks.'

'Weeks? Don't be stupid. Who are you, anyway?'

'I'm Ian Kennedy. My mother lives on the same street as your parents.'

'Really! What a coincidence!'

'It's not coincidence. Your mother sent me to find you.'

She pouted. 'She shouldn't have done that. I'm not a baby. I told her I was staying.'

'She was worried about you. You didn't explain why you weren't coming home. Nobody knew where you were. Where *were* you, Amy?'

Her eyes darted nervously about the car, then she tucked in her chin and shook her head.

'Come on, I think you owe me an explanation.'

Her head jerked up and she stared at me. 'What do I owe you for? Take it up with my mother! I never asked you to come!'

'Actually, you did. You asked me to meet you on Halloween, and you sounded pretty—'

'Halloween?' Her eyebrows drew together, and she turned away to look outside, where she seemed to take in the bare trees for the first time. 'It's October already?'

'Today is the first of November.'

'No! It can't be. It's August, it must be, it can't be later than that. I only went with him for a few days.'

'Went with who?'

She drew a shaky breath. 'Three months?'

'Amy, who did you go with? Where did you go?'

'I'd better call my folks.'

'That's an idea. Why don't I take you back to The Rowans. I'm sure Mrs MacDonald could fix you up with something to wear, and—'

'I'm not going back there!' She began to shake. 'Don't take me back there, please.'

'All right, take it easy. I won't take you anywhere you don't want to go.'

'I want to go home.' She murmured the words softly, pathetically, and tears shone in her eyes as she looked at me. My heart turned over. '*Please* don't ask me any more questions. Please, just take me home.'

I didn't actually go so far as that, but I took her to Edinburgh, where the American consulate was able to sort out the problem of her missing passport and papers, and I bought her some new clothes. I did question her again, of course, but by then she'd had time to figure out her story, and, needless to say, it did not involve supernatural beings, or other worlds, or anything at all that went against conventional expectations. She'd met a man . . . she'd been very silly . . . finally, she'd run away from him, and got lost in the woods where I'd found her. There were coy hints of sexual perversity, drugs, and general excess. I suspected she wouldn't have minded giving me more details, but I didn't want to hear those stories. I wasn't sure she was lying to me, exactly; more that she was struggling with her own confusion, trying to find some rational explanation for her missing weeks. Maybe she'd already forgotten what had happened to her, maybe it was beyond understanding, beyond words – or maybe she knew perfectly well and decided not to share it with me.

I don't know. I'd finally accepted that I would never know what her experience had been. I hadn't seen Amy Schneider since the day I'd waved good-bye to her at Edinburgh airport, and she'd made no effort to stay in touch; vaguely, I remembered my mother sending me news of her marriage some years ago.

It was unlikely that Amy Schneider had given me more than a passing thought in years; impossible that she could be behind an elaborate hoax designed to mess with my perception of reality.

No, the truth was altogether simpler, and stranger, and one people down through the ages had always suspected: there was another world beyond our own, another reality into which people might disappear and from which, even more rarely, they might return.

I went straight to bed when I got home and slept deeply, and if I dreamed, I don't remember.

In the morning, although I thought I made an early start, Laura was ahead of me. When I checked my e-mail I found she'd sent me the name and address of a restaurant in central London, noting that she'd booked a table for one o'clock, and Polly Fruell's e-mail address. I gazed at it while I sipped my coffee, but it told me nothing. She used her own name rather than a cute nickname, and the service provider was one I didn't recognise. I decided to leave it for the time being, and get her phone number later. I thought a confrontation with Polly Fruell was pretty much inevitable, but I wanted it to be on my terms.

I could have filled the time before lunch with more database searches, but that seemed pointless. Instead, I dealt with other business. I cleared out my in-box, responding to enquiries from potential clients, writing inconsequential, chatty notes to a half dozen old friends, then I surfed and browsed the internet for items of interest. There was still no official announcement from the police as to the cause of Linzi Slater's death. I wrote to Baz, the only journalist I knew who'd treated Linzi's disappearance as a story. Not that he'd been able to do much with it, against the general indifference of managing editors; but I thought it likely he'd remained interested, as journalists often were in their orphaned stories, and might have some inside information to share.

I was finding it hard to settle, anticipating my lunch with Laura, so I left early, and hit a few bookshops along the Charing Cross Road. In one, I came across an old collection of Irish legends I hadn't seen before. Skimming through it, I found 'The Wooing of Etain', simply yet rather beautifully told. It was a nice-looking book, and not too expensive, so I bought it as a present for Laura.

The prospect of asking her to believe that her daughter's disappearance had been foretold in a fairy tale – more than that; that Peri was the living embodiment of an old fairy tale – had me pretty jittery. Maybe I should keep her in the dark; it might be simpler that way. After all, it was Etain's human husband who had fetched her back – her mother hardly figured in the story, except as the means by which she was reborn. Although Laura was my client, it was Hugh's help I needed.

In the end, I was almost ten minutes late for our meeting, and I saw immediately by the set of Laura's mouth that this was a tactical error. Stupidly, I responded by abasing myself, saying 'sorry' far too many times, then thrusting the book forward, as if it might buy forgiveness.

'What's this?'

'A present?'

She read the title and shook her head. 'Peri's the one for fairy tales. Not me.'

'There's a reason for it ... I'll explain in a minute.' I picked up the menu. 'Have you ordered?'

'I was waiting for you.'

'Sorry,' I said again before I could stop myself. Embarrassed, I looked around, really taking the place in for the first time. It was a sort of French bistro, with daily specials chalked up on boards and a bar at the far end of the room. 'I was just wondering about wine – red or white?'

'Not for me. I have to get back to work.'

My heart sank still further.

'I'm sorry, but there are a lot of things I need to do in the office before I leave London. This has to be a quick lunch. I know you've got more questions to ask, and I'll sign whatever I need to sign and give you a cheque so you can get started.' She looked around for the waiter.

Rather than waste any more time, I ordered a steak, medium rare, with fries and a glass of the house red. Laura asked for the grilled goat-cheese salad and sparkling water.

When the waiter had gone, I plunged in. 'The missing hours, the time you can't remember after Hugh says he dropped off Peri, that's got to be key. How would you feel about—'

'I've already tried.'

'Tried what?'

'Being hypnotised. Hypnotherapy. Isn't that what you were going to suggest?'

I nodded. 'You're saying it didn't work?'

She let out a brief puff of air, looked down, picked up her knife, and used it to carve a line in the tablecloth. 'It was useless.'

'You couldn't be hypnotised?' I guessed.

'Oh, no.' Her eyes flew up to meet mine. 'I went right under. I was very suggestible. *Very*.' The corners of her mouth turned down.

'So what was the problem?'

'Well.' She shrugged, and worked with the knife on the tablecloth a little more. 'Have you heard of fabulation?'

I waited to hear what she meant by it.

'I didn't know anything about it at the time. I kind of thought, like most people do, I guess, that you *have* to tell the truth under hypnosis and that being hypnotised allows you to access parts of your brain that you can't normally. That may be true, but it also sets your imagination loose. I read up on it afterwards. The idea that you can't lie under hypnosis is so much bull. I think in that state maybe you can't tell the difference between lies and truth. Your inhibitions are down, you're in a suggestible state, and you want to please the hypnotist. Which means giving answers to questions. Not necessarily the truth, but what you think the hypnotist wants to hear.'

'You're saying you think you were led? Who did you go to?'

She shook her head quickly. 'I'm not saying I was led. I went to two different people, a woman in Hampstead and then a doctor in Bristol because he was reckoned to be *the* best. I can give you their names if you want, put you in touch with them, but really there's no point. I'm not blaming them. This sort of thing happens, much more often than you'd think. Hypnosis does break down some barriers, but basically it's up to the individual, and if you don't want to deal with certain memories, hypnotism can't force you.'

'So ... it was just the two sessions? You didn't go into therapy?'

Her mouth twisted, and she suddenly put the knife aside. 'Oh, it was suggested. Strongly suggested. But I didn't, no. I wanted to find my daughter, not go digging through my own psyche.'

The waiter brought my wine and Laura's water.

I raised my glass. 'Here's to finding the truth, however impossible it seems.'

'It could never be *that* impossible.'

'I wouldn't be so sure.' I was aware of my heart pounding.

She frowned. 'What do you mean?'

'Tell me what you remembered.'

'I didn't *remember* – that's the point! I made it up.'

'How can you be so sure?'

She shook her head despairingly. 'Because it was totally

impossible, nonsense, a fairy tale!' She touched the book she'd left on the table and her eyes narrowed as she looked at me. 'Like Hugh's story about the disappearing night-club.'

'Are they connected?'

'You want to hear my story.'

I took a sip of wine, watched her, and waited.

'All right. I was regressed back to when I was sitting on the couch, watching TV. I heard Peri come home – I heard the downstairs door open, then I heard her on the stairs, and that's when I got up and switched off the TV. When she came in, I went with her over to the window, to wave good-bye, and I drew the curtains, just like Hugh said.' Her voice was steady and calm; she might have been talking about something she'd seen on TV.

'She went off to the bathroom or something, and I double-locked the door and put on the chain – the usual routine. I went to get myself a glass of water from the kitchen, and I was just about to turn off the lights and go up to bed when Peri came back in. I asked her if she was planning to stay up, but she didn't answer. It was obvious she was thinking about something and it struck me that she'd grown up. I hardly knew her. She wasn't my little girl any more. I asked if she'd had a nice time with Hugh, and she looked at me and said, "Mom, do you know, is it possible to be really, truly in love with two people at the same time?" '

'What did you say to her?' I asked.

She shrugged. 'Something stupid. Something vague. I

was playing for time; my mind was racing. I thought: she's got a boyfriend back at college. I thought: I was too quick to tell her she didn't have to go back. She doesn't know if she wants to go back or not. She doesn't know what she wants. I was desperate not to say the wrong thing. I wanted her to confide in me; I wanted to be able to help. All this, so many thoughts and feelings whirling around in a matter of seconds, and she said, "He's here."

'There was a strange man standing in my kitchen. He was just inches away, between her and me, and he hadn't been there a second ago. I almost screamed. And yet, although it was impossible, I wasn't really afraid.'

'What did he look like?'

She smiled wryly. 'Guess.'

'Incredibly handsome. Long blonde hair, old-fashioned clothes . . . ?'

'Right. I described the same character that Hugh had met earlier the same evening. Of course, by the time I was under hypnosis saying all of this, I knew all about that; I'd practically memorised everything Hugh had said.'

She sighed and rubbed the side of her face with one hand; the other still rested on top of the book, like someone taking an oath. 'He told me his name was Mider, and that he had come to take his wife home with him. He held out his arms to her, and she walked into them, a dreamy look on her face, then they both disappeared, right in front of my eyes.'

Our food arrived then. I could not have felt less interested in it, but Laura automatically picked up her fork.

'You saw her disappear. The end?'

She frowned. 'Then ... then I heard a noise and looked towards the window, and there were these two white doves on the windowsill. You know that kind of clattering sound pigeon wings make when they flap? I heard that sound, getting louder and louder all around me. I saw the birds fly out through the window, and as they went, I saw a single, white feather float down through the air. I caught it in my hands.' She put down her fork without taking a bite.

'There really was a feather. I found it a couple of days after Peri disappeared. It was caught between the couch cushions. A big white feather – not a dove's, more like a swan's. I have no idea where it came from, or how long it had been there.'

Looking a little more relaxed, perhaps just relieved to have finished her story, she began to eat.

'Did you tell Hugh?'

She frowned. 'No, of course not. Why should I?'

'Did you tell Polly?'

'Well, yes. It was her idea that I should try hypnotic regression, so of course ... ' She took a bite of lettuce and cheese.

'What did she think?'

Mouth full, Laura did not reply. She rolled her eyes.

'She thought it was true?'

'Well ... kind of. She didn't really push it, but she said it could be psychologically true, we could interpret it like a dream, as a subconscious understanding of what had happened to Peri.'

'Meaning?'

'Oh, that Peri had made her choice, that she had gone off with this man, this stranger, and I should accept it was what she wanted.'

'Did you ever read "The Wooing of Etain"?'

'What's that?'

'You'd recognise the story. It's an old Irish tale. Hugh read it, he told me, as research for *The Flower-Faced Girl*.'

'But that's based on a Greek legend. Demeter and Persephone.'

'That story in Peri's notebook—'

Laura looked wary. 'I told you, that didn't really happen.'

'It could be a modern retelling of part of "The Wooing of Etain".'

'Oh! Well, of course *she* might have read it, she might even have told it to Hugh. I told you, she always loved fairy tales.' Her glance fell again on the book beside her plate. 'Is it in here?'

I nodded.

'So that's why . . . You want me to read it?'

I sawed at my steak although I was too tense to have much appetite. 'You probably should. Everybody else involved seems to know the story.'

'I don't understand. How could an old Irish fairy tale have anything to do with us? Who is Mider, really? You have an idea, don't you?'

This was it, the moment of truth. I thought of Fred in that Scottish pub, telling me about the abduction into the Otherworld of Robert Kirk. I put down my knife and fork and took a deep breath. Her eyes were fixed on mine as she waited for my explanation, an explanation I already knew she would not be able to accept.

I exhaled. 'Excuse me a minute, would you? I have to go ...' I gestured towards the back, where I presumed the toilets would be. I got up slowly and even managed to smile at her before sauntering away.

The corridor that led to the restrooms terminated in a fire door. It didn't look to me like the door was alarmed, but even if it was, it was still an easy way out. All I had to do was push down on the bar and I could be outside the restaurant, free and away in a matter of seconds. How long before she'd realise I wasn't coming back? Of course, she could call my mobile, but she'd never reach me if I kept it switched off or threw it away. I had my credit card on me, and an all-day, all-zones travel card. I could be at Heathrow in an hour, or Gatwick, or Waterloo Station in twenty minutes. When I'd taken the Eurostar to Paris last year, nobody even asked to see my passport until I came back. It was easy to disappear; it was only a matter of having the will.

Those thoughts ran through my head in the few moments it took me to turn to the left and step inside the men's room, but I wasn't even vaguely tempted. I knew the many ways there were for people to disappear precisely because I'd devoted myself to finding them and bringing them back. That was what I did; I wasn't the one who ran away.

Leaving the table wasn't entirely a ruse to gain time –

I did actually need the bathroom – but I had an idea that Laura would make use of my absence to read 'The Wooing of Etain', and that suited me.

I washed my hands slowly, dried them thoroughly under the noisy blower, then took a deep breath and counted to twenty before I re-entered the restaurant.

Laura looked up from the book as I approached. I noticed her face was a funny colour, a pale yellow, and her eyes shone weirdly dark. Before I could sit down, she slammed the book shut and got up, her chair making a harsh, grating sound as it scraped across the floor.

'Polly told you. Don't you tell *me* you don't know her, because I never told *anyone* but her; there's no one else you could have heard it from. How could she? How could *you*? What the hell is all this about? Why lie? What did you think you were going to get out of me, huh?'

She was like a stranger, shaking, possessed. I shook my head in confusion. 'What are you accusing me of? I promise you, I don't know Polly. What's happened? Look, would you calm down? Just sit down, sit, please, and tell me what you're talking about.'

I kept my voice low. The people at the next table were watching us like we were the floor show.

Laura dropped her voice to match mine, but stayed on her feet. 'This story! All the details! How did you *know*?' She thumped the book with the flat of her hand.

'I didn't write it. That book was published long before I was born, and the story's been around for centuries. If you don't believe me, try a library.' I kept my gaze steady on her, and saw a flicker of uncertainty lighten her eyes. Finally she pulled out her chair and sat down.

'Now you see why I wanted you to read it.'

She shook her head slowly, but not in disagreement. 'Who is Mider?'

'A great king of the Celtic Otherworld. One of the *Sidhe*. Maybe a god.'

'I mean really. In the real world.'

'I have no idea.'

'Probably Irish, right, since he's so obsessed with old Irish myths. And he must be awfully rich ... '

My heart sank as she went on rationalising into existence a bizarre yet human villain. Ridiculous though that was, it was still easier to swallow than the truth. How could I tell her Mider was the king of the fairies?

'But how did he know about Peri?'

I looked at her blankly, but she must have read some meaning into my expression, because her eyes widened, and she gasped. 'Polly! You think Mider knew Polly!'

She rushed on. 'They must have been involved – she always had terrible luck with men – she was too trusting – she must have told him – she's the only one who could have told him – nobody else knew – I never told *anyone* but Polly.'

'Told her what?'

The normal colour had come back to her face, and her cheeks flushed pink. 'It's silly, I know. You asked about Peri's father, and I said she didn't have one – that's true. When I got pregnant, I wasn't in a relationship. By the time I realised I was pregnant I thought it *was* impossible. When the doctor told me the due date, and I counted back ... ' She looked down, fiddling with her fork, the flush in her face turning darker. 'I hadn't slept with anyone that whole week – longer. And what I remembered most from that week was being at a party, a cookout on a patio. I was drinking punch, and a fly landed in my cup, and ...' She wrinkled her nose. 'I swallowed it.'

'And that was Peri's conception,' I said neutrally.

'I know it sounds crazy, but, yeah, that's what I thought. Of course, later I realised the doctor must have miscalculated, or I had. It's not like I'd been *totally* celibate for months on end. *Of course* Peri has a biological father; she was conceived in the usual way. I wish I'd never told Polly about that damn fly. If she hadn't told this Mider guy—'

'We don't know yet if your friend has anything to do with him. I'll need to talk to her—'

'Fine. Maybe you should just fly straight to DFW, rent a car, drive out to the ranch, and confront her; don't give her any warning,' said Laura. She leaned intently towards me. 'You might get more out of her that way.'

'Maybe.'

'But you have another idea?'

I nodded. I reached for my glass and drained the rest of the wine from it, hoping it could give me courage. 'I suggest we start in Scotland, in the area where Peri was last seen.'

She cocked her head, waited.

I took a deep breath. 'You remember I mentioned my

very first case, a girl who went missing in Scotland, had some similarities to this one?'

She nodded.

I had never told anyone Amy's story. Once, feeling myself in the right, sympathetic company, I had started, but for some reason the words had dried up and stuck in my throat.

That didn't happen this time. I took it slowly, went into lots of detail, emphasised my own total disbelief when I was first treated to stories about the being known as the love-talker and the legends that had accrued around a genuine historical figure like Robert Kirk.

At first, she was with me. The waiter came to clear away our plates and brought us coffee; but she didn't touch hers, too caught up in the narrative, her eyes fixed on mine. I felt a wonderful sense of mastery; I loved the fascination on her face. And then, I guess it was as I started to go into a little too much detail about the stories Fred had told me of all the different people who'd been to the Otherworld and back, the expression on Laura's face began to congeal. She dropped her eyes and concentrated on stirring cream into her coffee, adding sweetener, then drinking it in slow sips while I talked on and on.

I began to hurry, then, to stumble over my words and rush along, eager to get to the good part, the successful rescue, the happy end. I was losing Laura's attention, but still imagined I could compel her belief. When I finally finished, the silence between us was like a dead thing on the table.

She sighed and set her empty coffee cup back in its saucer with a decisive click, the dull sound of shattered bone. I waited for her to protest, raise objections, ask questions – some point of entry into an argument. She looked me in the face with a kind of resigned contempt and said nothing.

'It's true,' I said stupidly. 'That's really what happened.'

'You think Peri's in Fairyland.'

'We can get her back.'

'No. Not "we". There's no "we". I don't want anything more to do with you or your crazy fantasies. I would never have hired you if I'd known you believed in fairies.'

I forbore to point out that she had not, in fact, hired me. The contract I'd brought along was still unsigned, and she'd paid me nothing, despite the work I'd already done. Actually, she owed me, not that it was the time to point that out.

'You're not working for me, you're fired, understand? I don't want to hear from you again.' Her voice remained level and cold; she was furious, but I wasn't worth even the heat of her anger.

She got up and left the restaurant without looking back, leaving behind the book I'd given her, and of course leaving me to pay for lunch. As far as she was concerned, I was off the case. I, of course, felt differently.

Practicalities

Best times:
Twilight
Midnight
The hour before sunrise
Noon

Best days:
Halloween/Samhain (31 Oct.)
Beltane (1 May)
Midsummer (21–24 June)
Lammas (1 Aug.)

For safety:
Keep your wits about you.
Do not eat or drink during visit.
Carry about your person: St John's wort, churchyard mould, bread and salt, an iron dagger and/or a staff made of rowan wood

Polly

It was like returning to full life after a long period of drowsy hibernation.

I wasn't surprised that Laura had been unable to accept my story, and I didn't blame myself for not having been careful or convincing enough in the way I'd told it. For whatever reason, she was totally wedded to a rational, materialist view of the universe, which made her more blinkered than any honest sceptic. This was a woman who had seen her own daughter disappear before her very eyes, an event that did not fit into her perceptions of how things are. Rather than changing her attitude, she'd blocked the memory. There was nothing anyone could do to change her mind.

But that was OK. I didn't need her.

Although I will admit to disappointment that what had seemed like a promising new friendship (with the added *frisson* of sexual attraction) had died such a death, I didn't waste time or energy brooding on it. I had a job to do. As soon as I'd put lunch on my credit card (I would figure out how to pay *that* bill later), I shot over to nearby Cecil Court, where there was a bookshop specialising in theosophy and esoteric books. I picked up a few that were new to me and looked as if they might be useful, and further burdened my credit card before heading home. I planned to spend the next few days in research and reading, soaking myself in the old mysteries once again.

But first, I tried to call Hugh.

Selfishly, I would have preferred to find Peri and bring her back all by myself, but I knew that might not be possible. It never pays to ignore the old stories, no matter how illogical and downright contradictory they can be. Sometimes, a particular hero is designated, and no one else can do the job. It was hard to imagine Etain going back for anyone but her human husband.

I couldn't get through to Hugh that afternoon. All three of his phone numbers led me, through call diverts, to the same electronic voice mailbox. I left my name and number, and said it was urgent. There was no more I could do.

Turning on my own answering machine to field calls from the fitted-kitchen, package holiday, book club, and double-glazing salesmen that so often punctuate my day, I made up a pot of coffee from the last of the fresh-ground roast and dug out the map box.

During my first year or so in Britain, when I'd travelled far and wide, searching for other spots as liminal as Doon Hill, I'd acquired a complete set of the Ordnance Survey 'Pathfinder' series of maps. Each one covered a small section of the country in minute detail, on a scale of two and a half inches to the mile (or, as we're supposed to reckon it now, 4 cm to 1 km), with every hillock and spit of land given its local name, and every church, fort, well, and ancient ruin plainly marked.

To anyone who has grown up in America, Britain can appear almost ridiculously small. A tourist can confidently expect to 'do' it in a week, or to visit all major sites of interest in a month. I suppose you could even manage to drive from John o'Groats to Land's End in a single day. Yet although it is small in physical dimension, it is complex, nearly infinite in detail. Every field and hill has a name and a story behind it, and although most may have been forgotten in this age of mass media, and the once-intelligible, straightforward Norse or Gaelic or Old English place names long since corrupted into nonsense sounds, with time and patience and a bit of imaginative research it was possible to restore the original meanings and once again catch a glimpse of the magic lurking beneath.

Along with the maps I'd stored my notebooks and travel diaries from those days, jottings that described my impressions of psychic and emotional atmospheres as well as physical descriptions of the spots I visited. I hadn't looked through them in years – frankly, I'd almost forgotten about them – and as I got them out I felt a tingle of the old excitement and felt absurdly pleased with myself for having kept this careful record. This would really cut down on the time needed for research; I'd be able to read my impressions of the area where Peri had last been seen, probably pinpoint the very hill or stone circle that was the local entrance to the Otherworld in a matter of minutes.

My smug pride quickly evaporated as I realised I was wrong. Although I thought I'd been 'everywhere', there were spots I'd missed on my leisurely grand tour, and the twenty- or thirty-mile radius around the public phone box where Peri had briefly materialised was one of them.

For its size, Scotland still has relatively few roads, and much of the west coast consists of long, skinny tendrils of land projecting out to sea, served by a single, narrow road that connects to nothing. At first, I was determined to drive down every obscure byway but as the months wore on – and particularly in the short cold days of lashing rain – I gave that goal up as impractical. Even though there was a ruined castle that might have tempted me down to the end of the winding road where Peri had last been seen, something else – probably snow or hail – had countered that temptation. I'd decided that particular side track didn't fit in with my schedule, was too far out of the way, didn't offer enough of interest.

I cursed my younger self, although it had probably been a sensible decision at the time. The more closely I'd explored this country, the more it expanded, like some magical box, bigger inside than out. A whole lifetime would not be enough to investigate every nook and cranny of this island.

At least, although I hadn't seen much of North Knapdale, I had the Ordnance Survey map, and a copy of that useful little pamphlet, *Place names on maps of Scotland and Wales*, to help me make sense of it. I needed it, because almost nothing in that part of Scotland – apart from 'caravan site' and a few cottages owned by in-comers from the south – was labelled in English.

The first name to catch my attention as I pored over the map was *Cnoc na Faire*, but a quick check told me that 'faire' had nothing to do with fairies. It meant 'watching', and in connection with 'Cnoc' ('a round hill') translated as something like 'Look-Out Hill'. I couldn't see anything with *sidh, sidhean*, or *sith* in the name to indicate the traditional connection with the Good Neighbours, but there were several ancient sites within walking distance of the caravan park – three duns, a ruined chapel, and several cairns, as well as an indication that there were caves along the rocky shoreline. People had lived along this coast for many centuries, and I was sure there must be places they'd told stories about, woodland with a reputation for being uncanny, heaps of stones once sacred to a now-forgotten god, a magic well, a cave where someone had been seen to go in but never to emerge again . . .

I spent hours, long into the evening, moving from a close study of the map to the dustiest books in my library, searching out old collections of folklore as well as more contemporary surveys with titles like *Mysterious Britain* and *Haunted Scotland*. Few gave any mention to Knapdale – which didn't feature much in the more ordinary guidebooks, either – and when they did, the reference was always to something located on another shore, or across the loch, twenty or thirty miles or more from where Peri had been seen.

Finally, in a book about the remains of prehistoric Scotland, I found a description of *Dun a'Chaisteal*, the Iron Age 'Fortress of the Castle' and precursor to Castle Sween (which overlooked the contemporary caravan park). It was described as 'associated, traditionally, with the mythical Celtic heroine Deirdre of the Sorrows, who fled from Ireland to this part of Scotland with her lover, Naoise McUisneach.'

Deirdre and Naoise were both humans, entirely mortal, unlike Etain and Mider, yet the reference to this ancient love story gave me hope, for it seemed possible that a story about one pair of lovers might well be hidden or disguised by another.

Then I found this:

> *Dun a'Bhuilg, or Dunvulaig, The Fortress of the Quiver (or, perhaps, the Fortress of the Bag), the crumbling remains of another Iron Age Fort, was at one time avoided by locals, who believed it a dwelling place of the Daoine Sidhe, fairies, who could be seen on moonlit summer nights silently plying their delicate, eggshell boats with translucent green sails, in Kilmory Bay below.*

With a deep sigh of satisfaction I carefully marked the book and laid it to one side with the map and my notes. All of a sudden, I was ravenously hungry. The pot of coffee was long gone, and that skinny little steak at lunch might have been consumed in another lifetime.

I went down the road to get a hamburger. I name no

names, but one of the major American franchises had an outlet on the corner opposite the underground station, and although I'd been known to fulminate against globalization and the evils of standardised, mass-produced fast foods, not to mention the litter problem, there were times when all I wanted was the opportunity for quick, anonymous, no-hassle refuelling.

I went out into the light, balmy evening. The air smelled, not unpleasantly, of garbage and traffic and humanity, that summer-in-the-city smell. There were lots of people around, strolling along by themselves, or hanging around in clusters outside the closed shops, or queuing for takeaways at the kebab shop, the pizza place, the Chinese. Although it was late, it still wasn't completely dark. For no reason at all except the season, my mood was suddenly one of ridiculous optimism. Except for those years in Texas, where it was already far too hot in June, and you knew it would only get worse, midsummer has always been my favourite time of the year. Maybe it's because it was when I was born, but it has always felt special; a time out of normal time, without regimented schedules, when day and night blend together seamlessly, and anything is possible.

Halloween was a dark and dangerous night, when spirits of the dead roamed the earth, but midsummer's eve was the haunt of a different type of spirit; it was for lovers. All at once I felt convinced that we were going to find Peri and that Hugh was the one to bring her back.

With the warm and comforting weight of food in my

belly, the taste still in my mouth, I hurried home, impatient to talk to Hugh and convince him he could win back his long-lost love.

As soon as I got in I saw, as if in response to my thoughts, the winking light on my answering machine. One call, in the brief half hour I'd been out. But when I pressed the replay button there was only the faint hissing sound of the tape winding on before the buzz of the dial tone when the caller hung up. Hugh didn't seem like someone who'd do that, but I was reluctant to give up my belief that it was he, so I called him straight back.

Once again, I got his voice mail and left my details: 'I really need to talk to you. Call me as soon as you get this. *Any time*, on my mobile.'

I added that, because I only had one landline, and if I had to keep that free for his call, I wouldn't be able to use the internet. It was long past time that I upgraded, I knew. At the very least, I could have a separate business line. I'd considered it before, but somehow I never seemed to be in a position to expand and take on more expenses, even the most minor ones. Over the past few years, everything had gone up except my income. And now that Laura had fired me, my search for Peri had become something else to put down under personal expenses rather than possible income. Even worse, as long as I was looking for her, I wasn't going to be able to do anything else that might bring in some money.

Oh well, it looked like I was going to be running up a little more debt on my credit card. A straightforward loan would be cheaper, but what would I put down as the purpose of the loan? 'A trip to Fairyland'. Yeah, right.

As I checked my e-mail again – that nervous tic of modern life – my attention was caught by the earlier message from Laura, with Polly Fruell's address. On a whim, I entered Polly's details into a search engine.

Seconds later, I was staring at her obituary, from the *Fort Worth Star-Telegram* of 2 March, 1995.

The next hit was on an article from the *Dallas Morning News*, from a couple of days earlier, describing the horrific freeway pileup in which three people – among them, Polly Jean Fruell, forty-three, of Jacksboro – had lost their lives, and seven others were seriously injured.

I bounced around to check out the other hits, but there was no doubt in my mind that this was Laura's Polly, and that she'd been dead for years.

Was it possible that Laura had been taken in by an ordinary imposter pretending to be her long-lost friend? Somebody who was in reality an associate of the man who called himself Mider, both of them criminals involved in Peri's kidnapping . . .

I could imagine Laura's mind running along such lines, but it made no sense. People invented complex scams in the hope of a large reward. There was no way anyone was benefiting from this – not in the ordinary way.

Polly was dead. She'd been dead three years ago when she turned up on Laura's doorstep on Christmas Eve.

The connection between death and the Otherworld appeared again and again in the old stories. Although it wasn't a straightforward equation, fairies were sometimes confused with spirits of the dead. The tumuli that were supposed to be entrances to their underground homes were in actual fact ancient graves, chambered tombs, and many first-person accounts from people who claimed to have visited Fairyland mentioned seeing people they had known but believed to be dead. In addition, some of the people stolen by fairies appeared first to die, like Robert Kirk or Mary Campbell Nelson, although that death was explained away as an illusion if they were later rescued.

I wondered how Laura would explain this away, how deep in denial she'd have to go, and I imagined her comatose with shock, and shuddered. Well, I certainly wasn't going to be the one to tell her that she'd spent several weeks entertaining a dead woman in her flat; a dead woman who continued to send her e-mails.

I closed the internet connection, closed the program, and shut down my computer. Sometimes I left it on all night, but I didn't feel like doing so that night. Then I got up and made sure the doors were locked and bolted shut, and set the burglar alarm, too, even though such things are well-known to make no difference to the dead.

In my dream, I was going to meet Jenny. I was on foot in a city that was both familiar and strange to me, and the journey was taking much longer than I had expected as I made one slow, circuitous wrong turn after another. The city was a puzzling jumble, bits of Milwaukee and Dallas mixed up with London, and nothing that I recognised was quite right. Eventually I arrived at a park with a high wall around it. The tall, square gateposts were topped with pale grey stone statues of hooded figures. It looked more like a cemetery than a public park, yet I knew this was where Jenny had asked me to meet her, so I hurried through the open gate.

As I approached the small hill at the centre of the park I could see Jenny was already there, waiting for me, standing there like a beacon. She had on the dark red suit she used to wear when she wanted to impress, as it made her look both businesslike and sexy, with its short skirt and the high heels she wore to flaunt her shapely legs and add height. My heart leapt at the sight of her, and I hurried forward, my arms going out to hug her.

She turned and she wasn't Jenny, she was Fred.

I stopped in confusion, but she caught my hands and nodded encouragingly, inclining her head. I saw a door in the side of the soft, green slope. Although she didn't say anything, I knew from the nod of her head that Jenny waited for me inside the hill.

I stepped forward confidently, and as soon as I was inside, the door slammed shut and I was trapped in a small, pitch-black, suffocatingly close space. In a panic, I flailed my arms, struck the wall, and woke up.

The room was filled with light that seemed searingly bright after the darkness of the dream. My hand throbbed. I shook it and flexed my fingers: bruised, maybe, but no serious harm done. I peered blearily at the clock and groaned when I saw it was only just after five-thirty. My reaction to the dream had pumped so much adrenalin into my system, I knew there was no way I'd be going back to sleep.

I got up and stumbled downstairs, but as soon as I walked into my bare, chilly little kitchen, with its permanent scent of damp never quite covered by the ghosts of cooking past, I remembered that I'd forgotten to buy more coffee, or indeed anything to eat, and had to make do with a glass of water before going back up to shave, shower, and dress.

I didn't think any of the local shops or cafés would be open so early, so I decided to head into central London and get breakfast there. I had no plans for what I was going to do after that; but the residue of that dream, plus what I'd learned about Polly Fruell, made me unwilling to spend the day cooped up all by myself in my office. Until Hugh got in touch I had the frustrating feeling that there was nothing more I could do.

There wasn't much traffic on the road, and there were few people about as I walked down to the underground station. I wasn't even sure it would be running yet, but it was, and I had the rare, almost unique experience of riding in a carriage that remained empty almost all the way to Leicester Square.

That's where I got out to walk through the quiet, waking streets, past the shut-up shops in an eerie blaze of daylight. There were other people about, most of them probably heading for work, although some of them looked both bright and confused and were probably tourists, and there were also a few staggering shufflers who seemed left over from the night before, caught out by the morning's sudden arrival. I saw one coffee shop open for business, but it had a queue of customers spilling out the door, so I passed. The next early-morning café also looked overcrowded, and another one, although still shut, had attracted a huddle of sleepy-looking potential customers.

I kept on walking, even though I was starting to feel definite signs of caffeine withdrawal, but the thought of Golden Square guided my steps. I didn't know why I should go there, but maybe I'd pick up some clue, see something I hadn't noticed before that might tie in that particular little corner of London with an ancient Irish myth. If not, well, the square had benches, and I could rest until I decided where to go next.

Only a scattering of people were using the benches at that early hour, and some had probably been there all night. They were all men. I didn't look directly at any of them – this was the city; we allowed each other our privacy – but made straight for an unoccupied spot, head down, purposeful, projecting, I hoped, the image of someone who should not be bothered with requests for spare change or cigarettes.

'Ian.'

The sound of my name, spoken quietly, lifted the hairs on my neck.

'Over here.'

I turned and saw Hugh Bell-Rivers sitting on a bench.

As I approached, he held up a large styrofoam cup with a lid. 'Want a coffee?'

I stared. He had two cups with him. A little hesitantly, I sat beside him and took the cup he offered. 'Waiting for someone?'

'I thought you might turn up.'

'And this was easier than calling?' I gave him a hard look. 'How long have you been waiting?'

'I just got here.'

The coffee, steaming hot, seemed to confirm that. But it made no sense. 'What made you think I'd come here? Hey, did you get my message?'

He nodded.

'I didn't say "Meet you in Golden Square," did I? I didn't know I was coming here myself until ten minutes ago.'

He shrugged. 'That's OK.'

'No, it's not OK. I asked you to phone me.'

'I would've if you didn't turn up. It's still early.'

'Who'd you get this coffee for?'

'You.'

'Just in case I turned up.' I was getting irritated. 'This is stupid. I didn't come here to play games. In fact, I don't know *why* I came here. But you do, it seems.'

'I thought you wanted to talk to me.'

'I do. But I don't normally expect just to bump into the people I want to talk to at opportune moments. That's why God gave us telephones. What am I supposed to think, that you planted a posthypnotic suggestion that I'd come here this morning and be spooked out that you *knew*?'

'I didn't make you come here.'

I laughed harshly, not amused. 'As if!'

He sighed. 'I'm not trying to prove anything. There's nothing to prove. OK? Why don't you just drink your coffee and say what you wanted to say to me.'

I frowned. 'First I want to know what made you think I'd be here.'

'OK.' He stared at me with those big, blue eyes. It was not a guileless, faux-naive stare, but a weary, open gaze. 'I saw us here together. I mean "saw" us.' Still holding his cup, he managed to make quotation-mark hooks of his fingers. 'It happens to me sometimes, I have these sort of visions. I don't mean hallucinations, and I know they aren't happening now; they're more like really vivid memories, but of things that haven't happened yet.'

'And do they always come true?'

'I don't know yet.'

'It sounds like the Second Sight,' I said. The Second Sight was a gift, or curse, of the Highland Scots, and it was connected to the ability to see fairies. 'Were you born with it?'

'Definitely not.'

'How long, then?' But as I asked, I knew what he was going to say.

'Since Peri disappeared.'

'A gift from Mider,' I guessed, thinking of the strange wine. 'Maybe a gift he didn't want to make, but he had to trade you *something* for Peri.'

'Oh, he gave me a lot more than that. There was the money.'

I peeled off the lid of my cup and took a cautious sip of the hot liquid. It was delicious, a strong, rich roast, uncontaminated by milk or sugar, as if Hugh's Second Sight extended even to the details of how I liked my coffee. 'That cheque for five hundred thousand pounds? I thought you gave it back.'

'I did. At least, I thought I did, but he didn't take it.'

'What happened, did he slip it back into your pocket?' I brightened. 'If you had a cheque, we might be able to trace him through the bank.'

'It wasn't a cheque. It was a lottery ticket. My share of the winnings turned out to be five hundred thousand pounds.'

I whistled admiringly. 'Some coincidence.'

He shook his head. 'I never bought that ticket. My mother found it in my jacket pocket about a week later; she's the one who thought to check the numbers. It came from a local newsagent's, where I used to buy my copy of *Time Out*. The guy who worked there even identified me, said he remembered me buying it. Well, he remembered *me*, no doubt, I was in there every week, but I never bought a lottery ticket. I just didn't. But there it was, I won the money.'

Half a million pounds and the ability to see into the future. Good deal, I thought.

'So what about these visions?' I asked. 'Are they always as exciting as knowing when and where you're going to run into somebody like me?'

He smiled reluctantly. 'Go on, mock. Some of them are like that. Sometimes I don't even know what they're about – they're that inconsequential. I "see" something, out of context, then a week or two later I realise that it's happening. It's kind of like *déjà vu*. Other things – well, some are to do with other people.' He grimaced. 'I knew one of my sisters was pregnant before she'd done the test, and I knew when she miscarried, before she'd told anyone. And some of them are still ahead in the future.' He shrugged. 'Whether they're going to come true or not, there's bugger-all I can do about it.'

I frowned. 'What do you mean? You didn't have to come here this morning.'

He looked surprised, as if staying away never occurred to him. 'But you wanted to talk to me.'

'So?'

'I guess I wanted to talk to you, too.'

I sighed. 'Well, what if I hadn't turned up?'

'But you did.'

'But how long would you have waited? Would you have come back again tomorrow? I thought you didn't know exactly when something was going to happen. How long would you have kept coming here with your two cups of coffee, trying to make your vision come true?'

'It's not like that. It's just a feeling ... it was easy for me to come here today, I woke up early anyway, and it's near my work. If you didn't show up, I would have phoned you.'

'Well, thank you for returning my call,' I said, drinking.

'And thanks for this – I was about ready to kill for a cup of coffee.'

'So what did you want to talk to me about?'

I wondered if his visions included sound. 'What do you think?'

'You want me to rescue Peri.'

'I want your help to bring her back.'

He didn't respond to this distinction. 'Do you know where she is?'

There was no reason to pull my punches with someone who'd just confessed to Second Sight. 'I think she's in the Otherworld – whatever *that* means – with Mider.'

'But do you have any idea how to find her?'

'I have some ideas. There are certain places, and certain times, when there are ways through, and these places usually have stories attached to them, local traditions. I'm guessing there's some kind of link, or doorway, not far from where she was last seen. If we go up and scout around about, oh, say, a twenty-mile radius of that phone box, I think we could find it.'

'I think I'd know something like that if I was near it.' He put his empty cup down and toyed with his earrings for a moment, frowning. 'In the story, it's not clear that Etain wanted to go back.'

'If she gave her husband a sign, she did.'

'But if she didn't? If she stood by and said nothing and let him take his own daughter to be his wife – how sick is that?'

'Maybe she couldn't speak. She was under a spell.'

He winced as he tugged at his earlobe. 'Exactly. So she couldn't speak. She couldn't even choose to go away with Mider in the first place – he had to trick her husband into giving her up. She never had any say in what happened to her. It had nothing to do with what *she* wanted. It's all about the contest between the two men, or rather the god and the man, each a king in a different realm. Etain isn't a woman, she's a *thing*. It's not just that her desires don't count; they don't exist. She might as well be a magic box, or a prize cow that the men are fighting over.'

'Give that man an A-plus in feminist criticism,' I said.

'Peri is not an object. I won't treat her like one.'

'I'm not asking you to. Etain is obviously a symbol. But Peri's real, even if she's caught up in some ancient story.'

'She's not my property. I didn't give her away and I can't take her back. Only if she wants to come back with me. I don't want to bargain with Mider over who gets the girl; I won't play that game. If Peri needs my help, she only has to ask. I'd do anything she asked.' Raw emotion was naked in those last words, and I knew then that he'd never stopped loving her.

'What if she can't ask?'

He frowned and shook his head, fiddling again with the earrings, pulling them in a way that had to hurt. 'He'll have to let her talk; if I see him again, he'll have to. It's her decision.'

'What if she thinks she doesn't need rescuing, but she really does?'

'According to who?'

311

'People can be deluded, deranged ... you wouldn't let her destroy herself?'

'Take her away and lock her up for her own good, is that what you mean?'

I bristled at the contempt in his eyes. 'Who said anything about locking up?'

'Drag her back here, then. Force her to live the way somebody else says is right. No. If she wants to stay, that's it. We don't have to understand her choice, just respect it.'

I'd finished my coffee. I stared across the square at some strutting pigeons. The sun was warm on my face, the top of my head, my hands. Hugh was with me, whatever his supposed moral reservations, and we had a mission; I should have felt great. Instead, I felt weary, and a little frightened. I was aware of an aching, hollow emptiness in my chest, which seemed to have been with me for most of my life, and I thought of the dark, tomblike space in my dream where I'd found myself imprisoned, having lost both Jenny and Fred.

Out of the silence, I thought I heard a bell ringing – distant, muffled, as if sounding from another world.

I shivered and tried to ignore it, forcing myself to speak. 'What happened to change your mind?'

He looked puzzled. 'How do you mean?'

'You wouldn't help me, before. According to you, she'd made her choice and left you. Now you think she *might* want to come back to you.'

He took a deep breath, nodding. 'I've seen her. I mean,

"seen" her, living with me. I don't know how far ahead it might be, but – there's a baby.'

I could still hear the bell, ringing far away. For a split second I imagined I was back on that Scottish hillside in the dark cold of an October night and that everything since then had been just a dream.

Hugh was looking at me with an odd expression. 'Are you going to answer that?'

Belatedly, finally, I recognised my own telephone's ring tone and scrabbled to dig it out of my pocket. 'Hello?'

'Ian – oh, Ian–' a woman's voice, American, Texan, tearful; almost unbearably familiar. For one heart-stopping moment I thought it was Jenny.

'I have to talk to you – you have to help me – I'm afraid I'm going crazy!'

'Calm down, Laura. Take a deep breath. You're not crazy. Tell me what's wrong.'

'Polly's dead!' She gulped and fell silent.

'I know.'

'You do?'

'I read her obituary last night, on the internet. Your friend died in a car crash in Texas in 1995.'

'But I *saw* her! How can she be dead? I know there was an accident; she *told* me she'd been in a terrible accident, it was how she'd lost her leg.'

My eyebrows went up at that. I was certain Laura had never mentioned her friend was a one-legged woman.

'I tried to e-mail her last night and it bounced back. I went to find her phone number – she wasn't listed, but there was one for her sister. When I called her, she told me Polly died years ago – long before Peri disappeared! I didn't believe her – how could I? – after a while she got pissed off and didn't want to talk to me, but she faxed me a copy of the obituary, and a piece from the local paper, and also the phone number of the mortuary, and the crematorium and the public records office if I needed further confirmation.' She broke off. I could hear her breathing raggedly.

'Laura, I'm so sorry. You must be in a state of shock.'

'It gets worse. There's more. Just now – this morning – look, I hate talking into this dinky thing – I'm outside the underground station – can I come see you? I need to talk to you. I'm sorry I fired you. I need your help. I've changed my mind about everything. Everything.'

'I'm in the West End right now. Soho. Just having a talk with Hugh Bell-Rivers. Why don't you meet us for breakfast?' I glanced at Hugh as I said this, but he wasn't paying attention. His eyes were fixed on the other side of the square. I followed the direction of his gaze, towards Number 23, but there was nothing going on.

'Soho? Where?'

I suggested an American-style diner, which she knew, and it was agreed.

Putting the phone away I raised my voice to get Hugh's attention. 'What's so interesting?'

'I just saw someone go into the basement of Number 23.'

'Really?' I jumped up. Hugh didn't move.

'No point. I've seen her before.'

'So who is she?'

He sighed. 'You still think we're going to find a *real person* behind all this? A mad, all-powerful, millionaire obsessive playing mind games with us?'

'What did you see?'

'A woman. She opened that gate as if there was never a lock on it and went down the steps. I saw her as clearly as I see you now, but not in the same way. I can't explain it, but I know. It used to freak me out, seeing people, and things, that weren't really in our world ... but I've kind of got used to it.'

'The first time I met Laura she told me you saw things other people didn't see. She figured you for a fantasist.'

He nodded. 'Laura sees less than she could. Less than she should. She insists on such a rigid, narrow view of the world that she makes herself crazy.'

'That may be about to change.'

He looked at me, and a gleam of mischief shone in his eyes. 'Oh, and you're the man for the job? Good luck, mate!'

'You said you'd seen that woman before?' I inclined my head towards the house across the square.

'That's right, change the subject.' He crushed the styrofoam cup absently in one hand. 'Yeah, I saw her coming out of that same basement just a few days after Peri disappeared. I was keeping watch on it, just in case. I followed her down the road, to see where she went. I had my brand-new, state-of-the-art video camera with me – Christmas present from my dad – and so I used it. I even got a full-frontal shot of her when we were on the underground – she never seemed to notice me; I was sure she never had a clue I was following her, and I followed her all the way.'

'All the way where?'

He looked me in the eye. 'All the way to West Hampstead. To Laura's. I watched her go in.'

The hairs rose on the back of my neck. 'Polly Fruell?'

He nodded. 'So she said.'

'Did you tell Laura?'

'I tried. I was all set to show her the proof on video but, guess what? She wasn't *in* the video. That was when I realised that there were things I could see that wouldn't show up on tape. When Laura asked her, Polly denied ever having been in Golden Square. She said she didn't even know where it was. She didn't seem flustered, just bewildered. She said she hadn't even gone by underground, she didn't do a lot of walking because of her bad leg. I must have mistaken her for someone else. Laura thought she was being too kind to me. That's when she became convinced I couldn't tell the difference between fantasy and reality.' He stood up. 'I should go.'

'Come and have breakfast. There's things I need to tell you.'

He hesitated.

'That was Laura on the phone. I said we'd meet her.'

'Oh, well, you don't want me along . . . .'

'Yes I do. Yesterday Laura fired me. Today, she's hired me again. She just found out that her old friend Polly Fruell died in 1995.'

His eyes widened.

'The limits of her reality have just expanded. Come on, Hugh. We need to talk. You're not the only one who's had contact with the Otherworld.'

For the first time since I had known her, Laura looked less than perfectly turned out when she entered the diner. Her clothes were smart, as usual, but had an air of having been thrown on without much thought; her hair hung limply, without its usual shine and bounce, and her face was bare of makeup. For the first time, she really looked her age, the mother of a grown-up daughter, someone who had struggled, and suffered, and lost.

She kissed Hugh on both cheeks, but for me there was only an awkward nod as she slipped into the seat beside him, across from me.

'I have to apologise—'

'No, forget it. I'm all in favour of the sceptical mind – still try to keep mine that way. Why don't we order breakfast; then we can talk.'

Hugh and I both went for the Good Morning America special: scrambled eggs, bacon, sausage, and hash browns. Laura asked for a fresh fruit salad.

Then she began her story.

Learning of Polly Fruell's death had been disturbing, but it didn't push her into what historians and theorists would call a paradigm shift. Everything could still be explained in human terms. After all, why couldn't a competent actress have convinced Laura she was the friend she hadn't seen in over eighteen years, especially when there was no reason for her to be suspicious? The reason for this pretence was harder to understand, but must be connected with the man who called himself Mider, and, no doubt, given time, she could have concocted a plausible explanation.

But there'd been no time for that.

'I got up this morning and found her in the living room, sitting on the couch. I was amazed. At first, I wasn't even scared, because, well, it was *Polly*. I was just so happy to see her, to find out that the story about her death had been a terrible mistake, it was all so easy and natural to find her in my flat, that I was afraid I was still dreaming.

'But I knew I was awake. It's only in dreams that you think you might be dreaming, isn't it? And then I wondered how she could have got in. Even while I was still relieved to see my friend alive, I glanced at the door, and the chain was on, just like the night Peri disappeared.' Her voice wobbled slightly, and she paused to take a steadying breath.

I reached out to touch her hand, which was lying on the table. It felt very cold as I covered it.

Laura looked startled, and her eyes flashed to mine. I thought I'd overstepped, and started to take my hand away, but hers turned and caught mine and held it tight. The rush of pleasure this simple act gave me took me by surprise. I saw the faintly mocking smile that curved Hugh's mouth and tried to pretend I was alone with Laura.

'All of a sudden, instead of being relieved, I was scared.

"What the hell's going on?" I said. "What are you doing here? How did you get in? *Who are you?*" I was between her and the door. I was trying to look aggressive – well, I might be little, but I'm fit, and I've got both my legs. I was staring at her, demanding to know the truth, and all of a sudden, she just vanished. I mean, one minute I was looking right at her – I really was wide-awake, this was no dream, she was there – and then the next second, she just wasn't.

'I totally freaked. Well, not totally. I nearly went running out barefoot, in my bathrobe, but I managed to keep it together long enough to race back upstairs and throw some clothes on, and make sure I had my phone and keys and everything. I was so afraid she'd *be* there again when I went downstairs that I really thought about calling the police from my bedroom – but then I'd've had to go down-stairs to let them in, and I'd've felt like a complete idiot if there was no one there, and after all, this was *Polly*, not some maniac stranger who'd broken in . . . ' She sucked in a long breath, and squeezed my hand.

Her squeeze felt like a warm shot of whisky. 'Was she there when you went back down?'

Laura shook her head. 'No. But I'm sure I saw her the first time – I'm sure I didn't just imagine it.'

'I'm sure you didn't.'

'She was a ghost,' Laura said. She shook her head. 'I don't understand, how could that be? Was she a ghost the first time, when she stayed with me? Hugh, you met Polly.'

He nodded without comment.

Laura frowned. 'That video. You said you'd followed her from Golden Square until she went into my house. But she didn't appear anywhere on it.' She pulled her hand away from mine to cover her mouth. 'Oh! I touched her. She hugged me. She was real, we went out and around London together – ghosts don't do that; how could she be a ghost?'

'Not a ghost,' I agreed, missing her touch.

'Then what?'

'Someone from the Otherworld, a shape-shifter, someone friendly, I think; someone who wanted to help you and took Polly's form because it would make it easier for you to accept her.'

She stared blankly.

'A one-legged woman. Long blonde hair?'

Hugh and Laura both nodded.

'Did she wear a purple dress by any chance?'

Laura frowned. 'Actually, she was wearing purple this morning. She did like that colour, and she nearly always wore long skirts, because of her leg, I guess.'

'To hide her missing leg,' I said. 'Who does that remind you of?'

I could see that Laura still had no idea where I was going with this, but Hugh did.

'Queeny,' he said.

'Bingo.'

Laura looked from Hugh's cool smile to mine and back again. 'Who's Queeny?'

'One of Peri's Guardians.'

Laura seemed to hold her breath as she looked at me. 'You're not talking about Peri's old toys.'

'I'm afraid I am.'

'Oh boy.' Her shoulders slumped, and she sighed and shook her head. 'Oh boy, oh boy. Ghosts and fairies and talking toys. You really do think my daughter is living in Fairyland.'

'You could think about it as another dimension,' I suggested. 'Another world that has always coexisted with our own. It's not crazy; physicists have been theorising about alternate realities for at least a century, and before that – well, it would explain a lot of things if there really was another realm, another state of existence somewhere. Usually we can't sense it, it's completely cut off from us, but just occasionally the barriers open, and people from one world can slip across into the other.'

'And they can come back again, right?' She fixed her gaze on me. 'You've brought one woman back.'

That caught Hugh's attention. 'You have?'

The waitress arrived with our meals before I could reply. Once we'd all been served and our coffee mugs and water glasses refilled, Hugh said, 'I'd like to hear about that.'

So, with an apologetic shrug to Laura for putting her through it twice, I told him about Amy and how I rescued her. It was easier this time, and I told it more economically while we all ate.

When I got to the end, Laura had a question.

'What happened to Fred?'

'I don't know.'

'You didn't go back to look for her?'

'Of course I did!'

She looked taken aback and I quickly apologised.

'I'm sorry. I thought you were blaming me – and, God knows, I've blamed myself, letting her slip away like that . . . As soon as I'd said good-bye to Amy at the airport, I went straight back to Aberfoyle.'

It was late afternoon when I arrived, and already the long November evening was gaining on the day. But I went up Doon Hill anyway, quite fearless now, and spent a couple of hours searching fruitlessly for any sign of her. Afterwards, without much hope, I went to the caravan where she'd lived during her stay in Aberfoyle. It stood, dark and clearly unoccupied, in the side yard of a little white bungalow on the edge of the village.

I knocked at the front door of the bungalow. After a few seconds it opened and a short, balding, elderly man peered up at me suspiciously.

'I'm looking for someone who was living in your caravan . . .'

He interrupted me with a grunt, turned his head, and shouted back into the house, 'Betty!' before shuffling away.

I waited on the doorstep and soon a thin, nervous-looking, white-haired woman appeared, wiping her hands on a dish towel. 'Can I help you?'

'Well, I hope so.' I smiled, trying to put her at her ease. 'I'm looking for Fred.'

'Fred? There's no one by that name here.'

'Uh, the woman who rented your caravan?'

'Oh! Do you mean Miss Green?'

'Yes,' I said, although Fred had never told me her last name.

'I'm afraid you're too late. She left a few days ago.'

'Did she say where she was going? Leave a forwarding address?'

She shook her head, then cocked it. 'No, but are you Ian Kennedy?'

I almost sighed with relief. 'She left a message for me?'

'A parcel. Quite a big box, actually. It's in the caravan. Shall I take you there?'

'Yes, please.'

I had been inside the caravan with Fred only twice, very briefly. It might have been reasonably comfortable in the summer, but the only heating available was that provided by a small, two-bar electric heater, and even by early October it was scarcely adequate. Now, after two or three days of being left empty and unheated, there was already a smell of mould and decay filling the damp, chilly interior.

'Here. This is what she left you.' A cardboard box salvaged from the local supermarket stood on the table. It was filled with books, Fred's personal library. I glanced around the cramped, bare interior, wondering what had become of her other things, her clothes, any other possessions she might have owned.

'Will you take it now?' She jingled her keys, impatient to get me out.

'Did she leave anything else? A message?'

'Just this. Everything else she took away with her.'

'Um, would you mind if I had a look around?'

The little woman drew herself up, affronted. 'I cleaned and tidied as soon as she'd left. If she forgot anything, I would have found it and put it aside. There wasn't anything else.'

I believed her. Fred had owned little enough, as far as I could tell, and I was willing to bet on her being single-minded enough to have discarded everything she couldn't carry before she went up Doon Hill on Halloween, shedding her old self like a used skin. I was touched that she'd thought enough of me to leave me her books – but maybe it had nothing to do with me. Maybe, like a lot of bookish people, she just couldn't bring herself to throw a book in the garbage.

'Thank you,' I said, backing down before the woman's basilisk glare. 'I appreciate your keeping this for me. I'll take it now.'

When I got a chance to go through the box I found no letters, notebook, or personal scraps that might have told me more about the woman who had owned them. Two of the books had names written on the flyleaf, but as one was a man's and the other included Christmas wishes from 1923, I didn't think they would help me find Fred. Several of the books were from libraries, one from Huddersfield, one from Aberdeenshire. Probably they'd all been acquired secondhand. Although reading them made me feel a little closer to her in spirit, they didn't help me find her.

Nothing did. The name Fred (Winifred? Frederika?) Green was not much to go on, even if – as seemed very unlikely – that was ever her legal name. As far as I could find out – and I spent months trying, learning my trade on this unpaid, personal pursuit – no woman of that name had been reported missing in Scotland, England, or Wales. Maybe her real name was nothing like it, or maybe there was no one who cared sufficiently to notice when she went missing. I was convinced that she'd managed to perform her vanishing act as far as society was concerned long before that Halloween.

I continued to look for her even as I researched the subject of unexplained disappearances, and particularly visits to Fairyland, or the Otherworld in any of its guises. Where was it? *What* was it? How did people get there? When did they come back?

'I went back to Aberfoyle the next Halloween and spent the night on Doon Hill. I felt like I owed Fred that much, just to *be* there for her if she wanted to come back.'

'But she didn't,' said Hugh.

I shook my head. 'I don't know. I never saw her again. Never heard from her. Nothing happened to me that night – except for getting very wet, because of course it rained.'

I stopped. My story was done. I wished I could have

ended on a more upbeat note. Success is supposed to be what matters, but it doesn't live in the memory like failure. It's the unanswered questions that remain.

'Hey,' said Hugh. His voice was gentle, and there was a note in it I hadn't heard before. 'You did your best.'

I shrugged and pushed a bit of toast around my plate. 'Which wasn't good enough.'

'Don't beat yourself up. You saved Amy. You had to let Fred go – that was her choice. You can't save somebody who doesn't want to be saved.'

Caroline

John Roy was a Scottish Highlander, living in Glenbroun, in Badanoch, in the early 1700s. One evening as he went to bring in his cattle from the hillside, he was passed by a large, rapidly moving flight of fairies carrying something in their midst. It was not his nature to meddle with otherworldly creatures; he wanted nothing to do with 'the Good Neighbours', yet he feared they might have abducted a local child and left behind a mere stock in its place. Fortunately, he had learned a few tricks at his granny's knee. He knew, for example, that if a human being should offer to trade with them, the 'people of peace' cannot refuse the exchange.

Quick as thought, he threw his cap into the thick of the swarm, crying out 'Mine be yours and yours be mine!'

Thus compelled, the fairies fled, taking John Roy's cap, and leaving on the ground before him a beautiful lady dressed in fine white linen. She was in a swoon, half-conscious and feverish. He lifted her in his arms and carried her back to his cottage, leaving the cattle to fend for themselves this one night.

John Roy's wife was startled indeed to see what her husband had brought back from the hillside, but she was as goodhearted and generous as he, and immediately set about tending to the poor lady. They soon restored her to health and learned that, whoever she was, she was no Highlander, for she could not speak or understand a single word of Gaelic.

Gradually, over the months, the lady learned some Gaelic, and taught the Roys a bit of her own language, which was English. She told them her name was Caroline, that she had lived in a fine house in England, as a gentleman's wife, and had been carried off while on her sickbed. Never a believer in fairies, she had thought her abduction a feverish dream until the passage of time, and her improved health, had demonstrated otherwise. But surely her husband, seeing her gone, would have searched for her?

But John Roy knew that the fairies would have left a stock in her bed, an image of herself that would have seemed to die, then been buried. Her husband must think her dead.

Caroline sank into a deep depression for a time, scarcely able to bear the thought of life in this remote and savage land so far from everything she had known and loved, never to see her husband or her dear children again. Yet, live she must. Although poor in material goods, the Roys were rich in hospitality, and shared all they had with Caroline, accepting her into their family.

And so the years went by, until, in 1725, King George sent his red-coated soldiers to build roads and 'civilise' the savage Highlanders. Most locals were far from pleased by the sudden influx of foreign soldiers, but John Roy, who had learned English from Caroline, thought he might as well make the best of it and offered lodging to the English captain and his son.

The sound of English voices lifted Caroline's heart, and she stared at the two Englishmen as if she couldn't bear to take her eyes away. The captain was too polite to stare at a strange woman, but the younger man met her eyes, and felt something jolt his heart.

'Sir,' he exclaimed, tugging at his father's arm. 'If I did not know my dear mother was dead these many years, I should say I saw her again now.'

'Do you say so?' said Caroline. 'Why, if miracles could happen, I should say that I saw my little child grown into a man and standing before me.'

At the sound of her voice, the English captain gave a start and looked at her face. He thought he could see the likeness to the young woman he had married – and buried! – so many years ago. He at once demanded of his host how an Englishwoman came to be dwelling in a remote Scottish clachan, and John Roy told his story.

Still scarcely daring to believe it was true, the Englishman questioned the woman, asking for details of the place where she had lived and other things only his wife would have known. She answered him readily, until forced to stop by tears of joy. At last, they fell into each other's arms and wept together. And so, after many years, the stolen lady was finally restored to her husband, who took her back home where she belonged. Never to their dying days did they forget their gratitude to John Roy.

Peri

A week later, the three of us were on our way to Scotland, hoping to rescue Peri at midsummer.

It was still a few days shy of the twenty-first, but that gave us time to investigate all the possible sites and settle on the right one. Was midsummer's eve significant? I didn't know. Some of the old stories were quite specific about dates, but not so the story of Etain, in which the passage of many years had more significance than mere seasons. Peri had been taken in December, and returned, briefly, at the end of May. That might mean something or nothing at all.

When he turned up at the airport Hugh looked haggard, almost shockingly thin, his blue eyes more prominent than ever in his narrow face. Laura had told me that he'd been working all hours to get the editing done on his film before we left. She worried that there was something sinister in this – maybe Hugh was planning to stay if he managed to find his way through to the Otherworld. I didn't think so. Hugh was riding high, on his way to fame and fortune in the career he'd always wanted, and I couldn't see him giving up his human inheritance just to step into the unknown. He believed in the Otherworld because he had the ability to see it, but that didn't make him particularly interested in it.

As I looked at his gaunt countenance I thought of Lancelot du Lac, or a male Joan of Arc, and wondered if, like a Christian knight of old, Hugh had spent the last night in fasting and prayer rather than with one more critical viewing of the film he'd made. The rings in his ear had gone, and there were specks of dried blood on the fleshy lobe. I almost flinched at the thought of his amazonian girlfriend in a jealous fury, ripping them out and cursing his faithless heart. What would she do if Hugh returned to London with Peri in his arms? Would loyalty to the new girlfriend stop him from doing all he could to save the old?

As we sat in silence waiting for our flight to be called, I told my companions a story.

'Robert Kirk tells of a woman he knew personally who was stolen away by fairies. They left an image in her place, and it appeared to wither away and die, and so was buried. But after two years, the woman managed to escape and returned to her husband. Fortunately, he recognised her and believed her story. He was still grieving over her loss, and so he was naturally delighted to welcome her home again, and so it all ended happily.

'But Kirk couldn't help speculating on how things might have gone wrong. What if the husband had remarried? It would have been perfectly legal; his wife was dead as far as he knew, dead in the eyes of the world and the law. But when she turned out *not* to have been dead after all, if he had remarried, would he have been obliged to divorce the second wife? Kirk reckoned that he would, because as the first marriage had never been terminated by death, it was still in force, and the second marriage had no legal status. Of course, in those days, a divorce was a much bigger deal. The scandal of it, especially for the second wife, would have been awful. Probably, she'd be like a fallen woman, and probably, unless she was very rich, no one else would have wanted to marry her. Her life would have been ruined. It's lucky that things are easier now, isn't it?'

Laura looked nervously between me, with my faux-innocent smile, and Hugh's frowning glare.

'Your Reverend Kirk was interested in the legal and theological implications. In his day, they would have been serious. This is totally different.'

'You didn't marry Peri or Fiona. You're all free agents, sure. But somebody's still going to get hurt.'

'Yeah? Well, even if you're right, it's not your concern.'

'Actually, it is. Peri's my concern.'

'You've never even met her. Laura hired you to do a job – that's all.'

'Hey, guys,' said Laura anxiously, but our eyes were locked, horns down, each of us testing the other for weakness, goading.

'Sure, so it's my job to make sure she gets back. I don't

want you deciding it would be too much trouble to bring her back, not wanting to mess up your nice lifestyle with an out-of-date girlfriend . . . '

'You're talking out your arse. I *loved* Peri – I'd do anything for her. I still would.'

'Which means letting her go if that's what she wanted – does it include taking her back to London, marrying her, if she decides she wants that? No matter what it does to Fiona?'

His cheek twitched, it might have been in remembered or anticipated pain.

'What about Fiona?' I persisted. 'Your girlfriend?'

The flight to Glasgow was being called. In quick, nervous response, Laura got to her feet. Hugh and I stayed where we were.

'I care for Fiona,' he said quietly. 'I won't just dump her, no matter what happens.'

No, I thought, you won't have to, because if she's got any pride, she'll dump you first. 'Loved' vs. 'care'. No contest.

'Does she know about Peri?'

'Sure.'

'About what's happening?'

He shrugged uncomfortably. 'Not really. She knows Laura hired you, and that I'm helping . . . but she doesn't understand why I have to help. So she is kind of jealous.'

'With good reason.'

'No!' He frowned. 'I'm not cheating on her. I wouldn't.'

'You want Peri back. Otherwise, why are you here?'

His frown deepened. 'Look, mate. You know why I'm here. I'm here because you can't do this without me.'

Laura, hovering anxiously, now descended, sinking into the seat beside Hugh and resting her hand on his. 'He's here for *me*.'

Around us, people were moving sluggishly in a rough line towards the gate, or waiting with bovine patience to be herded on board. We were the only people in the boarding area still seated.

Beneath the warmth of Laura's approval, Hugh's fierce frown relaxed and he nodded agreement.

'That's bullshit,' I said harshly.

Hugh's eyes flickered, and Laura's mouth dropped open in surprise.

'Forget it,' I told Hugh. 'You're not Laura's proxy, and you're damn sure not mine. There's only one reason for you to go after her, which is that you still love her. If she still loves you, she'll come back. But if you're going to pretend, so you can shrug and whine that you did your best, sorry – no way. I won't have Peri tricked into coming back, and I'm not having you let her down at the last minute. If she needs saving, *I'll* save her. I don't need you.'

Emotions battled in his face while I ranted at him: incredulity, anger, and hope.

'You? You think you could win her? You think she'd even look at you?'

As he spoke I seemed to feel again Amy Schneider in my arms, and an unexpected pang of loss. I'd never loved her, never even known her, really.

Hugh leaned forward until he was right in my face, then he said, practically spitting, 'I'm going to bring her back, not you. And don't think for a minute that I'm doing it for *you*. You keep out of my way.'

He jumped up and, without looking back at either of us, pushed his way forward to the front of the queue. People gave way before him, not even annoyed by his presumption. He had the natural authority, the innate arrogance, of someone who deserved to be first.

I realised that the loss I felt was not for Amy, but for a younger, bolder self, someone not yet worn down by failure.

'What'd you go and do that for? What if he *had* gone home? We *do* need him.' Laura was staring at me, obviously annoyed.

'It's no good unless he loves her. And he had to know that. If we just needed somebody to bargain with Mider – hell, I could do that. But if Peri comes back with Hugh, it'll be for love.'

'How can you be so sure of that?'

I thought of all the stories in which visitors to Fairyland, dragged back into reality by well-meaning, interfering friends, had simply pined away and died, like the maidens abandoned by the ganconer. People needed something more than everyday life to live for, they needed some sort of magic to give it meaning, and love fitted the bill. But looking at Laura's tight, anxious face, I thought she might not understand. Hadn't her own life been dedicated to shutting out all possibility of magic, the supernatural and, probably, romantic love as well?

I shrugged and got to my feet. 'This is a fairy tale, isn't it? Come on, we should be boarding.' I tried to give her my arm, but she wouldn't touch me.

In Glasgow, a rental car had been reserved in Hugh's name – he was paying for it. He and Laura both took it for granted that he would drive, and I should have had no quarrel with that: years of living as a pedestrian meant I was out of practice, and the traffic on the roads around the airport was even worse than I remembered. But when I crawled into the tiny back seat to sit alone, the feeling of being not merely unnecessary but actively unwanted intensified. Laura had been cool to me throughout the flight, and Hugh was ignoring me.

The noise of the car made it difficult to follow any conversation in the front seat, and it became impossible once Hugh turned on the radio. Leaning forward all the time was uncomfortable, and as most of my contributions received no response, I gave it up to sink back in my seat and into my own thoughts.

We quickly bypassed Glasgow and left its suburbs for open country. As we travelled steadily west, my heart lifted at the sight of the green hills on the horizon. What is it about *scenery*? It sounds such a negligible thing, mere distant background, and in fact I, like most people, spend most of my life in rooms, or on streets lined with parked cars and buildings, scarcely ever lifting my eyes to anything more than a few feet above my own head. I'd never claim that I needed nature, or wilderness, or wide-open spaces in my life; certainly, in all the time I was in the city, I never felt 'scenery' was something I lacked.

But at the first glimpse of wide green pastures dotted with grazing sheep, of sloping, dark green conifer forest behind an open stretch of water gleaming in the murky daylight, I felt something inside me relax and expand, and I wondered, with faint surprise, how I had managed to survive without it for so long.

When we reached the shores of Loch Lomond, Laura sighed, 'Oh, God, it's so beautiful.'

Even on a dull day, beneath a low, grey sky, the water of the loch gleamed like a silver mirror, reflecting back the steep hillsides. In the narrowing distance down the water, mountains stretched away, the peaks rising until they disappeared into low cloud.

'Like the cover of some bloody fantasy novel,' said Hugh.

It was true, we were entering another world. Rocky slopes rose up on one side of the road, and the gleaming water of the loch stretched away on the other. The radio signal was by then very weak, the sound annoyingly patchy and scratchy. Finally, Hugh switched it off and the eerie silence of the mountains settled upon us.

As the road rose, twisted and turned, taking us farther into a haunted, unpeopled, mountainous region, my brain buzzed. This landscape affected me more powerfully than any art or music I'd ever encountered. It was real, it was natural, yet, like art, it worked on my emotions and my imagination as if it meant something more than itself.

We passed a ruined house – only the chimneystack and a few low, stone walls remained standing – and the sight of that ruin, lonely in a little glen, shadowed by the dark hills, stirred feelings of loneliness and loss. I thought vaguely of the Highland Clearances – the long, sad history of people forced out of their houses and off their land, dispossessed. My own great-great-grandparents might have been among them.

I gazed out of the window at a shadowy woodland, full of hiding places; at rocks and trees and ancient stone walls; at a stream that became a waterfall and fell, like a long, silver chain, down the flank of a dark green hill, and I thought of Fred. Where had she gone? Did she find what she wanted? Was she happy? Would I ever understand?

We'd been travelling for almost two hours when Hugh and Laura decided to stop in the village of Lochgilphead. They wanted a meal, but I was feeling somewhat carsick after so much rolling around – Hugh was not a gentle or a timid driver – and, besides, I'd eaten the snack lunch served on the flight, so we went our separate ways, agreeing to meet back at the car park in an hour.

I felt better as soon as I stretched my legs and walked around in the open air. Lochgilphead was attractively set at the head of a loch, bordered by a long, narrow green common where people walked dogs and children played on swings and slides. The village itself looked rather drab and far from ancient, but it seemed quite a bit bigger than Aberfoyle and was alive with people and activity on a warm, dry afternoon.

Across from the parking lot I noticed a bookshop, sandwiched between a wineshop and a store selling large electrical appliances. I went in and made for the 'local interest' section, where I found just what I'd been hoping for, a locally published guide to walks in Knapdale, including the history and folklore of the area. After I'd paid for it, I took it down to the waterfront and found a seat by the grey stone war memorial. At first it was just a rehash of things I already knew, information I'd picked up from the books and maps in my own library. The sites I'd noted from the Ordnance Survey maps were described: Dunvulaig, with its connections to the mythical *Sidhe*, and the Iron Age *Dun a'Chaisteal* associated with the tale of Deirdre of the Sorrows. And then I found something new:

The material for many of the beautifully carved stones and crosses of Argyll was taken from the ancient medieval quarries of Doide, on the shores of Loch Sween, the site of which lies just north of Doide Bay. Here the seaward cliffs have been riven and split by centuries of natural erosion into a fantastical array of massive rock-slices, pinnacles and overhangs.

One of the strangest natural formations to be seen in this wonderfully fine-grained rock is the Cachaileith na Sith, *or Fairy Door, a small square recess furnished with incredibly realistic side jambs and lintel, situated in a promi-*

nent outcrop of rock by the east side of the road above Doide Bay. This most unusual physical feature (not marked on the map) has for long enjoyed the uncanny reputation of being an entrance into the 'other world' of the Daoine Sidhe, the sweet wild sound of fairy music having been heard issuing from it on various occasions by folk still living in the locality.

I felt a distinct shock of excitement when I read that, but whether that was intuition, or the more academic pleasure that comes with any discovery, I didn't know. I was wary of trusting my own intuition, anyway, always preferring to act on reason, so I was eager to hear what Hugh and Laura thought, and shared my find with them as soon as we met back at the car.

Laura frowned. 'A rock formation that looks like a door? So?'

'Whether it's a rock or an ancient burial mound isn't the point,' I said. 'It's the fact that there are stories told about it; tradition connects it with the Otherworld, that's the point.' I looked to Hugh for support, but he hadn't forgiven me for what I'd said at the airport.

'Where is it?' he asked coldly, giving no hint of his feelings.

'On the road to Loch Sween, before we get to the caravan site.'

'Fine. We can check it out on the way. Let's go.'

'Hang on,' said Laura. 'There's not much else between here and the caravan site. I saw a couple of hotels in this village – why don't we book rooms for the night as long as we're here?'

'Sounds like a good idea,' I said.

Hugh included us both in his stony look. 'Not for me. You can do as you like, but I'm not stopping.' He unlocked the car.

'I'm not talking about stopping,' Laura said. 'But we're going to need somewhere to stay tonight, and we'll have more choice if we don't leave it till the last minute.'

'I'm not on holiday. I didn't come here to sleep in a hotel while Peri's lost.'

'Look, we've got plenty of time,' I said, deliberately calm. 'Midsummer's eve isn't—'

'What is it with you and midsummer's eve? There's nothing about a specific date in the story of Etain; it was just a matter of her husband finding Mider and forcing him to deal. It didn't even happen at *night*.' He wrenched the door open as he spoke and got in.

I quickly followed suit, guessing that it wouldn't take much for Hugh to drive off and leave me.

'Laura?' Hugh leaned across and opened the passenger door for her.

'She's my daughter,' she said quietly, not moving. 'This isn't a holiday for me, either.'

He bowed his head. 'I know. I'm sorry.'

She got in the car. 'OK. I couldn't find her my way, so now it's up to you. Just tell me when there's something you want me to do.' She spoke looking out of the window rather than at either one of us, and I guessed she meant to include us both.

We drove out of Lochgilphead on the road that ran beside the Crinan Canal, going north for a little while before jogging off to the west. This part of Scotland had once been the heart of the ancient kingdom of Dalriada, settled by the Irish, who had brought their culture, their gods and their tales of the Otherworld with them.

Soon we turned off the main road – which was narrow enough – onto a rough, single-track road that would take us the length of one of the many long, thin peninsulas that made up this part of the west coast. I noticed – and saw Laura's eyes register, too – a place offering 'Farmhouse B&B' with a lower sign, swinging a little in the breeze off the sea, promising VACANCIES. Neither of us said anything. The plan we'd agreed on was to drive to the caravan site, looking out for the Fairy Door along the way, then park the car and go on foot to Dunvulaig, where we would camp all night if necessary.

After that farmhouse there was nothing, just empty hilly heathland to the left and the arm of the blue-grey sea that had been designated Loch Sween to the right. I had the map open on my lap; but as natural formations, even when given their own name and story, weren't marked on it, I didn't refer to it as I gazed out at the passing countryside.

Hugh gave a sudden cry, swerved the car, and stopped on the road.

'What's wrong?' Laura and I spoke together.

He twisted around in his seat to look at me, his eyes blazing. 'Why didn't you warn me? Didn't you even *see* it? Some guide you are!'

'See what?'

'What?' Laura echoed.

Hugh put the car in reverse and whipped it backwards into a passing place. 'Are you blind?'

Maybe I was. I could see nothing special in the rough, rocky heath that rose up beside the narrow road.

'That's it – look, a door in the hill. Could it be more obvious?' He switched off the engine and, without waiting for further response, got out and walked a few yards down the empty road, then stopped.

I scrambled out after him, wondering if this was another evidence of his Second Sight. But when I reached him, I saw it, too: a huge, stone doorway set into the hillside. I couldn't imagine how I'd missed it until, as I shifted around trying to get a better look, I realised how the undergrowth and the rocks on the hillside combined to camouflage it. You had to approach from just the right angle to see the door in the hill, but when you did, the impression was incredibly powerful. As I stared up at it, even knowing it was an illusion, the hairs rose on the back of my neck.

It would have made a suitable entrance to a castle, or some great hall, yet there was no building attached; the doorway went into the hill. Clearly, it had been created long ago, and was no longer in regular use, because the flat surface of the pale grey stone that framed it was pocked and pitted, heavily patched with reddish brown and flaky grey lichens, overhung with weeds, sprouting dandelions, and long, tough grasses. Inside the rectangular recess created by lintel and jambs there was no door, but only more of the rocky hillside. Grass grew there along with green mosses and a few spiky bits of heather clinging grimly to the rocky soil.

'The Fairy Door,' I said as Laura came up between us. 'Amazing. A natural rock formation, according to the guidebook, but it really looks like a door.'

'It *is* a door,' said Hugh. 'That's the door Peri went through.'

'How could she?' Laura objected. 'Are you saying it leads into a cave or something?'

'I'm going to check it out.' Hugh left the road to climb up the rocky slope. I started after him, then paused and turned to offer Laura a hand up.

She pulled away, her mouth a tight, angry line. Although her mind had been opened to other possibilities, I had the feeling it was open only a crack and could slam shut again at any minute.

Up ahead, Hugh gave a shout, and bent, then straightened. He was holding something tiny that flashed silver between his fingers. 'Look at this!'

Had Peri worn a ring? I hurried to join him. It was just a coin, an ordinary, modern twenty-pence piece. His excitement baffled me. 'So?'

'Peri had twenty pence to make a phone call.'

'That was two years ago! Anyone could have dropped it.'

'It was Peri.' He sounded certain. He gazed up at the

door-like formation. 'What can we do to make it open for us?'

I knew some of the traditions: threaten to burn the thorns on a fairy hill, or dig into it until the owner comes out to speak with you. I didn't think either of those would work there. I couldn't see any hawthorns, or even brambles, and, anyway, this wasn't an ancient grave-mound. Doors, unlike graves, being meant to open, must require a different approach. A key? A magical password? It could be anything, and I hadn't a clue. I shrugged helplessly. 'Maybe, if you knock ... or call for Mider ... ?'

'What's going on?' Laura had joined us.

I tried to read her expression and failed. 'Hugh thinks the door must open sometime. That it did for Peri and might for him, too.'

She didn't say anything, but suddenly she rushed forward and began to clamber up to the looming rock formation. As I watched, she squeezed herself inside as best she could, flattening herself against the rocky, grassy earth and feeling about it with her hands, probing for any hidden nooks or openings. Finally, she inched back out again and stepped down carefully, slipping once or twice on loose rock, but eventually rejoining us. She was slightly breathless, her face was flushed, her hair tousled, and she'd managed to scratch her hand: I saw the tiny drops of blood beading up against her skin as she put it to her mouth.

'That's not a door,' she said.

'It is sometimes,' said Hugh.

Laura looked at me to judge. I thought of the old riddle – when is a door not a door? When it's ajar. But that was wordplay; this was a deeper riddle. I sighed. 'I think we have to go with Hugh's perceptions.'

Laura nodded, her mouth turning down.

'But you don't have to stay.'

'Of course I do! I'm Peri's mother. There might be something ... she might need me ...' She waved her hand uncertainly. 'Maybe this is craziness, maybe not. Anyway, I'm staying for as long as it takes.'

I had brought a waterproof groundsheet to sit on, but otherwise we were not well prepared for spending a night in the open. Leaving Hugh to keep his solitary watch in broad daylight, Laura and I drove back to Lochgilphead for supplies: drinks and snacks to keep us going through the night, a bottle of insect repellent, and some yellow candles that were supposed to ward off midges.

Midges: tiny, bloodsucking furies impossible to avoid. Individually they are so tiny as to be practically invisible, but they gather in clouds wherever there's a warm-blooded, breathing creature, and their bites swell and itch every bit as much as those of the bigger mosquito. Laura, Hugh and I reeked of insecticide, which we slathered on liberally, but if the strong smell discouraged a thousand midges, there were thousands more who weren't so fussy. Even when they weren't biting, the midges were a horrible pest: crawling on your face, in your mouth, ears, hair, everywhere. They arrived around five o'clock, and were our constant attendants on the hillside except when there was a breeze strong enough to blow them away. The evening was cloudy, still, and warm. There was no sense of immediately impending rain, but the sky was like moist cotton wool hanging low overhead.

Only after the sun finally went down, very late, did the wind pick up, blowing in freshening, salt-flavoured gusts off the loch, finally dispersing most of the midges as darkness wrapped itself around us.

Although not far from the road, we weren't disturbed by traffic. Occasional cars went past during the day, but between nine and midnight there were, I think, only two cars, and after that the road remained empty.

As it grew a little cooler in the still, oddly light dark, Laura wrapped herself in her dark brown pashmina and we huddled closer together, talking quietly, while Hugh stalked the hillside like a restless spirit. Occasionally he planted himself directly in front of the door and shouted, but something about the acoustics caused his voice to be swallowed by the rocks: I couldn't make out his words.

I tried to keep track of Hugh, but occasionally I lost him among the rocks and heather. I'd brought along three small but powerful torches, but he did not use his, preferring to let his eyes adjust to the gradual darkness. It was a cloudy night, but behind the cloud cover was a full moon, so the darkness was never absolute.

I'd felt during the day that Laura was withdrawing from me, from both of us and our fantastical ideas about her missing daughter, but there was nothing else to do to pass the time as we waited but talk, and, inevitably, perhaps, as we talked we were drawn closer. As the night drew on I felt her relaxing a little more. Although we didn't touch, we were sitting very close on the groundsheet, and I could feel her body heat.

From talk about travel and restaurants and movies and books and politics and culture we soon moved on to more personal details. It was easier to talk intimately in the dark, and somehow especially in the open air. It felt as if we were floating in space, detached from the rest of the world and from our ordinary lives: it became possible to say almost anything to each other.

As she told me about her life both before and after Peri's disappearance I got the sense of someone fragile and lonely, someone who had made herself strong and self-sufficient not because it came naturally, but because it was necessary. Peri had needed her, and she'd been determined to live up to that need. Afraid of failure, she had not allowed herself any weaknesses or dependencies; she'd never let herself entirely trust anyone.

'So, no boyfriends?'

'I've dated from time to time. But Peri always came first, and by the time she was grown-up, I guess I was too much out of practice. There's never been anyone serious ... I haven't been in love since before she was born.' The anti-midge candles had all been blown out by the wind, and by now I could barely see her, but I felt it when she turned towards me. 'You don't have any children.'

'Not that I know of, anyway.'

She gave a soft snort. 'Men!'

'Women,' I countered. 'You never have to wonder if a baby's yours. A man has to take a woman's word for it.'

'Not now. Now all you need is a few skin cells to find out for sure. I couldn't believe it when those billboards started going up all over in English and Spanish. Who'd have thought there were so many men worried about paternity?'

'Billboards?'

'You must have seen them, they're everywhere. Not *here* – in the States. Well, certainly in Texas.'

'I haven't been back in ten years.'

She gasped. 'Why?'

'No reason.'

'Don't you have family?'

'My mom's come over here a few times; she loves it. I keep in touch with my sister by e-mail.'

'Why'd you come in the first place?'

'I told you about Amy.'

'Yes, but if she was your first case ... How could you just up and go? What made you decide to do it? Didn't you have a job? A girlfriend?'

'I did have a girlfriend.' I hesitated. 'It's a long story.'

She laughed softly. 'A long story would be perfect right now.'

So I told her about Jenny, how I'd felt, how she'd changed me, changed my life; how special our relationship had been, until it became just ordinary, but how I'd gone on loving her anyway. It was easy to be honest, to open my heart like that in the dark; it was intimate and safe.

'And then one day she left me – she just moved out without a word of explanation. I couldn't see the point of staying on in Dallas without her – I'd been wanting to leave for ages anyway, and I was fed up with my job, so when my grandmother died, and I found out she'd left me a lot of money—'

'Wait, hang on. What do you mean? Jenny left you? You just let her go?'

'She didn't give me a choice.' I felt the old bitterness, which should have been long dead and buried, surge up like sickness.

'But how did she leave you? What went wrong?'

'You really want the whole story?'

'Of course.'

Jenny

I had no idea anything was wrong on the day Jenny left me.

She wasn't in when I got home from work, so I checked the calendar that hung on the wall above the phone. There, written in her rounded hand, was 'Weaving Circle', so I knew not to wait for her for dinner. I shuttled something from the freezer to the microwave and ate it, with a beer, in front of the television. A little later, *Rear Window* was on one of the cable channels, and I watched that with my ear half-cocked for the sound of her key in the lock.

At eleven o'clock, when she still wasn't home, I started to worry.

By midnight I was nearly frantic, imagining her unconscious, trapped in the wreckage of her car in a pile-up on one of the highways, imagining her dead. For the first time in my life, I phoned city hospitals, asking if anyone of Jenny's name or description had been brought in.

Jenny regularly met up with other weavers, women she had met through craft fairs and classes; but that was a part of her life that didn't involve me, and I knew little about it. I had no idea where the 'weaving circle' took place. I had met a few of the women, but most of them weren't even names to me.

The one I did remember was Pamela Schule, with a husband known as Deet. We'd been to dinner at their house in Carrollton, and they'd come to us in return; one of Jenny's attempts to broaden our social horizons. It hadn't taken, but I found D. T. Schule listed in the phone book, rang the number, and woke ol' Deet out of a sound sleep at a quarter past twelve. He passed me to his wife, who sounded sleepy and bewildered. No, there hadn't been a weaving circle Wednesday night. They only met once a month, and the last time was just two weeks ago. Yes, she'd seen Jenny then; she hadn't said anything about plans for tonight. Or – she corrected herself deliberately – she should say *last* night.

I kept her awake a little longer to get the names and phone numbers of the other weavers out of her, even though this was starting to feel like a false lead, one deliberately planted by Jenny.

What was going on? Was she having an affair? Had she fallen asleep in another man's bed?

Jenny kept a journal, a habit she'd maintained since high school. It was personal, which I'd always respected. But I felt no scruples. If she was betraying me, I had a right to know. I stalked into the bedroom, straight to her bedside table, and pulled open the drawer where she kept the journal.

It was gone. In fact, except for a clip-on book light and a box of cherry-flavoured cough drops, the drawer was empty. She had taken not only her journal, but her jewellery, the soft blue rabbit she'd had since infancy, silver-framed pictures of her parents and sister, her auto-graphed copy of *A Wrinkle in Time*, photograph albums, a wooden bowl, a silken patchwork cushion ... her under-wear drawer was practically empty. I opened the closet and saw the big gaps among her remaining clothes.

I rushed into the spare bedroom, Jenny's weaving room. The big wooden loom still stood there among the baskets of yarns and strips of cloth, but the rug she'd been working on was gone.

She'd left me.

I was stunned. I could hardly believe it, in spite of the evidence staring me in the face. It wasn't like Jenny to slip away quietly. She'd always been a fighter. And straight-forward: if there was something she didn't like, she'd tell me. 'Shape up, Buster, or I walk!' She hadn't given me a chance. And no explanation, not even a 'Dear John' letter stuck to the avocado-green surface of the refrigerator with a pineapple-shaped magnet. That would have been bad enough. This sudden vanishing was impossible to accept.

I called in sick the next morning and drove to the place Jenny worked instead.

She wasn't there. They told me she had resigned more than a week earlier; she hadn't even come in yesterday; Tuesday had been her last day at work. She'd *planned* this. And, unlike my father, who had left everything – except money – behind, Jenny had carefully packed her most precious belongings. I wondered how many trips she'd made between apartment and car, while I, in blissful ignorance, was out at work.

The honest, loving Jenny I'd known was beginning to seem like a fantasy. What happened to make her change?

None of our friends knew anything about it. They all seemed as shocked and mystified as I was. Of course, these were *our* friends, mostly couples, and she might have known she couldn't expect them to keep her secret from me. Apart from the weavers, Jenny had one close woman friend, Deborah. I had nothing against her, but I'd always felt she didn't like me, and I found out I was right when I called her.

'Yes, I know where she is, and no, I'm not going to tell you. It was her decision to leave, and I respect that decision.'

'Deborah, all I want to do is talk to her. I think I deserve an explanation. I'm worried.'

'Tough.'

She hung up on me. I didn't bother to phone back.

There was only one other person I could think of who would know where Jenny had gone: her sister Maddy. Jenny had always been close to her sister. I couldn't imagine her not telling Maddy where she was going; in fact, it seemed most likely that when Jenny needed somewhere to run, that's where she would go.

I didn't call first; I wasn't going to risk alerting Jenny that I was on her trail. As soon as I'd managed to square things at work, which took a few more days, I left Dallas late one evening to make the drive to San Antonio.

It was a long way to go, but I liked long-distance driving, especially at night. Traffic was light, and I enjoyed the silence, speed, and freedom of being on the move, steadily covering the vast distances of Texas. I liked the anonymity of being alone in my car. I could go anywhere. No one was expecting me; no one in the world knew where I was. I'd shucked all my usual responsibilities with the simple, ordinary action of climbing in behind the wheel. There was no reason why I ever had to stop. I could just keep driving, let the road take me to new places and a new life.

I stopped in Waco to fill up with fuel and coffee, but by the time I got to Austin I was flagging. It was almost two o'clock in the morning, and I hadn't slept well since Jenny had left. More caffeine wasn't the answer; I needed to rest. I took the next farm road exit off the interstate, then pulled off that road as soon as I found a place to park. I reclined the seat and crashed out.

Sun on my face, gathering heat, and birdsong all woke me. I drove on to San Marcos, where I got breakfast and cleaned myself up in the restroom before the last leg of the journey.

I'd been to Maddy's house once before, with Jenny. It had been built in the early 1980s, in a suburb on the outer western rim of the city, convenient to the Air Force base where Maddy's husband worked.

I drove slowly through the quiet streets lined with practically identical houses and was reminded of the neighbourhood in Minneapolis where I'd found my father. Acid churned in my stomach. I couldn't live in a place like this; it would kill me.

On the way out of Dallas I'd talked myself into believing I'd get Jenny back. I loved her, and she loved me; that was all that really mattered. We could change the things that didn't work. The heady exhilaration of driving away from the city had convinced me. Maybe when I picked up Jenny we'd keep going on to Mexico. To hell with everything else. I had my credit card. Why shouldn't we live on the beach for a while, swim, make love, go fishing, improve our conversational Spanish, drink too much, and learn to scuba dive?

But now, peering at the house numbers, trying to remember if there was anything to mark out Maddy's from all the rest, I thought of Jenny's wish for a house, her desire to settle down. What if *this* was what she wanted, what her sister had, this middle-class suburban life-in-death, with a couple of kids and life on the treadmill of getting and spending until death?

I didn't want to live like that – I wouldn't – and she knew it. Maybe that was why she'd run away.

Then I saw the birdhouse like a little castle, perched high on a pole in the front yard. She'd given one just like it to Jenny one Christmas, even though we had no yard to put it in.

Maddy was only four years older than Jenny, but it might have been ten from the way she'd let herself go since having kids. She wore loose, unflattering clothes in a vain attempt to disguise her extra weight, and she'd stopped bothering with makeup. Her short hair was speckled with grey, and there was a deep line between her heavy eyebrows.

Those eyebrows drew together at the sight of me on her porch; she looked almost pained. 'Ian?' She sounded uncertain.

'Hi, Maddy. I'm looking for Jenny.' I looked down at the tiny, dark-haired child who clutched her leg and peered up at me, and guessed this must be Adam, who had been a tiny baby the last time I'd seen him. I waggled my fingers at him. 'Hi, guy.'

'She's not here.'

'May I come in?'

She sighed. 'Adam, please, Mommy needs to move.' The little boy clutched her harder, then abruptly let go and ran away into the house. 'She isn't here,' she said again, but stepped back and allowed me to enter.

'May I use your bathroom?'

She gestured. 'End of the hall.'

The bathtub was littered with bright plastic toys, and most of the counter beside the sink was taken up with a changing mat, baby wipes, Vaseline, and other infant paraphernalia. There were some grown-up things in the cupboard, but I didn't spot Jenny's toiletries bag or makeup kit anywhere. After I'd used the toilet I peeked into the other rooms: one was a nursery, another a small child's bedroom, the third was the master bedroom. They didn't seem to be entertaining any overnight guests at the moment.

Maddy was in the big, family-room-style kitchen, in a rocking chair with a baby in her arms. The sound of its suckling seemed very loud in the quiet room, and I looked away, embarrassed.

'Make yourself some coffee if you like,' she said. 'The machine's right next to the microwave. Coffee's in the blue canister; filters in the drawer underneath.'

'Thanks.' I didn't need any more coffee, with my stomach as acid as it was, but I was glad to have an excuse to do something besides look at her. Adam had disappeared, and I couldn't think of the baby's name. The silence in the room grew heavier.

'Do you know where Jenny is?'

She didn't say anything. I looked at her and saw she had bent to nuzzle the baby's downy head.

'Come on,' I said. 'I'm really worried about her. She took off without a word to anyone, no explanation, no forwarding address. I have to find her.'

'I'm sure she'll get in touch with you when she's ready.'

I frowned. ' "Ready"? What did she tell you?'

'Nothing.'

'Nothing? Really? She didn't say why she was leaving me like that?'

'No.' She stared at me.

'And you didn't ask?'

'She said she didn't want to talk about it.'

'Didn't that seem strange to you? Aren't you worried?'

'Jenny doesn't have to justify what she does to me.'

'Or me?' I held her gaze. She looked uncomfortable, but lifted her chin defiantly.

'You're not her husband.'

'Not *legally*. But, come on. I sure wouldn't have left her like that.'

The eyebrows drew together. She tried to hide her face by bending over her baby again. 'I can't get involved in this. It's between you and Jenny.'

'It ought to be. But you know where she is. I don't.'

'She's my sister. If she doesn't want you to know, I have to respect her choice.'

The coffee was starting to perk, but I walked away from it, towards Maddy. 'I think she *does* want me to know. I think she wants me to find her. I think that's what this is all about. Did you know, when I was a kid, my father left us? I spent years looking for him, and I finally found him. It's a big thing in my life. Jenny knows that. If she really wanted to leave, if she thought it was over, she'd have told me to my face. She would *not* have done it this way.'

There was the faint sound of bare feet slapping against the floor. Adam streaked into the room, took one wide-eyed look at me, and streaked out again.

'Come on, Maddy, give me a break, please. If Jenny wants me out of her life, all she has to do is say so. She doesn't have to hide from me like this. I'm not a psycho. I've never hit a woman in my life. She's not hiding 'cause she's scared – this is a game, a test, or something. She

LISA TUTTLE

wants me to prove I really love her by finding her. I'm sure of that. Did she tell you not to tell me where she was?'

'She didn't have to.' Maddy was looking thoughtful, and I knew my argument had got to her. 'But if I tell you where she is, doesn't that spoil the test? I mean, isn't it kind of like cheating?'

I gave her a wide-eyed stare. 'You might give me a clue, at least point me in the right direction. I'm assuming Jenny hasn't left Texas, but it's still a big ol' state. I could spend years looking for her – but that would kind of ruin the point, too, wouldn't it?'

'I'm not going to give you her phone number,' Maddy decided. 'And I don't have her street address. She's got a PO box in Austin. You can write to her.'

My heart soared. I remembered Jenny saying, 'Dell's hiring.'

'I hope I'm not going to regret this,' Maddy said with a doubtful look.

'You won't, unless you hate me. Because I want the best for her, and I'm going to get her back. I'm going to be a part of her life forever.'

When she smiled, Maddy looked younger, prettier, more like her little sister. 'Invite me to your wedding?'

I gave her a warm smile back. The irritation caused by her assumption that Jenny was just like her was such a small, swift wave, I could pretend I didn't feel it. 'You bet.'

I headed for the door.

'Are you going already? You didn't even drink your coffee.'

361

'I've got a long drive ahead of me,' I said. 'I'll come back with Jenny, next time.'

It took about an hour and a half to drive to Austin. The zip code identified the post office, which was in a neighbourhood near the university, an area of mature trees and old houses, some of them recently expensively remodelled by upwardly mobile yuppie owners, others shabby and run-down, overflowing with impoverished students.

I arrived at midday and parked in the small lot and settled down to watch the customers come and go. All I had to do was wait, and she would come. But all too soon, my bladder forced me to go in search of a toilet. Before returning I paid a visit to a convenience store and bought a selection of snacks and drinks, including an extra-large iced tea in a lidded cup. When I finished the drink, I'd use the cup to relieve myself; that way, I wouldn't risk missing Jenny.

It was hot, and I was soon very uncomfortable, sweating like a pig and bored out of my mind. There was nothing to do but eat and drink, and that would only hasten the dread moment when I had to use the empty cup. I didn't mind peeing into a cup; it was more the idea of sharing the car with my own urine that discouraged me. I put the radio on for a little while, but I didn't want to run down the car's battery. Although I had a couple of books in my bag, if I read, I couldn't keep watch. All I could do was think – daydream, really – and of course all my thoughts were about Jenny. I tried to plan what I was going to say to her. I wanted to fantasise about the wonderful future we were going to have together, starting by driving down to Mexico, but I was too hung up on the mystery of her disappearance. Until I knew why she'd left me, I couldn't know what would make her return.

And the longer I thought about it, sweating away in the car beneath the blazing Texas sun, the more I realised how little I knew, not only about Jenny, but about myself.

What did *I* want? I thought I was ready to change my life, but how? Did I really want Jenny at any cost? What price was she asking?

A brilliant gleam, sunlight on glass, seared my eyes. Squinting against the painful light, I peered around, and there it was, the one other car I knew as well as my own. My chest got tight. Oh, Jenny. I could just make out her shadowed profile through the tinted glass, the big sunglasses covering almost half her face. I watched as she pulled into an empty space near the door, almost the full length of the parking lot away from me, and I opened the door and got out.

My legs felt numb from the knees down, so I stood where I was, half-leaning on the open door, and stared across the parking lot as Jenny got out, paused to lock her door, then marched up the short ramp to the heavy glass doors.

An odd little phrase went through my head. It seemed like a quotation, but I couldn't place it: *That is Jenny, but she is not herself.*

Her black hair was scraped back into a ponytail, but a

few tendrils had been allowed to escape to float artfully about her face. Not her everyday hairstyle, but one I'd seen before. I also recognised the sunglasses, the red sandals, the silver bangles on her wrist, and the dark pink Mexican dress. It was one of those long smocks with embroidery across the yoke and around the hem, and I had seen it on her often enough, but today it seemed to fit her differently. As she turned away from the car the dress clung briefly to her body, and I saw that her figure had changed. Her breasts were fuller, and her belly noticeably higher and rounder.

My heart seemed to plunge down a deep shaft towards the centre of the earth, leaving my chest empty. I fell back in the car and sat there, panting and staring at nothing like the slack-jawed idiot I was.

Once upon a time, Jenny and I made love every day of the month. We couldn't share a bed without having sex. I'd always known exactly where she was in her cycle, as aware of everything about her physical being as if she'd been an extension of me. Gradually that changed. We made love now mostly on the weekends, if at all. I had no difficulty in remembering the last time we'd made love, because it had been immediately following the big argument that started at the model home in Apache Springs, but I had no idea when she'd had her last period.

How long had she been pregnant?

Why hadn't I noticed before?

I tried to remember what clothes she'd worn recently, or the last time I'd seen her naked, even the last time I'd really *looked* at her, drinking in the familiar sight of her as if she was as necessary and desired as cool water on a hot day. Instead, I recalled how busy we'd been at work in the last few weeks, working overtime. I remembered mornings when we'd been more like roommates than lovers, scarcely speaking before rushing off to work in our separate cars, and those Saturday nights when I sat up nursing a beer and watching old movies on cable, long after she'd gone to bed without me.

Why hadn't she *made* me look? Why hadn't she told me?

I was still sitting, half-slumped over the steering wheel, in a state of shock, when she came out of the post office. As she got into her car I snapped to, straightened up, and started the engine. What I had seen changed everything, and I had no idea what I was going to say, but I couldn't let her get away.

I let another car get between us before I followed her down the road, because I didn't want Jenny to see me before I was ready.

Shock was turning to anger.

How could she do it? Even if (best-case scenario) it had been an accident, and she'd only recently realised she was pregnant, why hadn't she told me instead of running away?

I followed her onto Forty-fifth Street, but let her go when she turned again onto a quiet cross street. I drove down to the next possible turning, meaning to circle the block, only to discover that the next street was a dead end. I took my time about going back.

There was her car, parked on a gravel driveway beside a white clapboard single-storey house. It hadn't been yuppified, but was obviously old and still comfortably shabby. The gutters needed work, and the screen door had a rip in it. There were a couple of pecan trees in the front yard, and the short grass was withered and yellowing in the summer heat.

I parked across the street and one house over and sat and looked at the house where Jenny had gone to ground. I wondered if she had rented it, or was staying with friends I didn't know. As I watched, a squirrel raced across the shadowed grass and straight up the trunk of one of the pecans. I saw it crouch on a branch, quivering, and I felt as twitchy as the little animal.

I didn't want to walk up the gravel path to knock on the door. I didn't want to hear what she didn't want to tell me, what she had run away rather than confess. But I knew I had to do it. I had come so far to learn the truth, how could I drive away without it now?

I don't know how long I sat there, hardly moving, not thinking, doing little more than breathe. Time passed, unmarked by me, and eventually another car – new and foreign – turned onto the quiet street, drove up to the house, pulled in, and parked.

A tall, fair-haired man wearing a short-sleeved shirt with a tie hopped out. He leaned back into the body of the car and emerged with a pizza and a bottle of wine. He took these goods with him up to the house, whistling as he went. He didn't knock. He opened the door and went in.

I didn't stick around after that.

Once back in Dallas, I packed up all Jenny's things and called her friend Deborah to take them away.

I never heard from her again.

Peri

'And that's it?'

'Yeah.'

'You never found out why she left you?'

I snorted. 'I could guess.'

'I can't believe you didn't talk to her – confront her, demand to know the truth. How could you just leave her like that?'

'Hey, wait a minute – she left me.'

'To make you pay attention. She wanted you to prove you loved her by tracking her down, isn't that what you thought?'

'It's what I wanted to think.'

'What if that was *your* baby?'

'She should have told me.'

'Should, but maybe she thought she didn't have to. Maybe she thought you knew, and you weren't happy. You didn't want to be a father, you didn't want to be tied down with responsibilities. Maybe, when you didn't come after her, she thought you'd made your feelings plain, and she was too proud to beg, ever think of that?'

Of course I'd thought of it. There were times I'd even come close to believing it and hating myself for what I'd done, but by then it was too late. And at that moment I had something much more immediate on my mind.

'Where's Hugh?'

'Isn't he just over there?'

I stood up, peering into the darkness. I held my breath as I strained to hear the small sounds of someone moving, but there was nothing. I didn't expect to find him; somehow, I sensed he was no longer with us.

I was excited, and frightened, and also mad at myself. To think that while I'd been wallowing in a failure from my past, I could have missed the very moment when someone disappeared – before my very eyes, if I'd only been looking!

Then, as I peered into the darkness, I saw something moving, a light. I took a step forward, uncertain if my eyes were playing tricks on me. But there it was again, no doubt about it: something that glowed, no bigger than a firefly, and dipped and bobbed along just a couple of feet above the ground.

Fixing my eyes on the little light, I moved cautiously towards it, sliding my feet forward, anxious that I shouldn't trip over anything or make too much noise.

As I got closer, I saw that the light was a tiny, glowing, sparkling globe, about the size of a grape, and that it was carried by a little man who was barely two feet high. I couldn't believe what I was seeing. To make certain, I raised my torch, switched it on, and shone the beam directly at him. As the light hit him, the little man peered up at me, his face screwed up evilly, and hurled the burning globe right into my face.

Instinctively, my eyes shut and my hands flew up to protect them. I dropped my torch and stumbled. I felt myself falling, and threw my arms out to break my fall. But I didn't hit the ground. Instead, I seemed to be falling off a cliff, or down a very deep, wide hole.

A moment later I opened my eyes. They felt sore and dry, and I couldn't see anything. Had I gone blind? In desperate terror, I flailed out with arms and legs and, although I felt nothing but the rushing air all around, my efforts began to slow my fall. I discovered that, by flapping and kicking with all my might, I could affect how I fell. I could change direction, moving myself a little to the left or right, and not only could I slow my fall, I could reverse it. Although it took a huge effort, eventually I felt myself beginning to rise. Panting and gasping, I kept up the struggle although, in the dark as I was, I had no idea where I was going or when I could rest and be safe.

Then, off to my left, I glimpsed a faint light. I concentrated on moving in that direction. The pale glimmer became a soft, steady glow, and I was aware of curving rock walls all around me, and knew I was in a tunnel.

But even though I could see the ceiling and walls, I still couldn't see my own arms and legs. Calmed a little by being able to see again, I wondered how I was moving. I wasn't walking, crawling, or swimming – did that mean I could fly?

I stopped struggling, stopped working the arms and legs I could not see, but my steady forward movement did not stop; if anything, it became faster. Some sort of powerful, invisible, intangible force had me in its grip and carried me along, and there was nothing I could do about it.

Faster and faster I flew, until I shot out of the tunnel into a big, subterranean hall, softly lit by an unknown source and empty except for a single human figure: Hugh.

No sooner had I recognised him than my wish to go closer was granted. I went zooming in. As I drew nearer, Hugh bulked larger, becoming huge, a positive giant. Hovering in the air just below his right eye I realised that he was his normal size and I was the tiny one, no bigger than a fly. In fact, I *was* a fly.

Now I knew I must be dreaming.

In the past, whenever I'd become aware that I dreamed, I woke up. This time, however, the dream went on. I tried to wake myself, imagining Hugh calling for help while I lay snoring on the hillside. I blinked hard and fast. 'Wake up!' I shouted, without making a sound.

Hugh waved a hand beside his right cheek, and the gust of air knocked me halfway across the hall.

End over end I tumbled, and flapped wildly until I stabilised. As I spun around in the air, determined to keep my eye on Hugh, I saw that he was no longer alone. He was surrounded by a crowd of women, forty or fifty of them, all giants like him, and all absolutely identical.

Now I understood. This was Hugh's test. He had to pick out the real Peri from a host of imitations, and maybe I was there to help him. Although I'd never met her before, there might be some small, identifying mark, some tiny discrepancy that would be apparent from my fly's-eye view.

As Hugh began to inspect them, one by one, I swooped in for a closer view at the other end.

The first girl I saw immediately was not a girl at all but some sort of animatronic dummy. Very lifelike at first glance, her eyes shining, lips slightly parted, even her chest rising and falling in the normal rhythms of breath. But as soon as I landed on her skin, I knew it wasn't real. It was the wrong texture, without warmth, and it had no smell or salty, meaty taste.

To taste the skin I rested on was instinctive behaviour; it was also embarrassing for someone who believed himself more man than fly. I moved on quickly to the next girl, and found another dummy. The same with the third, the fourth, the fifth, the sixth ... oh, this was easy!

I continued my tour of inspection, but spared a glance at Hugh, surprised to see how slowly and seriously he took his task. Wasn't it obvious to him? Even without sniffing or licking the life-sized dolls, couldn't he see there was something wrong? Were his human senses really so dull? By then, I was pretty sure that all of these robots were exactly the same, but I visited each one in turn, expecting to be proved wrong.

And then I'd counted fifty artificial Peris, and there were no more.

Even from a distance I sensed Hugh as a warm-blooded, hot-breathed, living, stinking human creature, the only one in the whole cave. The illusion of a crowd of living women was a trick. They were convincing only to the eye. And they were all absolutely identical; not one was mortal. Whatever had become of Peri, she was certainly not among this crowd. None of them showed any awareness of me, not even when I buzzed past their eyes or crawled into the caves of their ears. Occasionally, when I looked at Hugh, I saw him frowning, twitching, even batting at the air around his head, and I wondered briefly if in some weird way he was feeling what *they* should have felt. Then I saw that there was another fly, besides me, in the cave. Was it Laura? Or just an ordinary fly, drawn to Hugh as the only warm-blooded creature around?

Didn't that give him a clue?

No, it seemed he was still convinced that at least one of these images was really alive.

It was up to me. I flew back to Hugh, desperate to get his attention. I had to tell him what he obviously didn't know, that Mider was trying to trick him. Yet as soon as I came close enough to his head to make him aware of me, his only response was to swat. I glimpsed the other fly, which was managing to avoid his clumsy blows, dancing in and out of his reach with elegant skill. I wondered again if this was Laura or a real fly, but had no time to find out because I had to make Hugh understand.

I shouted into his gigantic ear: 'Hugh, it's me, Ian! Listen to me!' and in my desperation I grew careless. This time when he swung at me the side of his hand just clipped my wing, and I was sent tumbling and spinning to the ground. I lay there winded, feeling groggy and sick, as the long, slow seconds crawled past. And when at last I recovered and stood on six feet before I rose from the ground, the situation had changed.

Most of the artificial women had disappeared. Only one remained, locked in a passionate clinch with Hugh. It could have been a happy ending, maybe he had managed to find the real Peri after all – but although I was too far away now to be certain, I didn't believe it. Even his famous Second Sight hadn't helped Hugh this time – I wondered why. Maybe it worked only on his own ground, or maybe, as with ordinary vision, it could be fooled.

As I was speculating on this, flying towards the lovers to get a closer look, I suddenly sensed danger. I spun around in midair, on guard, and found an enormous, terrifying male face staring at me. I saw the hairs in the huge nostrils quiver, then a great, hot wind struck me, lifted me, and sent me flying, utterly helpless, away down a long, dark tunnel.

I emerged into bright sunshine, finding myself hanging in midair above a man and a woman lying asleep and fully clothed on the ground. The man was lying on his back, his mouth hanging open as he breathed slowly in and out.

The wind that had supported me for so long now died, and I fell, dropping into that great, gaping cave of a mouth just as he sucked in more air. I fell into a warm, wet darkness.

Eilian

There was a girl called Eilian, a beautiful golden-haired girl, who went into service in the household of a skilled midwife and her husband, a farmer, at Garth Dorwen in Wales. It was Eilian's habit, on dry nights, not to sit in front of the fire and spin with the rest of the household, but to take her spinning out to the meadow and spin there by the light of the moon. One such evening she did not return, and it was widely reported that she had escaped with the *Tylwyth Teg*, as the Fair Folk are known in Wales. The meadow where she used to spin is known to this day as 'Eilian's Field' or 'The Maid's Meadow'.

Sometime after Eilian's disappearance, there came a gentleman to the midwife's door, wanting her services for his wife. He was a stranger, but the old woman went with him on his horse, a long way through the mist, until they reached a place piled high with rocks and stones and fallen boulders, what seemed the remains of an ancient fortress. There they entered a cave, and the gentleman led the midwife along a passage to the finest room she had ever seen in her life, and there she attended the man's wife as she laboured.

When the baby was born – fine and healthy – the husband returned with a bottle of ointment, and told the old woman to anoint the baby's eyes with it, but to take care not to get any in her own eyes. The woman did as asked, yet, after she set the bottle down, she felt one of her own eyes itch and, without thinking twice, rubbed it with the ointment-coated finger.

Immediately, she saw she was standing not in a fine room, but in a bare, chilly cave, with nothing but stones and dry rushes for furnishings, and she recognised the lady she had attended as her own former maidservant, Eilian. Yet, with her other eye, she could still see the beautifully furnished bedchamber.

She didn't mention anything about this to Eilian or to the gentleman, who helped her back onto his horse and took her safely home.

Some weeks later, attending the market at Carnarvon, she happened to see the fine gentleman again, and asked him, 'How are Eilian and the baby?'

'They are well enough,' he said. 'But, tell me, with which eye do you see me?'

'With this one.'

Quick as a flash, he struck her there, and she was blind in that eye forever after.

Peri

I opened my eyes, and immediately had to shield them against the bright sunlight. I rolled onto my side and pushed myself up to sit.

Hugh and a young woman in a rather ragged black dress stood with their arms around each other, looking down at me, and I was my normal size again.

Beside me, I heard Laura cry out. 'Peri! Oh, sweetheart!' She scrambled to her feet and rushed, arms open, towards the girl, who shrank back against Hugh, a look of alarm on her beautiful pale face.

'Hey, it's OK, that's your mum,' Hugh murmured. 'She's just glad to see you. Go on.'

If he hadn't given her a small push forward, would she have let Laura hug her? Because she certainly didn't hug back. I saw how her arms hung down limply, how she stood there unresponsive, passive in her mother's embrace, so different from the way she'd clung to Hugh.

Laura was crying, her whole body shaking with sobs, and it seemed to me that these were not tears of joy, but that, maybe for the first time, she'd really let herself feel the magnitude of her loss, all the grief and terror she'd kept locked inside.

Peri shot a desperate look at Hugh and pulled away. I couldn't bear the thought of Laura so bereft. In two long steps I was beside her, my arms around her, and she was crying into my chest.

'We should go,' said Hugh.

I looked at my watch over Laura's shoulder. Surprise made me swear. 'It's afternoon! What happened to the morning?'

'It was a long way back,' he said. 'We've been walking most of the night.'

For the first time, I really looked at Hugh. His eyes were bloodshot and red-rimmed, he looked exhausted, and there was an angry red weal across his brow.

'You're hurt!'

'I'm all right. I thought at first I'd gone blind. Come on, let's go. We're not safe here.'

I believed him. We paused long enough to gather up the blanket and water bottles, but left the burnt-out remains of candles and hurried down the hill.

At the car there was an awkward moment, as Peri hung back.

'I'm driving,' Hugh told her. 'You go in with Laura. It's not for long.' He spoke in the firm tones of a parent, and Peri obeyed without a peep of protest, although her face said she was not happy.

This put me in the front seat beside Hugh, which suited

me. He had some explaining to do. 'What happened?'

He didn't answer, frowning out at the empty road as he turned the car completely around.

I repeated my question, and he sighed.

'It's hard to describe.'

'Try.'

'I'm tired, and I'm driving.'

I ground my teeth. 'I'll bet you can talk and drive at the same time. How about some answers? You said you'd let us know as soon as anything happened, but the first thing I knew was you'd disappeared!'

'I'm sorry. But when I saw the door open—'

'You saw it open?'

'I didn't actually see it open, no, but it was. I saw this dark space stretching away inside the hill. I was afraid if I called out, or looked away for even a second, it would disappear. It might be my only chance, so I took it and went in. I was in a tunnel. I couldn't see where it went, but there was light ahead, so I went on towards the light, and after a while the tunnel opened out into a cave, and . . . there was a dead body in it.'

'Human? Male or female?'

'Neither. I mean, I don't know.' He frowned, gripping the steering wheel more tightly. 'Look, could we talk about this later?'

'Later you won't remember.' I felt sure of that. 'Tell me now. How did you know it was a dead body?'

'The shape of it, lying sprawled on the floor. The smell. It had been dead a long time. I didn't want to go near, but I had to go past it or turn back. As I did, it suddenly sat up. And then it stood up and came towards me – Christ! I felt like running! – and then, I don't know—' He faltered and shook his head in remembered confusion. 'All of a sudden I recognised Mider. And there was no way he was dead – I couldn't work out why I'd ever thought that, because he was more alive than anybody I'd ever met, more alive or, anyway, more *powerful* than I was. It was kind of like, I don't know, if I touched him, the shock might kill me. That's when I realised he wasn't human,' he went on more calmly. 'And I really shouldn't have been able to see him, or to be there, but somehow I was. And I could tell this made him furious – he didn't like it that I was there – but he couldn't deal with me the way he would have liked; he couldn't just casually destroy me, because . . . well, because. I don't know why, but it was all to do with the fact that somehow I *had* been able to get there, to beard him in his own den as it were, against his will. I had my own kind of power, I guess. I didn't know the rules, but at least I was pretty sure there *were* rules and they applied to him as well as to me. So, we started—'

He slammed on the brakes. Another car had appeared from around a bend, and was heading straight for us. Glancing into the rearview mirror, Hugh began reversing, fluidly and fast. The approaching car never even slowed, and would likely have hit us if he'd paused or hesitated at all. As Hugh backed into a passing place the other car sped past, the driver waving one hand in royal salute.

I let out my breath and turned to look in the back seat. Peri was curled half on her side, her head resting on Laura's shoulder, as her mother gazed tenderly down at her. They were both utterly unaware of our close brush with death.

'I have to stop soon,' said Hugh. 'I need food and rest.'

'We'll find somewhere around Lochgilphead. Anyway, you were saying?'

He sighed. 'I can't remember.'

I clenched my fists and breathed deeply. Not yet! 'Try! What did Mider say to you? What did you say to him?'

'Oh . . . hmmmm. I'm not sure I remember his words, exactly but . . . he challenged me. Asked me what he'd done to deserve this invasion, or something. I told him I'd come to take Peri home. He said *this* was her home because she'd been his wife since before she was born. We got into a big argument.' He sighed wearily. 'Blah, blah, blah. He would say she was his, not mine; I'd argue that she wasn't anybody's property, so he'd say in that case she'd made her choice by going with him freely; I said I wanted to hear that from her, and I wasn't going to leave until I saw her and asked her myself, and finally he said he'd make a deal with me. If I could find her, I could take her back with me.

'Then I saw her, at the far end of the room, coming from the tunnel there. At least, I thought it was her. I almost ran right over and grabbed her, but luckily I waited, to make sure, because right behind her was another girl who looked exactly the same. And then another, and another . . . in the end, there must have been fifty of them.

And all of them absolutely identical. Down to every detail. In fact, they were so completely alike that after a while, as I looked from one to the other, they seemed less and less like the Peri I'd known, more and more like strangers. They were all identical strangers – and I started to think that maybe none of them was my Peri.

'It had been too long. I should have done this, gone after her, as soon as she went away. Then, I might have had a chance. But now, I couldn't be sure I remembered what she was really like.'

He fell silent as the road became more twisting, and I let him concentrate on driving. We'd passed the farmhouse B&B, and were moving inland, away from the sea. Another couple of minutes, and we'd reached a T-junction.

'Which way?'

'Right,' I said. I hoped memory served because the map was bundled away somewhere.

He turned right onto a slightly wider road and continued.

'Anyway, they all just stood there and smiled at me, or pouted, or frowned, or stared down at their feet, but apart from the way they were looking at me, or not looking at me, they were absolutely the same. I couldn't see any differences between them. But I kept trying.' He shook his head, impressed by his own tenacity. 'I went from one to the other, sniffed her hair, looked inside her ears, stared into her eyes ... I don't know how long it went on, but Mider got impatient. I could feel his annoyance building up like a bad smell, and finally he said, with a real threat in his voice, "Make your choice. Find your woman, or choose one of these to take away with you and let that be an end of it."

'And then I remembered what I'd decided before I came to Scotland, and that was that I wasn't going to choose. I wasn't going to let him make me choose. This wasn't about me, it was about Peri, what she wanted. *She* had to choose. I couldn't know which of these clones was the real one unless she let me know. And if she didn't want to come back with me, she wouldn't reveal herself. So I'd let her stay, I'd leave alone rather than risk making the wrong choice.'

'You didn't come back alone,' I pointed out.

'That's right. I realised finally that I could only rescue Peri if she let me. She would have to show me who she was. As soon as I thought that, she did. Look, I'm stopping, we can get lunch here.'

I saw the hotel sign in front of a modest, white, two-storey building.

Hugh swung the car smoothly around onto a shell-covered drive and parked between two other cars, just beside the portable sign advertising in gold letters on brown that Costa Coffee was served there.

'What did she do?' I asked.

'I just told you.' He looked absolutely exhausted.

'Not exactly. Did she wink, or nod, or what?'

He sighed and shrugged wearily. 'I don't know. No. Of course I do. It was her look; the way she looked at me. So I knew it was her.'

A look. The hardest thing to be sure of, so easy to misinterpret, especially in poor light or between strangers. He'd so desperately wanted to find Peri that he could not allow himself to fail.

I left it for the moment. I had no choice, really, as Hugh was getting out of the car.

'Where are we?' asked Laura from the back. Peri blinked sleepily.

Hugh pushed the driver's seat forward and helped her out.

'It's a hotel,' I said. 'We can get something to eat.'

Inside, we were directed through a dark, book-lined bar to the bright, warm conservatory at the back where lunch was served. The meals listed on the chalkboard sounded substantial but strange: lamb-and-apricot casserole, venison stewed with prunes, seafood lasagne. When Hugh asked Peri what she wanted, she shook her head.

'I'm sure they'll do you a sandwich. Or just have a starter. Soup? A salad?'

She kept shaking her head.

'Come on, choose, or I will. You have to eat *something*.' He sounded angry.

'She's tired.' Laura spoke up defensively. 'She needs sleep more than food, if she was up all night. I'm not hungry, either. I'll go see if they can find a room for us. Come on, sweetheart.'

Without seeming to notice Hugh's threatening scowl, she led Peri away.

'She can't do that! Peri's not a child. She has no right

to treat her like that!' he burst out, rising from his chair.

'Because that's your job?'

He flushed, subsiding. 'She *does* need to eat. We were walking for hours. I'm starving!'

I shrugged. 'So'm I, and all I did was sleep. Vivid dreams, though.' I looked up at the young waiter, who was staring at us wide-eyed. 'I'll have the seafood lasagne, please.'

Hugh nodded. 'Same for me. I'll want a starter first, something quick ... er ... the venison pâté. With a glass of the house red.'

'Want to split a bottle?'

'Sure. We'd better hope they've got rooms for us, though, because I won't be in any shape to drive – not even as far as the next village.'

'There are rooms available,' said the waiter eagerly.

'Good.' Hugh rubbed his eyes, which were still very bloodshot. I noticed though that the mark on his brow, so vivid when I'd first seen it, had already faded.

'How'd you get that mark on your face?'

'Mider.' His mouth twisted. 'A little something to remember him by, I guess. I'd just gone into the tunnel with Peri when I heard his voice saying, "You've had your will, now I'll have my way." And then this horrible pain, like the worst headache ever, and a bright flash – and I was really scared that he'd blinded me. For ever, I mean, because I was definitely blind for a little while. Peri said she could see a light up ahead, so I let her lead me towards it, and gradually, after a really long time – I mean, we must have been walking through that tunnel for at *least* an hour – I began to see a kind of greyish light, and by the time we came outside I could see perfectly normally.'

The waiter was quick with the wine and a basket of bread and butter. I waited until Hugh got some food and drink into him before I asked a much more difficult question.

'Are you sure that's really Peri?'

'Of course.' He frowned, puzzled. 'Laura recognised her, too.'

'I'm not saying she doesn't *look* like Peri . . .'

'*Please* don't tell me you think that's my daughter! You do realise that if I had one, she'd still be a baby?'

I had been thinking, not of mythical incest and the story of Etain, but of stocks: the illusions traditionally created by the Good Neighbours to cover their tracks when they stole someone. Stocks didn't always appear to be corpses; occasionally they could move around for a brief while before sinking into a decline and seeming to die.

'Of course it's Peri. Who else could it be?'

'Nobody. She's not real.'

'Are you insane?' He pushed his empty plate to one side. 'You never met Peri before today. And you weren't even there.'

'Actually, I was.' I told him of my experience in some detail, ending just as our lasagne arrived.

'That sounds like a dream to me,' he said dismissively.

'So does what happened to you.'

'But I saw you, fast asleep on the ground. You didn't

see me. No.' He held up his hand like a traffic cop. 'Forget it. How would you know? You don't know Peri; I do.'

He dug into his steaming plate and began to eat.

We didn't talk much after that. Clearly, there was no way I could convince him he was wrong. And maybe he was right. I wished I could believe that.

Laura turned up when we'd nearly finished and took the empty seat between us. 'Peri's asleep. I got a room for us, and one for you guys. I didn't think you'd mind sharing just for one night.'

Hugh pushed back from the table. 'Any bed, anywhere. I've got to crash, now. If you'll excuse me.'

'Sure. Here's your key.' Laura handed it to him, and he stumbled away.

The waiter came over to ask if I had finished, and if Laura wanted to order anything before the kitchen closed.

She shook her head. 'I'm good.'

When he'd gone, I indicated the wine bottle. 'Have a drink?'

'Why not.'

I poured some wine into one of the unused water glasses, then raised my glass and paused to think of a toast.

'Are we celebrating?' she asked, looking unhappy.

'What do *you* think?'

She shook her head. 'It's crazy, what I'm thinking, but . . .' She trailed off, staring into the distance.

'What happened to you last night?' I asked.

She watched me warily. 'What do you mean?'

'After I got up and went to look for Hugh.'

'You didn't go anywhere.'

I raised my eyebrows.

'You said you'd seen him. Then I heard Peri calling.'

'You heard her voice?'

'Yes. Well.' She frowned into her glass. 'Maybe not. Maybe I was already asleep, because what happened next must have been a dream. It seemed to me that I called back to her, then got up and went in the direction that I'd heard her voice. Somehow, I wandered into a cave. I could hear her crying, the way she sounded when she was really little. I called but she didn't answer – I thought maybe the acoustics meant that I could hear her but she couldn't hear me. I went from one tunnel to another, looking for her, all night, or so it seemed, but it must have been a dream, because suddenly I was awake, sitting on that rug beside you, and there she was, with Hugh, in broad daylight.

'At least, I thought it was her.'

My pulse quickened. 'And now you don't?'

'Oh, it must be, I know, I'm just . . .' Her voice trailed off. She shook her head, frustrated. 'She's like a stranger, but that's only natural, isn't it, after so long? Of course she's changed, she's not like I remember; but it's Peri, really, it must be. She looks just like her, and who else could she be? It's only this feeling I had, sitting upstairs, that my Peri is still missing.'

'You could be right.'

'Then who is *she*?'

'Maybe no one. Maybe an illusion that will fade away in a few days, seem to die, or just disappear.'

She didn't react with the knee-jerk disbelief or anger that I'd come to expect; she'd learned to take the impossible seriously. 'What does Hugh think?'

'Hugh thinks he can't be wrong. He made his choice, and he's sticking to it. I think – no, I'm sure – Mider tricked him. The clue's there, in Hugh's story. Most of it's fairly vague, but he quoted Mider exactly. Mider said, "Find your woman or choose one of these." '

Laura caught her breath.

I nodded. 'Yeah. How that translates to me is: Look for her somewhere else, or take one of these as a consolation prize.'

'He chose one of the illusions?'

'He's convinced she gave him a sign, but I think he's kidding himself. He said he wasn't going to let Mider force him into the choosing game, but that's just what he did. It never occurred to him that the choice itself could be a trick; that Peri could be hidden somewhere else – in another room, or in another form.'

I stopped, recalling the other fly in the room, buzzing around Hugh's head. That was her.

'So that's it? He failed? She's gone for good?' Laura gazed at me in anguish.

'No way. We're going back there tonight. And this time we'll bring her back.'

William

William Noy was a respectable young farmer who lived near Selena Moor in western Cornwall in the early 1800s. He had courted Grace Hutchens, and the two had been very happy, intending to marry, until one day she went missing. Several days later, her body was found on Selena Moor, with no evidence of how she died.

However, that tragedy was three years in the past when this story begins, and William Noy was a sociable bachelor well liked by his neighbours. When he failed to return home after visiting the local inn one night, he was soon missed, and the alarm raised. The local people all turned out and searched for him for three days.

Finally, in a treacherous, boggy area only half a mile from his home, the searchers heard dogs howling, and when they went to investigate, discovered William's horse tethered to a thornbush in a grassy spot, with the dogs, thin and starved-looking, crouched trembling nearby. The dogs led them to a ruined barn, where they found the missing man asleep.

When they woke him, he was confused, surprised it was morning already, and astounded when his friends told him he'd been missing for more than three days.

He said he'd decided to take a shortcut home from the inn, but had lost his way on the moor and had wandered for many miles through a country strange to him, unable to recognise a single landmark although the moon was bright. Eventually he was cheered by the sound of music, and distant, glimmering lights. But his horse shied and refused to go on, so he dismounted and tied it to a tree. The dogs shrank back and whimpered and would not follow him, so he went on by himself. He came to a fine orchard, where he admired ripe plums hanging from the branches, and wondered who owned them. Beyond the trees he glimpsed a house where some sort of party was going on – perhaps a Harvest Home supper, he thought. The place was lighted by hundreds of candles, and there was a crowd of richly dressed folk on the lawn. Some sat at tables, eating and drinking, while others danced; still others played musical instruments or sang. His eye was caught by one particular girl playing a tambourine. She looked taller than any of the others and was dressed all in white. As he began to approach, she signalled him urgently to stay back.

He stopped and waited, and saw her give the tambourine to one of the others; and then she walked in his direction, murmuring as she passed, 'Follow me to the orchard.'

He did, and there, in the moonlight that filled the quiet grove, he recognised with a shock his old sweetheart, Grace, whom he thought dead. He made a move to kiss her, but she drew away nervously and warned him not to touch her, and not to eat or drink anything if he wanted to see his home and friends again.

She told him what had happened to her:

Searching for a strayed sheep on Selena Moor one evening, she had heard the sound of her lover's voice, calling to his dogs, and so she had decided to take a shortcut past his house, in hope of meeting him. But somehow she got lost and wandered for hours before she eventually came to this orchard. Feeling hungry and thirsty after her long walk, she'd plucked a beautiful golden plum. As she began to eat it, it turned bitter in her mouth and she'd fainted away. Coming to, she found herself surrounded by a crowd of people, all of them smaller than she, who were excited at having found this strong young girl to be their servant.

She had been bitterly unhappy at first, and found it a trial to serve these people who had little sense or feeling but lived what seemed to her false, unnatural lives. They were not Christians, but star-worshippers, and took pleasure only in appearances, and in memories of what had pleased them when they had lived as mortals, perhaps a thousand years ago.

She told him: 'People believed, and so it seemed, that I was found on the moor dead; what was buried as me, however, was only a changeling or a sham body, I should think, for it seems to me that I feel much the same as when I lived to be your sweetheart.' More recently she had discovered she could take the form of a small bird, and fly about near her old sweetheart and others she had cared about during her mortal life, and this made her more content with her fate.

From beyond the orchard the small people began to call for Grace to serve them more ale. She begged her sweetheart to keep himself hidden, and promised to come back and help him escape very soon.

But William felt himself in no danger, and hoped he might find some way to rescue her. He'd never given much credence to fairy tales, but now he racked his brain to recall some helpful detail. Unfortunately, he had no holy water or churchyard sod about his person. Plucking up his courage, he took his gloves from his pocket, turned them inside out for luck, and going out of the orchard, he hurled them into the midst of the fairies, calling out boldly, 'Let her that was mine be returned to me!'

Immediately everything vanished, including Grace, and he found himself standing alone in the ruins of an old barn. He felt something strike him on the head, and fell to the ground, and knew nothing more until his friends discovered him.

Peri

Laura went up to her room to get a few things and joined me at the car, at which point we realised Hugh had the key. She would have gone back to wake him up, but—

'Let's walk,' I said.

She rolled her eyes.

'I'm serious. It won't be dark for hours. If we keep moving, we might shake off a few midges. Those boots of yours, are they just for show?'

She looked down at her brown leather lace-ups. 'I don't mind walking. But if we're hiking all evening, we'll be worn-out when we get there.'

'It won't take that long. Two hours, max. Honest.' I saw the doubt on her face, and pulled out my trusty OS map. 'We're not going back down the road. There's a forestry track we can take instead, and it's more direct. Look.' I spread the map out on the bonnet of the rented car and showed her.

'What's that?'

She pointed, squinting uncertainly at a line of lettering

midway along our route – the very thing I'd noticed that made me decide on this walk.

'It's a chambered cairn.'

'You mean one of those ancient graves, the ones called fairy mounds?'

I nodded.

She hoisted her large, soft-leather bag more firmly across her shoulder. 'OK, let's go.'

It was wonderful weather for a walk. Yesterday's clouds had cleared away and with them the oppressive humidity. It was warm and the sun still shone strongly out of the clear blue sky, but a regular breeze kept the air refreshingly cool and also drove away the midges. We crossed the road and entered a forest. Silence enveloped us, as palpable as the cool brush of air against skin. I could hear nothing but the rustle of our clothing, the soft padding of our feet, the sound of my own breath.

I had no particular plan in mind, only, as I'd told Laura, a disinclination to spend the rest of the afternoon doing nothing. And I didn't even know that going back to the Fairy Door would work a second time. It was Hugh who had recognised the Fairy Door for what it was; it had opened for Hugh, not me.

There was more than one way into the Otherworld. When I'd seen the unnamed chambered cairn marked on the map and tracked with my eyes the obvious route between it and the Fairy Door, I'd remembered Laura's story of searching through many tunnels, and what Hugh said about how far he and Peri had walked before they came out on the hillside again. I wanted to have a look at the cairn, so old and so long-forgotten in the forest that nobody now living could put a name to it. Maybe, once upon a time, it had been known as Mider's *sidh*.

We'd been walking, mostly with an easy, comfortable silence between us, for nearly an hour when we came upon it in a clearing in the woods. Although there was no marker or sign to identify what it was, and it had long been overgrown with moss and weeds and the ubiquitous giant ferns the British call bracken, there was no mistaking it. A shaft of sunlight fell through the leafy canopy overhead onto the rocks at the summit of the hillock. Veins of white quartz in grey stone caught the sun and burned like fire.

The hairs rose on the back of my neck for no reason, and I cleared my throat nervously.

'Let's rest here for a while,' said Laura. She looked around. Spotting a substantial tree stump, she tested the surface with her hand, then, finding it neither too rough nor too damp, sat down. With a small sigh she eased her bag off her shoulder and let it slip to the ground. 'I hope you brought water.'

'Two full bottles.' I shrugged out of my rucksack and unzipped it to get the water. As I handed her one, my eyes were on her bag, which looked pretty full, and was obviously no small burden. 'What did you bring?'

'Oh, various things.' She uncapped and took a long swig. 'Thanks.'

I kept staring at her fallen bag. It was moving. She'd

set it down on a slope, so I reckoned the contents had tumbled over; but the longer I watched, the more I thought something inside was trying to get out.

'Like what?' I asked. 'Live mice?'

Laura looked down and caught her breath. As we both watched, astonished, something greyish and hairy pushed through the opening. A moist black nose, the gleam of an eye, the shape of the narrow head, and then two hairy paws that scrabbled for purchase on the mossy ground before managing to haul the rest of itself out of the bag. It was some sort of wolfhound: large, brindled black and white, very shaggy. While I was still struggling to accept the evidence of my eyes, something even more impossible happened, as a full-sized horse erupted from the bag. How? I have no idea. I felt I was witnessing some incredible birth. Seconds later, the leather shoulder bag lay limp yet whole, and a large, chestnut-coloured mare and a big dog stood beside us in the clearing.

Laura looked as dazed as I felt.

'Peri's Guardians.'

In response, the horse whinnied softly, and the dog's tail wagged furiously.

I cast a sidelong look at the bag. 'Did you bring the doll along, too?'

'I couldn't find it.' Her voice was soft and faraway-sounding.

The dog came over and thrust its long snout into my hand. Being a well-trained human, I stroked behind its ears. It leaned against me and panted happily. The horse dropped its head and looked at Laura, who didn't seem to notice. She stood still, zoned out.

'Maybe they'll take us to your daughter,' I said, speaking sharply to get her attention. 'Come on.'

The dog pulled back and gave a short, sharp bark, watching me eagerly.

'Yes? Peri? You know where she is?'

He barked again.

'Come on, Laura. This is what we came for.' I moved towards her, meaning to take hold of her if I had to, but she was moving, finally, bending down to pick up her bag, recapping the water bottle and dropping it inside. Then she looked at the horse and reached out a tentative hand to touch its neck. A shudder ran through her as, I suppose, she felt its undeniably warm and living flesh against her own. The horse snorted gently and as it moved away, Laura followed.

The dog trotted after the horse, with a look around at me to make sure I was coming, too.

We left the forest and emerged onto rocky, open moorland. I could see no sign of any path or track, but we didn't really need one as long as we had the animals to follow. I still wanted to have some idea of where we were going, so I looked around, trying to get my bearings and fit together this bit of countryside with what I remembered of the map.

I couldn't do it. Of course, one bit of Scottish moor looks, to the stranger, very much like any other bit: rough ground, projecting lumps of rock, tough springy heather, and spiky gorse bushes punctuating every stretch of open land. Not a lot of distinctive landmarks, especially not to a visitor. But normally I have a pretty good sense of direction, and that, coupled with my knowledge, from the map, of the general contours of this area, should have let me know if we were heading westward towards the coast or instead walking farther inland; if we were circling back around the forest through which we'd come or heading away from it.

Unease crept through me as I realised I had absolutely no idea where we were or which way we were headed. I turned to look behind us, but already the forest was out of sight, and all I could see was more of the same uneven, open moorland. I couldn't even take my bearings from the sun, because it was hidden by low cloud and the sort of mist that forms on Scottish hillsides unexpectedly at any time of year.

I stopped walking and broke out into a sweat. I made myself stand absolutely still, because if I kept walking it would be all too easy to go faster and faster until I was running, and once I began running I didn't think I'd be able to stop. It was safer to stand still.

On my watch, the digital display flickered between zeroes and eights. Only then did I realise, finally, what had happened.

The understanding broke through my paralysis, and I could move again. But I'd lost sight of Laura, the horse and the dog, and without a guide I had no idea which way to go.

Before I could get into another panic, I heard a welcome bark, and, moments later, saw the dog racing back to fetch me. I hurried forward, my eyes scanning the horizon and finding nothing but more of the emptiness ahead. I was just wondering how Laura and the horse managed to move so quickly out of my range of vision when I heard her call.

'Ian! I've found her! I've found Peri!'

I looked all around. The mist was gathering more thickly, and lower now, not far above my head. There was no sign of anyone – only the dog at my side – although Laura's voice was so clear I was sure she could not be far away.

'Where are you? Laura?'

'Here we are.' Laura came out of the mist with the horse beside her, her hand twined in its mane. She was smiling, radiant with happiness. It took years off her, and she looked so beautiful, and so *familiar*, that my heart gave a great painful thump and I couldn't say a word for the sheer delight of looking at her. In that moment I suddenly knew what she meant to me. I understood why Jenny had been so much on my mind recently, why Laura made me think of her. It was not that the two women were alike, but my feelings for them were.

'I *found* her,' Laura said again, jarring me out of my self-absorption.

'Where?'

She gave me a strange look. 'Here!' She turned her head towards the horse.

Until then I hadn't raised my eyes from Laura's face. Someone rode on the horse's back; a little girl, no more than three or four years old, with long blonde hair.

'Who's that?'

The little girl smiled down at me. 'I'm Peri,' she said in a sweet, high voice. 'What's your name?'

'Peri, sweetheart, this is Ian. Ian Kennedy.'

'No.'

'What?'

'Laura, that's not your daughter.'

'Don't be ridiculous! Of course it is! Don't I know my own child?'

'Peri's not a child. She's twenty-one. That's a little girl. I don't know where she came from, or who she is, but—'

'She's my daughter!' Laura glared at me, absolutely sure of herself.

'Laura, think about it, please. Trust me. This isn't—'

'It is! Why should I trust you? This is my child, and I'm taking her home.'

'How are you going to find your way back?'

I saw her shoulders tense as she stiffened her back. 'Is that a threat?'

'A threat?' I stared at her in pained disbelief. 'Of course not!'

She relaxed a little and allowed me a tentative smile. 'Don't worry. I'll bet the horse knows the way. We don't want to stay here any longer.'

'Laura, we do. That' – I nodded at the beautiful child – 'whoever she is, that's not the woman who eloped with Mider. This is some kind of trick, a distraction. I'm not saying you should abandon her – maybe she's your grandchild!

– but we still have to find Peri; don't forget.'

Before I'd finished, I knew I'd lost her. What I'd said was impossible. In her mind, probably, she was a young mother again, relieved to have found her missing child; how could she trust someone who told her that the little girl she dreamed of, the little girl she thought she'd found, was gone forever?

'Peri and I are going home,' she said flatly. 'You can do what you want.'

It tore my heart to watch her walk away, but what else could I do? No argument was going to change her mind. It was up to me to save Peri.

The dog started to go after the horse, but stopped when I didn't move. He turned and gave me a mournful look, whining softly.

'Stay, boy.'

He fidgeted, and his whines grew louder and picked up in tempo.

'Come on, boy, I need your help to find Peri.'

The other three were just about to vanish into the misty distance. The little girl turned around and waved at us. With a groan, and without another look at me, the dog lunged after them. One heartbeat, two, while I wondered if I'd made a terrible mistake, and they were all out of sight.

The mist was closing in. I couldn't see more than a few yards in any direction, and the silence was as oppressive and ominous as the lack of view. I was just drawing breath for a shout when a voice spoke behind me.

'What are you doing here?'

It was a cool, aristocratic male drawl. I turned and saw a man dressed in the faintly anachronistic gear of the Scottish outdoorsman: tweedy jacket with elbow patches, oddly shaped trousers with high socks and gaiters, even the deerstalker cap. And, of course, a gun. I was happy to see he kept it resting against his shoulder, not pointed at me.

He repeated his question and added, 'You don't belong here.'

'I'm sorry. Is this your land?'

'It is.'

He had a natural arrogance about him that went with the voice and the outfit. He was good-looking, of course, in a very noble, northern European way: narrow blue-grey eyes, high cheekbones, sharp nose. There was something naggingly familiar about him, although I was sure we'd never met.

'I'm real sorry. I kind of got lost, I guess. I didn't mean to trespass.' I laid the American accent on with a trowel, trusting it would gain me a warmer welcome.

'Didn't you?' He raised an eyebrow, and as he looked directly and rather mockingly into my eyes I understood that, despite appearances, this was no mere mortal landowner, and remembered the gigantic face I'd seen in my dream.

'You're Mider.'

'I am. What do you want with me?'

'I've come for Peri. Peri-Etain.'

'My wife? Do you mean to challenge me?' His eyes narrowed, and he shifted the gun's position as if to draw my attention to it.

'No.' He didn't say anything to that, so I rushed on, desperately. 'I'll trade you for her.'

'What do you propose to trade me?'

According to the old stories, fairy morality required them to accept any trade a mortal offered – a handkerchief, a cap, the unknown contents of a sack – but looking into Mider's immortal eyes I knew he'd treat any such offer as an insult, and even if he didn't blow my head off for it, I'd be blowing my chance.

So, knowing that it was dangerous, but feeling I must risk everything, I said, 'Anything you want.'

'You think you have something I want?'

I waited, feeling that to answer either way would put me in the wrong, and he nodded. 'Perhaps you do. Your life for hers? A soul for a soul; that would seem fair.'

'But if you take my life, how can you give me Peri?'

'A fair question. And I might ask you another: Why do you think she's mine to give?'

'You took her.'

He shook his head. 'She chose to come with me.'

'Meaning that she could choose to leave you? You wouldn't stop her?'

'She has a foot in both worlds. It's she who decides which foot to lift, and when.'

'Let me see her. Let me speak with her.'

'Is that a demand?'

I bowed my head, terrified and trying not to show it. 'A request. Please. I'm not seeking Peri for myself. She belongs in the mortal world, where she was born. With the people who love her. Of course, it's her choice.'

The silence went on for a long time. Finally, I raised my head and saw he was gone. I looked around. The mist pressed even closer, damp and chilly. I was alone in a place I didn't know.

Anger, disappointment and fear all welled up, battling for supremacy. Mostly I felt mad, which was better than being scared. What sort of answer was that? *Had* he taken my life after all? Had I just disappeared?

Before I could make a move, I felt a warm gust of wind stir the mist, then I heard a voice, quite plainly and clearly, close to my ear, although I could see no one.

'If I find you here again, I won't let you go so easily. Remember this.'

The wind blew harder and harder, whipping up dirt and bits of dead vegetation so fiercely that I had to shut my eyes. Then, just as suddenly, the wind dropped. I opened my eyes and found that the mist had blown away.

It was a beautiful evening. Away to the west the setting sun dyed the still waters of the narrow sea loch pink and gold. An empty, narrow road snaked along beside it, far below me. I knew immediately that I was back in my own world and, as I gazed to get my bearings, I recognised the road and the shoreline, and realised that I was standing on the high moorland somewhere above the Fairy Door.

My watch had recovered its powers and told me it was

21:56. The position of the sun suggested it would very soon be dark. I decided it would be safer to follow the road, so I made my clumsy, sliding way down the slope.

I wasn't the only person out walking so late; ahead of me was a woman: long blonde hair, black dress. She moved so slowly and awkwardly that I thought she must be drunk or physically disabled. I didn't have to run to catch up to her.

At the sound of my footsteps she turned. I knew her face.

'Peri!'

A tiny frown wrinkled her brow. 'I'm sorry ... '

'Peri Lensky?'

'Yes, but ... do I know you?'

I thrust out my hand. 'Ian Kennedy. We haven't met before, but I know your mother.'

'Oh! You do? How is she? Where is she?'

I thought of Laura as I'd last seen her, walking away from me, into the mist, and pushed the thought away. 'I was hoping I could bring you back to her.'

Her face cleared and she beamed at me. 'Brilliant! I'm fed up with walking. I lost my shoes, see?' She indicated her bare feet, and I understood the reason for her crippled gait. 'Where's your car?'

I grimaced. 'Back at the hotel. But don't worry; I'll call Hugh and ask him to come and fetch us.'

Her animation stilled. 'Hugh Bell-Rivers?'

I nodded.

'You know him, *and* my mother?'

'We've all been looking for you.'

'He still loves me?'

'Did you think he didn't?' I asked gently.

She dropped her gaze. 'I wouldn't blame him. I left him, you know. You do know?' She met my eyes again.

I nodded. 'He told me about your last night in London, and meeting Mider.'

'And he still wants me back?'

'I'm sure he does.' I hesitated, not wanting to mislead. 'But ... it's complicated. He has a new girlfriend, and ... He must wonder about *your* feelings, don't you think? I mean, even if Mider kidnapped you, even if you had no choice—'

'It was my choice. I went with him because I wanted to. He never forced me to do anything.' She spoke fiercely.

'And now you want Hugh.'

'I never stopped loving him.'

'But you left him for another man.'

'Not another *man*. Mider isn't a man, he's ... ' But even in the magical, Celtic twilight it seemed she couldn't bring herself to say it. Maybe she was afraid it would sound silly, or maybe none of the words we use in English could properly express what he was.

She shook her head and went on. 'I wasn't choosing between men. It was so much more than that. Mider was offering me another world. How could I refuse? Would you?'

I thought of Fred, of the impossibility of arguing her out of what she'd set her heart on, and shook my head.

'I would. Unless my life was so miserable that I couldn't stand it. I wouldn't leave a promising future and somebody who loved me, for vague mystical promises.'

She gave me a long, cool, doubting look and shrugged. 'Maybe. But you're old. It's weird, the way old people get more cautious, the nearer they are to dying anyway! I wasn't giving up, I was going for it! If I hadn't gone, I would've regretted it forever.'

'So you don't regret what you did?'

She sighed and turned away from my nagging question, my incomprehension. 'How far is it to a phone?'

I pulled mine out. 'Right here,' I said, pressing in Hugh's mobile number.

'Where are you?' he demanded as soon as I spoke.

'I'm on the road near the Fairy Door. Can you bring the car?'

'Is Laura with you?'

I hesitated, and Hugh rushed on. 'She's got her phone switched off, and nobody's answering in their room. I'm worried.'

'Don't be. Peri's here with me.'

'What? How? Never mind. I'll be right there.'

'Hugh's coming for us,' I told Peri, putting my phone away. I nodded up the road. 'Let's go wait in that lay-by.'

We made our way along the road in silence. Darkness was gathering, thickening the air. There was a large, smooth boulder at the edge of the road, not far from the black-and-white-striped pole, and Peri leaned against it. She lifted one foot and massaged it slowly. 'I used to walk around barefoot all the time when I was little. I don't know how I could stand it.'

'Why did you come back?'

She put the first foot down and lifted the other, rubbing it gently. After a while she said, 'It was wonderful, at first; just like he promised. I was so happy I couldn't think about anything else. I didn't want anything else. And then one day I thought about Mom. I wasn't sure exactly how long I'd been away, but it must have been weeks since I'd spoken to her. It was so weird. My whole life, I don't think I'd gone more than a single *day* without talking to her. Even when she moved to London, and I stayed on in Houston to finish high school, even with the six-hour time difference, even then we managed to talk every day. And when I went away to college it was the same. And then I went away with Mider, and that all stopped. I had no idea what she was doing or thinking. It was almost like she'd died.'

'He saw I was missing her, and told me I could go back and talk to her if that's what I wanted. I could go out into the other world as often as I liked, but not for too long. The door would only open for short periods, and if I stayed away for more than an hour and a day, I'd be locked out forever.'

She gave me a stern look. 'See, I could have left any time. But I didn't want to. I just missed Mom, that's all; I wanted to hear her voice again.'

I looked at Peri's face, like a pale moon in the gathering dark. There were so many questions I wanted to ask, so much I wanted to know, and I was aware that this might be my only chance, this brief time of waiting before Hugh turned up and swept her back into his orbit.

'So, you walked through the door . . . what then?'

'Well, I had no idea where I was. I'd expected London, somewhere I'd recognise, but instead I was in the middle of nowhere – I didn't even know what country! At least there was a road, so I started walking, figuring it would eventually take me somewhere. I had no idea it would be so *hard* to do something as easy as phone home!' She gave a rueful laugh and shook her head. 'Such a long walk! That's when I ruined my shoes – they were these silly little dressy heels, not made for walking. I got blisters. It was horrible!'

She sighed. 'You'll think I was a total wimp, but, see, that was the first time I'd felt any kind of pain, well, physical discomfort, since I'd gone away with Mider. It freaked me out. I was hot and sweaty and thirsty, with nothing to drink. My feet hurt like hell, and my back was aching, I couldn't get my breath, and – well, it was totally weird, because until I came back here I didn't even know I was–' She stopped.

'Pregnant?'

She gasped. 'How did you know?'

'People saw you.'

'That lady who gave me a coin for the call? Yeah. I was pregnant, pregnant enough to show; but, believe it or not, I didn't even know it.'

'What happened to the baby?'

I couldn't make out her expression in the gathering dark, but she shifted her stance uneasily. 'It was born . . . I gave birth . . . maybe prematurely, I'm not sure; it might even have been a miscarriage. It all happened so quickly, not like you hear about. And then they took it away. I never even got to—'

'They?'

'The ladies.'

'What ladies?'

She sighed impatiently. 'The others. It wasn't just Mider and me, you know; there were lots of others. I didn't really make friends with them, but . . . they were company. One of them told me that babies were very rare among them. And that when they were born, they didn't often thrive.'

Far away down the winding road I glimpsed a flash of headlights.

I moved a little closer to Peri. 'Why did you come back? If life was so pleasant and easy there—'

'That's why.'

I frowned.

'It was all too comfortable. Does that sound perverse? I mean, it's not like I *wanted* to be sad, or uncomfortable, but – well, some things just ought to make you feel unhappy, don't you think? There, nothing really mattered. I wasn't even sad about the baby. It didn't seem real. I wondered, if the baby had lived, would I have been able to love it? Also, I was starting to forget things. My old life started to seem unreal, too, like a story I'd heard a long time ago, not part of me.'

I could hear a car approaching, noisy in the night-time stillness.

'After Mider told me that I could come back whenever I wanted, I meant to go lots, to keep in touch. But I forgot. I was starting to forget everything – except maybe my mom. I did remember her, and sometimes I really wished I could be with her, but I don't know, there wasn't any urgency about it. Then I dreamed that I saw Hugh again, and the feeling I had – well, I realised I still loved him. I didn't know how he felt about me, if he even remembered me, but I knew then I had to come back, before it was too late. Even if it *was* too late, it was what I wanted to do. This is where I belong.'

The car came around the final curve, headlights glaring, blindingly bright, and then swept past.

'How long have I been gone? Tell me the truth. Five years? Ten?'

'Two and a half.'

'So it's not too late?'

Brakes screeched; then the car went into reverse and began to roll back in our direction.

'It's not too late,' I promised.

MacRoy's Wife

A Highland crofter by the name of MacRoy one day paused in his work around noon and sat down on a little hillock to rest. And as his gaze swept about, he saw what appeared to be a cloud of midges hovering just above the ground, but as he concentrated he saw that what at first appeared to be insects was in fact a whirling, tumbling storm of wee folk, all dancing madly. Rousing himself from his fascination, MacRoy snatched up a pebble from the ground and threw it into the midst of the throng, shouting, 'Let all that is within be mine, in God's name!'

Immediately, all the little people vanished, leaving behind a beautiful woman, as naked as the day she was born. MacRoy gave her his plaid and turned his back to spare her modesty as she fixed it about her. When she was as decently attired as she could manage, he led her to his cottage and gave her bread and water. She could not remember her name or where she'd come from; but she was a beautiful woman in need of protection, and he

413

was a man in want of a wife, and so, very shortly, they were wed.

The years passed happily enough until one day a cattle drover and his son, passing through on their way to a market in the south, stopped by the door to ask lodging for the night. This was granted. The son, a boy of about twelve, was very taken with Mrs MacRoy, and could hardly take his eyes from her. As well, he kept tugging his father's arm, and telling him to look, until soon the father was staring as hard as the son.

MacRoy was not pleased by this discourtesy. 'You must see something very strange about my wife to stare at her the way you do.'

'Indeed,' said the drover. 'And had I not seen my own wife die at noon on' – and here he mentioned the day and the year – 'I should say that was she!'

MacRoy gaped in wonder at this coincidence, for the hour, day and year corresponded exactly to the time when he had found the woman who had since become his wife. Drawing them all near about the fire, he proceeded to tell the story. In response, the drover related incidents from his own life: where and how he had met his wife, how he had wooed and won her, when and where they had married, and how they had lived together. As she listened, the woman felt as one waking from a dream. Now she recognised the drover as her husband, and the boy as her son, and, leaning forward eagerly, began to ask for news of other family members, calling them by name. As they talked, more and more details came back to her, more and more vividly, until finally she remembered the whole of her previous life quite clearly.

It soon became obvious to them all what had happened: the woman, lying ill, had been spirited away by the fairies, who left behind a substitute image that had seemed to die. Now the only question was what should be done.

'Let her decide,' said MacRoy to the drover, 'whether she will stay with me or go with you.'

They waited, and watched her tensely. The woman looked at neither of the men, but only gazed tenderly at the boy. After a long pause she said, 'I will go to my bairns.'

And so MacRoy was a bachelor once again.

Jenny

Laura was not waiting for us at the hotel, and the room she had taken for herself and Peri was empty.

I stared at the two beds, one of which appeared to have been slept in, and wondered what had become of Peri's simulacrum. Vanished, of course, as illusions do. But if we'd only imagined her, if she'd been some sort of shared hallucination, then what had disturbed the bed?

'Mom's not here,' Peri said.

I looked at Hugh, who wore the same dazed, uncomprehending expression he'd had since picking us up at the roadside. He hadn't asked any questions; in fact, he'd hardly said a word, but from the way he looked at Peri I could tell that he recognised her, and also that he felt utterly bewildered. All his former assurance had deserted him. He still loved her, that was obvious. But her feelings remained a mystery to him, and he was afraid of making the wrong move.

'Well, where *is* she?'

They both looked at me accusingly. Of course, I had

been the last person to see Laura. I remembered too well how she'd vanished in the mist with the horse and the child even as I recalled the old stories of fairy morality. For a few seconds, I panicked. What if Mider had let Peri go in exchange for her mother? Bewitched by the fairy child, Laura might have gone anywhere.

'Maybe she got lost coming back – she could be wandering around out there in the dark – we'd better go look for her.' I tried to sound calm, but they picked up on my anxiety at once, and we made a mad scramble to get outside and across the road, searching in the dark for the path Laura and I had taken hours earlier. Hugh and I had our torches, but there wasn't a spare for Peri.

'Keep close together,' I warned. 'We must *not* get separated, got that? Peri, I want you to hold Hugh's hand.'

I was trying to think ahead, trying to remain rational and make plans, but luckily it wasn't necessary, as our quest took no more than a couple of minutes.

We found Laura almost immediately. She was fast asleep on the ground at the edge of the woods, lying curled up at the base of the sign that marked the start of the circular walk. She'd used her soft leather shoulder bag as a pillow, and I could see at a glance that it was emptier than when we'd set out, and guessed that the Guardians, having brought her this far, had not resumed their toy forms but vanished back into their own world where, perhaps, there was another golden-haired, magical child it was their duty to protect.

'Oh, Mommy,' said Peri in a high, soft voice, sounding

for a moment very much younger than her actual years.

I hung back with Hugh, carefully angling my light so the beam wouldn't glare in Laura's face, and watched as Peri crouched down and gently stroked her mother's hair, then kissed her cheek.

I saw signs of rapid eye movement, suggesting Laura was dreaming, and her lips curved into a smile a few seconds before her eyelids fluttered and she woke. For a long moment mother and daughter gazed into each other's eyes; and then, with a little, gasping cry, Laura sat up and flung her arms around Peri, hugging her tight.

I looked away. Reunions always choke me up. Under almost any other circumstances I'd have taken that moment as my chance to slip quietly away and leave them alone together. But we were four people in the remote Scottish countryside, in the middle of the night, with just one car among us, and besides, I still had questions.

I cleared my throat. 'Come on, you guys, unless you *like* being eaten by midges. Let's get inside.'

So we walked back to the hotel, mother and daughter clinging together, hugging each other as they walked, unwilling to be separated again for even a moment. I proposed drinks, but Laura and Peri declined. It was obvious they had no use for us and only wanted to be alone together. Hugh and I exchanged a look, two super-fluous males, and went back to the comfortable, book-lined bar, where we sampled an interesting range of single-malt whiskies. We didn't talk much. I wasn't going to say, 'I told you so,' and I guess he didn't want to admit he'd been fooled by asking me how I'd managed to find her. Far more important to him than what had happened was what would happen next, and that wasn't something I could help him with. It wasn't even my business. Now that I'd met Peri, I was confident of her ability to cope with whatever the future had in store.

I'd hoped to have a chance to talk to Laura privately the next day, but she still had no attention to spare for anyone but her daughter. The feeling was obviously mutual, and I guess it was pretty understandable, considering how long they'd been separated, but it was frustrating all the same.

I saw how Hugh watched Peri as we drifted around the airport shops, killing time before our flight, and I suspected there was some of that same yearning in the looks I cast at Laura, looks she didn't seem to notice.

Finally, when Hugh went into W. H. Smith, leaving us next door in Accessorize, watching as Peri mused over the merits of a beaded purse shaped like a butterfly against one shaped like a toadstool, I said to Laura, 'Could I have a word? Privately?'

Her eyebrows went up; then, with another glance at her daughter, she followed me out of the shop. 'Of course! We need to settle up.'

'Settle up?'

She made a writing gesture with her right hand. 'Your bill. I've got my chequebook.' She was reaching into her bag when I stopped her.

'Oh, no, no, that's not necessary. I didn't really find her, you know. She came back of her own accord.'

Laura frowned. 'What do you mean?'

'Didn't she tell you? I mean, did she tell you what happened? Haven't you talked about it?'

'Yes, of course. But, Ian, that's not the point. OK, maybe you just happened to be there at the right time in the right place in the end, but you figured out where that place would be. And I hired you. I hired you to do a job, and you did it. Of course I'm going to pay you!'

'Laura, how much do you remember about last night?'

'What do you mean?' She eyed me warily.

'I mean about finding Peri. Do you remember finding her?'

'No, of course not! I didn't find her – I was asleep.'

'When did you fall asleep?'

'Well, I don't know.' She stopped and really thought about it. Hugh approached, holding a newspaper, then veered around us and into Accessorize, heading for Peri.

'We went out after Hugh went to bed. There was a footpath. We were going to an old cairn in the woods that you thought was connected with the Fairy Door in some way. We stopped to rest.' She paused and shrugged. 'Then I guess I nodded off, because that's all I can remember until Peri woke me up.' The tender smile returned to her face. 'And I don't care what you say, I'll always be grateful to you.'

'Don't you remember the Guardians?'

'Peri's old toys?' She reached for her bag, startled, then

stopped and shook her head. 'Yes – I took them with me – but they're gone. That's right. Did they fall out of my bag? What happened to them? Not that it really matters. Peri's too old for toys.'

'Don't you remember the little girl? The little girl you thought was Peri?'

She stared at me. 'I dreamed she was a little girl again – she was lost, then I found her. But you're not talking about my dream?'

Over her shoulder, I saw into the shop. Hugh was paying for something at the cash register, while Peri smiled up at him, love shining in her eyes.

I looked down at Laura and smiled at her. 'It doesn't matter. You're right. What matters is that she's back.'

Finally, she completed that much-arrested reach into her bag. 'Tell me how much I owe you.'

I managed to stop myself from insisting that she owed me nothing, remembering just in time that I was far too broke for such largesse. 'I don't know yet. I need to add up the hours and figure out the VAT. I'll invoice you. I've got your address.'

'Don't forget, I'm going back to America next week.'

'Oh, right. Well, how about if I call you tomorrow?'

'And then, maybe, we could get together for a drink or something, I mean, if you're not too busy?' She looked away as she spoke.

My pulse quickened at her sudden shyness. 'That would be great,' I said warmly. 'I'd really like to see you again.'

She smiled back, meeting my eyes, and I knew then

that the intimacy I'd felt between us during that long night on the hillside had been no illusion.

'Call me,' she said.

We got into London just in time for rush hour and parted in a crowded underground station.

'I'll call you tomorrow,' I called after Laura as she was swept away with Peri and Hugh – who were now, I noticed, holding hands.

After the wilds of Scotland, Turnpike Lane looked even seedier than usual, and the body odours of massed humanity surging through the lavatorial-smelling tunnels made me feel slightly sick. Even at street level the air was no fresher, choked with traffic fumes, human exhalations, the aromas of overused cooking fat, rotting garbage, and dog shit.

Arriving home, I discovered someone had filled my council-supplied wheelie bin to overflowing with their rubbish, while several beer cans, a plastic milk bottle, one styrofoam hamburger carton, and the papers from what must have been six or seven fish suppers littered the little paved area at the front. Oh, the joys.

Inside, I gathered up the scattered papers that had come through the letter box during my brief absence: no real mail, but lots of advertisements for local businesses, cards for taxi firms, specials at the nearby pizzeria, startling news about a revolutionary new hearing aid, and urgent requests from three different estate agents. Two offered free valuations; the third, more enterprising, had added a handwritten note to advise me how much he reckoned he could get for my property, should I wish to sell.

The figure was enough to make my eyes bug. Of course, it wouldn't go far if I wanted to keep living in London, but as getaway money it was more than decent. I put that note on my desk; everything else went onto the recycle pile on the couch.

The light on the answerphone blinked: one message. I pressed PLAY and listened to my mother's voice, wishing me a happy birthday in advance. She said she might call again on Wednesday, but she assumed I'd be out celebrating with my friends . . . For the first time, I could hear age cracking my mother's clear voice, and I felt an almost painful rush of love for her. Her last visit to London, and the last time I had seen her, had been nearly two years ago. I really should see her again, before it was too late. My eyes went back to the note from the estate agent.

I made a pot of coffee before booting up the computer. There were forty new messages in my in-box, but only one got my attention right away, and that was from Baz, the journalist I'd asked about Linzi Slater's death.

Not a murder investigation, he wrote, *but I'm sure the cops would love to find out the name of her pusher. They found gear (syringe, etc.) and drug residue at the scene, plus a bottle of pills, which makes it look like a deliberate OD.*

I shut my eyes, as if not seeing the words could somehow change them, and began to swear, monotonously and unimaginatively. With murder, there is someone to blame, someone to hate, and something to do: you hunt down the killer and bring him to justice, one way or another. There's no such comfort in a suicide; there can never be any justice. Nothing is left for the survivors but guilt and pain and a lot of questions.

Why did she do it? Why was life so unbearable for her? Was there anything anyone could have done that would have made a difference? Could she have been saved?

I would never know. Linzi Slater had been lost before I ever heard her name.

So, I tried to put it behind me and got on with the things I could do. I answered e-mails, paid bills, and drafted an itemised invoice to the attention of Laura Lensky. I did it again and again, revising downwards to reflect how little I'd had to do with Peri's return, then, remembering Laura's taunt about how self-deprecating and un-American I'd become, revising the final figure back up to more accurately reflect my professionalism, my commitment, my years of experience and research . . . yeah, right. I had that letdown feeling I often got at the end of a case, the low that comes after a high, the sense of an ending that brings, as payback for any satisfaction I dared feel, the certainty that it would be the last; that nothing good or interesting would ever happen to me again.

Fighting the blues, I made myself go out to eat, and wished, while I picked at the tasteless food, that I was with Laura. The prospect of seeing her soon did not cheer me. I might wish for a relationship, but how could anything get started when she was just about to leave the country? And, anyway, she was out of my league, older, richer, more successful.

Later still I slumped in front of the TV and channel-surfed mindlessly, bored and restless, reluctant to go to my solitary bed, but finally too depressed and tired to do anything else.

I didn't expect to sleep, or not for a long time, but as soon as I lay down, hypnogogic images began to play on the screen of my eyelids, giving me the sense that I was already dreaming.

I saw faces, the faces of women and the lost girls; the missing, the mysteries. Peri, Linzi, Jenny, Fred . . .

I was sitting beside Fred. I knew I was dreaming. We were on my bed together, and she looked younger than I'd ever seen her, a teenager like Linzi Slater.

'It's easy,' she said. 'It's really easy. Lie down and close your eyes.'

I did as she said.

'Now tell me what you see.'

I was looking across a grassy field at a low hill. On top of the hill was a grove of trees. The sun was going down behind the hill, turning the trees to black shadows against the peachy gold of the sky.

I opened my eyes. Fred's face was very close. She frowned and reached her hand out towards my eyes. I shut them quickly. There, waiting for me, was the grove of trees on the hilltop.

'Don't look at me,' said Fred's voice. 'It's not allowed. Concentrate. You have to forget about everyone. Just concentrate on the place you see behind your eyes. The place where you want to be. You just have to want it enough to give up everything.'

I was aware of the threatening implications behind her words, but they didn't frighten me. What was there to give up? My debts? A failing business? A string of shallow, temporary relationships? Who would even miss me if I disappeared? Even my mother was used to me not being around.

I didn't try to look at Fred again. I knew she wasn't really there, anyway. I went on looking at the low hill with its mysterious, solitary grove of trees. It was a fragment of landscape I had never seen before, yet I was coming to know it intimately. It seemed to take a very long time for the sun to set, but finally it began to grow dark, and I knew the moment was near, the moment when I'd have my answer.

Then, out of the darkness, a bird sang.

My heart gave a painful lurch and began to pound harder. What kind of bird sang at night? Was it nearly morning? Already? But I hadn't been anywhere, I still didn't know anything. It wasn't fair.

The bird gave another long, warbling call, and this time I recognised the sound as the telephone.

Groping along the bedside table until I found the cordless phone, I thumbed it on and fumbled it to my ear. My mouth was so dry my lips were sealed together.

'Hello? Ian?'

It was Laura. I managed to croak a single syllable.

'Ian? Are you OK? You sound terrible!'

'Just.' I sniffed. 'Just woke up.'

'I woke you! I'm so sorry! For some reason I thought you got up early.'

'S'OK.' I peered at the clock – 9:23. 'Overslept.'

'Well . . . should I call back later?'

'No, no.' Keeping the phone clamped to my ear, I edged out of bed and into the bathroom for a glass of water.

I heard her take a deep breath. 'I'm sorry to bother you. It's just – you did say you were going to call.'

A haggard, grey, heavily stubbled face stared back in surprise at me from the mirror. She couldn't wait a few more hours? She seemed astonishingly eager to hear from something that looked like *that*. I gave myself a wink over the water glass. *You dog, you.*

'I was going to call,' I said. I forbore to point out that it wasn't even 10 a.m. and repeated, 'I overslept. Sorry.'

'That's all right. It's just . . . things have been put ahead. I thought I'd be leaving on Sunday, but it turns out they want me at a meeting in New York on Friday afternoon. I don't suppose you're free for dinner tonight?'

'Free as a bird. What do you fancy?'

'Do you know a good Chinese place?'

'Lee Ho Fook.' She didn't know it; rather than spend more time figuring out the directions, I suggested we meet in a pub near Leicester Square at six o'clock. I would happily have gone on talking to her, having her voice so intimately close in my ear, but I was bursting to go to the toilet, and that was an intimacy I did not wish to share.

During my shower I felt shaky, and diagnosed low blood

sugar, so I dressed quickly and went out for breakfast, scooping up a surprisingly substantial pile of mail on my way out.

I ordered the 'full English' in my favourite café, and, before looking at my mail, glanced through the newspapers I'd paused long enough to buy on the way. Of the broadsheets, only the *Telegraph* carried the Linzi Slater story. It seemed that she had ingested an unknown number of sleeping tablets and paracetamol, washed down with an alcopop, before injecting the heroin. I was about to read the brief story through again when I was distracted by something odd. The date on the newspaper was Thursday, 22 June.

I checked the other papers. They had the same date.

'Here you are, my friend, full English,' said the café owner cheerfully, setting down a white china plate brimming with fried eggs, bacon, sausage, tomatoes, and mushrooms.

'What is today?' I asked him.

'Today's date? Is the twenty-second. Thursday.'

I had gone to bed Monday night, slept what felt like a normal eight or nine hours, and awoken on Thursday morning. I'd slept through my birthday. More than two full days had passed.

No wonder I was starving. I ordered more bread and more coffee, and began to work my way through the food before me, trying not to wonder what would have happened if Laura hadn't phoned. Or, if I'd left the ringer switched off, and the answerphone on so I wouldn't be disturbed. Would I *ever* have woken up?

I shuddered as I recalled Fred's calm voice telling me to forget everything.

The smoked, salty tang of the bacon dipped in unctuous egg yolk, the smell of strong coffee, plaintive foreign music and voices, and spatters of hot fat frying in the background, the way the sunlight glittered on the ashtray on the next table – all these things were life, and, no matter how prosaic or lonely it could be, I knew I wouldn't willingly sacrifice a single half hour of it for whatever peace there might be beneath that hill.

Two days I'd spent staring at that skeletal grove of trees, watching the light bleed out of the sky; two days and two nights and another great handful of hours . . . No wonder it was etched on my brain like a part of me.

It wasn't Doon Hill that I'd dreamed about, nor was it the rocky, treeless slope in Knapdale where I'd met Mider; as far as I could recall, familiar as it seemed, that particular low hill, topped with about a dozen deciduous trees of some kind, was not a place I knew or had ever visited in my waking life. But it was real, real enough to make my chest tighten as I thought of my narrow escape.

I didn't want to die. That seems so obvious that it should not need saying – doesn't everyone feel that way? – yet every day people kill themselves, often for incomprehensible reasons. Many more are driven to flirt with death. I thought of Sylvia Plath's self-mythologising, and of all the young people drawn by that fantasy. Had Linzi Slater wanted death, or only an escape from her own narrow life? Had she imagined there was something better waiting for her on the other side?

I could understand the urge to disappear. Even when I was younger, even though I'd told him I didn't, I *had* understood why my father had gone. He'd run away because it was easier and more exciting than staying. Men often took that way out, had done so for centuries. They ran away to sea, or just over the hill to the next village. Women, traditionally, were the ones who stayed put and tried to work things out. But times had changed. Maybe Jenny had left me for the same reasons my father had left my mother.

I finished my breakfast and only then remembered I still hadn't looked at my mail.

Despite its promising bulk, most of it, as usual, was junk. The only personal letter was a thick, square one from my mother. It felt suspiciously like a card, and I winced at the prospect of a second birthday card, another birthday cheque, and wondered if my mother was getting forgetful in her senior years.

But inside it was another envelope, this one light green, addressed to me c/o my mother in handwriting I recognised immediately: a neat, rounded, girlish hand that stabbed me to the heart. I peered closely at the stamp, which showed an old-fashioned aeroplane and a man decked out in fur-collared coat, flying helmet, and cheesy grin – but I couldn't make out the postmark. I turned it over in my hands, feeling oddly lightheaded.

'More coffee?'

'Yes, please. Oh, and could I have a glass of water?' My

mouth was very dry, from nerves now as well as dehydration. I waited until he'd brought my water and gone away again before I opened the green envelope.

There was a card inside. On the front of the card was an atmospheric, arty photograph, a misty scene of a low hill topped by a small grove of trees, outlined against what might have been sunrise or sunset. With a deep, foreboding chill, I felt myself back inside that timeless dream.

It was an effort to turn the card over to look at the acknowledgements on the back. They were there, as for any normal photograph: the name and logo of a publishing company, the title ('Morning Mist'), and the photographer's name. The man's name meant nothing to me, but maybe this was a famous image, maybe I'd seen it on a poster or a book cover. It was an odd coincidence, but surely not sinister. Without looking at the picture again, I opened the card and read the message written there in dark blue ink in Jenny's familiar hand.

Dear Ian,

After dreaming about you three times in the past month I finally decided to listen to my subconscious. I would like to see you again, in real life, and talk to you about what happened to us. I'm not asking for anything more than a meeting. I am happy, and my life is good in a lot of ways, but I guess turning 40 is one of those milestones that makes you look back over the way you've come and think about what might have been. I wonder if you're feeling the same way? Or maybe you think that the past should stay dead and buried. I wouldn't blame you. It's your choice. You don't owe me anything. I'll be in New York City early in September, and I'm planning to visit The Cloisters on the 6th. If you're there between 11 a.m. and 1 p.m. I'm sure we'll find each other.

Your
Jenny

That was it. I read the brief note again and again, but there was no more to it than that. No address, no phone number, no way of contacting her unless I accepted her challenge and met her in New York on the day we'd always celebrated as our anniversary.

Celebrating the first anniversary of our first date – seventeen years ago! – I'd taken Jenny to New York. It was the first time she'd ever been, and she'd thought nearly all of it was wonderful, but her favourite place by far was The Cloisters, a collection of medieval European art and artifacts in Fort Tryon Park. As I tried to remember it now, I couldn't recall how to get there, or what the building looked like. My one sure memory of that day was the awe shining on Jenny's lovely face as she gazed in mute wonder at the magnificent Unicorn Tapestries.

I looked down and read the note again. This was so typical of Jenny, I thought, she hasn't changed at all.

No mention of her marital status, any children, or what

she'd been doing for the past ten years: as far as *we* were concerned, none of that mattered. No promises, of course, although she signed herself 'Your Jenny'. No room for me to manoeuvre: As I had no way of getting in touch with her, I couldn't argue that my job, bank balance, wife, or any other commitments prohibited a trip to New York on that date. If I *cared* I'd be there. If I wasn't there, I didn't care. Did *she* care? I'd have to wait and see.

She was still an absolutist, still the emotional dictator . . .

And I knew from the pain in my chest that what I felt for her was more than just curiosity or regret. I wanted a second chance. But to have to wait, and do nothing, for nearly three months was impossible. I would have to find her before then. Why should I let her make all the rules?

I wouldn't. I would find her first. After all, finding people was what I did.

I paid the bill and went home to begin my search.

It was still too early to call most people in America, but my mother was always an early riser, so I took the risk.

'Sweetheart, how nice to hear your voice! How are you? Did you have a nice birthday?'

As if I was still into birthday treats. 'Mmm, quiet. I mostly just slept.'

'Really? Well, I guess you must have needed it. I'm glad you took the day off, at least.'

'Mom, do you remember my old girlfriend, Jenny Macedo?'

'Of course I do! Did you get her card?'

My heartbeat quickened. 'The one you forwarded? Yes.'

'Oh, that's good. I wasn't sure it would arrive on time. Wasn't that nice of her, to remember your birthday.'

'How did you know it was from Jenny?'

'What do you mean?'

'There's no return address on the envelope.'

'Of course there was. One of those little sticker things. I'm sure I remember that.'

This news sent me hurrying across to the couch where I'd dropped my armload of papers when I came in. The outer envelope would be there, and maybe the address label had fallen off inside it. Clamping the phone to my ear with my shoulder, I began excavating. Bingo. But the envelope was empty.

'Well, it's not here now. Must've fallen off your end. Can you remember anything about the address? The city?'

She made the little humming sound she used to signify thinking. 'Well . . . you know, you might be right. Maybe there wasn't a return address. There *was* a sticker, though; it was on the back flap, like a seal. It said "Jenny" in fancy script, and there was a little picture, no, a design, it was sort of like a logo, I think. Sorry, I can't remember it exactly. Anyway, I saw her name, and made the assumption it must be from *your* Jenny, and I was right, wasn't I?'

'My Jenny as was.'

'I always liked her. I was sorry it broke up the way it did. It's nice that you're back in touch. What's she up to these days?'

I shook my head helplessly. 'I don't know. Thinking about the past, I guess, but I don't know why.' I spent the rest of the day at my computer, trying to find something more about Jenny, but made no progress. Everything I learned was a negative: no phone number for her in Austin, Dallas, Fort Worth, or San Antonio; no Jenny Macedo listed on the website self-advertised as the largest cyber meeting place for rug-weavers; no definite hits on any of the search engines. Surely anyone who sold anything these days had to have a website, but if she ran a business or had a design trademarked as 'Jenny' (this had occurred to me following my mother's comment about the sticker looking like a logo) I hadn't yet found it.

I felt sure she'd changed her name. It was the easiest, and most ordinary, way to disappear. Most women still took their husband's name when they married, especially if they had children, and it made them practically impossible to find.

I tried to find Jenny's sister, but there was someone else living at her ten-year-old address, and there was no listing for her in the greater San Antonio area. Maybe her husband had been transferred to another state, or overseas, or maybe she'd left him and changed her name, too.

It was a relief, really, when I had to stop my compulsive web searches and get ready to go into town for my meeting with Laura. I knew I needed a break. Tomorrow I'd take a slightly different tack and dig through my memories and old address books for everyone I could recall who'd once known Jenny, and I'd track them all down. They, in turn, would suggest others, until, finally, the magical combination was reached and the connection made.

I knew I could do it, and I tried to put it out of my mind, to concentrate instead on the evening ahead. But what should have been pure pleasure, a date with Laura, had become a duty, a distraction from what I really wanted to think about. Before leaving, I slipped Jenny's card into my breast pocket, where I could feel it against my heart.

Approaching the pub Laura had named, I saw a slim figure in green just vanishing through the door. Immediately, all other thoughts fled as I hurried after. She was wearing the same leaf-green linen dress she'd worn to our first meeting, but instead of anxiety on her face, this time I saw happiness.

'You look great,' I told her, bending to kiss both cheeks, inhaling her fresh and sexy scent with pleasure.

'Thank you.' She smiled and tilted her head coquettishly. I was ambushed by emotion, startled by how quickly my fantasies about Jenny had been displaced by desire for the woman standing in front of me.

'What would you like to drink?'

'They're advertising Pimm's Cup, to celebrate summer. Shall we? Something appropriately English for my last night here.'

I heard her with a pang of loss. 'I hope this won't be your last night in England.'

'No – of course it won't. I'll probably be flying back and forth between London and New York a few times over the next few months. And that's just on business.'

I bought our drinks and we moved to a table in the back corner, which fortuitously had cleared.

'Cheers,' I said, raising my glass.

Instead of responding, she dipped into her big shoulder bag and brought out something wrapped in plain brown paper. 'Happy birthday, even if it is a day late.'

I was startled, embarrassed that I'd mentioned it, but oddly pleased she'd remembered. 'You shouldn't have.'

'It's no big deal. Just something I happened to see that I thought you might like.'

It was a book. The sight of the cover made me smile: it was faded red, with the image of an American Indian with a writhing green snake in his mouth. *Weird America: A Guide to Places of Mystery in the United States.*

'Oh, wow, this is great! I had a copy when I was in high school, but it disappeared a long time ago. Thank you!'

She ducked her head, smiling. 'You're welcome. I thought maybe, as a change from the mysteries of the British Isles, this might tempt you back to explore your native land.'

'As a matter of fact, I have been thinking about going back.'

'Really?'

I nodded.

'Whereabouts, exactly?'

'Well . . . I have a reason to go to New York . . . ' I touched my breast pocket and hesitated, wondering whether to tell her about Jenny.

A faint pink flush appeared in her cheeks, and her eyes

sparkled. 'I guess you do,' she said softly, gazing at me.

She thought I was flirting. Damn. I felt like a complete heel, but I had to tell her. 'I'd love to visit you, but—'

She went very still at that 'but'.

'Something's come up. Some old business. Personal business. I told you about Jenny.'

'The girl you left behind.' She took a large swallow of her drink.

'The girl who left me. Whatever. I had a card from her today. She wants to meet and talk about what happened to us. She's going to be in New York on the sixth of September – that was our anniversary.'

'So you're going to meet her.'

'I think I have to. She didn't give me any way of getting in touch with her before then, but I'm working on it.'

'What's her situation?'

'I don't know. She didn't say.'

'What are you expecting to happen?'

'I'm not expecting anything.'

She gave me a hard look.

I shrugged. 'OK, at the least, I'm expecting some answers. Why she left me. Why she never tried to get in touch before.'

'If you're a father or not.'

'Well, that's something I should know, don't you agree?'

'Of course.'

I longed to touch her but knew I didn't have the right. 'Laura, I want to be honest with you.'

'Honesty is good,' she said, her tones measured. 'Is that why you never bothered to call me?'

'I meant to. I overslept.'

She gave a delicate snort. 'You overslept by *two days*.'

'I went to sleep Monday night. I dreamed I saw Fred, and she told me how to go under the hill and disappear. Then I heard a bird singing. It was the phone. It was you. I might never have woken up without your call. You saved me.'

I saw her battling with disbelief. Almost against her will, it seemed, she decided to believe me. 'Is this because of Peri? Are you in trouble for going after her?'

I shrugged. 'She decided to come back. It wasn't anything I did. But I guess I have been playing with fire. And you know what they say about that.'

She looked at the garish cover of the book lying on the table. 'I shouldn't have given you that. You should get out of this business.'

Might as well tell me to get out of my life, to stop being the kind of person I was, drawn to mysteries. I drained my glass and nodded at hers, which was nearly empty. 'Want another drink?'

'No. No, thanks. I'd rather have something to eat.'

We made our way through busy streets, the warm and vibrant circus of London in the summertime, to Chinatown and Lee Ho Fook's. Not a particularly romantic place to dine, which was probably just as well given the state of play between us, but the food was reliably great.

After we'd settled in and decided what to order, I asked Laura how Peri was doing.

'She's good. Great. She's more like her old self again, but different. I mean, she's a lot like she was when she first came to London, before she went off to college, but with that, she's, I don't know, older, I guess. More grown-up. More settled, somehow. Hard to explain. But she's good.'

'Has she talked about what happened?'

'She doesn't want to dwell on the past. She's here now, this is her life, that's what's important.'

'She hasn't told you anything?'

Laura frowned. 'I didn't say that! Of course we talked, that first night up in Scotland. We had a good long talk and she told me a lot about it.' She shook her head. 'Strange, though.'

I leaned forward, eager to know more. 'Strange, how exactly?'

'Well, strange mostly that it wasn't stranger, I guess. The way she talks about it, she ran off with this rich and powerful man because she couldn't resist knowing what she'd be like with him, in a completely different life. She lived in his house, met his friends, went to parties, listened to music, went horseback riding – he had a whole stable of gorgeous horses, and she was always horse-mad ...' She trailed off, sighing, then went on.

'I don't know, it sounds not so different from what might happen to a beautiful girl swept off her feet by an eccentric, foreign billionaire. The only thing that made it different was the way she was completely out of touch with me and everyone else she'd ever known. No letters, no phone calls, no turning up at Christmas. And even that, she claims, was mostly her fault. She *could* have kept in touch; she just forgot. Forgot.' She shook her head in wonder. 'And she talks about it like she was only away for a few months. That's what it felt like to her: months, not years.'

'Is she living with Hugh?'

'Not yet.' She busied herself fixing a duck pancake. 'She's been staying with me. He had a few things to take care of.'

'The other girlfriend?'

She frowned. 'His *film*. He's been working day and night. He's not quite finished yet. She doesn't have to move in with him right away; the lease on my flat has another month to run. I wanted to renew it for another year, in her name, so she'd have somewhere of her own, no pressure, but the landlord wouldn't agree; he's decided to sell.'

'So Fiona's out?'

'It's really none of my business,' she said with excessive gentleness. 'But I don't think she ever actually *lived* with him.'

I thought Hugh would be advised to get his locks changed, and take any other precautions he could think of to keep the two women apart. Fiona might not be a sorceress like Fuamnach in the story of Etain, but she had just as much reason to feel jealous, and jealousy could be a dangerous emotion.

But I didn't say any of that to Laura.

'They are definitely an item, then – Peri and Hugh?'

Her face softened. 'Oh, yes. It's like before – they're completely besotted with each other. I'm glad. It makes it easier to leave, knowing she'll be with him, and happy. I've been encouraging her to think about college, but I don't know what she'll decide to do. Right now, just being with him seems to be enough for her.' Her smile was wistful.

I wanted to know more about Peri's experiences in the Otherworld, but there was no point in pumping Laura about it; even less than there'd been in quizzing Peri. Whatever she told me would simply be just another second-hand story, her experience, always at a distance from me, something I could not understand. This was my obsession, to want to know something that couldn't be known. I might as well accept that the Otherworld would always be a mystery to me. Some people, a very few, were privileged to go there and return to tell the tale, but I was sure now that I would not survive the experience.

So I let Laura change the subject. We chatted about New York and London and enjoyed the food. She had insisted on paying, pointing out that she'd invited me. It was still early when we left, and the daylight streets were full of noise and life, people coming and going, talking and laughing, spilling out of pubs and restaurants as if all were part of one huge, communal celebration of midsummer. The magical golden dusk seemed to hold such promise, as if the whole long evening were just beginning, stretching out ahead of us, alluring and full of endless possibility. Standing on the street corner, I inhaled the warm, fume-laden city air like an intoxicating perfume. I was clearheaded in spite of all the drinks I'd consumed, and I felt more wide-awake than ever before in my life.

I touched Laura lightly on her bare arm. 'Where to now?'

'I have to go home and finish packing. I'm off to New York in the morning.'

'So this is good-bye?'

Conflicting emotions flickered in her eyes, and she made her decision. 'Ian, I'd like to stay in touch.'

'So would I.'

'I'd like to know what happens with Jenny. You'll let me know?'

'Of course.'

Suddenly her eyes widened, and she gasped. 'I haven't paid you!'

'Forget it.'

'Don't be silly! Did you bring your bill?'

I thought of the two draft bills, still on my computer. I shook my head. 'Really, it's on the house. Peri would have come back anyway. I'm not out-of-pocket – you paid for everything in Scotland, and now you've just paid for dinner.'

'That was for your birthday.'

'OK, then will you grant me this as a birthday wish? I don't want to be paid. I'm happy if I helped. I did it for love – or friendship. You don't owe me anything.'

When I'd finished my little speech she stretched up on

her tiptoes to kiss me. This was not a perfunctory peck, such as I'd given her on meeting; this was full on the lips, and it was warm and promising. When I put my arms around her, she seemed to melt against me. If we hadn't been on a busy street corner, surrounded by people, it might have developed into something much more. It was the best kiss I'd had in years.

My head was spinning when we parted. 'Shall I—'

She shook her head. 'Not tonight. Come and see me in New York, Ian. Whatever else happens.'

'I will,' I promised.

I watched her descend into the Leicester Square underground station and didn't follow. I couldn't bear the thought of going tamely home alone. I was too wide-awake, too restless and hungry for life.

So I walked. I was walking as a way of thinking, and exploring the territory inside my head meant I paid little attention to which way I turned. I was alert enough to keep out of the traffic, and my course was northerly because that would eventually take me home. Apart from that, I might have been in another world. I daydreamed about Laura, that promising kiss, and fantasised about where it might lead. I imagined us exploring New York together, as, many years ago, I'd explored it with Jenny. Then I wondered what Jenny looked like now, and what she expected of our meeting, and if she still had fantasies about me.

With my mind so pleasurably occupied, it's not surprising I lost track of where I was and where I was going. All of a sudden it was dark but for the yellow street-lamps casting their unnatural glow, and I found myself on a street I didn't know.

It was a quiet, residential street of substantial brick terraces, heavily parked with cars along both sides. It looked in no way a major thoroughfare, and I didn't recognise it as being along any of my usual routes. After a moment of uncertainty, I kept walking. When I got to the corner I should be able to find the name of the street and get my bearings.

Before I reached the corner, though, something caught my attention, movement glimpsed from the corner of my eye. Looking around, I saw someone coming out of the house across the street. That sounds ordinary enough, but somehow I knew immediately it was not. The door, as it shut, made no sound. The figure emerging from the front gate onto the pavement was that of a woman, not very tall, wearing a long dress. She was carrying something wrapped in a blanket cradled against her chest. Although I couldn't see anything of it, from the size and the way she carried it, I felt certain it was a baby.

As the woman passed beneath the streetlight, her hair gleamed a brassy, improbable colour in the glow, and I had a clear glimpse of her face.

It was Fred.

For a moment I was rooted to the spot, too astonished to call out. Surely I was mistaken. Then, as she continued to move swiftly away from me towards the end of the street, I became determined that she shouldn't get away, and I ran after her. My footsteps sounded clearly in the still, quiet air, yet Fred made no sound at all. And although I was running, and she seemed to be moving at no more than a quick walk, not only did I fail to catch up to her, but the distance between us grew rapidly greater. By the time I reached the end of the street, she had disappeared. I ran out into the middle of the road and looked around wildly, and there she was, moving at the same, even pace down the next street.

I chased after her, past more of the sleeping terraced houses, hearing only my own footsteps and my own panting breath. I couldn't catch up to her. Again she turned the corner well ahead of me, and again passed out of my sight. This time, the street ended in a little square, filled with a gated, communal garden. I was just in time to see her open the gate and go inside.

There was no hurry now. There was unlikely to be another exit.

I crossed the street slowly, looking around at the houses whose windows overlooked this little private park, trying to see if there was anything I recognised, trying to recall if I had been here before, on my way to visit Laura. Was this the garden where Hugh had filmed Peri the summer before she disappeared?

The gate, when I reached it, hung slightly ajar, just waiting for a push from me. I stared through the bars, trying to see into the garden, but it was scarcely possible. Bushes had been planted thickly around the entrance and trained into an arbour. Just now it felt like a tunnel.

Perhaps, in daytime, there might have been a view of the garden through the arbour, but now, in the dark, I could see nothing but shadow, and I could only guess where the tunnel might take me.

I might walk through and find myself in a night-time garden, alone.

Or it might take me to wherever Fred had gone.

My heart pounded erratically. I pressed my hand against it and felt the card in my breast pocket. I thought of the picture on the front of it, the silent landscape from my dream; and then I thought of the real and living woman who had chosen it, perhaps on impulse, or for some unknown personal reason, and I remembered, word for word, the message she had written inside. I imagined Jenny walking up and down the cool, stone corridors of The Cloisters, hoping I would come, fearing I would not, as the day wore on. Was she alone, or was there a child with her? My son? My daughter?

I thought of the promise I'd made to Laura, and imagined her anger, and her anxiety, if I never called. Would she come looking for me?

I thought of all the mysteries of my own life, waiting to be solved, and wondered how I could let myself be so distracted.

I don't know how long I stood there.

ACKNOWLEDGEMENTS

The lines from "Mider to Etain" at the front of the book and the quotation on page 142 are both from Jeffrey Gantz's translation of "The Wooing of Etain" in *Early Irish Myths and Sagas* (Penguin Books, 1981).

The letter and some lines of dialogue on pages 238-241 are from "Nelson, Mary" in *An Encyclopedia of Fairies* by Katharine Briggs, copyright 1961; she gives as her source Sir Walter Scott's *Minstrelsy of the Scottish Border*.

The "quotation" on pages 340-341 is adapted from a description in *The Land of Knapdale*, No. 13 in the West Highland Series, a pamphlet compiled and illustrated by Mairi MacDonald F.S.A. Scot., copyright 1986.

My thanks also to Lewis Shiner, who planted a seed years ago when he let me read his unpublished play *Neverland*, and Faith Brooker, who showed me Sydenham Hill Woods.

Author photo © Léon Cuervo

Lisa Tuttle was born and raised in Texas, but moved to Britain in the 1980s. She now lives with her writer husband and their daughter on the side of a Scottish loch. She has written more than a dozen fantasy, science fiction and horror novels. Her earlier novels, *The Silver Bough* and *The Mysteries* are published by Jo Fletcher Books, and book one in the forthcoming Jesperson and Lane series will be published by Jo Fletcher Books in 2016.

You can visit her at www.lisatuttle.co.uk.

THE SILVER BOUGH

Lisa Tuttle

Appleton is a small town nestled on the coast of Scotland.
Though it was once famous for the apples it produced,
these days it's a shadow of its former self.

But in a hidden orchard a golden apple dangles from a
silver bough, an apple believed lost forever. The apple is
part of a legend, promising either eternal happiness to the
young couple who eat from it, secure in their love – or a
curse, for those who take its gift for granted.

Now, as the town teeters on the edge of decline, the old rituals
have been forgotten and the mists are rolling in. And in the
mist, something is stirring . . .

Jo Fletcher
BOOKS

THE SOMNAMBULIST AND THE PSYCHIC THIEF

Lisa Tuttle

For several years Miss Lane was companion, collaborator and friend to the lady known to the Psychical Society only as Miss X – until she discovered that Miss X was actually a fraud.

Now Miss Lane works with Mr Jasper Jesperson as a consulting detective, but the cases are not as plentiful as they might be and money is getting tight – until a wife's concern for her husband's nocturnal ramblings piques their interest.

But there's more to it than an oblivious somnambulist, for mediums are disappearing all over London and the Psychical Society suspects the supernatural.

There is only one team with the imagination and intelligence to uncover the nefarious purpose behind the vanished psychics and the somnambulist's wanderings: Jesperson and Lane, at your service.

Jo Fletcher
BOOKS